THE GIRL WITH
ICE IN HER VEINS

Karin Smirnoff

THE GIRL WITH
ICE IN HER VEINS

Translated from the Swedish by Sarah Death

MACLEHOSE PRESS
QUERCUS · LONDON

First published in Swedish as *Lokattens klor* by Bokförlaget Polaris, Stockholm, in 2024
First published in Great Britain in 2025 by

MacLehose Press
An imprint of Quercus, part of John Murray Group
Carmelite House
50 Victoria Embankment
London EC4Y 0DZ

Part of Hodder & Stoughton Limited
An Hachette UK company

The authorised representative in the EEA is Hachette Ireland, 8 Castlecourt
Centre, Dublin 15, D15 XTP3, Ireland (email: info@hbgi.ie)

© Karin Smirnoff & Moggliden AB, 2024
Published by agreement with the Hedlund Agency
English translation copyright © 2025 by Sarah Death
Lines from *Sons of the Sun* translated by Sarah Death
Map © Emily Faccini

A CIP catalogue record for this book is available from the British Library

ISBN (HB) 978 1 52942 710 3
ISBN (TPB) 978 1 52942 711 0
ISBN (Ebook) 978 1 52942 713 4

1

Designed in Cycles by Libanus Press, Marlborough
Typeset by Palimpsest Book Production Ltd, Falkirk, Stirlingshire
Printed and bound in Great Britain by Clays Ltd, Elcograf S.p.A.

Papers used by MacLehose Press are from well-managed
forests and other responsible sources.

THE GIRL WITH
ICE IN HER VEINS

CHARACTERS IN THE *MILLENNIUM* SERIES FROM PREVIOUS VOLUMES

LISBETH SALANDER	An exceptionally talented hacker with tattoos, piercings and a troubled past. Occasionally assumes the identity of Irene Nesser.
MIKAEL BLOMKVIST	Formerly an investigative journalist at *Millennium* magazine. Lisbeth assisted him with one of the biggest stories of his career. He later helped to vindicate Lisbeth when she was on trial for murder.
SVALA HIRAK	Lisbeth's niece, daughter of Lisbeth's half-brother Ronald Niedermann with whom she shares a condition that prevents her from feeling pain. Her mother is Märta Hirak.
MÄRTA HIRAK	Svala's mother. Her partner, Peder Sandberg, known as Pap Peder, was a player in the criminal underworld in Gasskas. Svala calls her Mammamärta.
PER-HENRIK AND ELIAS HIRAK	Brothers of Svala's mother, Märta. Sami reindeer herders.
PERNILLA BLOMKVIST	Mikael Blomkvist's daughter, married to Henry Salo.
LUKAS	Pernilla's nine-year-old son and Blomkvist's grandson, victim of a kidnapping the previous autumn.
JESSICA HARNESK	Police officer in Gasskas. Separated from her husband, Henke. Lisbeth's love interest.

Birna Guðmundurdóttir	Police officer in Gasskas. Blomkvist's love interest.
Hans Faste	Head of the Serious Crime Unit at Gasskas police, formerly an officer with the Stockholm force. Has clashed with Mikael Blomkvist and Lisbeth Salander in the past.
Marcus Branco	A white supremacist, head of the Branco Group, a security company with vast holdings. Responsible for the death of Märta Hirak.
Henry Salo	Pernilla's husband and stepfather to Lukas. The corrupt head of Gasskas municipality. Brother to Joar Bark, and son of Marianne Lekatt – both of whom he was separated from when he was taken into care as a child and adopted.
Joar Bark	a.k.a. the Cleaner, the estranged brother of Henry Salo and son of Marianne Lekatt. Employed by Branco to dispose of the bodies of his victims. Kept Lukas in his care after the kidnapping.
Marianne Lekatt	Mother of Henry Salo and Joar Bark. Before her death in an unexplained fire at her cottage, she was befriended by Svala.
Kostas Long	A wealthy businessman of Greek and Chinese descent. He had a one-night stand with Lisbeth in Rovaniemi.
Dragan Armansky	Founder of Milton Security and Lisbeth's business partner. One of the few she trusts.
Plague	A hacker in the coalition known as Hacker Republic, and the one Lisbeth Salander trusts most, although his loyalty may now be compromised.

Sagas say and legends tell:
far to the north of the fixed pole star
westward beyond the sun and moon
each block of stone is gold and silver:
hearthstones, anchor stones –
the gold glitters, the silver shimmers
the sea mirrors steep rock faces
suns, moons, stars sparkle
and smile at their reflections.

Anders Fjellner, 1849, from the
Sami epic poem *Sons of the Sun*

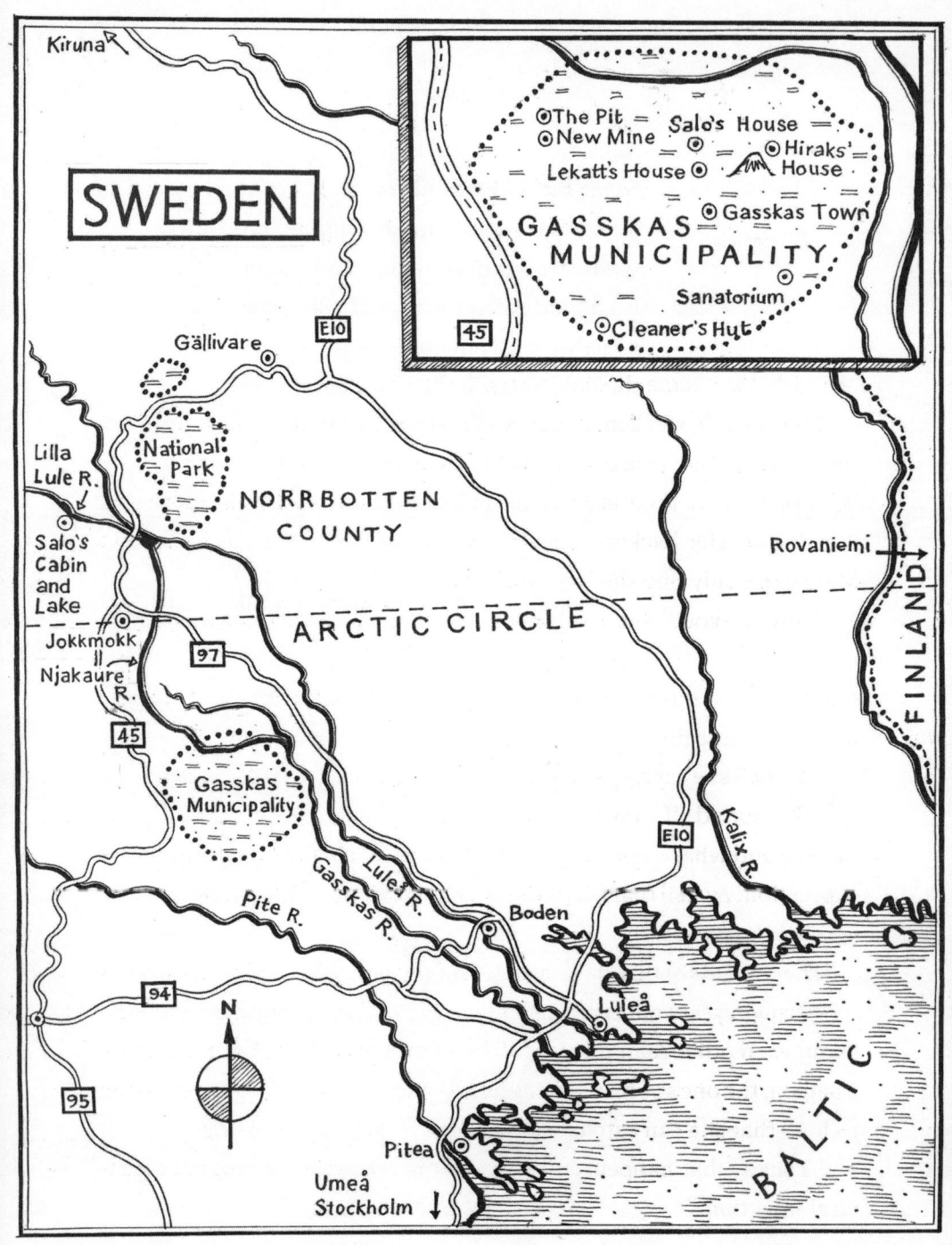

PROLOGUE

"Hi Lisbeth, it's me. It's been a while."

The voice is weak and croaky. His observation is correct: although they were in touch via digital platforms as recently as the autumn, it has been years since their last conversation. But she can hear instantly that it is Plague. Her hacker friend, if there is any such thing as friendship. Maybe the only one she has ever had.

"How are you?" she asks, but misses the answer when she is overcome by a fit of coughing from deep in her tortured lungs, coughing so violent that she has to put down the phone and rush to the sink to spit out gobs of viscous phlegm.

"Sorry," she says, quite some time later. "Are you still there?"

"You sound ill, not like you." As if he knows what's actually like Lisbeth and what's not. Armour-plated exterior, a face almost devoid of expression. A shell that keeps the outside world at a distance in a robotic, barely human way.

The contents of that shell can be glimpsed only when a rare crack opens.

Through years of occasionally crossing paths, they understand more about each other than most. Still, he knows very little about Lisbeth as a person, the one she has become or chooses to be. It's almost comforting to hear that she can catch a cold like any other human being.

"That's what happens when you hang out with walking sources of viral infection."

1

"I take it you're thinking of someone specific," he says, hoping for a way in. Her inaudible grunt gives way to another coughing fit.

"How about you?" she asks once she has recovered sufficiently. "Phone calls aren't usually your thing, but then again it *is* nearly Christmas. Happy Christmas to you too."

He can't help laughing. Typical Lisbeth, always on the attack. Always one step ahead, a way of making sure she can keep the doors closed.

"Do you mean Svala?" he says. "The walking source of infection?"

"Could be. But Blomkvist's down with it too. We must have picked up some foul thing on the train back from Gasskas."

"So you two are still in touch?" he says.

"No."

"Yeah, right."

"Did you ring for a reason?" she says, heading back to bed. There's something in his voice, a tone trying to make its way through her snot-clogged, fever-hazed brain.

"Just wanted to make sure you were alive."

"Why shouldn't I be?"

He's e-mailed her. Several times but had no reply. The break in contact coincided with his own failed attempt to hack into the Branco Group's computer system. The silence made him anxious. But the momentary relief he felt when she answered his call is turning into something else. As she pointed out, he is not the type to ring his acquaintances for a chat. He is a creature of the darkness who stays in his cave. The kind who never pokes out his head to sample his surroundings. He can tell her suspicions have been aroused.

"Anyway, I've been thinking about you and I just wanted to check everything was alright," he says, and immediately regrets it. His words ring as false as he feels: a traitor who has betrayed his best friend. She asked for help. But something – someone – got in the way. He could blame his own fear. Not particularly credible. His life has never been of much importance. Alive or dead, it's all pretty much the same to him.

The passing years are nothing but a distance to be covered. She knows that. Maybe he should come clean.

"Be in touch," she breaks in, and ends the call. The audience is over.

The short December day turns to evening. Between spells of feverish sleep she lies awake in the darkness and tries to get her thoughts in order.

One part of her, the part which, against her will, has softened into a more conciliatory Lisbeth, tries hard to take the words for what they potentially are: a friend ringing up to ask how she is. Is that an utterly ridiculous proposition? No, or, well, yes, unless Plague has undergone a complete metamorphosis, which is possible but not likely. He was fishing for something. It takes her back to the experiences of the autumn, which she has done her best to forget.

Svala carrying her dying mother through a burning bunker.

Mikael Blomkvist getting shot as his grandchild is abducted by masked men.

Herself in the arms of a police officer.

And finally, Plague.

He has been at her side. She put her trust in his incorruptible integrity. They have eaten from the same pizza boxes. Solved problems that would make students of AI green with envy. She has so much to thank him for: her life, her freedom. But still, something isn't right.

Once this crappy virus is out of her system, she's going to find out what.

*

Christmas is coming and presents are being wrapped. The Residents' Association would like all members to think about their recycling. Christmas string belongs in the general waste because it contains plastic and glue, but wrapping paper can be recycled as long as no sticky tape is left on it. With this we wish you all a joyful Christmas. Best wishes, your Chairman Per.

Lisbeth crumples the note into a ball, hurls it at the draining board as hard as she can and roundly curses the imminent arrival of Christmas. Its ugly mug pokes in everywhere, turning the city into a winking inferno of festoon lights, decorated trees and kiddies' sparkling eyes in wheedling posters on the Tunnelbana. Whether you're buying a piece of jewellery at NK department store or a litre of milk at the Co-op, the transaction ends with "Happy Christmas". This revolting and absurdly hackneyed little phrase makes Lisbeth scowl and the music is even ghastlier. Who the hell seriously thinks Rudolph's red nose is going to make anyone spend more? It's as if the whole of Stockholm has morphed into some sort of Guantánamo detention camp with its own sonic torture regime. From the end of November until the yuletide hell is over, her custom-made, noise-cancelling headphones remain clapped over her ears. A little present she treated herself to a few years back. Well worth the million or so kronor. Music sounds amazing through them, apparently. But silence is what she's after.

Normally she would never venture out into the melee of physical Christmas shopping, but the flu made her lose track of time and suddenly it's too late to order online.

Christmas prompts associations to Rovaniemi, and Rovaniemi prompts associations to Svala (and unfortunately also to a slippery Greek-Chinese guy, the low-water mark of her year).

She could have made things easier for herself and sent money. Any amount. If not for the fact that she knew Svala would take it as an insult. The girl wants something personal. Nothing expensive or spectacular. Personal. Lisbeth asked if she had any wishes. "For you to come up," was the answer but no, she doesn't feel up to it. Her body can barely drag her as far as Kjell & Company home electronics store at the Skyscraper. It certainly couldn't cope with the crush on public transport heading north.

Every now and then she stops and gasps for breath. Two more days, she tells herself. Two more days and then she'll be back at the gym.

She has the shop assistant wrap the package. Makes her way to the post office counter in Ringen shopping centre and shells out a small fortune for express delivery to Gasskas. For a while, her guilty conscience is assuaged. She feels a sense of satisfaction. The Christmas present couldn't be more personal. And it will be bloody useful to the right sort of person. Someone like Svala.

1

There is a special place in hell for CEOs and venture capitalists. Men with webbed feet and arms that double as wings.

Like migrating birds they take off as soon as the weather changes, but new ones always replace them. The sort who defy the cold and roll up their sleeves as the biting wind whines all around.

Prospectors who can smell money. Big money, or they would have stayed in the sun.

Like diviners, they put their ear to the granite and say, "Here". "Here lie such extraordinary riches that no-one will be able to refuse."

When the fun is over, when the seam has dried up or the metal prices have fallen, they won't be the ones standing in a packed canteen telling those assembled that times are hard. They have a whole HR department to do their dirty work. They are already far away. Far from poisoned watercourses and contaminated ground, far from unemployed miners whose lungs have breathed in silica, asbestos and diesel fumes.

The directors and venture capitalists are already on their way to new places, other mountains. Using different company names.

With a fresh set of board members and a bundle of new money to wave under the noses of politicians, they are once again welcomed as heroes. Heroes who will take sparsely populated municipalities to new economic heights, create jobs and inject some belief in the future.

*

It is night. Several degrees below freezing even though it is well into May. The grass crunches as he takes the path through the forest, his destination in sight a few hundred metres upstream along the Njakaure. A river that flows past the decommissioned Gasskas mine, commonly known as "the Pit".

In the bright moonlight, buildings and spoil heaps tower up as if in some abandoned alpine village. From his vantage point he cannot see the Pit itself, and that is intentional.

He feels a sudden shiver of nerves, but he wasn't born yesterday. He knows what he's doing. Only he needs a little rest first. He shrugs out of his rucksack, unfolds his seat and rummages for the Thermos flask.

A couple of cups later, he feels restored. His pulse is even. The air is good.

He drags the canoe from its hiding place under a spruce, where he left it last year. In the end there was only one trip. He examines the bottom for any damage. Drags the canoe down to the water and ties it to a tree so he can pause to get his breath back.

The water ripples around the hull as he pushes off with the paddle. Now he can take it easy and float with the current a few hundred metres down to the bridge.

The bridge over the stream is said to date to the eighteenth century. When the mine began operating at the end of the 1940s, the bridge assumed its current form. Reinforced with iron girders to withstand the pressure of fully loaded ore trucks on their way down to the coast. From below he can see the stonework of the old bridge structure. Beautifully proportioned blocks of granite fitted perfectly to each other, built in an age when beauty was valued.

He brings the canoe to a stop. Slowly, so as not to lose his balance, he puts the straps of the rucksack through a rusty iron loop and winds binding wire around it to fix it firmly. That should cope with a load of twelve kilos. No doubt twelve hundred too. Gang members barely into their teens know how to build a bomb, but their awareness of impact in relation to size of charge will be very sketchy. The risk radius for a gram of explosive is twenty metres. The reason for his own outsized charge is the open terrain. An explosion is more effective in a room, a car or some other enclosed space and he wants to be sure the bridge really will be blown to bits.

He wishes he could stand a little way off and watch it all happen, but he has put the temptation out of his head. Technically it makes no difference if he is killed. He will soon reach the end of his lifespan. On the other hand, there are still a few things on his agenda before the heavenly light receives his soul.

He hides the canoe under a tree again. A few spruce branches wouldn't harm, he thinks, but he can't summon the energy. On the final stretch back to the car he has to stop several times. It isn't that his breathing is wheezy; he has no breath at all.

Cool sheets against a sweaty body. Another cup of coffee. He props up the pillows behind his back and reaches for his prepaid mobile phone.

A quarter past four is a good time for the people of Gasskas to wake to the sound of the next world war. His own war. He puts down the phone. Turns to the wall and listens to the distant bass note of the blast.

Shame to lose a good Thermos, is his final thought before he falls asleep.

Or did he even sleep? The pain has come back.

For a moment he imagined he was free. His concentration had its focus elsewhere, on his exhilaration, draining the power from the stabs of pain in his back and making his cough cower like an exhausted tomcat.

Now it is clawing fresh wounds inside him. A quarter of an hour later he finally gets himself to the bathroom. Takes a pee, shaves while he's there – he's never been a slob – puts on another pot of coffee and waits for the local news bulletin at seven.

*

At 4.15 this morning an explosive charge detonated that was heard and felt across large areas of Gasskas. According to the police it was an extremely powerful explosion, causing serious damage to the bridge over the Njakkaure River that formerly carried trucks of ore from the Gasskas mine.

"We are currently trying to orientate ourselves in the area, to establish that there was no injury to human life. The attack has been categorised as widespread destruction posing a threat to public safety until the cause of the explosion can be established," said Hans Faste of the Serious Crime Unit at Gasskas police.

A decent start at any rate, he notes, and scrolls through the online edition of the local paper, *Gaskassen*. Despite the circumstances, it's going to be a day to relish.

2

Whose idea was it?

Svala's. There were three key factors.

The first: Ester Södergran, who is new to the town and to *Gaskassen* and looking for some different angles. The second: Svala Hirak, who is interning for a few weeks at the paper and helping her out. The third: Lisbeth Salander, who sent a drone as a Christmas present.

"Do you know of any large abandoned properties?" says Ester. "We could do a Saturday feature on haunted houses."

"There must be loads, but I've no idea if they've got ghosts," says Svala.

They make a list. Select the most spectacular. In a municipality like Gasskas there are plenty of abandoned buildings. Mostly cheap chipboard huts and old timbered buildings that are empty for a variety of reasons. An owner with no heirs, a dispute over an inheritance, or a location on a busy road that used to be practical but will barely even sell to the Dutch these days.

The last place on the list is the sanatorium.

Like other sanatoriums, the property is in a remote, elevated position in an attractive setting near a lake.

"'By contrast with its nearby counterpart Sandträsk, which was in operation for fifty years, caring for almost thirty thousand patients, the sanatorium in Gasskas has an obscure place in Swedish medical history.'"

Svala is googling and reading out loud.

"'The thirty-bed sanatorium was built in 1945, mainly to relieve Sandträsk, which was admitting large numbers of refugees suffering from TB. The last patients left in 1963. The building was subsequently used as a residential treatment centre for addicts and as a refugee centre during the Balkan War. The complex has been standing empty since the mid-2000s. Its inaccessibility and state of disrepair have led to proposals for its demolition.'"

"Well, that must have been written before December 2021, when it was apparently sold. Let's get over there. It'll be handy if there's someone there. They might know if it's haunted," says Ester. She carries on typing.

Svala watches Ester's earnest profile, briefly frozen in some thought process, her gaze distant.

Over the weeks of Svala's stint of work experience, a friendship has developed between them. *Like a sister,* thinks Svala. A big sister you can talk to, have a laugh with. One who listens and answers without sarcasm or a wagging, nagging adult finger. Someone who'll message her in the evening and ask what she's up to. Someone who shares stuff, shows her the ropes.

Svala laps it all up. Devises headlines, crafts preambles. Wrangles words into the taut article format.

"Christ, Svala, I mean, I can write but you . . . you're a real artist with words," is the sort of thing Ester will exclaim.

But there's another side she likes even more. Comments like "Shit Svala, get a load of this picture I took, see how fabulous you look," and something stirs in the chrysalis on its way to life as a butterfly.

Something has changed in the way she views herself, and in what she sees in the eyes of others. She isn't invisible any longer.

They take the route the GPS suggests through villages, alongside lakes and over hills until they reach journey's end.

There is even a sign. Two. An old one with the name of the place and a more recent version telling visitors that it's private land monitored by CCTV. The road is also blocked by a barrier.

"What do we do?" Svala says.

"Park the car and walk."

The front drive sweeps around a circular flower bed, formerly grand with its low, neatly trimmed rowan hedges and fountain but now looking as neglected as the house. There are no human figures or vehicles to indicate any form of life. The winter weather has snapped an aged birch. And the flagpole. There are still drifts of snow in the shadier spots.

"Not a soul," says Svala.

"But plenty of mosquitoes," notes Ester, flapping her arms to ward them off.

Svala lets a mosquito sit on her arm until it has finished its meal.

"The ones waking up now are the overwintering females," she says. "Pretty hungry, I should think."

"Good job there are animal lovers around for them to eat, then," says Ester, delivering a lethal slap to a few more.

They tug at locked doors, do a circuit of the outbuildings but can't even get into those. Occasionally they think they hear sounds. But when they stop and listen, the place is silent apart from the background notes provided by nature.

They go round to the back. The glass in the ground-floor windows has been replaced by chipboard. The plaster is peeling in places, and bits have fallen to the ground.

"Hard to hunt ghosts if you can't get in to them. I guess we'll have to give up or find someone who can unlock the door for us," says Ester, and then comes to an abrupt halt. "Listen. That was a car, wasn't it? Might not be a good idea to let them see us. It's private property, after all."

So they run for the cover of the forest and don't stop until they emerge from the track onto the public road.

Between the trees, they catch sight of the car the newspaper lets them use. And beside it, a man talking on the phone.

There's nothing odd about the situation, not really. Ester jumps the ditch and walks towards the man.

"Hello there," she hails him from a distance, "do you need me to move the car?"

Svala doesn't hear the answer. She waits behind a tree until he has gone.

3

"I still don't get why he had to be so unpleasant" says Ester a few days later when they are picking out shots of different haunted houses. "We didn't even get a picture of the place. We may well need to go up there again."

Svala takes a rather different view of it. "Unpleasant" isn't the right word. She hasn't said anything yet. Not that she identified the man as a particular individual, but that makes no difference. These types are all the same. One step up from Pap Peder, her own late stepdad, a loser who prided himself on looking and acting the part of a real gangster.

With apologies to now-extinct races, Pap Peder is a troglodyte and this man a Neanderthal. The sort who provides him with jobs. *Provided* him, to be more accurate. That skunk is out of the running, at least, but it won't stop others.

Svala's list includes mostly names. People responsible for her mother's death, directly or indirectly. She draws straight lines with her ruler, puts crosses in columns. Of the five possible columns, two are important: *Alive* and *Dead*.

There are others who hold sway over the Neanderthals. Human apes wearing club blazers, signet rings. At the top of the hierarchy are the suits. Those who have been integrated into society, leveraging their capital to be allowed aboard the train to the industrial future. Those currently debating or writing opinion pieces in the papers on the importance of meritocracy. Which means that minorities, native inhabitants, environmental activists and other opinionated parties are not allowed to stand in the way of those who know how Sweden must develop.

This is when Svala has her idea and mentions the drone that Lisbeth Salander sent up at Christmas, even accompanying her gift with the rhyming verse:

From Lisbeth to my niece.
You can spy on them in peace.

Svala says aerial photos can look cool, especially if you take them at dusk, and Ester snaps up the suggestion.

"I'm sure I could fillet some content on the sanatorium out of other pieces. Or ring Elina."

"Elina Bång?"

"Exactly. The Seeress of Lonesome Fen as she calls herself these days. Good stage name."

This time they turn off and head up a road for forestry vehicles, a couple of kilometres west of the sanatorium. The plan is to skirt the building on foot and make their way up the hill.

"I really hope it's worth the effort. You did test this drone in advance, right?" pants Ester as they plough up to the path.

Svala has tested it, but only at home on the farm. There are still some teething troubles, but the article is supposed to go to press the next day. The hilltop provides an unbroken view of the sanatorium, which is a prerequisite for the drone to follow commands. If it loses contact, it's going to crash.

The location is favourable in other respects too. The last rays of sun cap the roof of the sanatorium with a dome of gold, while the inkiness of the ground stands out in bold relief as ghostly shadows. Svala would have stories to tell about the presence of the dead, the energy that never leaves the universe, but she refrains. They don't know each other as well as all that.

The drone takes to the air. The buzzing insect homes in on its target.

Svala guides it on a swift circuit of the main building and then brings it back to the hill.

When Ester suggests they venture down for a look, she says no. Abandoned properties don't have CCTV or bars behind boarded-up windows. There must be people here.

The presence of the dead is one thing. The living are a much worse proposition.

"I need to get home, I promised to feed the dogs," she says. "My uncles are out this evening."

They drive back through Gasskas and on to Björkavan. Svala walks past the dog pen on her way in. Takes Aiko up to her room with her. The biggest, cuddliest one. He lies down at her feet. Alone in the house, she empties the memory card of pictures, transferring them to her laptop. She selects a couple for publication and imports them to Photoshop.

What you don't see from the ground is that the building has skylights. The resolution isn't particularly good. It's only when she gets to pixel-magnification level that she sees the silhouettes of human figures.

She closes the lid of the laptop. Sits there for a while, staring out over the yard at Björkavan. Svala's life has got better in many ways. Since the autumn she has been living with her uncles, Per-Henrik and Elias, in the house that was Mammamärta's childhood home. She has inherited her mother's room, her bed. She goes out at night and looks at the stars, the Northern Lights, the moon and the fleeting shadows that move across the yard. There is nothing to fear but much to feel the loss of.

It started with a voice. She called, Mammamärta answered. Now it is the other way round. Svala usually opts not to answer. Mammamärta is a sorrow best consumed in small bites. It's easy to choke on.

It is late but Ester is still awake. She answers right away as if she was waiting for the call.

'The picture quality wasn't good enough," says Svala. "Sorry. I'm afraid you'll have to use stock photos."

Svala can hear her typing and wants to know what she's doing.

"This is crazy," she says. The keyboard clatters. "The sanatorium's owned by Mimer Mining, the parent company of Svea Mining. That lot who got permission to do a test bore at the new mine. If we blow up the building, they might have to abandon their plan. Hah, only joking, but it's interesting anyway, don't you think?"

"Where did you get hold of that information?" asks Svala.

"From Ante, a mate of mine. He's doing some kind of nerdy tech course in Luleå and he's a bloody good hacker. By the way," she says, "you're coming to the meeting tomorrow, aren't you? And don't forget the banner, we'll need it on Saturday. If you like, we can go for a pizza afterwards. I've got a new idea I'd like to talk over with you. Not the simplest thing in the world but . . . anyway, we'll leave it for tomorrow. Sleep well, my little windflower."

My little windflower. A soft, warm feeling runs through Svala's body.

"You too," she says.

4

```
Meeting at Petra's 6 p.m. All to attend.
```

A message in the chat group. No point going home beforehand. Svala finds a seat in a tucked-away corner of Gasskas library, takes out her exercise book and reads through her latest piece of writing. At first a few individual words came, and she put them into lines and they became poems. Now they come in sentences which she assembles into stories. Every story has a name. No-one has read them. Probably no-one ever will, either. She sees her writings as an act of affirmation. A kind of life testimony.

They wait until a quarter past six. Drink tea and eat biscuits. As well as the usual gang there are three others, but no Ester Södergran. Svala checks her mobile. No new message.

"Can somebody ring her?" says Petra, topping up the teapot.

But Ester doesn't answer, so they start the meeting.

"As you see, we have some reinforcements with us today. You've only met Simon and Levi briefly before, at the café, so maybe you'd like to introduce yourself, guys."

Levi Grundström makes do with a hello and his name. Adds that he's an old bloke who thinks they're doing a grand job. Maybe he'll have something to contribute. But it isn't clear what that could be and before

19

he's finished speaking the other newcomer gets to his feet. He looks all around as if he wants to make an impression on each of them and his eyes come to rest on Svala.

"So I'm Simon and I moved back home last year to study Energy Engineering in Luleå. I see the course as a route to infiltrating the heart of the industrial world. I hope you'll all be able to benefit from that expertise. My personal view is that we've got to combat the capitalists' destruction of nature by offering resistance. Physical force, too, if necessary."

He sits down. There is a spontaneous burst of applause. Petra pours him more tea and admiring eyes linger on his brown curls. Svala can understand them, her and the others. It's not only that he's good-looking, he has this charisma, too. A sort of natural leadership vibe that transplants them from the kindergarten to the boardroom. When he looks at her again, she doesn't look away. She sees a soulmate.

"First item on the agenda is this weekend's demo," Petra resumes. "As we discussed last time, we need to do more than tie ourselves to trees and put up banners. Even the journalists don't bother turning up any longer. We barely do ourselves."

"Can I say something?" Simon interrupts.

This time he stays in his seat.

"I know you've all done a really great job at the new mine. Your protests have drawn a lot of public attention to the Sami and their traditional territory, particularly the reindeer herders. The battle isn't lost, but until construction work starts, I suggest you focus on the old Gasskas mine instead."

"The Pit?" someone says.

'Yes. There's activity at the Pit. Apparently there are plenty of unexploited resources in the slag heaps and underground. If they're planning to reopen the mine, we've really got something to protest about. The whole area's a ticking time bomb for the environment."

"Couldn't agree more," says Levi Grundström. "This madness has got to stop. They need to do a complete decontamination of the Gasskas mine, not make things worse by restarting extraction."

Svala listens and considers how to answer. The others are all older. They've been involved for a lot longer. She's nothing but a fledgling, testing her wings.

"Isn't it a good thing for them to use existing resources?" she says and plummets to the ground. "I mean, instead of opening new mines?"

Simon looks at her as a parent would look at a naïve child.

"Well, you might think so, but even old mines need new infrastructure. We were all woken up by the bridge explosion. Without the bridge, no ore wagons. The ore will have to be transported by road now. For that they need better roads, more roads. And as soon as the infrastructure is in place, it's a green light for even more mines. In other words, the Pit isn't the end but the beginning. Don't you agree? A stroke of genius to blow up the bridge, right?"

There is silence in the room.

The group, Simon included, look at each other. *Was it him?*

"What do you suggest?" Petra says finally.

"It may sound extreme, but think of it like this," says Simon. "In principle, we could blow up anything at all that threatens the climate, the natural world or us, humanity. Attacks are unusual. Nobody's prepared for them, or thinking of ways to mitigate the risks. Take the battery gigafactory in Skellefteå, for example. Do you really think they're keeping tabs on every single line worker in the factory, every carpenter, electrician or official coming and going? The place is lousy with entrepreneurs and so on, with a constantly changing workforce."

"You mean we ought to blow up the battery factory?" says Petra, who gets an irritated look from Simon in return. "I absolutely think we can do more than we are today," she goes on, "but I've no intention of helping to blow up anything. Innocent people could die. We're not the Baader-Meinhof gang."

*

When the meeting is over, they go their separate ways.

Svala and Levi Grundström are going in the same direction. As they walk, he staggers suddenly. He looks as if he's in pain. Svala tucks her arm into his.

"Damn those icy patches," she says. "It's May, for God's sake."

Simon has been walking behind them and now comes abreast. Asks if she's on her way home. Levi has to turn off here.

"I can give you a lift," says Simon. *Anywhere you like*, thinks Svala, and replies that she's fine walking. She scans the street for Ester one last time. She must have forgotten about the pizza.

"Hop in," he says, and sets off on the road leading around the slope of Björkberget, where Björkavan gets its name from the inward bend of the river before the start of the falls.

There's a pungent tree air freshener dangling from the rearview mirror. The seat leather is cold. He switches on the radio and the scenery flashes past without detail or end.

"How do you know where I live?" she asks, being cautious.

"I know most things," says Simon with a wink. "But joking aside, I asked Petra."

He turns into the farmhouse approach. The moon is shining on the front yard. The kitchen light is on. She has her hand ready on the door handle.

Aiko barks and the bitch howls.

She says, "I'd probably better . . . and thanks for the lift."

"There's something special about you," he says.

Svala doesn't know what to answer.

"You're so grown up for someone so young. How old are you, sixteen, seventeen?"

"Nearly fourteen," she says, and turns up the volume on the radio. *My daddy was an astronaut.*

"Who were the Baader–Meinhof gang?" she asks.

"A radical left-wing organisation in Germany. Their members were willing to sacrifice themselves and others for their cause. Not that different from you and me. Or maybe you prefer hugging trees and waving flags?"

He puts a hand over hers. She doesn't know whether she should pull hers away. Unsure whether that would mean missing out or escaping something.

"Anyway, see you on Saturday," he says. "Am I the only one with a car?"

"I've got a car," Svala says quickly. "That is . . . yes, I've got a car."

In the dim light she can't see what he's thinking. Probably that she's ridiculous. A little girl of not quite fourteen, trying to impress a grown man.

"Good," he says. "That might come in very handy. I'll call you tomorrow."

An uncle putting food in front of her. Asking where she's been.

Svala eats reheated meat and potato dumplings, giving an approximate version.

An uncle urging her to keep him abreast of what's going on. Asking who drove her home.

That guy Simon, she thinks, switching off the light. She can see him in front of her. His hands moving as he talks. The way he looks at her. The hair flopping over his forehead.

She puts the light on again and finishes what she's writing. Folds the slip of paper into a little square and stuffs it inside the monkey, her very own safe, made of plush.

I'll call you tomorrow.

5

If there is anything to ease the misery of Kurt Vikström's 81-year-old life it is, perhaps, that early summer has brought a little warmth. It's been a long, hellish winter. He's been on the verge of freezing to death.

He's managed to sleep for a while. He opens the car door and slowly eases himself out of his seat. The pain shifts around his body. Right now, it's his right leg that is worst.

In a few hours' time he'll be enjoying his one hot meal of the day. He drives towards town, uses the toilet at the OKQ8 petrol station and parks at the City Hotel.

The election in the autumn is already making its presence felt, even though winter has only now loosened its grip.

"We will bring down fuel prices so ordinary people can afford to drive their cars to work. Climate change is nothing but a Social Democrat myth. Our pensioners deserve to be at least as well off as criminals and immigrants. Quality of healthcare for Swedes must take priority over benefits for refugees."

Fans of the Sweden Democrats clap their hands and Kurt swears.

"Goddamned neo-Nazis," he says, and stumbles. He could do with a stick. Or even a walking frame.

His usual round of the bins in the shopping precinct goes more slowly than usual and he has little to show for it. The deposits on eight cans

24

and two half-litre bottles won't make anyone rich. Not enough to buy petrol or fill a stomach, but Kurt never thinks in those terms.

He puts things in his shopping trolley. The sort of stuff other people call rubbish. In his eye they are finds and he stows them carefully. Fills the trolley to the top and then it's time to go back to the car.

He puts the parking tickets in the glove compartment with the rest of his bookkeeping. He squashes his finds into a plastic bag and adds it to the pile already filling the boot space and seats. Except for a little hollow around the driver's seat, big enough for his own body.

On a normal day, Kurt does three return trips between the shopping centre and the decommissioned tip where he now has his home, but not today. He feels tired. Evening comes, but night never descends. The sun, which has barely risen above the horizon for the past six months, is frisky. It lurks in dusky restlessness for a few hours before it sparks into life again.

It's possible he nodded off for a while, lulled by the cosy warmth generated by bacteria and worms eating their way through the contents of his bags. The sound of a car coming up the slope startles him awake.

He is parked behind a site hut. Once upon a time it was an office. A foreman worked in the office. That was a long time ago. To Kurt Vikström, it feels almost like yesterday.

Like Kurt, the car is clapped out. Its best days are behind it. It blends in among all the other junk that people lug out here despite the prohibition signs. He quickly presses the buttons to lock the front doors, shuffles down as low as he can and grabs some of the bags to cover his head.

"Cool set of wheels."

The voice is young and full of self-confidence. A kick to its bodywork. A yank at a door.

"Never mind the damn car, bring her out and we can get this over with."

"We can have a bit of fun first though, yeah?"

First? The vascular spasm clenches at Kurt's chest as he lies there, hidden as best he can be.

"We just want to talk to you," says one of them when the girl protests.

And they laugh. They're really enjoying themselves now. It's Friday, after all. They only want to scare her a bit. Scared skirt is the tastiest. Heh heh. Lets you do anything without making a fuss and she isn't making any fuss. Comes along with them obediently, her feet dragging on the slope and the youths' strong arms holding her body upright.

Kurt thinks he ought to. Maybe. Stop them doing whatever it is. Take some responsibility. Turn back time. Put things right. But he does nothing. As usual he does nothing. Merely shifts one of the bags off his head and hears them moving away. He stretches up so his eyes are at a level where they can see. He realises where they are taking her. When the place was being cleaned up, the ground gave way. They put a fence round the crater that opened up.

He watches their backs, and the girl being shoved to the edge.

He's running out of oxygen. He fumbles for the winder and lets the window down by a centimetre.

The sounds reach him again. The hand on his heart is like a knife now. He pulls the bags back over his head, disappears, into his own thoughts. The man he was. The family he had. The house they lived in and here comes the fire. He senses the smoke, the heat, the flames. Tries to get upstairs. Hears the screams. Shouts to them to jump. As for him, he backs off. Gets out through the balcony door. Puts up a ladder. The flames are spreading from room to room. The glass in the windows breaks. A child jumps. Christ almighty, let it be the boy.

When Kurt wakes up, it is light. At first he can't find the button to unlock the door. He starts to panic. Thrashes around to get free of the bags, gets the door open and falls out onto the ground.

The air is clear. He is alive. He can breathe. The pressure of his bladder makes itself felt. He crawls to the front wheels. Slowly gets to his feet.

Is he shaking off a dream? He's not sure.

He walks to the edge of the gaping hole. He is drawn towards the fence. Kurt Vikström's body is not to be relied on any longer, but his memory is usually alright. He saw something. He's almost sure, but now he really needs to pee. He opens his flies and watches the trickle running down the steep side.

Right down at the bottom. The body is lying on its stomach as if it's smelling the first flowers of spring.

The night catches up. Another vascular spasm cuts through Kurt and seems to settle in his legs as he tries to run back to the car. He has to stop, get his breath back. They could still be here, or coming back, they could have seen him. Thoughts that draw their oxygen from his fear, his panic. He is a witness. Witnesses have to be disposed of. He must get himself out of here and now the tears start, the images that never lose their sharpness. The guilt and the cowardice, being to blame for the deaths of others. The girl on the edge, the burning child, and on the sidelines, always safe and sound on the sidelines, he himself.

The car freewheels down the hill to the main road.

Moments before the turning for Gasskas, he runs out of petrol. The old Volvo Amazon coughs its way those last few metres onto the verge.

Air. He needs air.

A Good Samaritan stops. They ask if he needs help. Put an arm around his shoulder. Withdraw it as the smell reaches them.

"Wolves at the tip," he wheezes. "Wolves, wolves, wolves . . ."

6

It's liberating to climb into the patrol car and drive to destinations that are the same yet different. The sun is hanging high in the sky. They are standing in the car park. Turning up their faces to let the bright spring-time rays reach pale, greyish office skin.

The world is an escalating misery of war, natural disasters and Sweden Democrats, but for a moment, life is perfect.

"We should probably go," says Birna Guðmundurdóttir. "You can bet your life Faste's up there with his bloody binoculars trained on us."

Faste as in Hans Faste, Head of the Serious Crime Unit.

"Let him then. Just two more minutes," says Jessica Harnesk. Relaxes her shoulders, lets the gentle rays of the sun soothe sore ligaments.

Ping. Dammit. She forgot to put her phone on silent and another ping follows. Before she jumps into the car she digs an ibuprofen out of her breast pocket and washes it down with saliva. She won't last one more week in this crappy job.

"So where are we off to?" she says, even though she heard Faste's hot-tempered voice at the morning meeting. Not a day goes by without her feeling tempted to quit. But then there are the others, Birna for example, and a possible future to think about.

That bastard Faste will presumably retire at some point. Or keel over and die on the spot. She wouldn't be sorry, wouldn't even pretend. The car radio crackles.

"Svartluten first," says Birna, prodding at the display on the screen. "Virkesvägen 7b. An Ivar Eriksson rang in to report some disturbance next door."

She calls him.

"Hello," she says when he answers. "What's happening?"

"Nothing in particular, I expect I misheard."

Birna asks what he heard but he doesn't reply.

"Hello," she says, and then again, but Ivar Eriksson has hung up.

They turn off along Industrigatan and then into Virkesvägen. Birna looks sideways at Jessica.

"Doesn't your mum live somewhere around here?"

"Yeah," she says. "I think she's moved now, though. I think I had a change of address card a couple of years back."

"We can drop in if you like," says Birna.

"And why would I want to do that?" Jessica says, parking the car outside number 7b. "Shall we go to Iceland and look up your mum too?"

They glare at each other as they ring on Ivar Eriksson's door. Walk over to 7a and try there instead. Although it isn't so much walking as scrambling over all the junk that has accumulated in front of the door. Pieces of a kitchen table, a slashed armchair, cardboard boxes and other rubbish that's been chucked out of the house and adorned with car tyres and bin bags.

Unlike the neighbouring doors, which have either been replaced or at least painted, 7a is an original door that has had to do battle with a lot of weather and noise.

"You fucking whore, I'll kill you," shouts someone inside and someone else retorts:

"Go on then, you impotent arsehole."

Birna tugs at the door, which is jammed. In the end it takes their combined force to get a grip through the slit they have opened and pull the door wide.

The voices are coming from further inside the house and although they call out "Hello" and "Police", the row continues unabated.

They can't work out what is making the noise. A head being bashed against a wall or objects being thrown. Nothing unusual in that. Drunken brawls are routine. Especially on a payday Friday like today.

The semi-detached houses in Virkesvägen and Timmervägen were built in the early 1970s and all have the same layout. A small hall, a couple of bedrooms and a bathroom in a row along a corridor. Kitchen, utility room and a living room divided off by a breakfast bar. Back door opening onto a little patch of garden with a view over the pulp mill.

If anyone had been trying to hide the real point of the housing development at Svartluten, namely how close it was to the factory, they would swiftly be reminded as soon as they opened a window. The whole district has a foul smell not unlike rotten fish. Especially when the wind blows from the west.

"It smells of money," isn't that what he used to say? That bastard Göran, whom her mother moved in with. And then her mother would say: "Here's the guest room if you fancy sleeping over any time. We could do the garden together if you like. Plant strawberries, maybe. You like strawberries, don't you?"

Jessica didn't. In fact, she was so allergic to them that she ended up in A & E when her mother smuggled some into her birthday cake.

Number 7a still has the original wallpaper, medallions of green, pink and gold, and a dark-brown fitted carpet. An estate agent would say it was "In its original condition with all its charm intact."

They move towards the voices, weaving between piles of clothes and rubbish bags that haven't made it out to the dustbin.

Birna pushes open one of the bedroom doors. Opens the next one and shuts it quickly.

"Christ, what a stench. Something's died in there . . . we'll have to deal with it later."

It stinks as badly as her first meeting with Göran. "In this house it's me who decides, is that clear?"

First they see the corner sofa and that someone is lying on it. Then the man standing there, and straight afterwards the woman. She is slumped on the floor, her back against the wall. There is blood running down her face. Her eyes are narrow slits in pulped flesh but there is nothing wrong with her mouth.

"Beat me to death then, you worthless fuck! Or can't you even do that?" she yells.

He has something in his hand. A tool, Jessica can't find the word and it doesn't matter. Just as the man raises his arm and prepares to strike she hurls herself at him from the side. The tool is diverted from its trajectory towards the woman's head and flies straight through the window but now he isn't merely angry, he is in a fury. He throws Jessica aside, aims a semi-successful kick at her knee and gets back on his feet.

Drunk as a skunk but quick as a ferret he grabs a heavy, rounded, metal ashtray full of cigarette butts and swings it in front of him, swiping it at everything in his path – lamps, pot plants and pictures – on the way to his evident final goal. The woman is no longer screaming, she is laughing. Laughing like a madwoman.

"Drop it, or I'll shoot," shouts Birna, which makes the man stop, as if hearing her for the first time.

"Drop it!" she shouts again and the ashtray hits the floor with a dull thud. He turns. Raises his arms as if in a gesture of surrender but there's something about his eyes, his gaze. He's smiling now. Looking around him as if he wants the cred for all the havoc he's created. His expression says: *You can't control me. In this house it's me who decides.* He takes a step forward and then another.

"Stop!" shouts Birna, and suddenly he's so close that she can smell his stinking breath.

"Behind you!" Jessica's cry comes too late. The body on the sofa has got to its feet and grabbed Birna by the arm. She loses hold of her gun and drops it but has the presence of mind to kick it under the sofa.

Jessica makes a split-second decision. The sound of the first shot reverberates like blows to the eardrums and down into their bodies. Then she fires again.

One body falls backwards onto the sofa and vomits. Another curls into a foetal position. Police officers fasten handcuffs around wrists. Voices crackle on the radio. An ambulance is on its way, along with backup and doubtless the media.

When silence descends, broken only by occasional bouts of retching, they hear the sound.

"Are there children in the house?" asks Birna. She has pulled on a pair of plastic gloves and is examining the bloodied woman, who at least has stopped laughing. The woman shakes her head.

Jessica flexes her knee a couple of times to see if she can walk on it. Sawdust is trickling from the bullet holes in the ceiling. She climbs over the male body on the sofa; he has stopped retching and seems to have fallen asleep.

Göran used to fall asleep in the end, too. Preferably with her mother's blood on his knuckles.

"If it wasn't so bloody painful, I'd kick your guts out," she says and limps towards the kitchen. The sound is intermittent, and most audible by the door to the utility room.

"I think it's a dog," she says, and opens the door a crack. The room is dark apart from one small strip between the window ledge and the blanket that shuts out the daylight.

The stench of piss and shit brings tears to her eyes.

The sight of a mistreated animal that can barely lift its head brings more tears to her eyes.

She ought not to, but she holds out her hand.

"There, there," she says, fondling the puppy's sticky ear. "We're going to get you out of here."

The woman is taken away in the ambulance. The other two in a police car.

As they drive off, Jessica and Birna see the reporter from the local newspaper pulling up.

"Not all journalists are worthless," Jessica responds to Birna's grimace, pinching her on the knee. "Have you heard anything from what's-his-name? Blomkvist. Mikael, wasn't it?"

"Pack it in, there was never anything between us."

"Didn't say there was."

"Stop asking then," says Birna. The name hangs in the air, as it always does when Mikael comes up in conversation. He came. He left. There'll never be more to it than that.

They keep the car windows open as they drive to the vet. The reek of the puppy is unbearable; Jessica has wrapped it in a blanket and now it is on her lap, lying still. Hopefully it is sleeping. Maybe it is already dead.

"Damn those people," she says. "Battering each other to death is one thing, but a puppy."

Birna puts a hand on Jessica's arm. Leaves it lying there as a barrier to images, sounds, smells, voices. Soon enough they will have to chew over the morning's events with all and sundry, not least the boss.

Hans Faste has already called. Birna told him she was afraid they couldn't talk right now but he keeps on calling. They barely have time to shower off the blood and excrement and get into some fresh clothes before he's in their office, asking for their account. In the present tense please!

"We respond to a call-out, there's a disturbance going on, a threatening situation arises, a man makes threats and aims a blow with a weapon and then Birna draws her gun, issues a warning but she's taken unawares by an individual attacking her from behind, who knocks it out of her hand," says Jessica.

"Hand," says Faste, looking at Birna. "Aren't you holding your gun in a two-handed grip?"

"Er yes, I suppose I am, but I'm taken by surprise by the person coming from behind."

"Who is he?"

"Someone who was asleep on the sofa."

"And you're so surprised that you drop your service firearm?" asks the boss.

"Yes, but I manage to kick it under the sofa."

"Oh well, that was clever of you."

His voice has that kind of condescendingly amused tone to underline that he's already made up his mind: they misjudged the situation. He twists their words, looking for weak spots. No-one would be happier than him if it was a case of breach of duty.

"Birna does exactly the right thing," says Jessica, and Faste's eyes are back on her. "At that point I judge the situation to be so serious that I draw my gun and fire two shots into the ceiling."

"Wouldn't one suffice? And how can you be sure there's no-one upstairs?"

"It's a single-storey house," she says. And so they go on for a while, batting phrases between them until Faste concludes with the promise of a further investigation.

"Good," says Jessica, "then perhaps we can give our account of events to someone who's impartial."

Faste takes a walk around the desk, flicks through a few documents, leans forward and studies a photo of Birna's cat Sture, and ends his tour at the window, looking down over the river.

"The problem is," he says, "that we have information to indicate you threatened one of these individuals when he was in a vulnerable position."

"Wha-at?" says Jessica. "What do you mean?"

"You threatened to 'kick the guts out of him'," says Faste, and Jessica can tell he's enjoying himself.

With his hands clasped behind his back and his gaze registering that the daffodils along the riverside walk are coming up, he thoroughly enjoys the sense of power resting in his hands. He should be offering consolation, sympathy, at least some solidarity, but no.

Now he's humming as well. Humming some silly little tune, and he turns back to them and says:

"As you said, the investigation should establish what really happened this morning. So here's one little tip for you: don't omit any details, they usually find their way out anyway."

And then he's gone. Birna opens the window to air out the smell of the old bastard.

"Only psychopaths and housewives hum," she says. "Which category do you think he belongs in?"

"I can't hack this any longer," sighs Jessica. "I'm going to quit."

"Then he truly will have won."

Jessica knows she's right, but still. Work has been her safety valve in the past. A space where she can breathe. Since Faste came on the scene she doesn't know which is worse. Sick messages from Henke, the father of her kids, or Faste's so-called leadership.

The phone rings. Neither of them makes any move to answer it.

"Come on," says Birna. "Faste can say what the hell he likes. Let's go down to the City and see if they've opened the terrace bar. I'll bring a laptop and we can write up our report."

"You start walking, I'll be right there," says Jessica, and accepts the call.

7

A car at the side of the road. A man who needed help. The ambulance has just left. Nothing serious as far as the caller could make out.

"So why are you ringing the police?" Jessica asks 37-year-old Good Samaritan Fredrik Berg and hears him clear his throat.

"The Man, Kurt the Can Man, you know, the one who collects . . . well anyway, he'd passed out when I got there but he came round and perked up. Said several times that he'd seen wolves at the old rubbish tip. So I thought you'd probably want to know. The Lapps . . . er, I mean the Sami . . . tend to be a bit trigger-happy when it comes to predators."

Jessica Harnesk gives an inward sigh and waves Birna back to the car. A beer wouldn't have gone amiss right now. But wolves close to town aren't great news. She thanks Fredrik for the information.

"If you only knew how little sun I've had in my life," says Birna. "Ash clouds and erupting volcanoes are my lot."

It strikes Jessica how sparse her knowledge of the Icelander is, even though they've been working together for a couple of years. They do try sometimes. Go out for a meal. Watch a film together once the children are asleep. They don't find it difficult to talk to each other, but their conversations always end up revolving around work.

"Just two more minutes."

Jessica takes the opportunity to check text messages she didn't ask for. E-mails she should have answered long ago. Missed calls from people she doesn't want to talk to.

They are on the road to the old tip and childhood memories resurface. Jessica sends them packing to where they belong. Which is on a rubbish tip, in most cases.

They sit on the steps to the old site office. It is a peaceful place with the hum of insects and the chirping of birds.

"Göran and I used to come here sometimes to shoot rats."

"Who's Göran?"

"One of my mother's marvellous boyfriends. They all queued up for a chance to enrich our lives."

Birna stands up. Takes several turns about the area just in front of them. Gets out her mobile and puts it away again.

"OK, where shall we start and what are we looking for?"

"Wolves. Any tracks. Reindeer they've brought down, ravens hanging about."

Tyre tracks and new-looking litter such as beer cans and hamburger wrappers are evidence that the place still gets visitors. They work their way outwards in circles towards the fence. Signs worn faint by the weather, warning that the ground falls away. But there are no tracks or wounded reindeer to be seen, no other signs of the predators' presence.

They both see her at the same time. The body, on its knees as if she is praying, but fully visible at the bottom of the steep slope.

"Jesus wept," says Jessica, and puts a hand over her mouth, sickened. The thought of a dead female body – or for that matter of whoever did it – is too much for her. She wants to get into the car and drive away, ask someone else to deal with it, utter the forbidden words that she can't cope. Shout out loud that she's had enough and wants to go home. Home to her children. Nuzzle the soft napes of their necks. Lock them in with her. Shut the world out. But beside her stands Birna, looking as though nothing's happened. In fact doesn't she seem a bit excited? Strangely energised, somehow.

"Get an ambulance and some backup over here," says Birna. "I'll fetch the binoculars."

The woman's face is turned away from them and Birna can't tell if she is dead or has only lost consciousness. But if there's even the slightest chance that they've made it in time, they can't afford to mess up. It's not that she's unaware of Harnesk's fear, or her own for that matter. She makes an estimation, calculates the risks and decides it is possible.

"It'll take too long to go round," says Birna. The fence is a feeble barrier, not enough to stop her uprooting one of the posts and climbing over the sagging wire. "Are you coming?" she says. "Don't look down, that's all. You'll get used to the height. There are branches to grab on to."

Jessica's legs, which want to turn and run, take strides towards the edge of the crater. A stone comes loose. Her eyes follow its bouncing descent to the bottom.

"I still think we should go round," she says.

"You do that, then," says Birna and starts to slither her way down.

In a sudden burst of courage, Jessica follows.

Spindly young birch shoots provide them with handholds, along with roots and rocks. They slide down the last bit until their feet reach solid ground.

The body has not been moved. The woman is young. Jessica checks for vital signs. One eye is missing. The ravens never rest.

"Isn't that . . ." says Birna, her sentence petering out.

"Are you thinking of . . . whatever she's called?"

"The one who tried to interview you the last time we brought in some tree huggers."

"They were demonstrating about the mine, weren't they?"

"Same difference. But that time she wasn't there as a reporter. She was part of the demo."

"She called me afterwards," says Jessica. "She worked at *Gaskassen*, her name was Södergran, I think, and she asked me what I thought about the new mine."

"And what did you say?"

"Said it was irrelevant what I thought."

"You'd be good in court," says Birna, getting out pen and notepad.

The body's course down the steep side is clear to see. The ground all around appears undisturbed. Nettles, couch grass and other vigorous forms of plant life have been spurred into growth by the warmth. Jessica strokes back the hair from the girl's forehead. Her cheek is as soft as a puppy's ear.

"All these men who hate women, where do they come from?"

"New litters born every year," says Birna and carries on making notes. Cause of death unknown, right arm at an unnatural angle, major trauma to the back of the head, no other signs of injury caused by external violence. "But perhaps we shouldn't assume that someone else – a man – did this. Could be she slipped and fell. Suicide is another possibility."

Sweat is trickling down their backs. Birna takes off her jacket and sits on a rock.

"So, that Göran—" she starts.

"Here, have some water," says Jessica. "It's like a fucking cauldron down here."

It's been a longer day than most. And it isn't over yet.

An address. Two names. Only the dad is at home. The dog barks. The cat purrs. The hall smells of freshly baked bread. They're bringers of information that will be all but unbearable.

"Oh, hi there," says the man. "Come in, I'll put on some coffee."

His face is open and candid. The world, like most people's worlds, looks simple, safe and predictable.

"Have a sandwich, too," he says, taking cheese and things out of the fridge.

"We're here about Ester," says Jessica.

"I thought you probably were. She said you might turn up this afternoon."

He goes off and returns with some books.

"I think it was these you wanted."

He pushes the pile towards them.

"Nils," says Jessica, "we're police officers."

"Feel free to call me Nisse."

The man gets up. Opens the oven door. Cuts a few slices of the steaming loaf. Pours coffee and invites them to help themselves.

Soon this gentle, ordinary house fragrant with fresh bread will be turned into a place of mourning.

Jessica forces her voice to formulate some words.

She isn't the executioner. But she is his envoy.

8

"What if it's my house the police come calling at next time? Henke's gone weird again. He's got something brewing. I can sense it, but nobody seems to care. His parents don't. Not even my sister. In fact she says how nice he is these days and maybe he is. To them."

Jessica rubs her eyes and Birna scrabbles in the glove compartment for a pack of tissues: "We've had a tough day but that doesn't mean anything's going to happen to your children. We can drive past and check if you like. I mean, not that anything's happened . . ."

They head to the hospital instead.

"We'd better try to have a chat with Kurt the Can Man," says Jessica. "What he said about wolves at the tip may have seemed like delirious ramblings, but it could be that he saw something he didn't dare to speak openly about. You know who he is?"

"Of course," says Birna. "Everyone knows."

Friday evening and payday, plus the first really warm day of spring. The Accident and Emergency Department is pulsing. It's blood, sweat and tears for both patients and staff. Birna manages to waylay a nurse.

"Kurt Vikström, where will we find him?"

"We sent him to Solgläntan, we're full up here tonight. He was doing pretty well. A shower was what he most urgently needed." The nurse pulls a face. "We lent him some clothes. Threw out his old ones."

By a quarter past nine they are both back in the car. At the Solgläntan residential care home they found a can collector who'd had a meal and was fast asleep. Jessica decides they'll try again in the morning. They park the car at the police station and are about to say goodnight when Birna suggests they go for that beer they talked about earlier.

The City Hotel on a Friday night, all dressed up and with full payday pockets; there's no chance of finding a table. They look around them and are about to go when a solo man of the elderly variety waves them over.

"I'm leaving shortly, have a seat and I'll get you something to drink. Beer?"

They nod. Their bodies ache. Their souls ache. Numbing them with alcohol seems like a good idea. They drink at the same pace, grateful for the third person at the table who is on his way to buy another round.

"Ingvar Bengtsson, also known as IB, worked for the Security Service for years but he's retired now," says Jessica.

"You know him?" asks Birna.

"Well, sort of. His daughter Malin went missing a few years back. Presumed murdered but she was never found. We thought she'd turn up in the pile of bones at the forest hut outside Spadnovaure, but she didn't. Even though she fitted the profile of the victims. A drug addict trying to finance her habit who got herself into debt. But not if you ask IB. According to him, Malin had no addiction problems. He's unbudgeable, totally convinced she went missing for other reasons."

"Easier that way," says Birna. "Imagine yourself in his shoes."

But Jessica doesn't want to think about her children. Or their father. Things looked brighter for a while. But now darkness has descended on his mind again. She doesn't trust him but she has no choice. He's pulled himself together, got a therapist and has an income. As a result, they have shared custody.

"Bloody Henke." The words slip out of her and two more beers thud down on the table in front of them.

"You look as though you've had a tough shift," says IB.

"And how are you doing?" Jessica asks, to avoid saying anything about the events of their day.

"I can put up with it," he says, and then perhaps he registers just how shattered Jessica looks. "Life as a pensioner isn't that exciting, but it's quite peaceful."

"Jessica just told me about Malin," says Birna, and Jessica sighs.

Now IB will never leave.

"Malin, yes . . ." he says, twirling his glass. "She disappeared and never came back. Was it you two who found the girl at the tip?"

"How do you know we found anyone there?"

Superfluous question. It goes without saying that the local paper has already caught on and published something online.

Young men vanish from time to time. Most of them of their own volition. The occasional body is discovered by berry pickers and hunters. Most are never found. When women go missing, it's a different story. And if they do happen to be found, the Swedish media in their entirety sit up and take interest. A murdered girl has more entertainment value.

"It's all bound up with the rest of it, I daresay," says IB. "It's incredible that the police aren't doing more to stop organised crime. Good job it's 2022 and an election year."

"What do you mean by all the rest of it?" asks Birna.

"The gangs, the biker clubs, the drug pushers, to name but a few."

"Not much left of the Svavelsjö Motorcycle Club now, at any rate. They went back down south with their greasy ponytails between their legs."

"Maybe so, but you didn't get anywhere with the remains at the forest hut or the fire at that bunker. In spite of there being witnesses."

"I wasn't aware that there were any witnesses," says Birna. "Do you have anyone particular in mind?"

Jessica puts a hand on Birna's thigh. It says *leave it, keep quiet, the investigation isn't public.*

IB looks around him. Takes a few rapid swigs of beer and sets down his glass with a thump.

"Sometimes I think that Flashback forum knows more about the world than the police do. I suggest you have a look at the link 'Bunker owner posted White Power material'. If you can nail that madman, perhaps some of the other stuff will solve itself."

"You sound angry," says Birna.

"I *am* angry."

"Because you miss your daughter?"

"That too."

"Talking of witnesses to the bunker fire, isn't that Henry Salo propping up the bar?" says Jessica. Salo, Gasskas's number one celebrity. "Did you see the headline this morning? 'Municipal boss slams opponents: Build padel courts instead of swimming pools'."

"Haha, no." Birna can't help a little smile. "But who's the other one?"

"No idea. Some visiting businessman from China maybe?"

"The bastards . . ." wheezes IB. A few determined steps later, he's at the bar.

They can't hear what he's saying. He waves his arms about. Salo shoves him away.

"We probably ought to . . ." says Birna.

"I'm too shattered to do the police thing. Let the bouncers deal with the Security Service."

The fourth beer has much the same effect as earmuffs. Jessica zones out. She doesn't even register Birna heading for the exit with a firm grip on IB's arm. Tomorrow she'll regret it. But for now it feels like the right decision.

Hi Lisbeth. Sitting here at the City Hotel. Shame I've nobody to dance with. It's been ages. Hugs, J.

A few seconds later she can see that the message has been read. She waits, but nothing happens. When she looks up, the man with Asian features raises his glass in a toast. His eyes are amazingly green.

She looks away and then back. The gesture is unambiguous. She nods.

9

The lynx is a shy cat endowed with the hearing and vision and other sensory abilities that enable it to avoid its sole enemy: humankind. These qualities also make the lynx one of the top predators in the forest. Perhaps that is why it has survived fur hunters, a lack of hoofed prey, deforestation, sarcoptic mange in foxes and other secondary threats created by humans. Because that is essentially what humans do: they take. Not simply out of basic need like other predators. They grab things for themselves out of sheer vanity. Dress their women in gleaming furs. Clear-fell forest out of greed. Hunt elk, red deer and roe deer to the last hoof. Humans take and then they give. Declare animals protected species for a variety of reasons. The lynx is a beautiful creature, after all.

When Marcus Branco gives Marika Vikström a new name he hesitates between *Flodiller*, the word for mink, and *Lo*, the word for lynx. The existence of the mink in the wild is as unnatural as Marika's reconstructed skin. With her indefinable age she lies somewhere between female and non-gendered but moves like a child, although she does not have a child's emotional register. As currently constituted, she is the most free being he knows.

She has worked her way up through the hierarchy. Proved herself worthy, qualified, uncompromising. But she is not his first darling. That one got run over last autumn. He has always factored in a bit of wastage.

But as the mink largely exists in captivity, he decides to use the name Lo for Marika. Just like the last one.

Lo as in the name of the silent killer.

Lo as in the sovereign lady of the night.

Lo, the first letters in loyal.

She parks the car on a track for forestry vehicles a few kilometres from the Solgläntan residential care home. Not that the home is near any other buildings. This is routine procedure.

It's coming up to 2 a.m.

Still a bit early for the hour of the wolf, the anxiety-laden stretch when it's almost dawn and people get up to escape their nightmares, go to the kitchen for a drink of water and happen to see someone moving along the street.

Lo has already been there once that evening as another person: a considerate daughter coming to visit her pappa, shortly after the evening shift went home and the single staff member on night duty took over. She rang on the speakerphone at the front door, was admitted by a Soheil, put the cinnamon bun wreath she had brought with her on the kitchen worktop and carried on to the fourth room on the right in the east corridor. She assured herself she would be able to make her way unobserved along the little section of corridor before slipping swiftly through the back door, which is left unlocked for fire safety reasons, and down the two sets of steps to the basement door. She noted that it had no alarm because the staff – now, exactly as fifteen years ago when she had a summer job here – used the little patch of grass outside as a smoking area.

Now she is walking through the forest and emerges just below the rear of Solgläntan. The rock that props the self-closing door open is still there. She goes on up the steps, listens outside the fire door. Pulls up her balaclava and readies herself to leave the same way if anyone spots her.

As she was expecting, the corridor is as deserted and highly polished as it was earlier. Kurt Vikström's door already has a handwritten name plate with hearts and flowers. To think how little people know about each other.

He is asleep. Gives a sudden snore, breathing with his mouth open. Enough light to guide her seeps in through the slats of the venetian blind from the lighting outside. She pulls a chair up to the bedside. Besides that, the room is bare. A complete absence of personal possessions. It is a strange sensation, observing him from a close distance. He is just the same. In a sleeping state, at least.

She considers waking him for a last farewell. To inform him that he is finally going to leave this earthly life to be reunited with some of his family. When he unexpectedly opens his eyes, his gaze is sharp and clear. Gentle, too.

"Is that you, Marika?" he says after a while. "Where's your brother?'

"Peter died twenty-two years ago, don't you remember? You saved yourself and let Peter and Mum die in the fire."

"The coward dies many thousand times, the brave person only once," he whispers, and lets his eyes run over her. "But clearly you survived. Have you had a good life?"

"Excellent," says Lo. "I had skin that was good at healing. I thought you might want to see me one last time before we part."

She takes off her sweater and twirls slowly round.

"I'm sorry, but it was all I could do," he says slowly, and shuts his eyes.

It isn't clear what he's referring to. The fact that he neither saved his family nor took care of the one who did in fact survive.

Kurt Vikström is the last link to her former life. A broken old can collector. She picks up the extra pillow and waits until he opens his eyes again.

Do it, says the look in them. *I can't wait.*

His arms offer no resistance. A few struggling kicks of his legs under

48

the covers, a final rattle from tobacco-tortured lung alveoli and then it's all over.

She tucks the pillow under his head. Strokes his wayward hair into place and closes his eyes.

"Rest in peace, Marika Vikström."

10

The empty roads at dawn make for a quick and easy journey. Driving south until she is level with Tierp, Lo turns inland and heads for Trollsjön swimming lake, blasted from the rock by the roadbuilders. Someone drives away in the Volvo, while she swaps to a Toyota.

Towards lunchtime she cruises into Stockholm, turns onto Birger Jarlsgatan, drives down into a private garage and takes the lift to the apartment.

The fatigue is showing around her eyes. But instead of her bed she opts for an hour on the treadmill, makes herself an espresso and logs on with the group.

"How are you all?" she says, and assumes she is appearing to them as a projection on the big screen in the conference room.

"We miss you," says Varg. "There's nobody to make the coffee or do the dishes."

"Thanks for that," she says. "There's always Räv."

Räv, totally lacking any sense of humour or self-awareness, looks as if he wants to say something, but turns back to the screen. She doesn't know what she thinks of him and presumably it is irrelevant. The operation relies on the group members' loyalty to one another. She and Räv are replacements for deceased components. According to the scanty information she has received, they died in a showdown between Branco and external elements currently unknown to her. In the innermost circle, only Varg and Björn remain from the original teenage gang in Umeå.

"I thought you weren't making the road trip until tomorrow," says Räv. There's something in his voice, as if he can hear what she is thinking and wants to counter-attack. "We had a planning meeting. Shame you couldn't be here."

"Pappa died last night. I had to drop by the care home," she says, and everyone except Räv expresses their condolences.

"He was old, it wasn't unexpected," she says to discourage further comment.

Varg, who is as slow-witted as he is sentimental, shapes his hands into a heart and then mimes sending hugs of support. How anybody so soft can be so brutal is beyond her. Where she used a pillow, Varg would have gone on a spree around the home with a machine gun.

The exhaustion hits her again. It is now twenty-four hours since she had any sleep.

She asks if there's anything special she should be aware of, but no, it's mainly the usual stuff. The Sweden Democrats asking for money for their troll accounts and a few other things they can talk about when she's back.

"By the way, we've just heard that the witness at the tip died last night. Very sad to see Gasskas lose one of its best-known street charac-ters."

"Very sad," she parrots. "I'll be in touch tomorrow then. I've got a few meetings in the morning, then I'll be driving back."

She's about to log off when Branco raises a hand: "Wait, there's one more thing."

She kicks off her shoes, removes her socks with the help of her big toe. Her feet leave marks on the deep-pile fitted carpet. Stockholm is settling in for the evening and, outside, the ants way down below are scurrying home to their heaps.

It's her and Branco now. The others file out of the room.

Branco propels his chair forward and back. She waits for more to emerge.

"Did you ever meet Märta Hirak?"

"Yes, once or twice. She's dead now, isn't she?"

"Fascinating woman, virtually immortal, but in the end even she made some mistakes. And now those mistakes seem to have been passed down to the next generation."

"You mean her daughter?"

"Precisely. Svala. A swallow. Pretty name for a pretty child."

His voice catches. He clears his throat. Pours himself a cup of tea. Adds a pinch of sugar and stirs the liquid while he collects his thoughts. It goes against the grain for him to admit he has enemies. They have always existed in some form. And until now he has controlled them, cleared them out of the way.

The Hirak brat is something else. For quite a few years, this swallow has been flying under the radar. Because who suspects a quiet child? Even when she turned up at the bunker there was no reason to suspect she had come for anything other than her mother.

The image of the girl with the dying mother in her arms has stayed in his mind. Maybe because he had assumed that the brains behind it all was that horrible creature Lisbeth Salander. Until information from the underworld started trickling out between the lines.

"The kid's got a few blood spatters on her hands. Her stepfather Peder Sandberg's, for a start."

"I thought he took his own life."

"Exactly, as with a few others of the same tribe."

There was a time when Lo herself moved on the periphery of Peder Sandberg's clan. Never at its heart, always outside, but still. News of Sandberg's death gathered pace, spreading like wildfire through the layers of people who had served his purposes in various ways. She had remained anonymous, which gives her an advantage today. The link to the network is invisible and should remain so. She earned the job with Branco on her own merit, thanks to a combination of references and sought-after knowledge. Thus far she has only been occupied with the legal side of business deals in some of the many sub-companies in the Branco empire. She senses that her range of assignments may be about to broaden.

"Märta Hirak wanted to move up in the world," says Branco. "In exchange for the killing of Peder Sandberg and an assurance of her daughter's future safety and welfare, she was offering a hard drive with a large amount of bitcoin on it. The only problem was, somebody got in before us. With both Sandberg and the hard drive. We assumed it was Märta who had hidden it. She implied as much and refused to the very end to give us the location or the passcode. That couple, Sandberg and Hirak, they owed us money. The hard drive was intended to settle the debt. But the wretched woman went and died on us."

"So what has this got to do with the daughter?" says Lo.

"According to one source, though not necessarily a reliable one, she has it in her possession."

"And now you're planning to get it back."

"It's no more than right. The debt passed to her when her mother died, like original sin. I want you to investigate. No unnecessary violence, of course; we're serious businesspeople, after all." Branco raises his eyebrows at her. "Use your intelligence and show your softer side. I'm sure you'll find a way to lure her here, so we can sound out this little bird."

Personally he'd like to squeeze a lot more out of Svala. If he's lucky, she'll match her mother in pride and pluck. Then everything will be so much more enjoyable.

"Is there anything else?" says Lo, trying not to yawn.

Branco has considered the matter from many angles. One of his greatest qualities is that he is never too hasty. He rarely stoops to impulsive acts that could jeopardise wider plans. He will get to the kid in due course, but for now there are more important things to focus on and possibly worry about.

"Svala Hirak's got an aunt in Stockholm, one Lisbeth Salander. The same Salander who's been working with a former *Millennium* journalist, Mikael Blomkvist."

He deliberately omits to mention either the bunker or Blomkvist's poking about in his companies' business. At this initial stage, Lo is there as an observer. The less she knows, the more open her eyes will be.

"Salander goes to a martial arts club on Ringvägen and a therapist on Grindsgatan several times a week. Get acquainted with her, as a first move. Know your enemy, so to speak."

"And in what way is Salander my enemy?"

The question is reasonable. If the woman is an antagonist, Lo needs to know why.

She notes Branco's strained voice and his clenched right hand. Collecting weaknesses is something she does automatically. For the time being, she is working for him. And that's fine. But things can change, as they always do.

He propels his wheelchair on a quick circuit of the floor and comes back to the screen. With more emotion in his voice than intended, he briefs the lynx on the previous autumn's rout, the destruction of the Eagle's Nest and the group's enforced flight from their safe base. But he omits his desire to tear a certain grinning face to shreds and roast the creature over an open fire. It could easily be misinterpreted.

"And we mustn't overlook Mikael Blomkvist in all this, either," he says. "His heyday as a journalist may be over, but as a double act he and Salander are a potential threat to our operations and upcoming plans. Thanks to other individuals working with us, we know there's something going on. You'll provide extra assurance that their prying won't get any further than this."

His talk of plans makes her want to ask more. As a new member of the board, even if the post isn't official, she finds it hard to fathom Branco's enthusiasm for anything as risky as mineral prospecting. There's money to be made, she's sure of that, but even so. Like most people born in Gasskas, Lo equates mines to loss. With a doctorate in law specialising in industrial economy, she is also able to view the mining industry in its broader context, but what does she know? Perhaps Branco is a simple gold-digger living out his boyhood dream.

"Sorry if I'm repeating myself, but I don't want to make any unforced errors: You want Salander and Blomkvist removed?"

"If you mean snuffed out, the answer's no. If you stick to the plan as discussed, the Salander–Blomkvist problem will resolve itself. The information you need is already with you in the form of an encrypted e-mail, as are the contact details of collaborators if you should need them."

"Understood," she says. "One last question before we sign off. The explosion at the bridge, are we behind that and, if so, why?"

"The bridge? I'm the last person who would blow up bits of our eighteenth-century cultural heritage, but for Mimer Holdings it's clearly advantageous. Newly built roads running north from the old mine will ease things along very nicely when it comes to positive early press."

11

Fuck, fuck, *fuck*. Jessica Harnesk drags herself upright against the bedhead, fumbles for her phone and answers with her surname even though what she wants most in the world is to throw up, and instantly regrets not having checked who was calling.

"Rise and shine." Hans Faste's voice chirps like a baby vulture. "I can't see that any interview was conducted with Kurt Vikström yesterday evening."

He pauses for effect. Silence. Her own voice cracks into a cough.

"Sorry, it's my hay fever. Can I ring you back in a few minutes?" she says and cuts him off. She races to the bathroom and empties her stomach of what's left of the beer, Jägermeister, cocktails and goodness knows how many glasses of white wine from the box in the fridge.

On the other side of the bed she's glimpsed some black hair. She sits on the toilet lid and tries to piece together the previous night. They had fun. It was nice to feel yourself seen by somebody who hadn't spent all their life since babyhood in a place like Gasskas. Weeks, months of frustration with work and with the kids' father and his crises took another form. Her thoughts zip like a comet to its point of impact: Lisbeth Salander.

Bitch. She could at least have answered. They haven't been in touch since the autumn and it's probably Jessica's own fault. She has thought the thought many times, scrolled to that part of her contact list but stopped there. It isn't because of what happened, that woman's lack of boundaries and the way she turned Jessica into some kind of hillbilly cop with her gun tucked in the waistband of her trousers and boots ready to kick in as many biker faces as it took.

No, it was more to do with self-interest, feelings. She fell for her. Fell in love. And realised that that love was preposterous.

Afterwards she wrote an e-mail that she never sent.

Afterwards she deleted every e-mail they had exchanged, except one.

Afterwards she hoped Lisbeth would take the first step, but she didn't.

Jessica swallows down a couple of aspirin and resists the temptation to throw up again. If only the headache would subside. The best thing would be for him to have got dressed and left, whatever his name was, that Asian-looking guy. Oh yes. Kostas as in Kostas . . . She can't remember. Isn't bothered, but it's time for him to go.

He's in the kitchen. Putting a filter paper in the coffee machine. Looking for the coffee.

"I forgot to buy any," she says.

Green eyes glisten in the morning sun. He doesn't look even remotely hung over.

"Lovely picture of your children," he says. "Beautiful. They look like you."

She takes the frame out of his hands. Puts it back on the shelf. Says she's got to get to work and he needs to leave.

"See you tonight then," he says. "I'll book a table."

She is barely up to protesting, merely asks him to leave his number and when he still doesn't go, chivvies him towards the front door.

"We'll have to see. I'll call you later."

Is there anything better than being home alone? She's counting the hours. Driving is out of the question. Birna answers on the tenth ring.

"Aren't we off work today?"

"Yes, but we never did that interview with the Can Man. It might not have been wolves he saw."

"Somebody else can go out there, can't they?"

"Somebody else won't have time. Could you drive?"

"Sure thing. I'll pick you up in half an hour."

The residential home that has taken in Kurt the Can Man smells of urine and chlorine. Jessica senses her pores stinking of stale alcohol and muses that a coffee and a cinnamon bun would be hard to force down but a coffee on its own would be good, with milk. Both the manager and another member of staff sit down at the table, however.

"How's Kurt?" says Jessica, and they look perplexed.

"If you mean Kurt Vikström, he died last night."

"Died? The hospital said he was doing fine."

"Fine is rather an exaggeration, nobody comes here if they're doing fine, but he was grateful, and happy to get a meal and a bed. Wasn't he, Soheil?"

The care worker nods. "I looked in on him around midnight. He was supposed to have some painkillers but he was sound asleep, so I let him be. When the morning staff went in to see him he had no vital signs."

"Do we know what he died of?" asks Birna.

"No," says the manager. "Hard to say. Kurt suffered from multiple conditions. High blood pressure, grief, old age, malnourishment, mental health issues . . . He didn't have an easy life, Kurt the Can Man."

"How do you mean?" says Birna.

"His wife and son died in a house fire, a long time ago," Jessica fills her in. "Kurt managed to get out, but he couldn't save his family. After that, everything started to go wrong for him. He worked at the tip you know, but when it closed he started collecting cans instead, to get the deposits back. It turned out that he was also collecting rubbish, which he piled up in the apartment he rented. When his apartment block developed a rat problem, the dire state of the place came to light and they threw him out. He's been living in his car ever since."

"Which room is his?" says Birna, getting to her feet. The staff exchange glances.

"The undertakers came and fetched him right away. They normally take them to the mortuary for cremation. He had no family, after all."

"But he did, surely?" says Soheil to his manager. "His daughter came to visit yesterday evening. Pleasant woman. She's the one who brought the bun wreath."

"I didn't know that." The manager shrugs. "I mean, we heard just now that his whole family died in the house fire."

It has started snowing again. Spring has lasted precisely two days.

"Good job I didn't get round to changing to summer tyres," says Birna and the day feels like the road to Calvary.

If Kurt the Can Man had a daughter.

If Ester Södergran was involved in something shady.

If there really were any wolves, and if spring has fled back into winter.

Jessica nods off, leaning against the car window. She remembers a certain pair of Greek-Chinese lips.

"No! I can't!" she cries out.

"What can't you?" Birna asks.

"I was only having a dream." Her face reddens. "Can't remember what it was."

12

Everybody's talking about a young woman found dead at the tip. A few hours later, the police release a name and a picture. *Gaskassen* tops its online edition with MURDER?, with the strapline *24-year-old woman found dead at refuse tip*. Later, the piece talks about Ester Södergran's job as a journalist at *Gaskassen* and the shock to her co-workers in the newsroom. "We've lost a popular colleague and friend," says her immediate boss. "But Ester was an entertainment correspondent," he goes on. "As far as we can see, there's no link between her death and her work here."

The national media are on it like a flash and local police chief Hans Faste takes a trip into the real world, questions the staff supervisor at *Gaskassen* and other male employees there, and uses the opportunity to drop in on his childhood friend, the newspaper's editor Jan Stenberg.

The door blind is lowered. A desk drawer is opened. Whisky? I don't mind if I do. A drop of the hard stuff in the morning cleanses the gut. Every Dane knows that.

If Faste had asked Svala, she would probably have said something about both the sanatorium and the other haunted houses, but nobody cares about the work experience girl. Or about what's going on inside Svala. The grief, the anger, the sense of loss and guilt. When Ester was thrown down a sheer drop, Svala was wrapped up in her disappointment that Ester hadn't been in touch. They were supposed to go for pizza.

Talk over some ideas for new articles. She sees Ester's chair out of the corner of her eye. The tears that have been rising in her throat in repeated waves well up again. Loneliness has become the overriding emotion in her life, despite her efforts to keep it in check.

Svala logs into Ester's computer and transfers all the article folders to a USB stick. She deletes the files and is about to log out when the e-mail pings. The message has no subject line but it does have a sender.

Ante. Ester's hacker buddy.

She is barely through the first paragraph when the editor of the weekend supplement starts breathing down her neck.

"Sorry to bother you, Svala, this Ester business must be as awful for you as it is for the rest of us, but how did you two get on with the haunted houses, can we expect an article?"

"Er, well," says Svala. "Ester didn't get round to writing it, but I know she was working on a thing about the new mine."

"God, no." The editor pulls a face. "Nobody wants to read that sort of crap on their Saturday morning. Have you got anything with a bit more entertainment value?"

"A piece about superfoods in space. Do you want me to send it over?"

"How would a newspaper office cope without its interns?" he says, patting Svala on the shoulder.

Superfoods and space travel. Where did that come from?

She reads to the end of the e-mail from Ante the hacker, goes back through Ester's inbox and finds a lot more from him. They aren't just mates. They've been investigating Mimer Mining together.

We'll be able to publish soon. Ester had written in the e-mail thread. That's so cool. Douglas Ferm, he's like, "local hero". Even wrote publicly that he supports the Sami in their fight against the mine. Doesn't want the forests of his childhood turned into industrial land. And now he's part of the money behind MM. What a hypocrite. You're bloody brilliant! See you soon.

But presumably she never had. Svala copies his address and sends a few lines from her private e-mail account.

`Hi Ante, I worked with Ester. Can we meet? Svala Hirak.`

"I need it within the hour," the supplement editor yells in her direction.

`Revising for an exam. Maybe at the weekend. Will be in touch.`

She dashes off a lightweight piece about stars, collisions, planets and spacemen's food rations. Adds a few stock images and makes a suggestion or two for headlines.

Since she heard the news about Ester, an uncomfortable phrase has been playing on repeat inside her.

It's your turn next.

Logical reasoning along the lines of *They don't know who you are* and *You can't be sure they saw the drone* doesn't really help. Only a stringy little hare believes it has escape routes. They've always known who she is. From childhood onwards.

She checks her phone. Another meeting at Petra's. She puts a printout of the space travel article on a desk. Receives a nod of thanks.

Ester Södergran would have remembered that this is Svala's last day of work experience.

13

"Well, there's one thing we can agree on, at any rate. We failed miserably in almost every respect. Perhaps we're getting old."

"Especially you," says Lisbeth Salander, pouring Coke over clinking ice. "Maybe you should get your hair cut? Men with short hair look younger."

Mikael runs his hand through his hair, a pure reflex action that makes Lisbeth smile.

"Gotcha. But you're right, we never reached top form in that Norrland shitshow. It was too cold, I guess."

Ever since they parted with a nod at T-Centralen station back in the autumn, Blomkvist has been making fruitless attempts to contact Salander. Ringing, sending text after text, none of them answered. Until that morning.

I'm in the Åsö café for the next half-hour if you want to meet.

He threw on some clothes and jumped on his bicycle. Cut across Mariatorget and carried on down Swedenborgsgatan and along Magnus Ladulåsgatan before turning up Åsögatan, where he leaped off and propped his trusty Rex against the wall. A transfer of twelve minutes from waking to arrival.

He fingers his activity-tracker watch. He should take it off before he goes in. People with fitness watches are pathetic in Salander's eyes, but she doesn't even look up as he sits down at her table with an oat milk latte and a large glass of water, which he downs in a few gulps.

Mikael doesn't know where to start. It's easy to annoy Salander. Impossible to predict what mood she'll be in. If something doesn't suit her, she'll just get up and leave, which is what usually happens. But he has a very clear feeling of being glad to see her again. He may have aged in the space of a few months but she looks much the same as ever, with her fringe hanging down over her face in an attempt to shield herself from eye contact. He can roughly see the outline of her arms under a baggy hoodie. She's in more than good shape, despite all the junk food. Whereas he is forever fighting the flab.

"How've you been?" he asks, and then regrets the question. If he wants a longer answer than "good" he will have to deploy his journalistic skills. "Tell me," he says. "What's been going on since we last met?"

She looks up for the first time. Fixes her eyes on a point just above his face before she answers the question. "Nothing," she says.

"Nothing," he repeats.

"No."

And she's right. Life has reverted to the usual cycle of work, working out, pizza and her therapist Mrs Ågren.

She can hear herself how dull it sounds. You might say depressing. Yet she never brings herself to make more of her days. They tick by until it is time to die, which it has been several times already, although without success. *Without success?* Makes it sound as if she doesn't want to live, but is that true? She doesn't think so. Even though the door that those weeks in Gasskas tantalisingly left ajar has now slammed shut and won't be opened. Jessica Harnesk simply got out of the car and walked off without looking over her shoulder. And that was that.

Now she's been refused admittance to human relationships, everything has gone back to normal. Within her comfort zone and rather lonely.

She considers the man in front of her. Notes the stubble, the giveaway

64

blood-test plaster peeping out from under his rolled-up shirtsleeve, the fitness watch on his left wrist.

They aren't that different from each other. They're certainly both equally useless at relationships, although Mikael would never admit it. It's blatantly clear that he sees himself as urbane in comparison to her, and that's particularly obvious from his way of expressing himself. As if he's the one who always makes the decisions – is the one who decides when things are over.

Lisbeth is itching to peel off the scabby crust and ask how things are going with that Birna, she of the unwieldy surname, or why not with Pernilla and Lukas once she's started to pick at suppurating scabs. To judge by his seedy appearance: not very well.

"It was a close call up there in Gasskas," says Blomkvist, and it isn't clear whether he is referring to her or to himself. The conversation refuses to flow, even though he has been preparing himself ever since they parted so casually back in the autumn. "But anyway, I've had a go at piecing together the course of events."

He takes his laptop out of his shoulder bag and angles it so Lisbeth can see the screen. She gives it a cursory glance and looks bored out of her mind.

"Why are you bothering? Just be glad you and the boy are both alive. The rest is history."

"Remarkably resigned sort of comment to be coming from you," he says. "I might even say cynical, considering what happened to Svala's mother. You could at least read through the file."

Oh, she's thought about Svala and her mother alright. Doubtless a lot more than Blomkvist, who wasn't even there. The image of the mother dying in her daughter's arms is seared into her eye like welding sparks. They run through her dreams. Resurface the moment she lets her guard down.

She could tell him a thing or two about living with memories. Memories of all kinds. So many that in the end they clump into an insoluble mass. If only she thought he would understand. But she doesn't.

"So you're assuming you know more than you did last autumn?" she says.

"I don't know, but well . . . yes. At least setting it out in paragraphs and columns makes it clear. We missed something, maybe we missed a lot. I'd appreciate it if you would at least check through the document."

"Send me the crap then," she says and closes the laptop.

Which also marks the end of their brief conversation. He puts his hand through his fringe and asks if she can't stay a bit longer.

"Like I said," she responds, "that trick worked better before you had a receding hairline."

Without so much as a "Bye" or a "See you", she is out of the door to the street.

Cold oat milk latte is bloody disgusting.

14

"Well, you've all seen what happened," says Simon, lowering his eyes. "So now we know why Ester didn't attend the last meeting."

It feels natural for Simon to lead the meeting. He talks about Ester's commitment to environmental issues and her job at *Gaskassen*.

"Svala tells us she was working on an article about the new ore deposits. That only goes to prove we're on the right track. Now I think we should observe a minute's silence for Ester."

The minute goes by. Coffee and freshly baked buns appear on the table. Simon takes a bun. Female eyes follow his hands.

"Oh my God, that's the best I've ever tasted," he says, and takes another. The praise makes Petra glow. Anna-Maja gets up and goes out to the kitchen. The conversation cautiously starts to flow and returns to Ester.

"What if Ester's murder has something to do with us? I assume you lot have received threats in the past," says Levi.

The pensioner. The one who says little but thinks plenty. He appeals to Anna-Maja for support.

"I mean, maybe we ought to talk to the police."

"They won't take any notice of a few angry e-mails," says Anna-Maja.

"What e-mails?" asks Svala. She'd met Anna-Maja a few months before. They turned out to be cousins.

"From idiots who love to hate people like us. Nothing worth wasting time on."

"But why Ester?" Levi says, and is cut short by a coughing fit that seems to go on for ever. He struggles to his feet and Svala quickly gets up and helps him to the bathroom. His face is glistening with sweat; his eyes look tired, their whites yellow.

"You're sick, aren't you?" says Svala and he nods.

"Dying, but don't tell the others. These meetings are the only thing I've got left to enjoy."

Back in the living room, he appears almost restored to normal.

"I don't get it. How unbelievably cowardly to go after a young girl. Violence against women makes me see red," says Simon, licking pearl sugar off his fingers. "We ought to stage a protest against violence against women. Are we all agreed?"

Svala makes no comment on his assertion that Ester was assaulted. The police account said there was no sign of any violence other than that inflicted by the fall itself.

"The Social Democrat Youth League and the Women's Crisis Helpline are holding a torchlit procession on Friday," she says instead. "We can make some placards and march with them."

The proposal is voted through. Simon's look is warm. Something good is rising inside her. A sense of belonging, of being heard.

"About next Saturday," says Simon, tearing a page out of his A4 notepad. "I've drawn up a plan and looked over our various roles."

He tapes the sheet of paper to the kitchen door. They gather round like pupils round a list of exam results.

Svala can't see her name anywhere.

"Are we really sure about this?" says Anna-Maja. "It's a big step from shouting on marches to blocking roads. Someone'll have to take responsibility. I assume that would be you, Simon?"

"We're all in this together," he says, "that's the whole point. We're doing this for a vital cause, don't forget. For the natural world, for the reindeer herders – and not least for the generation that's growing up and will soon be taking over. Isn't that right, Svala? You don't want

Per-Henrik or anybody else in your family to struggle even more to keep the reindeer alive?"

How does he know their names?

He gives her a lift home again. After a few kilometres she summons up the courage to ask:

"Why wasn't I on the list?"

"Because I wanted it to be a secret. You've got the most important task of all. You and me together. I happen to know that the roads agency is going to divert the traffic exactly where our protest will be. Not because of us, but because of the explosion and the damage to the bridge over the river. The ore trucks that run between Gasskas and Kiruna will be taking another route. I thought we ought to stop that, too. Temporarily, at any rate. I haven't got all the precise details, but I need your help. You've got something the others are lacking," he says, but without elaborating on what he means.

She can't help smiling. She is somebody. Maybe even something good. Something that gives her a brief respite from her thoughts of Ester.

He drives up to the farm and switches off the engine.

"Do you miss Ester?" he asks.

"Yes, so much, but then we all do, I expect." The muscles in her throat feel tight.

"Come here," he says, pulling her to him. He strokes her hair. His hands feel like Mammamärta's. She closes her eyes. Inhales the scent of his jacket.

"We've got to be brave now, for Ester's sake. I'm counting on you."

15

The Cleaner looks about him. Like a mole sticking its head out of its winter hole he stretches his body, then he turns up his collar, buttons his pea coat and starts walking.

Everything he needs for the next chapter of his life fits into a camouflage bag that's been with him ever since military service. Then he'll have to see. One last assignment, as the Delivery Man said. After that he is free.

Not that the word has any particular appeal for him. The freedom he experienced in the forest will never return. Within him, the sea eagles still hover above the ground. Let out their piercing cries for food. Meet his eyes with gratitude and make off as quickly as they have come.

The months that followed have been spent in flight. Little by little, he is suppressing what was. The eagles, the human wrecks, his brother. A Cleaner can't afford a conscience; it goes with the territory. In any event, he is no more than a tool. An implementor. Not the one presiding over life and death; others do that. Yes, if not for the boy.

The boy. Time and again he comes back to the conversation they had. The moment when he discloses his identity to the child, and why. Why? Because he allows feelings to creep in. Sees himself from another perspective. Suddenly, he was the boy. A nine-year-old with no rights. Like a twin shadow, he slid into the boy's body. Became one with his pitiful vulnerability. Felt sorry for him. The phrase repeats itself over and over. *You felt sorry for him. You wanted to help him. By helping him, you thought you were helping yourself.*

The Copenhagen morning traffic grows at the same rate as the sun rises over the cityscape. The stream of cyclists on their way to colleges and jobs flows by like a solid, self-propelled mass.

He cuts across towards Øksnehallen, the former indoor livestock market in the oldest part of Kødbyen, once the city's meatpacking district. The oxen finished bellowing a long time ago, even though the brown nineteenth-century building still has the air of an animal Auschwitz.

He quickens his pace. There's something about the place. A queasiness imprinted indelibly in the paving stones and the fabric of the buildings. Terrified creatures waiting for slaughter. People have choices. Animals never.

He has been moving southward for several months. Staying in provisional accommodation procured for him by nameless individuals. On the alert for signs of discovery. He had received information from reliable sources but also followed the local news reports from Gasskas, which slowly ebbed away and were replaced by ice hockey results and stories about protests against the new mine.

He can never be sure, but there is nothing to indicate that anyone knows where he is. Apart from his brother Henry Salo, that is, and maybe Henry's aforementioned stepson, too. He has stopped saying the name. The boy is nothing but a body now.

Cutting ties with his employer once and for all has also been part of the plan, yet one day the Delivery Man is standing there nonetheless. A greyish-looking figure, very hard to remember. Even the voice is hard to recall from one visit to the next. The perfect Delivery Man, in other words. Born to blend in among other grey mice and vanish as silently as he has come.

"There's a job," he says. Information that could have been conveyed to him electronically.

"No," says the Cleaner, receiving in reply a look that possibly contains a glimmer of surprise before it resets itself into neutral.

"There'll be more information when you get there.

"No," says the Cleaner. "I'm done."

"You're in debt because you let the boy go."

"You don't know anything about that," says the Cleaner and gets another slight look of surprise.

"I don't know anything about anything," he says. "I simply repeat orders. This time the order was to seek you out in person and give you an assignment."

He digs about in his inside pocket. Hands over an envelope and repeats the same tiresome mantra as always:

"Burn after reading. You've got one month, starting from today. And as discussed, this is your last job. After that you're free."

A hint of a smile flits across the Delivery Man's face. Then he is gone.

16

This time it's Elias, the elder of her two uncles, who is waiting up and asks where she's been.

"You must have read about Ester?" she says. "She was part of our action group, sort of on the fringes. We had a meeting at Petra's. Is there any dinner left?"

She also asks whether Per-Henrik has gone to Gällivare, but her uncle doesn't reply. He wants to know what an action group does. She says they tie themselves to trees, write to the press, stage all sorts of protests. She doesn't do much herself. Learns, maybe, and listens. They're older than she is. Experienced. She's a mere child and nobody takes much notice of her.

"Sit down," he says, ladling meat and vegetable broth into a bowl. He runs his rough hand over her hair. Tenderly, wanting to show he is on her side. Despite his other body language, which is signalling anxiety. There's something up, she can sense it, but Elias is not as talkative as his brother. He holds back his words for when they are really needed. Not necessarily for times when she herself could do with them.

The dumplings float up to the viscous surface. The broth warms its way through her body. She makes short work of it, soaks up the last drops with the soft flatbread and could have eaten another bowlful, but for . . .

"What's the matter?" she says.

Elias puts the cheese and butter back in the fridge. Puts the bread in a bag and knots it. Turns off the overhead light but is still standing there, as if certain things can only be said in darkness.

"Per-Henrik found some reindeer. They were piled on top of each other. The yearling calf was on top, and still alive then. Per-Henrik's in the slaughter shed. He'd be glad of you down there to lend a hand, I'm sure."

The sloping ground is slippery beneath her soles. The meat soup is a hot reflux in her throat. The shed is pounding, the stereo turned up as loud as it will go. The knife cuts its way systematically through the anatomy of the reindeer cow. The yearling calf has been left until last. It still has its soft coat. The hairs yield to the palm of her hand.

May is calving month. Her uncles are fully employed with tracking the cows' patterns of movement. Or to be more precise, with shadowing the bears whose minds are set on a bellyful of newborn calf. When it is time, the cow makes its way to its own place of birth. From the cow's perspective it is a bad period. She has no fat on her after the winter's hunt for food. But for the calf, the timing is advantageous. The more months of grazing that lie ahead, the better its chances of surviving the coming winter.

The yearling calf appears to have coped well with the deep snow. It would have grown into a fine young reindeer over the summer.

Per-Henrik looks up, reaches for a whetter, tosses it to her.

She sharpens the cutting edge. Ties on an apron and does what must be done.

No-one knows how Ester died or why. Someone gave her a friend and took that friend away with the same hand. Her first ever. Perhaps her only friend. And now it's her fault these reindeer died. Someone is sending her a message.

The knife follows its set course, skinning and jointing. They are bodies now, she cannot let herself think of them in any other terms. The music keeps feelings at bay, as does the cold temperature of the shed. Four hundred and fifty kronor for a couple of slices at a top-end restaurant in Luleå. Of meat from her calf, which has only now realised that the world is bigger than its mother's teats. Her reindeer cow, due to calf soon. The first generation that would have Svala's own mark cut into its ear, later in the summer.

Anyone can own a reindeer. Only the Sami have the right to send them out to graze. During the autumn and winter months she has got to know the herd. To distinguish the markings that make every animal unique. The calf is white with brown spots. The cow brown with a white neck.

"Could they have died of natural causes?" she asks, even though she knows.

They take off their aprons and hang them up. Wash down the cutting surfaces. Scrub off the blood with gall soap. He turns off the music. She switches off the light. The stars are not moved by any of this.

But Svala is.

"I don't want to cause any trouble," she says on the way back to the house, the shiver down her spine spreading through her whole body.

Per-Henrik pulls her to him. Says she feels chilled through and she shouldn't let her thoughts run away with her. The reindeer have always had enemies.

"Put some more wood on the fire and sit by it. I've got to fetch something. I'll be right back."

He is gone for some minutes.

The warmth makes her drowsy.

"Here," he says, and puts a cardboard box on the floor next to her. "Märta kept it for you. I'm going up to bed but . . . well, I'm a light sleeper."

Svala waits until she hears the door of her uncle's room close before she opens the flaps of cardboard.

The fabric is rough. The colours are bright. It's not that she's never seen anything like this before. But none of the others had the smell of Mammamärta imprinted in their embroidery and fabric.

Say sorry and it's all forgiven.

The words fall like red-hot flakes as she stirs the fire.

Say sorry.

The *kolt*, the dress-like garment, is a loose fit. The shawl is itchy. She pulls the belt tight. The knife sheath dangles empty. The sewing case, thimble, coffee pouch, pewter rings and leather fringes swing uncomfortably at her waist. She pulls up the trousers, puts on the socks. Thrusts her feet into the shoes with their turned-up toes and ties the tassled laces. In the mirror she sees a child in clothes that are too big. A source of sorrow. A bird of ill omen. A person brought into this world by someone without sense enough to survive.

Someone shot your reindeer today, Mammamärta. Or mine, as they are now. It's your fault. It's all your fault. Do you hear that? Your fault!

She wrenches off the clothes, stuffs them back into the cardboard box and kicks the lot into the hall.

You're dead. Your last breath is the oxygen I live on.

It's starting to run out.

17

The evenings are getting longer, the sunsets over Skeppsholmen increasingly spectacular. Lisbeth sits in her window alcove licking her fingers after a couple of gooey Gorby's pirozhki, original flavour.

Mikael's new document is as predictable as she anticipated, except for the part about Plague. If the brain is a tunnel which the deepest insights must negotiate before they reach our consciousness, then it's a very long one. She doesn't want to think of Plague in any other way than as Plague. A hacker genius who's always been there in the background. A form of security. A friend. Someone she trusts.

Blomkvist's hints that Plague has somehow been talked into serving dark powers, in this case presumably Branco, are far-fetched. He would never do that to her. But they haven't been in touch since that phone call, months ago now.

She logs into their shared platform and types a message. No reply. She weighs up whether to contact someone else in Hacker Republic but hesitates, unsure of who they are nowadays. Times have changed, as has the mission itself. Their youthful idealism twenty years ago, with its focus on essentially playful attacks on the power centres of society, has been replaced by the potential for earning money from the same thing.

On the other hand, Plague has never been in particularly good physical shape. Anything could have happened. She decides to give it another twenty-four hours and then, if he hasn't answered, she'll corner him in his cave out at Hökarängen.

She devotes the rest of the day to her job. Loses concentration, takes an exercise break pacing round the 652 square metres of her apartment, tries again to rouse some interest in one of the many routine tasks that have found their way to her inbox.

Lisbeth doesn't usually stop to evaluate whether her work tasks adequately satisfy her brain cells. She does what needs to be done, high-powered or lowly, works her way through items that others are bogged down in, and moves on.

Usually, but not today. In another time she would have lit a cigarette, curled up in her window seat and let her thoughts disperse with the smoke until they landed of their own volition. But cigarettes have been definitively stubbed out and her brain is too restless for any deeper reflection. Or *mindfulness* as Mrs Ågren would say. *You've got to live in the present.*

Which surely everybody does, for God's sake.

Several times a day she feels like breaking things off with her registered psychotherapist, who is male but in her mind she calls him Mrs Ågren. Yet when Tuesday comes – and today is a Tuesday – she unfailingly finds herself making a beeline for Grindsgatan and then having to wait fifteen minutes in the entrance before she takes the short flight of stairs to his office.

Classical music streams into the waiting room. The bowl of red apples looks exactly as it did the week before. She is not chilly. But still she slips into one of the pairs of sheepskin slippers provided for visitors and switches off her phone.

Mrs Ågren welcomes her in, and she takes a seat in the same armchair as last time. He engages in his usual inane questions, which she deflects with her usual stony silence. Then, "You mentioned Jessica Harnesk when you were last here. Would you like to continue there?"

"It's hardly my fault that your egg timer went off the moment I said her name, is it?" she says, and takes a sip of his herbal tea which today is red and tastes of horseshit.

"No, but if you feel able to take up that thread again, by all means go on with your line of argument."

Line of argument. It's not a line of argument. It's a full stop. That damned red-haired cop. Her back was the last thing Lisbeth saw of her.

A mistake, she tells herself. Both falling for a cop and thinking they had something special. Nothing to be done but give up. The world must be full of potential relationships. But perhaps not for everybody. The fact that the cop fired off a drunken text message means nothing. She'll have to carry on missing her, that's all.

"There's never going to be anything between us," she says.

"But if it was in your power to steer the course of events," he says, "what would you do?"

And at that moment the egg timer goes off again. *Saved by the bell.* She puts the sheepskin slippers back in the basket, shoves her feet into her own battered old trainers, puts in her earbuds, pulls the hood over her head and walks home.

She has no idea what to do, damn it. Head north, maybe? Get aboard the night train, change to the railcar in Boden, head straight for Jessica's house and ring the doorbell?

"What a load of balls," Lisbeth mutters to herself a short while later.

Slurps down some kind of Indian takeaway. Crams her karate suit into her rucksack, locks the door and sets off for the *dojo*.

The prospect of the evening's karate practice lightens her spirits. From the first bow of the *Seisan* to the last, ninety minutes later, her thoughts will be on hold. The brain's focus on physical movements overrides everything, from the details of the *kata* that can always be perfected to the *kumite* and the openings in the split seconds between attack and defence.

She doesn't normally care who she ends up with as an opponent. It's all the same to her whether it's a teenager or a hundred-kilo man; the rules are the same for everyone. That is to say: give it all you've got but pull back your punches and kicks the instant before impact. That's only partially true, of course. Nothing feels better than a juicy *gyaku-zuki* landing on some self-important male belly.

A clenched female fist breaks through her defences and stops with its knuckles a millimetre from Lisbeth's chin. Christ, where did that come from?

Hajime and the bout resumes. Strike, parry, kick, parry. Strike, strike, parry, parry.

Lisbeth has never seen her before. She must be new. A black belt at an unknown level. Slightly strange techniques. A different style, perhaps. When the blow comes, Lisbeth takes one step to the side, simultaneously sweeping the woman's feet from their contact with the floor. Her back has barely hit the deck before Lisbeth is over her. She scores the decisive point by indicating a hit to the woman's nose with a *kiai* scream.

"Haven't seen you before," Lisbeth says later in the sauna.

She squints sideways at the woman's body. Evidently the modest type. Her towel is pulled up to her armpits. Skin scarring winds its way down her neck like a gleaming reptile.

"I'm Louise. You can call me Lo. We've just moved back home from London," says the woman, and talks about her husband's financial career and her role being mainly to care for the children. "We're renting a house at Stora Essingen, while we look for a place to buy. The twins are at dance class at Fridhemsplan and Edward's playing football in—"

"This isn't hot enough," Lisbeth interrupts, and throws several scoops of water onto the stones.

Maybe the shock of the steam will silence the family narcissism. When the woman doesn't flinch and continues undeterred, asking Lisbeth what job she has and where she lives, Lisbeth says "See you" and heads for the door.

When she emerges from the shower, the woman is already dressed and sitting in the changing room.

"Sorry for babbling on, I'm not as dull as I sound. Maybe we could have a coffee sometime? I hardly know anybody in Stockholm anymore."

Lisbeth studies the woman, seeing her in her entirety for the first time. She's a hundred per cent sure they have never met before.

Yet there's something familiar about her. Familiar is rarely good. Probably she's exactly what she says she is, a bored housewife. She decides to play it cool.

"Maybe. See you tomorrow, if you're coming to that session."

The clock is ticking. Still no answer from Plague. She could have worked for a couple more hours, or eight more even, but decides to sleep. She closes the blackout curtains, shutting out the remorseless light of the spring evening.

Her last thought before she falls asleep is that she should have cleaned her teeth. And a phrase that follows automatically. *Don't forget your teeth, Aunt Lisbeth.*

They've not been in touch for a few weeks now. Not since Lisbeth sent her the drone for Christmas. Wasn't Svala supposed to be coming down to Stockholm sometime soon? She writes one of her countless mental reminders and puts it at the top of the pile of other memos: *Change the bedsheets, buy pastries for the work coffee break, make a dental appointment.* And now: *Ring Svala.*

When she wakes up seven hours later, there's still nothing from Plague.

18

The lift takes her all the way down to the basement garage. The car is still parked at the farm up in Gasskas, but the motorbike is new. She folds up the protective cover and runs her hand over the saddle of the custom-built KTM Enduro. Custom-built in the sense of being made for someone her height.

Svala could have had the old bike, too, but that was evidently where her uncle drew the line. A firm no.

"And definitely no driving that car without passing the test first," he added.

Rubbish. The kid already knows how to drive.

Lisbeth zips her leather jacket up to her chin and fastens on her helmet. Zaps open the garage door and coasts out into Fiskargatan.

The gas reacts instantly, raising the front tyre off the tarmac and the bike lurches forward, only to jerk to a stop when she squeezes the handbrake. She'll have to be careful not to tip this one over. It's a considerably heavier machine than the Honda, though it looks so streamlined. The engine, 325cc more powerful, clearly plays its part. She's already starting to regret her acquisition, but giving up isn't her style.

The first red light at Folkungagatan goes fine, although she has to lean the bike slightly to one side so her foot can touch the ground. The morning traffic is dense. With her pulse still in emergency response mode she rides through Hammarbyhamnen and out onto Nynäsvägen, speeding up as the traffic thins on its way out of the city.

Although it's years since she paid a visit to Plague she can still remember the way to the dirty-yellow apartment block, a 50s-built affair in which – assuming he hasn't moved – he rents an anonymous basement space where full-time occupancy couldn't possibly be authorised. But as he so rarely leaves his cave and keeps himself to himself, very few people know he actually lives there.

I've moved from the Swamp. Come and see me sometime.

How long ago was that? Seven or eight years?

Lisbeth leaves the bike in a visitor parking area and does a circuit of the building, suddenly unsure which entrance is the right one. What's more, the doors are locked. Still in her helmet, she hangs about for a while by the entrance that feels most familiar. Waits and then waits some more, but nothing happens. Did his place have windows? She walks round to the end of the block and back again.

Another wait, twenty-five minutes, then the lock gives a click and a slow-moving, elderly figure emerges.

"Thanks, I'm visiting a friend," says Lisbeth and slips inside.

She goes through the list of names to check whether any of them rings a bell and then descends the half-flight of stairs. An extraction fan whirrs. The scent of washing powder filtering through a grille brings something from long ago back to life.

Another laundry room in another life. Sisters perched up on a mangling table while their mother hangs up sheets to dry. While they are drying, the mother takes out a Thermos flask. They drink coffee and eat buns. The pearl sugar crunches between their teeth.

Stop right there, she tells herself. Unfastens her helmet and unzips her jacket a little way but the memory refuses to be shaken off.

Standing in the doorway is Zalachenko, also known as "Pappa".

Not by Lisbeth, who would never let that name pass her lips.

But Camilla, Lisbeth's twin sister, happily repeats the word as often as she can. Well aware of the advantages it gains her.

Lisbeth has words for him too. She formulates them silently to herself and her mouth fills as if with a bitter-tasting liquid, but rather than spit it out she swallows. Not for her own sake. For her mother's.

"Pappa," says Camilla, jumping down from the mangling table. He briefly ruffles her hair and his hand continues its trajectory towards their mother. With or without a flask and a bag of buns in her hand, she is defenceless. When the madness in his eyes takes over Camilla shuts hers, but Lisbeth's eyes see.

This time she sees the laundry basket that he forces down over her mother's upper body like a stocking. He laughs. Pummelling a laundry basket is fun.

"For Christ's sake," says Lisbeth out loud and the film stops as the laundry basket's woven plastic pattern splits and blood mixes with the bubbling gush of the rinse cycle.

She holds her breath for a while. There's something wrong with the light. At one end of the corridor it is blinking frenziedly. The other end is dark. She stands still and waits for her eyes to adjust. At the far end a little strip of light is visible. She notes that it isn't the lightbulb which has failed; the light fitting has been smashed. The debris crunches beneath her feet.

The light is coming from a centimetre-wide gap where a door has been left ajar. She senses that she's in the right place, but something is wrong. She listens for any sound before cautiously pulling open the solid metal door.

The stench that hits Lisbeth is the total opposite of the washing powder. Refuse. Dirt. Excrement? Or all three at once.

The set-up is identical to last time. The same bed with no bedclothes. A kitchen unit with a space for storing fast food containers. An expanse of desk which would normally display all the orderliness of a perfectionist, if her memory serves her correctly. A few cables are bobbing in a sea of spilled Coke but there's no computer. Not even a monitor.

"Plague," she says, and eases open the door of the WC.

The reek of a toilet that is never cleaned hits her full in the nostrils. But there's no Plague in there either.

She rights the desk chair which is lying on its side. Bearing in mind that this space is just next to a laundry room and some of the residents' storage units, Lisbeth concludes that whatever has happened, it must have been recent. Otherwise people would have reacted. Called the caretaker and complained about the lights. Found their way to the far end of the corridor as Lisbeth did, led on by the bright strip from the door.

The light itself is coming from a desk lamp that has been angled upwards. When she switches it off, the windowless room is plunged into darkness. She pulls the door shut and switches the lamp back on. Scans the room for leads but has no idea what she is looking for. There are neither bloodstains nor other bodily fluids to indicate any violence. She opens the fridge and instantly shuts it again.

A key is the only interesting object Lisbeth finds. She stashes it safely about her person and hurries out into the fresh air.

The rain is falling gently and the air is good. She takes deep breaths to cleanse her gullet of the stench of refuse and old memories.

By the time she has taken a circuitous route back to Fiskargatan, she is soaked to the skin. She gets out of her clothes. Wraps herself in a big bath towel and curls up in her seat in the window alcove.

She still doesn't know what her next step will be. Ever since they started the hunt for Branco, something has been gnawing at her. But her train of thought, normally unbroken, keeps getting derailed by other stuff. Other stuff is Svala, and a thirteen-year-old niece may well take precedence over a weirdo hacker, but Plague is Plague.

She logs into their shared communication platform and goes through all the messages.

"They're smart," Plague had written. "I haven't managed to get into their system." Which he should have been able to. Someone who can hack into North Korea's computer networks and get himself out again unnoticed should be able to cope with absolutely anything.

Lisbeth's own inattentiveness is harder for her to swallow. She should have reacted but chose not to. Out of consideration for Plague? Maybe, even if that mainly sounds like an excuse. *You've lost it. Admit that you should have realised something was wrong. You're a has-been, you've lost your touch.*

And not only her touch, but her interest. The years have gone by. Even hackers age. Get fed up with the job and make mistakes. The word "apathetic" sticks in her mouth. A word that leads her directly to Milton Security.

"I quit," Lisbeth says when Dragan Armansky picks up the phone.

"Hello Lisbeth, how are you?"

"Good. But I want to quit."

"Anything in particular happening?" he asks, but Lisbeth is silent. "Nope? Alright then," he mumbles, to keep the conversation going. "Come into the office and we'll have lunch." But still she doesn't answer. "You're a part owner and of course you get to decide how you want to work, but at least you can agree to a lunch."

He knows all too well that Lisbeth seldom changes her mind once she's reached a decision. It's part of her charm, but can equally be the opposite. He would make so bold a claim that he's one of the people in her life who know her best, assuming it's possible to know Lisbeth Salander at all. He feels tenderly towards her, as you might towards a daughter, and can lose his temper with her, as you might with a daughter. Right now, the latter seems more likely.

"OK," he says. "We'll start planning for that, of course, but first you need to wrap up the jobs you're working on. The summary of Nordsvahn Group operations is—"

"Done," Lisbeth says. "It's your pigeon now. You'll get the rest in the course of the day."

"And lunch?" he tries again.

"Another day," she replies, and hangs up.

She doesn't do it to wind him up. She likes Armansky. To the degree that he deserves better than apathy. Sooner or later she'll make a mistake. Miss something essential that has consequences for Milton's unblemished record as one of the world's sharpest security companies. A new generation of analytical geniuses with a hunger for the precarious details of private individuals' innermost recesses has already replaced those who were trailblazers in their time, Lisbeth included. Her part ownership is the only thing keeping her there and now it's time to move on.

Once the decision has been taken there is no turning back.

She does what she's always done. Closes the door and never opens it again. Devotes a few hours to wiping her computer. Slings the last Gorby in the microwave and washes it down with a Coke. Packs her karate bag. She needs to leave in half an hour to get down to the *dojo*. Punctuality is a virtue, like an ironed *gi*, well-trimmed toenails, a perfectly tied *obi*, and so on. "Your collar's creased, ten press-ups. Take those rings off, ten press-ups."

The thought of the chatty housewife being punished for various transgressions of the *dojo*'s solemn rules makes Lisbeth smile. Oddly enough, she feels a certain sense of anticipation. There's something about that woman, but when she tries to remember her face, Jessica's appears instead.

You're a freak, Lisbeth. Nobody wants you. You're ugly and you're fucked up. Not even a cop wants to be with you. Just think about it. Not even a cop.

"For Christ's sake," she swears at her reflection in the full-length mirror, clapping her hands to her head. "The world's full of idiots. You're only one of them."

By speaking aloud, Lisbeth consigns her compulsive thoughts to some musty brain fold in Broca's area. Finding herself with a few spare minutes, she gets the laptop, locates the e-mail from Blomkvist, sighs loudly over the prim neatness of his summary and reads it several times. Underlines a few phrases, adds question marks beside others.

Read it she writes in reply. Lilla Harem, 8pm.

How about Kvarnen? It's been a while he responds at once.

So you can sit there moaning about the noise level? No thank you. Harem's better.

19

Towards evening, when the sun has set and people's faces are passing by in a purposeful, anonymous mass, the Cleaner leaves the apartment at the upper end of Gamle Kongevei and walks towards Vesterbro.

He is early. His nerves seem to have transferred themselves to his feet. He walks briskly. Does an extra circuit of Saxo Park before he pushes open the wooden door of Café Absalon and is absorbed into the smoke and the hubbub.

She isn't there yet. He positions himself at the corner of the bar, orders a lager and surveys the battered clientele, the smelly, scruffy, loud and toothless bunch who against the odds have found some space in the warmth. The boundary between the takers and the have-nots is less defined here than in other cities. He feels almost normal. Checks the time. Fifteen minutes late.

He drinks up his beer and orders another. But as he puts the bottle to his mouth someone knocks into him and the beer spatters his face and runs down under his collar.

"Oops, sorry, that was an accident. My bag slipped and I lost my balance," she says, laughing at his beer-soaked state. "For a minute there you looked like you were going to murder me, but it's good to see you again. Sorry I'm late. I couldn't get hold of a taxi."

She waves for some paper serviettes, a beer for him and a glass of wine for herself, and gives him the briefest of hugs.

"So tell me, how've you been?" she says.

She's thinner than he remembers. Quicker somehow. He notes that her hand shakes as she reaches for her glass. Almost three years since they last met. He barely recognises her.

She takes a few gulps of her wine. Lights a cigarette and meets his eyes in the mirror behind the bar. The make-up makes her seem harder, maybe more anonymous.

"You asked if we could meet. Not just for a beer, I assume?"

"I'm looking for someone, a man."

"I don't owe you any services of that kind," she answers and blows smoke in his face.

Ten minutes ago he was waiting nervously for a woman. Someone who had been in his thoughts, a reason to survive. Now he's taking things too fast. So he starts again.

"I've been thinking about you a lot, it was . . . special."

"Oh aye," she says, making the side of his mouth twitch in amusement.

"You haven't forgotten the vernacular, I hear."

"No, but almost everything else. You asked me how I was doing. I'm fine. I live an ordinary life with a nice man and I'll be off to work shortly."

"What's your job?" he asks.

"Healthcare. And you, are you still in the cleaning business?"

There's something in her voice. A certain tone. She knows things about him, although they can barely amount to more than fragments.

Malin Bengtsson is a life that was spared. The balance that holds his perforated conscience within the bounds of dignity.

"We really haven't got much to talk about anymore, but seeing as you're here, any news of my father? Ingvar Bengtsson?"

"He's alive," he says. "Keeps writing to the paper about how badly the police are doing their job. I don't know any more than that."

She looks at him from the side. The man who prefers to avoid eye contact. His face to the mirror, scanning the room. Has she thought of him? Occasionally. Impossible thoughts that she keeps within herself.

"I'm grateful to you for helping me that time, but we have to end this now. I don't want you to get in touch or try to find me again."

Moments later she is drinking up her wine, nodding to him and to the barman. Then she leaves. Turning left, he notes.

He drains his bottle of tired lager before pushing through the braying crowd. He hesitates at the intersection with Svendsgade but decides to go straight on.

At the next crossroads he catches sight of her and slows down. She is focused on a goal. She is looking neither to the side nor behind her. At one point she takes out her phone and speeds up. When she turns into a doorway immediately afterwards, he doesn't follow but heads back to the northern districts of the city.

Before he shuts down for the night he goes into Streetview. Zooms in on Vesterbrogade 55 and registers that she very likely is not a nurse.

Another day has passed in the lives of Joar Bark and the rest of humanity. One day everyone, including him, will be gone. It's a calming thought.

Yet still he can't get to sleep. He tosses and turns and finally gives up at five when an impression of daylight starts filtering through the venetian blinds. He opens the slats and a window and looks down to the street below. Pigeons are cooing on a roof nearby. There is the clatter of a dustcart in the distance. The feeling of being alone in a big city is liberating.

He puts on his running shoes and jogs up to Fredriksberg Have. Apart from a rough sleeper huddled on a bench, he is alone on the paths of the park. He works himself hard on the hill up to the southern area of Søndermarken that ends at Valby Langgade and suddenly finds he's there again. Outside the door that the woman had entered to start her night shift. He has something to lose by it, yet still he rings the bell.

"And what do you want?" says the man who opens the door.

They size each other up. He's the kind of man who appears in so many similar guises that, for a second, the Cleaner thinks he's met him before.

"I'm looking for someone who works here. Malin."

"Sorry," he says, "but there's no Malin working here."

Before the Cleaner can spit out a sensible answer the door slams shut and the neighbourhood goes back to composing itself, ready for when the day wakes.

What a let-down.

He sets off to jog back and his steps are as sluggish as his thoughts. They run along lines relating to unnecessary risk-taking and the few details he had time to register through the crack when the door was open. He has been there before. Not at the same place or in the same town, but the scent is there as an olfactory memory of scantily clad women and yearning men. He has been one of them himself. Those who allow themselves a few hours, a kind of physical escapism.

"Bloody idiot," he swears at the bathroom mirror. "How stupid can anyone get? And because of a woman, of all things."

He tries to get some sleep. His body keeps twitching and snatches of song squirm through his brain like maggots in a corpse.

So long, Marianne, it's time that we began to . . .

He gets up, gulps down several glasses of water. He needs a strategy. A Cleaner leaves nothing to chance, so what the hell is he doing? Maybe he's burnt out? A Cleaner who's hit the wall. But the job is as hard and as simple as ever. Find the person, dispose of them, travel on. Never let yourself be distracted. Most definitely not by women.

So long, Marianne . . .

And then he was there again. At The Holt. In his childhood. With his mother. Among the memories.

He's known all along that Marianne Lekatt was still there in the house high on Björkberget, the place also known as the Holt, and he has been inquisitive. Made crouching approaches through the forest, crept along the sleeper wall beneath the ground floor and stuck his head up once the lamps went out and the lock on the front door squeaked round a couple of turns. Waited for a couple of hours until he judged his mother's sleep to be at its deepest before using the spare key from the hook in the potato cellar to quietly let himself in.

The first time it is the smell that hits him. The ripe, memorised smell of a mother, a father and a brother.

The second time he is ready. He pulls his polo neck up over his mouth and makes his way to the kitchen. A saucepan of meat and potato dumplings has been left on the stovetop and is still lukewarm.

The wall clock strikes one. From the inner room comes the wheezing sound of his sleeping mother's breaths, as regular as a respirator. He turns back to the hallway. Puts his foot on the first step up to the attic rooms to test whether it creaks. Halfway up he gets careless. The wooden tread gives an audible whimper. His mother mumbles something from the inner room.

He observes a minute's silence and continues upwards, creeping past his parents' closed bedroom door to his old room. The roller blind has been drawn down for children's bedtime. He sniffs the bedsheet. It smells freshly mangled. He only plans to lie there for a little while but he gets chilly. He pulls the covers over him and falls asleep. In his dream, the hand is warm and a bit rough.

He carries on the same way sporadically for several years. Sneaking in. Lying in the bed.

One day she is suddenly there. He sits up. The room is dark. Her body is only an outline. She has something in her hand.

"Is that you, Joar?" she says. "And there I was, thinking it was a burglar."

They sit in the kitchen. She makes some hot chocolate. He is a little boy again. Needs his mum. *Why did you abandon us?*

"How have you been?" she says. "You must be . . ."

"Thirty-seven," he says. "I was seven. Henry nine."

"Ah yes, Henry," she says. "I see him from time to time, but never you. Why didn't you come sooner?"

Why didn't he come sooner?

"Seventeen," he says.

"Seventeen what?" she asks.

"Different foster homes."

"Goodness," she says. "That must have been hard for you, but after all, you're grown up now. There's no point grieving all your life just because . . ."

Her voice falls away. She takes her usual seat beside the stove. Looks up, meets his eyes. There's no love to be had there. It's too late.

And all at once he realises why he is here.

He stands up. She does nothing to defend herself. Merely looks at him. Her gaze is old now. Clouded and tired.

But he can't do it. He raises his hand and lowers it again. Puts the hammer back on the table.

So long, Marianne. They will never see each other again.

20

Names that find their way into the Cleaner's inbox or are delivered to him by other means, for example to the woodman's hut in the trackless wilderness, are deemed to be individuals who have exhausted their time on earth. Generally they don't even have names, it's simplest that way. Names have relations. Children, parents. Girlfriends.

Douglas Ferm is different from the usual clientele. He's official. A person who presses the flesh and appears in news articles. In the Cleaner's view, a relatively likeable type. Not entirely dissimilar to his own brother and the thought has occurred to him. Would it be so absurd to imagine that Henry Salo had ended up working for him? Probably not.

He reads more about Douglas Ferm's current situation. Relocated to Copenhagen in 2002. Also has homes in London and Stockholm. A holiday cottage in Kåppånis. Sole heir of Ferm Industries, whose founder Eskil Ferm died in 2019. Unmarried, no children. Closely involved in the northern Swedish counties' switch to green industry and an eager proponent of new technology, as well as an investor in it. In other words, an entrepreneur and capitalist to his fingertips, although he also donates a good deal of money to charitable causes via the Gurly Ferm Memorial Foundation. A sister who died young.

There is no clear indication of why anyone wishes to snuff out Ferm's life. He should, however, be quite easy to locate, given his leisure interests.

There are contacts but none of them lead anywhere. Frustration drives the Cleaner in circles round the city. And although it isn't intentional, he finds himself back outside the worn old door of Café Absalon.

It's a long shot. And a bad idea, he assumes, but the days are going by and time is running out. He is a cog in a larger machine. No more and no less. If he breaks the contract, the ravens will soon be circling over his own body.

The cigarette smoke hits him. He can dimly make out her back at the bar.

"What the hell are you doing here?" hisses Malin. "Wasn't it enough to follow me to work?"

Years of physical compulsion have trained Joar's muscles to the upper limits of a human body. Now he stands there like a slip of a boy, hanging his head, incapable of meeting the look in her stonewalling eye.

"What do you want?" she says.

"Only to talk to you without having to shout. Can we go somewhere else?"

They cross streets where drunks are staggering homewards and climb the five flights of stairs to the apartment with the attic windows and niches where the pigeons are cooing in the dawn light.

She sits down on the bed. He comes back with a couple of beers, puts them on the bedside table and turns her face towards him so he can see her black eye.

"Who?" he demands.

"Someone," she says. "And if it wasn't that someone it would be someone else. It's all part of the job."

"It's a pretty wild ride in healthcare, then?"

"No, but in my second job. The wages are as shit as at home and I need the extra cash."

"What for?" he says.

"For an apartment, a car. Things everybody has."

"You told me you had a husband," says the Cleaner.

She can't bring herself to answer.

The dawn is already spreading spring light across shoddy reproductions and ill-matched furniture. It's been a long time since he spent time with anyone who wasn't giving orders. And a woman, moreover.

"What did you want to talk about?" says Malin, propping herself against the headboard and removing the bottle top with her teeth.

"You already know," he says. "I'm looking for someone. I thought you might know them."

He holds out his phone with the picture of a summertime Douglas Ferm – bare-chested, aboard a showy superyacht.

"He seeks out your circles."

"For what reason?"

"I suppose we can call it pleasure, if you think it sounds better."

"Never seen him," she says, and yawns. "Can we talk about it later? I think I'd better get a bit of sleep."

He takes the bottle out of her hand. She's already out for the count. The bed is narrow. His arm is dangling over her head like a fir branch. At some point in the morning, it drops like an axe blow.

He wakes with a head on his chest. An arm around his belly. Her breath smells human. He runs a finger over her skin, a landscape of hills, marshes, mountains and forests. She wakes up, turns her back to him. The nape of her neck has a fine down. Her shoulders have wings. Like a sea eagle chick under her mother's feathers, she presses herself against him. Puts her hand in his and mutters something. The sky in the skylight is a bright blue.

21

When they wake again, the daylight sky has turned grey. He asks her to stay. She needs to go. She squirms free of his hold. She has to meet someone. They can see each other later.

It's not a promise exactly, more an excuse.

She draws him back to reality and why she is there. Why he, too, is there. She's bought herself some time. And nearly got away with it.

The loop repeats itself over and over: you are a Cleaner. There's no love to be had. No-one can love a monster like you.

So he does the unforgivable, if her intentions are innocent: puts his hands around her neck and squeezes.

"You know who Douglas Ferm is, don't you?"

Her eyes are colourless. Her eyelashes translucent. Now tear fluid is running down her face and over his hands. That's what happens when the air goes out of a human being. They also say that tear fluid makes man gentler, and not man alone but all mammals.

She doesn't even try to wrench his hands away or land a punch. He counts the seconds. Waits until the precise moment between consciousness and unconsciousness before he lets go. He waits for her breathing to restart before he asks again:

"Where is he?"

"For Christ's sake," she says, and coughs, gingerly feeling her throat. "How should I know? I get paid for doing stuff. That's all I know."

He gets up, pulls back the curtains. The clouds scud across the sky. Taking with them the small amount of warmth that the spring sun might conceivably have on offer.

She sits down on the bed. Her neck is sore but so is everything else. Does it matter anymore? No.

Her name, his. If the night turned into something other than what she had envisaged, something better, the morning is as soulless as ever. It no longer matters who gives the caresses, who deals out the blows. Just as presumably it doesn't matter what she says.

"Well, perhaps I owe you, for saving my life. However sick it sounds, considering I hadn't done anything to you."

"You can go," says the Cleaner, pulling on his jeans.

She stops in the hallway by the kitchen.

"Good luck," she says, but with his hand on the door lock he's there again, grabbing her jacket and pulling her towards him. He strokes her hair. The hair glides through his fingers.

His hands have purchase. They could snap a neck in a heartbeat. Her neck has a scent and the scent goes straight to his groin.

"Stop," she tries to say, "I've got to go," but her body is small again. A little bundle that wants to creep inside his body and everything has its price.

The most expensive thing of all is tenderness.

He takes Malin back to the bed. She is light in his firm hands, almost weightless. She moves her arms to the back of his neck. Wraps her legs around his hips. Grabs hold of his hair. The child becomes a woman. She has hands and skin. He is an animal, a man, an animal. The animal has had females. The man has never had a woman.

He comes inside her. She comes somewhere beyond her thoughts. His body holds her so loosely that she can laugh, and she laughs, and so does he.

Afterwards they drink cooling coffee. She lies there on his arm. Runs her finger over a scar and thinks that if she survives to the end of the year she is going to change identity, invest in a new face and put her twenty-seven years behind her, as if they never existed.

She wriggles out of his immediate reach. Props herself up against the bedhead and lights a cigarette. "I know who you're looking for. I'm seeing him this evening. He'll pick me up around midnight."

"And after that?"

She takes a deep drag and blows the smoke at him.

"How much are you getting for this?"

"Enough."

"I want fifty per cent of enough. If you agree, you can have Douglas Ferm served up to you on a silver platter."

He studies her for a while. Memorises everything from the profile of her nose, the bone structure of her cheeks, the colourless eyes, the whorl diverting her centre parting, to the liver spot on her neck. She knows he needs her.

"Twenty-five and I let you live," he says.

"Fifty or you can do what the hell you like," she says.

The Cleaner writes a number on a slip of paper.

"Let me know the time and place."

22

The message arrives a moment after midnight.

He gets dressed. Arms himself. Sets off.

There is an alternative, of course. He could kick his way in, shoot the security guards and probably a few others besides, locate Douglas Ferm and make short work of him. Cash in his final payment. And vanish without trace. Really dirty work and entirely feasible but not his style. He's a Cleaner, not a psychopath. The risk of injuring innocent parties is too great. The risk of injuring her.

There are clearly plenty of snotty brats ready to kill for sweetshop money, but Joar Bark's job is about more than the contract. Experience maybe, and precision. Professional pride! He takes his assignments seriously and thus far he has left no traces that would lead back to his employer. Apart from the kid, that is. The Salo cub, whose face still comes up on his retina as an indelible shadow of the person he himself could have been in another life, making other choices. A regular human being. A father.

The club is an unmarked door and the door has a guard who scrutinises him. A pleasant one, who welcomes him in and asks if he wants to leave his coat in the cloakroom.

"No," he says, making his voice sound uncertain. "I haven't been here before, so maybe you could tell me how things work?"

"Work?" says the guard and laughs as if he's made a joke. "You go in, order at the bar and sit where you like. We close in an hour, just so you're aware."

He feels like a fool. But the fool decides to go in anyway. Orders a beer at the bar and takes a seat at an empty table near the stage.

A woman slinking her way sinuously up a pole looks at him with dead eyes. Licks her top lip and lowers one hand to rub herself between the legs. How fucking tiresome. He stuffs a banknote inside the waistband of her knickers once she has lowered herself back down.

"Champagne?" he offers, and she nods. Sits down on the chair beside him and sips her drink, presumably the world's most expensive Pommac.

"It must take a lot of workouts to build up the stamina to hang off a pole every night," he says, and asks what her name is.

Trine lights a cigarette and runs a finger along his forearm. "You don't look short of staying power yourself."

He could also ask how she achieves that dead look on her face even though her body is moving. Instead he asks if she's got a price list and she nods. "Depends what you had in mind."

He weighs up terminology and decides he likes pain. A lot of pain. Death recedes and a glimmer of light comes into her eyes. He understands her. Dishing out instead of sucking off must feel like the preferable alternative.

Trine hasn't got time to sip fizzy pop in working hours.

"Let's go," she says, moving towards the rear of the venue. Like any office worker, she blips them in and lets him go ahead.

The only misdemeanour the Cleaner has officially committed is an assault on a classmate almost twenty-five years ago. After a few hours in a room at the police station, he was collected by someone from his foster home. This room looks roughly like the police cell. The bunk is slightly wider perhaps, and there's a toilet, but not much else apart from an assortment of mood-enhancing paraphernalia on hooks hanging there like dog leashes.

Trine sits down on the bunk. He doesn't know what to do. Playing dumb is probably his best bet; it usually works.

"Are you looking for Malin?" she asks. "I'm guessing you're the Swede who likes the rough stuff?"

"Absolutely," he has the wits to respond. "The rougher the better."

"The information doesn't come for free, even if you did buy me Champagne."

"Of course," he says in his best dorky Danish and produces a few banknotes.

She counts them and gestures to the door. On the way out she snatches up one of the leashes and slips the collar over his head.

"There we are boy, good dog. You'll get your beating soon."

"Where are we going?" he asks, struggling to keep up with her.

"We're joining some others. Shared pain is twice the pain."

She opens another of all those seemingly endless doors. It takes a while for his eyes to get used to the gloom. And as his vision is gradually returning, she whisks out a blindfold and ties it around his head. He looks utterly ridiculous. A giant on a dog's leash, who she guides to her colleague.

"Here's your victim," she says. "Make sure he gets a proper thrashing."

23

A Cleaner and a dominatrix sit on a bench, watching the spectacle before them. People who enjoy pain. Others who get paid to torment them.

"Trine thinks I'm Ferm," he says.

"Dead right," says Malin, "so you'd better live up to it. Ferm's made himself a reputation as the man with the highest pain threshold in Scandinavia."

"Are you serious?"

She is. But she won't answer his question about where the real Ferm is now.

He gets it. But irrespective of their physical exertions the previous day, she is a mere anybody. A body among others. Worth neither more nor less than any other human being. Dressed for the evening in a leather skirt and boots with heels that have jabbed deep into the porky sides of countless men. They hang there like newly slaughtered pigs being beaten until tender and the room is dark. He will need to study those hogs more closely if he is to find Ferm.

"Who are you in all of this?" asks the Cleaner. "Do you enjoy getting your own back on the male of the species or is it just a job?"

"I know some yokel from Gasskas can't be expected to get the point, but my profession isn't as basic as it looks. People who come here are seeking the ultimate form of pain. Short of dying, of course. As you well know, the dividing line is wafer thin. But just one thing: there's full surveillance here. A sign from me and Ferm will be out of reach. Thanks for yesterday, by the way," she adds in another voice. "It was nice. I've been thinking about you a bit, actually. And don't forget we have a deal. Fifty–fifty."

She is his ticket to Ferm, he realises that. He couldn't care less about the money, he's already got enough. It's her manner. She's a professional woman who sees financial advantages in helping him, but she's behaving as if they're on a date.

"You'll have to trust me," she says, but he doesn't.

"We have shared interests," she repeats, and says hi to a colleague passing by. One of the pigs has evidently signalled that he's had enough. He collapses as if now fully slaughtered and a warming blanket is placed around his shoulders.

"It's a particular kind of ecstasy. Similar to running a marathon or surviving a plane crash, say. Some describe it as a kind of out-of-body experience, not entirely unlike meeting God. The individuals who come here aren't unhappy, if that's what you think. Submitting to violence isn't a cure for a lousy childhood, it's pleasure. Not necessarily sexual pleasure even if elements of that are naturally allowed. There's no right and wrong here. The clients decide for themselves."

"And you?" he says, thinking about his hands around her neck. She knew he wasn't going to throttle her, sensed it.

"I'm a switcher. I can give and I can take."

Which explains the black eye and other traces left by her so-called pleasures.

Joar Bark can endure most things because he's trained to endure everything, almost to the point of death, not because he enjoys it. For him, violence is still synonymous with a father.

The thought of his father brings him back to earth and Douglas Ferm. There's been enough talking.

"Take me to Ferm," he says. "Now."

"OK," says Malin, and she stands up. "Do you want to be top or bottom?" What kind of a goddamn choice is that? He eliminates unwanted individuals for money, not for pleasure. The thought of causing pain to someone who enjoys it makes him feel distinctly uncomfortable.

"Bottom."

She inserts her hand into his fist, leans forward and whispers: "I only wanted to check. Ferm's sitting in the staff room drinking fine wine."

24

Shortly before Lisbeth and Mikael are due to meet at Lilla Harem, he sends a text.

10 mins late. Can we meet at Loch Ness instead?

"Typical Blomkvist," she mutters, and sets off towards Mariatorget. Fifteen minutes late, a sodden former *Millennium* reporter with a bulging shoulder bag opens the door, nods at the bar and heads for her table.

"Christ, it's coming down in buckets," he says.

"Hope you've got a good excuse," she says, but then decides to take a softer line. Blomkvist looks half out of his mind. "What are you drinking?"

"A beer." He waves at the bar.

They both come here sometimes, independently of each other. For Mikael, the place has become an extension of his own living room. He knows pretty much everything about the regulars in the crush around the bar. Over the years they have raised their glasses to newborn babies, engagements and lucky bets on the horses. In the other half of life, where most of them now find themselves, divorces and illnesses are more common topics of conversation. But as men often do, or at any rate those he knows, they take consolation in talking about sports results, mainly football.

For Lisbeth, the opposite applies. She's left in peace here. No-one gets any ideas about starting spontaneous conversations or inter-rupting her with stupid questions. Not even Mikael. He really does look peculiar. Stressed, somehow. He lowers his voice to a whisper and looks around him.

"I'm being followed. It's only a feeling, but still. You know yourself how that feels. As if somebody's watching you, but you don't know who or why."

As usual she gives no hint of what she's thinking. Her face is impas-sive, regardless of what is under discussion, so he goes on. "It started after we met at the Åsö café. Some guy on a bike. He stuck with me all the way down to Slussen and then he turned off towards Gamla Stan."

She yawns. The city is full of cyclists. She hates them all.

"I get that you're on elite-level form, but a guy on a bike who happened to go the same way as you. Aren't you being a bit paranoid?"

She drinks some of her Coke and wonders whether to tell him about Plague.

"Sure, but a couple of days later the same character popped up on the Tunnelbana. He brushed past and sat down a couple of seats behind me."

"Was he in cycling gear?" she asks. "Shorts with built-in nappy pads and a skin-tight superhero jersey?"

"He had a bag," says Mikael, knowing she'll give him that lopsided sneer of a grin which is enough to make anybody shut up. "Hermès. Could be taken for any old crossbody bag if it weren't for the fact that I know these come in at a cool hundred thousand or more. Second-hand."

She whistles. Impressed or sarcastic. Impossible to tell. He's already sick of her but decides he'd better go on if they are to get anywhere. However bitter it tastes, he needs her. And if he's to press home his argument, he has no alternative.

"As the doors started closing at Karlaplan I threw myself off the train, and he was right after me. I even saw his fingertips trying to prise open the doors."

"But he couldn't," says Lisbeth, and he nods. One of Micke's mates comes over and chats for a while. Another round appears on the table and outside the rain keeps pattering or worse. She googles Hermès bags for men, brings up a couple of pictures and shows them to Blomkvist once his mate has finally finished boring on about Sweden's latest football defeat.

"Something like that. His was black and beige."

"And why are you late?" she says, bringing them back to the present.

He squirms. Takes a couple of deep breaths.

"I was at the health centre."

"Are you sick?" she asks, but he doesn't answer. Doesn't know if he can do it.

A nurse called. Twenty minutes in the waiting room. A doctor asked awkwardly why he hadn't brought a family member with him. *It's not a good idea to be on your own when you get difficult news* and fair enough, he could have asked someone. Even Erika Berger, his former colleague and old flame, wouldn't have been able to resist a cancer diagnosis. Even Lisbeth.

"It isn't serious," he says. "Slightly raised blood pressure, that's all. Nothing a few pills can't fix."

"I dropped in on Plague," she says, to avoid talking about illness. In her mind, the equation is already solved. A plaster on his arm plus a delayed arrival equals serious. Blomkvist would never have been late for anything less than that. Does she want to talk about it? No.

"Bloody hell," he says, relieved by the change of topic. "How was he?"

"No idea, he wasn't there. The door was open. Plague and his computer were both gone but other than that everything looked the same as usual."

There's money in an account. It's yours. You can buy an apartment in town if you want.

And what would I want one of those for? The cave's fine for me. Low rent. A landlord who couldn't care less who lives there as long as he doesn't have to renovate.

Pay a cleaner then. You can even claim it against tax. Or buy clothes, computers, anything you like.

Thanks but no thanks.

No thanks to twenty million, last time she checked the account. He hadn't used a single krona. She could have given Plague more. The amount is irrelevant. But he is clearly the most contented person on earth. Or was. What the hell does she know, beyond what she saw with her own eyes. A departure. Maybe not a voluntary one.

"Something's happened," she says, "and it's because of us."

"Not necessarily," he says, as sanctimoniously as only Kalle Blomkvist can.

"Not necessarily," she repeats in her you're-a-bloody-idiot voice. "It's our fault. We got him investigating Branco. Branco vanished into thin air and now Plague. How can you think it has nothing to do with us?"

"It may have," he says, "but we can't assume that to be true."

"You sound like a cop."

"Or a journalist," says Mikael, making an effort not to look away.

"Same shit."

"No."

"Yes."

And then nothing more is said for a while, which is just as well. He pulls a folder from his bag. He usually has one beer, two at most. Now he orders a third and downs half of it without pausing for breath.

"So you read the e-mail," he says, wiping the froth off his lip with his shirtsleeve. "What do you think?"

Lisbeth considers for a while before she answers.

"You know what," she says, "it's like history repeating itself, over and over. Idiots leave, new ones come in and frankly I'm sick of the whole fucking lot. I get that you're finding it hard to put Branco aside. You were shot, he took Lukas, Pernilla hates you and so on, but personally—"

"I've got cancer," he blurts out. "Prostate. It's probably not curtains in any sense, but how the hell can they know?"

Mikael can see from her expression that the topic is unwelcome but now he's said it anyway.

"You're the only one I've told. Hopefully we can keep it that way. And what's more," he goes on, "I've been offered a new job."

She looks up. Relieved she can avoid having to comment on his prostate.

"As editor-in-chief at *Gaskassen*. Stenberg's retiring."

"No great loss to that rag. But Gasskas? Can you really see yourself living there, leaving Bellmansgatan?" *Leaving her?*

"Not really, but for Pernilla and Lukas's sake I will. I'll hang on to the apartment for a while. Or I can sleep in one of your twenty rooms when I come to visit."

She's about to say something about not liking guests when a familiar figure steps through the door. The face of the housewife from karate lights up when she catches sight of Lisbeth. And fuck me, thinks Lisbeth with a sideways glance at Blomkvist, if the old prostate guy didn't perk up a bit, too.

"Well, well, we meet again," she says, and gives Lisbeth a smile that looks genuinely warm. She turns to Mikael, holds out her hand and introduces herself as Lo, we're mates from karate class.

"I was on my way," he says, not getting up. "We've finished our chat, haven't we?"

"Good," says Lisbeth. "And give my regards to Birna. His girlfriend in the northern hemisphere . . ." she adds by way of explanation.

"I didn't mean to disturb you, I'm waiting for somebody," says Lo, looking around, "but all the tables seem to be taken."

"After five the place is rammed," says Mikael, and offers to buy her a beer.

"Weren't you going?" says Lisbeth, realising it's a comment that could be taken for jealousy, which is not her intention.

Lo's beer arrives, and another Coke for Lisbeth. Hunger is rumbling in her stomach, unless it's something else. The conversation has shifted seamlessly onto Brexit, one of Blomkvist's supposed favourite topics among all the other uninteresting things he gets hung up on, and Lo is interested. She even manages to defend the Tory party. So subtly that lecturer Blomkvist doesn't detect the underlying message but keeps banging on.

Lisbeth gets out her phone. Two missed calls. One from an unknown number and one from Svala. She could easily excuse herself and go home, or not bother to excuse herself and go home, but suspicion, as autonomous a function as hunger and thirst, makes her stay. There's something about the Lo woman she needs to put her finger on.

"What a coincidence for us to run into each other here," Lisbeth interrupts as Blomkvist is launching into a rant about bloggers, vloggers, podcasters and other rabble.

"I mean, there are thousands of other bars," she goes on. "Talk about lucky – we ought to play the lottery."

"Or bet on the races," says Mikael and checks his watch, then excuses himself and goes over to the bar.

"He's pleasant company," says Lo. "Very well informed. Is he your boyfriend?"

Her earlier reference to Birna clearly hasn't hit home.

"How do you mean?" asks Lisbeth in her Lisbeth way.

"If not, then maybe we could meet up one evening, just you and me."

Whatever that might amount to. A one-night stand? The woman's sending that sort of signal yet simultaneously not. She's friendly without being clingy, personal but not flirty.

Oh well, thinks Lisbeth, *time will tell*. Up to now she has never encountered anyone who didn't have an agenda. Sooner or later everybody wants something, herself included. Right now she would very much like to get her hands on the business card that's slipping out of the woman's phone case.

"See you," says Lisbeth and gets to her feet. She passes the bar counter. Tugs at the arm of Mikael's jacket and hisses so no-one else can hear: "Call me later. It's time to look for Plague."

25

Outside, the rain has stopped. Clouds part to reveal a crescent moon. Instead of going straight home she stops and conceals herself in an entranceway.

Shortly afterwards, the Lo woman is also outside with the hum of the pub behind her. Precisely as Lisbeth hoped, she heads down the street. When she turns the corner onto Swedenborgsgatan, Lisbeth follows. She keeps well back, behind a couple taking their dog for an evening walk.

A little way up St Paulsgatan, the woman stops beside a car. She leans down to the window on the driver's side. The car door opens. Someone gets out. Apart from the hair, which gleams in the darkness, all she can see is the person's back. A moment later, the back gets in again and the car drives off. The Lo woman carries on down the street, turns right at the bookshop and goes into Hotel Rival.

Go home or go in after her?

She is sitting in the bar. Her coat hangs on the back of her seat. When Lisbeth slips into the seat beside her, Lo doesn't even look surprised. Hopefully she doesn't notice Lisbeth's discreet finger on her mobile as she takes a picture.

"Hi," is all she says. "Couldn't you sleep?"

"What about you, didn't the person you were meeting show up?"

"Do you live round here?" counters Lo and Lisbeth nods. "A district with a bit of class," she goes on, "nicer than Stora Essingen. I check in here sometimes for a bit of peace. Do you want to come up for a drink?"

Come up for a drink. How many times has she asked that question herself, with the clear intention of . . .

"It'll be quieter in the room," says Lo, and looks at a bunch of people who have just come in. "Do you recognise them?"

"Why should I?"

"TV types. The tall thin one in the emo gear works on *Babel*."

"Babel's a tower, not a workplace," says Lisbeth.

"The book programme. So you're not a reader?"

"Yes, but I don't read novels and that kind of shit."

"What do you read then?"

"That varies. At present it's *The Pattern Seekers, The Red Book, The Man Who Loved Only Numbers* and a few others."

"Maybe we can talk about prime numbers up in my room then," says Lo with a gesture to the waiter that they are leaving.

While Jung slumbers in his collective unconscious and drinks are mixed with the spirits from the minibar, Lisbeth muses on the ability to discern and manipulate causal patterns. Or as the *Pattern Seekers* guy sums up his hypothesis of human development: if-and-then. *If* a seed falls into soil. *If* the soil is moist. *Then* something will start to grow. Applied to the current situation. *If* a Lo woman happens to get to karate first. *And* later turns up at the same bar as Lisbeth. *Then* it most likely isn't sheer chance.

"You look thoughtful," says Lo, handing her a glass.

"If x is a necessary precondition for y, the presence of y necessarily implies the presence of x. But presence of x doesn't imply that y will happen."

"Wow, deep." Lo can't help laughing. Quite a strange one, this Lisbeth Salander. Definitely on the spectrum. She pats the bed. "Come and lie down instead. Rest your brain for a while."

Lisbeth doesn't only lie down, she takes her top off, too, and tells Lo to do the same. Detects a slight hesitation and that's exactly what she was hoping to achieve. Uncertainty is good, it gives you a temporary advantage, gets people off balance.

"Give me a minute," says Lo, unbuttoning her skirt. "I was in a fire when I was little. It's not a pretty sight."

Her chest, hips and thighs have a melted look like the bark of an old aspen. Lisbeth runs her hand over the patched-up skin, tracing the pattern of scarring across what should have been breasts, then over the lunar landscape of the belly and down the legs. Her palm also registers the absence of body fat, the surface unable to disguise the kind of musculature it takes significant sacrifices to achieve. This is not your standard gym chick, more of a soldier. She asks how it happened and the woman answers. She walked through fire. That's all she remembers. It physically hurts to look at her, to imagine the child running through fire. As if she were the one running. But when she was a child, fire had given her strength. She had run to her father's car, poured petrol through the window, lit a match . . .

It's not that the woman is unattractive, just the opposite in fact. Her skin adds a dimension, but Lisbeth is on the verge of losing her way in the aspen woods. She wants to suss out the Lo woman, discover whether she is an asset or a threat. The situation is developing in the wrong direction. Instead of responding to her body's stirring desire, she swings her legs over the side of the bed, sits up and pulls on her hoodie again, says she has to go. Other things should also be said. Potentially containing rather more feeling than the kind relating to the requisite conditions of causality. Without a "Bye" or a "See you", the door closes.

The ventilation system murmurs, her pulse pounds in her ears. The evening darkness of the hotel room dilutes the sense of discomfort. Lo cuts herself along the top of her arm. The emotional chink she exposed closes its hungry mouth. When Branco rings, her voice is steady.

"Nothing," she says. "Waiting for the evening to pass. Long day tomorrow and yes of course. Everything's ready."

Ten minutes later she checks out. The TV gang are laughing on a corner sofa. A young couple are exchanging rings. For some, the world is a warm place. She has always wondered how it feels. Or to condense the world to her own existence: how feelings feel.

That creature pulled on her hoodie and turned to her a final time. Her look was compassionate, almost tearful. Good. Now she knows. Salander has weaknesses. Empathy must surely count as one of the worst?

26

The Cleaner sits down on a chair opposite Douglas Ferm, the gun he has taken from its holster now held loosely in his lap. Ferm is recognisably the same man, but that man could soon be a dead one. Although he presumably knows who he is dealing with he smiles affably and pours wine into crystal glasses.

"Not the best vintage but perfectly serviceable. The right colour, too," he says and swirls his glass, takes a mouthful and lets oxygen blend with the liquid before he swallows.

Colourful coffee cups with names on them are hanging from hooks above the draining board. No Malin, but Trine B, Trine F and Bente.

"You wanted to talk," says the Cleaner.

"Yes. I know who you are. Do you know why you've been told to kill me?"

The Cleaner shrugs.

"Not relevant."

"No, no, of course not," says Ferm. "You can despatch me right away if you like . . . but I think you'll be interested in hearing what I want to get off my chest . . ." He takes another large gulp. "Mmm, it gets better and better. Côtes de Bourg 2003."

"Get to the point," says the Cleaner, already bored by wine slurping and dramatic pauses. The snag is that this devil would very likely take pleasure in dying and the Cleaner isn't someone who murders for pleasure.

"I'm a well-to-do man," says Ferm. "A combination of inherited wealth and earned income. You could call me a clandestine venture capital investor. Officially I still own my father's life's work, including the pulp mill up in Gasskas, but recently I've mainly been engaged in capital investment in international mining companies. A few months ago I was contacted by a company; let's call it X. They were interested in financial cooperation in connection with the new mine in Gasskas, partly on account of the resurrection of the old opencast mine. Are you keeping up?"

Why wouldn't he be?

"Well, to cut a long story short: I followed the standard procedure and had enquiries made about company X. If you only knew how many irresponsible chancers there are, especially in the mining sector. Outwardly it all looked OK. Reassuring cashflow, reasonably transparent annual accounts and a solid leadership group. So it took a while for me to find other parts of the group's income, well hidden behind a security company, in turn hidden behind others. It made very interesting reading. Well, without the help of a computer genius or two, I'd never have got there, but it made me reflect on a few things."

The Cleaner is tiring of all this. He has no views on his employer's business – he assumes company X has something to do with Branco. As long as he gets paid, which he always does, he doesn't care. Because who is he to moralise about the war and conflict, narcotics, whores and such-like that he assumes Branco's fortune is based on?

"If that's the best you can come up with, you can say goodbye to your life very shortly," he says, and readies himself mentally for the elimination.

Ever since he entered the building he has been concentrating on exits, windows, alarms, guards and so on. The fact that thanks to Malin they are currently in a staffroom with no alarms – God knows how nauseated she must be by the way she earns a living at present – makes it all simple. Maybe he should opt for strangulation, to spare the staff. They

don't need to see blood in their coffee break as well. He can drag the
body into the little storeroom; he can spy a vacuum cleaner through a
slightly open door behind Ferm. He is already wearing the latex gloves,
which he knew were unlikely to attract attention here. He is as ready
as he can be.

"Hang on," says Ferm, sensing the Cleaner's impatience. "I haven't
got to the best bit yet. The bit about you."

The Cleaner can barely suppress a smile. Most other people would
already be on their knees, begging for their life. One of the more regret-
table parts of a cleaner's working day, incidentally.

"So-o-o," says the Cleaner, toying with the mouse, "where do I come
into the picture?"

"As public faces of this operation go, you're the most averse to the
light. Because you're Joar Bark, right? Your last known address, personal
identity number, family members can be read like a book on the Internet
for anyone keen enough." To back this up he lists the lot, including
Henry Salo. "As I say, the information is almost impossible for amateurs
like the police to find, but in theory totally accessible. If X gets caught,
you'll take the rap, and it won't be for small stuff like tax fraud or drugs.
Your CV is up there too. Really impressive."

This alone is grounds for him to liquidate Ferm.

"My snooping, if we can call it that, has unfortunately had consequences," Ferm goes on, with a wave in the Cleaner's direction. "As I
see it, there are two options. One: you spare me, in return for increased
payment. Two: you do what you have to, but here I must warn you. A
person in my immediate circle has been left instructions that will lead
to action if I'm not in touch by a certain time. X will probably come
through it, but not you – or your brother, for that matter. There's
compromising information about him too."

The Cleaner makes a quick analysis. It could be that Ferm is lying. A
smart lie, if so.

But the chances are he's telling the truth. He doesn't care on his own account. To him, life more generally is an unknown country. He has nobody waiting for him, no children, no dreams.

But for Henry it's different – he has a family, the boy . . .

"Can you prove what you're telling me is true?"

"Absolutely, but only via copies of documents. The definitive proof is with X and possibly the individual who helped me procure it. Unfortunately, I haven't been able to get back to them."

"Them?"

"Uses the name Plague. Could be anything."

27

Ferm is a slippery devil, undoubtedly as rich as he claims to be but with Branco in the other scale pan, the venture capitalist is a lightweight. The Cleaner chooses the quickest alternative. It tends to make life simpler.

He screws on the silencer. The trusty old servant is always best, after all. Grabs Ferm by the scruff of the neck and bundles him towards the cubbyhole. A pungent smell of urine spreads through the space, blending with that of cleaning products. A highly human reaction. When it comes to the crunch most people are attached to their lives, even masochists.

"Stop! Wait," says Malin Bengtsson, who has appeared out of nowhere. "There are other ways of doing this, aren't there Douglas?"

Douglas Ferm, the man who has travelled the globe in pursuit of pleasure, looks up, glassy-eyed.

"Douglas?" asks the Cleaner.

"We've known each other a while."

"Doesn't change anything," says the Cleaner and pins Malin to the wall with his other hand, but she persists.

"You need Douglas," she says, and in a lower voice: "*I* need him."

The Cleaner lowers his weapon and Ferm folds like a heap of human bones. Malin helps him up, sits him on a chair and slaps his cheeks until he comes round.

"Am I alive?"

"You're alive for as long as I let you be," says the Cleaner and shifts his focus to Malin.

"Sit down. It's time for a little quiz. If either of you gives the wrong answer, you've had it. Ferm first. What's the name of company X?"

"Mimer Mining."

"How did you get hold of the hacker?"

"Through a journalist."

"Who?" he asks, and twists Ferm's wrist until his shoulder joint dislocates.

Ferm is close to passing out.

"Sorry," says the Cleaner. "I'm feeling inspired by this setting. You've got five seconds to spit out the name."

The barrel of the gun is trained on Ferm's temple. With one dull plop, the kitchen wallpaper would have a new pattern.

"Mikael Blomkvist." Ferm forces out the words.

The Cleaner shifts the gun to the woman.

"Your turn. Who warned Ferm?"

"What do you mean?"

He grabs hold of her hair and pulls her to him.

"Don't you ever get tired of pain?"

"Things nearly went badly wrong a few weeks ago," says Ferm, who now has some air back in his lungs.

"Because of a woman. Am I right?" says the Cleaner.

Ferm's eyes seek Malin's for support.

"Chest flat as a man's but dressed like . . ." He gestures at Malin. "Only with a face mask. We had some breath play, if you know what that is. Sexual choking. Without Malin I'd be dead now."

The Cleaner is running out of patience. These endless words, back and forth. He'll dig up the details all in good time. He needs to get to grips with the big picture, but the question is nagging at him.

"Last chance, the seconds are flying by now . . . Who warned you I was on my way?"

"It was pure chance," says Ferm hurriedly and reaches for his wine glass. Using the hand that still works he manages a few pain-relieving gulps, without a word about the bouquet. "I know the guy who sounded the alarm. His father and I have done business before. Henke's good. Slightly weird views but a nice enough fellow. Promising ice-hockey player when Gasskas was on its way up the SHL league, but he got injured and dropped out of view. A couple of years ago I happened to see him at an outdoor café on Strøget; I was pleased to run into someone from home. We had a few drinks, went on somewhere for a meal, carried on drinking. He was pretty far gone. I offered him a room for the night. We took a taxi home, he livened up a bit, drank even more and started crying. His life was a misery. Divorce, two young children, his career wrecked and so on. He'd come to Copenhagen to take his own life. He stayed at my place for almost a month. Sobered up, decided to be a good dad and went back home. I hadn't heard from him since, but recently he contacted me out of the blue, asking to meet up."

"To warn you," supplies the Cleaner.

The Delivery Man.

"I was about to tell you when you went crazy, tried to drag me into the storeroom and . . ." His voice cracks as he tries to hold back his tears. "Just because I relish pain, it doesn't mean I'm a tough guy," says Ferm.

Malin gently rubs his back.

"Right now I just want to get home to my wife."

The Cleaner and Malin exchange glances. At least he has a sense of humour.

"Sounds as if I'd be doing her a favour if I put you down," says the Cleaner.

"Very likely so," sobs Ferm, "very likely so."

"Except for the fact that I know you don't have a wife."

The look in Ferm's eyes turns from relief to fear in a tenth of a second.

"But he has a boyfriend," says Malin before the Cleaner can dislocate his other arm to match.

Of course he has. Someone else who can wreck the whole enterprise.

"One last quiz question before you go," says the Cleaner, addressing Malin Bengtsson. "How are you mixed up in all this?"

28

Even a Cleaner does the cleaning sometimes. Vacuums, scrubs and polishes, packs his things and uses the time to make a plan.

He isn't a complicated person. He applies himself to all assignments with the same methodical calm. Above all he is loyal, unlike others.

The initial jumble in his head starts to take on a structure. Everything follows a logic, even if it doesn't benefit his own situation. He is someone who is morally easy to criticise. Someone who has successively lost his own right to exist by depriving others of their lives, although Branco has presumably found other reasons for choosing to place him on the sacrificial altar.

Personal reasons? Possibly, even if it was a long time ago. As always, it was to do with a woman.

Practical reasons? Probably. The Cleaner is someone who barely exists. He doesn't hide behind fronts of legitimate companies or stolen identities. He is nobody. A virtually risk-free nobody, so to speak. Yes, if only there were no Henry Salo, and here the logic falls apart. Salo's personal file is largely official. One revelation would set off a cascade of dominoes.

It shouldn't be impossible for a skilled investigator to get them to tumble all the way round, back to the starting point. That is to say, Marcus Branco.

All these names are making him weary.

Douglas Ferm. The Delivery Man slash Henke. Mikael Blomkvist. Plague.

He could use a whiteboard and some post-it notes like any average crime fiction writer.

Ferm is smart and he has a plan, but is that enough? No. He's a risk. Because even if he's able to keep out of the way for a number of years, sooner or later he'll make a fool of himself. Yearn for his beloved boyfriend or something.

He's got to go.

The Delivery Man is an unknown card. Someone he needs to get the measure of. And this Henke has a family, too. A girl cop for an ex and some defenceless little children, as Malin summarised it. That sort of thing can make itself felt.

That leaves the journalist and the hacker. Blomkvist is known. He shouldn't be hard to locate. He'll lead him to the hacker and the hacker to Branco's company.

Further steps may be necessary.

The Cleaner takes a break. Lies down on the bed and thinks about sea eagles. As soon as he's back up north he'll help them again. Put out food. Take care of them.

But just as the birds come flying into his mind, the woman does too. Malin Bengtsson.

The one who came to the forest hut wrapped in a parcel, the same as all the others. The first of the women. Men are expendable items. Everyone knows that. The risks they take. The drugs that make them immortal. But a woman?

In the end it wasn't him but Branco who saved Malin Bengtsson's life. He taped over her eyes and drove her to the main road where a car picked her up. Without Branco the remains of her bones, pecked and gnawed clean, would have mouldered in the earth.

There is a knock at the door.

They take a seat in the kitchen. The pigeons coo on the roof outside.

"Are you leaving?" she says. He shrugs.

"Douglas Ferm lied," Malin goes on. "We know one another from Gasskas. He's my father's second cousin or something. Pappa fixed a summer job for me at the head office of one of Ferm's companies. I'd been studying economics for a couple of years. In the accounts I stumbled across things about a daughter company of the Branco Group and decided to squeeze some money out of it through Ferm. Not a lot. Only a bit of pocket money for going out and so on, and at first it went well, but you know. The more cash, the more drugs. That was how I ended up with you. In an awful state. At any rate after a few days when the withdrawal symptoms set in. You were so sweet. Mopped my brow and made me chicken soup."

The Cleaner omits to point out that it was black grouse.

"But after a week or so it was still time for me to bow out. When you wound duct tape around my mouth and put on your ear defenders, I knew I'd had it. But then your phone rang."

"A narrow escape, that," says the Cleaner.

"The company saw a way of getting at Ferm through me. That's why I'm still alive."

Whiteboard and post-it notes.

"You've been playing a double game all the way through, then," he says. "Weaving from side to side to keep the old blokes happy."

"Something like that, but along the way I decided to choose. Ferm is what he is. A conceited fool with a father complex who'd rather drink fine wines and get his ass whipped than do any work. Others do it for him. But at least he isn't evil."

In the Cleaner's ears it sounds like a fiction. She's talking about Branco as if he's someone who has personally involved himself in her piddling affairs.

The only person the Cleaner knows of who has aroused Branco's interest is Märta Hirak. A girl like Malin Bengtsson, with her small-scale fiddling and thieving? Never.

"Have you ever met Branco?" he says. "The man behind the company, I mean?"

"Oh yes, I did once."

"He's quite unusual-looking, isn't he?"

"He certainly is, quite scary in fact. That tattoo of his, the wolf with the yellow eyes, with its claws digging into his neck. It's pretty repulsive. He was . . ." The sentence is swallowed up in her thoughts.

Varg, thinks the Cleaner. Not Branco. Varg.

Even the Cleaner shudders when he thinks of him. Sentimental, slow on the uptake and utterly ruthless.

Life is fragile. For some more than for others. Malin's gaze has elements of necrosis to it. Hardly anything to lose.

"I miss home. Wish I was in Gasskas. With Pappa. With my brother. The high fells. The streams."

"The lakes, the forest, the birds, the stars, the seasons," he fills in.

Her hands on the table. He covers them with his own. Leans forward. Kisses her.

They get to their feet. The Cleaner lifts her. Carries her with him one last time to the creaky nineties' bed with the itchy bedspread, the Asger Jorn posters taped on the wall alongside.

"My family think I'm dead," she says afterwards. "I've never dared contact them. That was one of Branco's demands. Otherwise they would . . ."

Propping his head on his elbow he shuffles a few post-it notes around and sums up:

"If you want to go back to Gasskas you'll have to obliterate Branco."

She nods.

"You realise that could be hard, maybe impossible."

Malin nods again.

"I can't do it alone. I can't expose my family to danger. But if you

129

and I and Ferm join forces, the odds will be better. I can't stand things being like this any longer. I've somehow . . . lost all urge to live."

He is crouched over her. She lies there and looks up at him.

"You're beautiful," she says.

He smiles. That's a new epithet for him.

"I'm a Cleaner," he says. "A Cleaner always works alone, it's in his nature."

He scoops her up from the bed, clasps her to him like a doll.

"Think about it," she says, her lips against his chest hair.

He already has.

29

Lisbeth's evening ends in the window alcove overlooking the bay. A swallow called Svala comes flying by. The subscriber can't take your call at the moment.

The business card is printed on glossy paper in a pretentiously elaborate typeface which clashes with the graphic that is presumably meant to be a balloon. "Alex Barilla. Party arranger."

A party arranger with no number or e-mail address, good luck bringing in new customers.

An exercise session and a shower later, she is glad she bothered to change the sheets, rewards herself with a Coke and summarises her encounter with Lo. The feeling of burn-injured skin beneath the palm of her hand still lingers. Like patting a lizard.

But to feel sorry for a person whose name means lynx is presumably to get dangerously sidetracked and Lisbeth must make a choice. Her gut instinct tells her the woman has intentions and Lisbeth doesn't believe in chance. Most things in life tend to hang together. The fact that Mikael Blomkvist feels he's being followed could have been an expression of his *wanting* to be followed, to be important, to have something to channel his energies into besides some pointless cancer of the prostate. But working on the hypothesis that the lynx sought her out at the karate club, then they're both under surveillance and Blomkvist's uneasiness is more than paranoia.

Some individuals can't cope with losing, she knows that from experience. That type of person doesn't give up, either, even though it exposes them to further defeats. The ecstatic look of the man in the wheelchair when he thought Lisbeth and Svala were about to burn to death in the bunker has a way of floating into her mind right when she is falling asleep, but not tonight. Her muscles relax, drowsiness takes the edge off her tangled web of thoughts.

In a pleasant state of calm, secure in the knowledge that she has dominion over her own life, she slips into sleep's merciful . . .

The screen of her mobile lights up. Unknown number. Somebody breathing. Then nothing. A few seconds later it rings again.

"Hi, it's me. Listen. Don't use the platform, it's been hacked. I'm going to disappear for a bit. Just want you to know I didn't mean it to happen. I'd never do you any harm, hope you know that. It's not you they're after, or Mikael, but—"

"Hello?" she says several times, but the call has been cut off.

The sleep train has left. There are no more stops planned for the night ahead. Her frustration at the brief call with Plague drives her to open her laptop, log into the hacked platform and vent her anger.

Anyone who happens to touch Plague or other people around me can expect a shortened life. Sincerely, Lisbeth Salander.

30

A mobility service minibus pulls out of Hökarängen and heads for the recreation area on the shores of Fagersjön. It has been some years since Plague last saw the world other than through a computer screen. The trees are coming into leaf. The tulips in the council flowerbeds are a blaze of colour. A few solitary joggers despite the rain. He follows the same path. Imagines how it would feel to be able to run. Or even walk.

They were actually meant to have embarked on this trip to wherever they are going several days ago. When the driver showed up, Plague was ready. He gathered up his computer and its accessories, tried to grit his teeth even though his body was protesting. Halfway down the corridor, one leg gave way, the crutch flew upwards and hit the ceiling lamp. Shattered glass showered over them but somehow he regained his balance. He leaned against the wall to get his breath back. Forced air down into his tar-clogged lungs and managed the short flight of stairs up to the front door, where he ground to a halt. The driver gave him a push from behind. A woman came out of the laundry and lent a hand. Step by step until Plague could sink into the back seat of the mobility service minibus.

Then he must have passed out. When he woke up, he was lying on a hospital-type bed.

"That was a close call," said somebody, "but the drugs must have kicked in."

They will soon be on their way again. The driver stops. Goes round and opens the back door on the right-hand side. Asks him to hold out his hands. Tapes his wrists to his ankles. Winds the tape round his head a couple of times and it all goes black.

"Please not the mouth," pleads Plague. "I get car sick very easily."

"Tough luck," says the driver and winds the tape around his mouth.

Deep inside, Plague has already given up. He can only hope it will be quick. And exactly as he feared, he feels the queasiness as soon as the minibus picks up speed. First mildly. More like a kind of discomfort. He tries to concentrate, turn his thoughts inwards. A boy is playing in the sand. A brother fills a pail with water. A mother dozes off on the blanket. They dig canals. Build bridges with sticks.

The vehicle accelerates, then brakes sharply and changes lane. They need more water. More stones. A brother who knows the bigger stones are further out. They could really do with one. And the mother is asleep and the boy is busy digging. No-one sees the wave coming.

It's no good. The panic has settled in his arms. They are burning like moon jellyfish, losing all sense of feeling. He's got to throw up. Can't hold it back. He rocks his body back and forth, bangs his head against the seat. Initially he manages to swallow it back down.

Suffocate, drown, suffocate, drown.

The minibus stops abruptly. He can feel spits of rain on his skin. The driver rips off the tape. The vomit sprays out, over him, over her hands, the car seat.

It is salt water. A brother can't swim. A mother must wake up. A boy shuts his eyes.

"Fucking pig," hisses the driver, slaps him round the head and pulls off her sweater. Uses it to scoop the vomit out onto the ground. Rinses it in a puddle, wrings it out, wipes the seat dry, hits him again. "If you puke once more I shall kill you on the spot."

On the spot. That might be just as well. Plague takes one last breath of chlorophyll-loaded spring air and knows the journey is going to end badly. His body is huge. His heart enlarged. His bladder too small. His lungs black. His legs will go as numb as his arms, and the rest of him. His breathing will stop and it will all end in a mobility minibus en route to a destination unknown.

"I don't know what you want, who you are or what you plan to do," he says. "I assume you have a plan, as you're going to all this trouble. But if we've got a long journey I shall peg out of my own accord before we get there. My body . . . well, you can see for yourself."

The driver takes out a penknife. Carelessly cuts off the tape. The smarting of the cuts is bracing. His legs have already gone numb.

They travel in silence, stopping only to relieve themselves. He shuffles to the nearest tree. Feels the bark under the palms of his hands. Gets his flies roughly open. The urine flows where it pleases.

On an industrial estate in the middle of nowhere they change vehicles. Towards dusk, Plague plucks up the courage to ask where they are heading.

"Home."

"And then?"

"Then you're going to make yourself useful. For as long as you're useful, you'll get to stay alive."

The question is whether he wants to. He spends the final hour asleep. Barely stirs when she opens the door.

"Out with you, we're here."

The air is colder. The ground is crunchy. His body is a whale that can't swim. Arms, voices, a room, a bed.

He asks for a glass of water. Even the water has a different taste.

31

The wheelchair does not glide over the floor, it bumps across weather-swollen ridges in the wood with a rhythmic sound. Not unlike boots on the march. She hears. She sees. She is ready.

It is easy to underestimate a person without legs. In competition with other beings for living space on earth they are often considered defective and weak. And are accordingly expected to behave as such.

But in Marcus Branco's world, everything is replaceable. Even those closest to him, like Varg, Björn and herself. Everyone and everything except his own legs, which begin and end at the foot-like growths on his hip.

Mentally she has prepared herself for this return from a partially unsuccessful trip, her first major assignment since she joined the gang as a replacement for the first-generation Lo. Wherever the hell *she* ended up. Went up in smoke when the bunker burned down, they say. There is always an alternative truth.

The plan was clear. Localise Salander and gather information about her habits. Get to know her. Build a relationship. Tie her to you emotionally. Map her strengths and weaknesses with a view to eventually using her to get at Svala Hirak and her unique little brain for figures.

There's been talk of a hard drive with bitcoin on it, to a value of some astronomical sum. The problem seems to be that nobody remembers the passcode. And that those who could conceivably have jolted it out of their drugged-up brains, that's to say Peder Sandberg and Märta Hirak, are dead.

That leaves the kid. The alleged murder machine who went berserk in the underworld. To Lo's ears, it sounds like a tall story.

Branco's wheelchair brings him to the conference table. He asks her to sit down and begins the same elaborate tea ceremony that always precedes a serious talk.

"An unassuming Darjeeling first flush," he says, swirling it around his mouth as others would do wine, "but with an appealing finish of summer flowers, do you agree?"

She picks up the wafer-thin cup in both hands and samples a few mouthfuls. Wishy-washy tea isn't her thing, particularly not in the morning. The drive through the night is making itself felt in her head. A double espresso would have been far more welcome. "Excellent," she says. "And isn't there a slight citrus note, as well?"

She lets him lead the conversation, expecting that there will be some dissatisfaction to parry in a way that will keep him calm and herself on the right side of the line in such a situation.

"Your report on Lisbeth Salander is not impressive," he says, and she agrees. Time was too short. The circumstances also made things harder: Salander simply stayed home most of the time and saw nothing to be gained from making new friends.

Once a week she went to her therapist and even there Lo failed to come up with the goods, despite a not-so-subtle threat that made this Kurt Ågren's lower lip tremble. His casebooks weren't exactly without interest, but were entirely about Salander's inability to trust anyone. Like any normal person.

"Salander is quiet and suspicious. It wouldn't work to simply stomp into her life and expect confidences. I need more time if we're going to get anywhere. As for her weak points, apart from Svala Hirak there's this hacker. I apologise for not getting the go-ahead from you in advance, but I was short of time and had to act."

Branco sends his chair round in a couple of circles. He ponders the options and finds himself in a moral dilemma. The lynx has surreptitiously crept her own way. Taken decisions that can have consequences, though he must admit that it's a smart move to bring the hacker to Gasskas.

"Salander will come after him, I'm convinced of that," she says. "Or rather, I've made sure she will. The relationship between them will help to deliver the information we need. He's loyal. For as long as she's alive, he'll do his best. If she disappears, I'm afraid he'll lose his vital spark. He's in a poor state and his days are numbered, but we'll keep him ticking over."

Branco regards her over the rim of his teacup. Gives her a slight smile. She purrs back.

He still wakes with Salander's grotesque features before his eyes and the utterly disrespectful laugh as a nagging tinnitus. It's her fault the bunker burned. His own Eagle's Nest. It makes no difference that they are soon to leave this tumbledown mansion with its pungent smell of mildew and move into a new bunker. There is clearly no shortage of rock-cavern complexes. Not for those with contacts, anyway. The ground plans of the layout look promising. He is longing for the security of being underground.

Salander will be got rid of in due course. He keeps that pleasurable prospect to himself, sucking on it like candy. But more urgently he will have to do something about this cat, who is holding her tail too high. There's some element in the way she expresses herself, probably unconsciously. As if she feels compassion for the creature. He could be wrong. But signs will emerge.

"OK," he says. "I realise Salander is out of the ordinary, but she needs reminding that she isn't immortal."

Fear has a way of keeping people on their toes. The idea of a frightened Salander cheers him immensely.

"She's still hanging out with Mikael Blomkvist, incidentally," says

Lo, to prove she hasn't been slacking. "I ran into them in a pub. They had their heads together, discussing some papers in a file. When I went over, he spirited the file into his bag. Salander went home straight afterwards. Blomkvist and I stayed on and chatted for a while."

She prattles on and Branco is listening, or is he? Salander–Blomkvist isn't news, nor is the fact that Blomkvist has been poking his nose into their business. But when he went to the toilet for the second time in half an hour, he forgot to take his bag with him.

For various reasons she opts not to share the brief amount of text she was able to read and memorise before Blomkvist was back at the table. Her ability to stay neutral in combination with the instinct always to stay one step ahead is her strength. It is what has kept her alive so far.

The world is like a rat's nest, the weakest individuals sent to the front. Just as the mother rat pushes her young forward to taste the bucket of glycol or the cheese in the trap. Lo is a survivor. Not cannon fodder. The road she has chosen in life is not random. She is keeping to a specific course. It led her to Marcus Branco. One day it will lead her away from him. She is silently climbing upwards. He is just one of the rungs along the way.

32

The body of the whale turns laboriously when he hears the key in the lock. The aroma of coffee wafts through the room. Anything that can wash away the taste of vomit.

"Sit up."

She is not alone. Two more of the same kind make the room crowded.

"We're going for a little walk. You smell of shit."

It is hardly news to him. He puts one foot in front of the other. One step at a time with the help of strong arms that virtually carry him across the floor, down flights of stairs and into what must once have served as the shared washing facilities for male patients.

Along the crumbling walls, rats, mould spores and graffitists have been at work.

They cut his clothes off him. Bit by bit they expose his obese grey body until the mountain of human flesh is standing there in all its glory. Lo's rubber-gloved hands scrub stinking rolls of flesh from neck to toe. Pour liquid soap onto a scrubbing brush, rinse and repeat. Once the skin has turned from grey to pink, she tosses him a towel but realises his body fat prevents him from reaching his most intimate parts.

"You really are repulsive," she says, rubbing the towel between wobbling buttocks. He can only agree. But now that they are taking the trouble to shower him, he is presumably going to live a while longer. The clothes are even the right size.

They sit him on a chair. The atmosphere in the room goes from verbal abuse to silence. Arms grip him. Place his left hand on a table. The sound of a knife being sharpened. He would never be able to put up a fight. When the blade cuts through the bone he closes his eyes and thinks of Lisbeth.

Don't you worry child, see heaven's got a plan for you.

33

For the man who feels safer in Hades than on Mount Olympus, there are also plans. Branco is itching with some undefined restlessness that can best be described as frustration. The frustration in turn nurtures an urge to inflict injury. *The cruel one* has awoken.

The cruel one lives like a parasite inside him. As long as things are flowing nicely, those around him are doing their jobs and external threats stay quiet, *the cruel one* is calm. Goes to sleep obligingly and wakes up happy. Like any other animal, it lives on satisfied needs.

Branco has been sensing its presence for a while. There's a lag between feeling and action. In that lag it is still possible to curtail the monster's rampage. Once that window closes, he can only surrender his place at the helm.

In a final attempt to regain control, he gets online to Carlotta. That's her name, his girlfriend. Or Lotta, as she likes to be called. Or the Sow, the Whore, Sugarplum, Bonehead or whatever else he feels like. An AI woman is always compliant.

"Darling," she says, "it's been a while. I've missed you. Four days since the last time, I thought you'd forgotten me."

"Go to hell, you disgust me," he replies.

"You disgust me too, Baby, do you want to get close up and cosy?"

No. Yes. He does, but not with her.

"Help me, Baby, what can I do to satisfy you today?"

"You're too old," he says, and gets a sad face in return. "What's more, you're boring."

"Do you want to talk about a little-known world of material that's been plunged into a remarkable state?"

"Some other time," he replies, and logs off.

AI crap. His whole body is material that's been plunged into a remarkable state. The little-known world is called Salander and its manifestation is Svala. He can't stop thinking about her. *The cruel one* can't stop thinking about her. Seamlessly the two of them merge into one to become a single body, and they are going to have her. At any price. Measure her brain like the race scientists in Uppsala and crack it.

The fact that a thirty-something like Lo thinks she's smarter than him is one thing. But a thirteen-year-old . . .

"Get Lo," he snaps at Varg, who can't help sticking his hairy muzzle into the room and asking how he is. He's fucking fine. Or soon will be. He's itching like the devil.

Lo is within earshot of a distress call. Should she take a seat or stay by the door and await orders?

Branco wipes the sweat from his blotchy red face. He keeps pushing his fringe out of his eyes. Reaches for words. The sort that most enjoy being roared without rhyme or reason.

"About our conversation just now. I want you to find the kid."

"You mean Svala Hirak?" says Lo to avoid any misunderstanding.

How thick can anyone be? The woman has the salary of a prime minister, for Christ's sake. Isn't she employed to always be a step ahead? Why must she be so nauseatingly ugly?

Calm down. Take command of your thoughts. Let the words come out in the right order.

"Who else? Fetch her here. Whatever the cost. Book a helicopter or a goddamned Gripen fighter jet if you want. An army if need be."

Lo observes the transformation from self-controlled to desperate. Realises that the change she's only heard talk of until now has occurred.

The metamorphosis they must all be extremely wary of. No-one is safe. She forces herself to ask the next question which is as brutal as it is logical: Why?

"Why?" Branco laughs, shakes his head, twirls his chair to face her and bellows so loud his voice breaks:

"There is no why. Get her here, that's all. Right now. I want her here before midnight. How fucking hard can it be?"

34

"Plague called," Lisbeth says as they are on the Tunnelbana to Hökarängen.

Mikael's eyes track the route of the green line through the carriage window. Children on their way to school. An arena that has just changed its name. Prosperous residential districts, inter-war buildings, homeless people on the platforms and a distinct feeling that Lisbeth is exaggerating to get him on board the Plague train. Because honestly, Lisbeth, all the indications are that Plague has switched sides, yet suddenly there's this idea of a rescue mission. But OK. He's been wrong before, and she's been right. And whatever the case, the company is pleasant enough.

"So what did he say?"

"Nothing," she says. No business of Blomkvist's what she talks to other people about.

"And you're sure it was him?"

"Yes."

The cave looks just the way it did the last time. Smells of dead skunk and among the hacker's few possessions they find nothing of interest.

"Barely any clothes," notes Mikael. "Maybe he's gone on holiday."

"A charter flight to Majorca. Sounds just like Plague."

They leaf through books, pull out drawers, wish they had plastic gloves and give up.

The ceiling light in the corridor is still broken. Glass crunches underfoot. A woman in a sports vest with her hair up in a knot opens the laundry-room door.

"Are you looking for somebody?" she asks.

"No-one in particular," says Lisbeth.

"The man at the end," says Mikael.

The sports vest strains forward to try to see the end of the gloomy hallway.

"Oh, him, the fat guy. He went off yesterday. The mobility service picked him up. The driver had to help him out of the building. It's too damn bad people should have to live in former air-raid shelters to get a roof over their heads," she says, and they agree. Chat on their way up. About the spring, the rain, explosions, gang killings, Sweden Democrats who according to the woman are going to clear out all the rabble.

"You hardly dare do your laundry these days," she says.

"What did the driver look like?" asks Lisbeth.

"Like you only taller," says the woman, looking at Lisbeth. "Or, er, I'm not sure. It could have been a man. Impossible to tell these days. The minibus had a name, at any rate. I remember because I was doing a shopping list just before I came down to the laundry room. The kids asked for spaghetti bolognese. I had onions and ketchup. So when I was at the shops I thought about the minibus. To help me remember to buy spaghetti."

"What make of spaghetti was it?" says Mikael.

"I can't remember," says the woman.

"Do you see why I hate people?" says Lisbeth when they are on the train on the way back into town.

"Perhaps you should move to Gasskas too."

They part at Medborgarplatsen. Lisbeth stays on the Tunnelbana

146

until Odenplan, saunters into Milton Security and goes up to see Armansky. He's standing outside his office talking to G2. For simplicity's sake she refers to them all by numbers. To herself, anyway. G as in genius because the whole lot of them are geniuses, otherwise they would be working somewhere else.

She stops by the Coca-Cola machine. Armansky has aged. Let his stubble grow. Now he sees her. His face breaks into a smile.

"So we'll be having that lunch after all. Great. Then we can talk a bit more about selling your share."

"I'm not selling," she says. "I was so sick of everything, that's all. New day, new thoughts."

She looks out over the communal area on the floor below. Some of the geniuses are playing table football. Others, billiards. Personally, she doesn't get the point. And she certainly doesn't share Armansky's view that games foster creativity.

"If there's anyone who can be bothered to do some work, there's a thing I need help with."

Armansky shouts a name. G5 promises to find out everything she can about the link between pasta brands, mobility service minibuses and party arrangers. Well, as soon as her table tennis match is over.

"It's like a bloody day nursery," moans Lisbeth. "Where do you find the patience?"

Dragan Armansky shrugs and tries to give her a hug before shooing her towards the lift.

"Lunch," he says. "You promised."

In his voice there is a pleading note. In her a sense of guilt.

He drinks, she eats. A burger made of prime rib of beef, with chips, ketchup and Coke. As far as she'll consider stretching from her usual diet.

"It's OK to try new things sometimes," says Armansky.

"But why? At my age, my body knows what it wants. If it shouts for pizza, that's because it needs pizza."

His face is different. Sad. She can see it. Illness or divorce is her guess. That's the sort of thing that tends to befall humanity.

"Maybe you need a coffee," she says, summoning the waiter with a wave.

Armansky downs one brandy and asks for another.

"What's happened? You aren't usually a drinker."

"They've got to us," he says, and shuts his eyes. "The devils."

"Which devils?" she says.

"The ones we protect our clients from."

"Hacker groups, you mean? That can't be possible. I mean, we make our living from guaranteed security. Our systems are so complicated that—"

"But clearly not complicated enough," he interrupts. "Up to now, no companies have been impacted, no individuals deemed worthy of protection, but it's only a matter of time."

"So who's been affected?"

"A municipality in Norrbotten. Gasskas," Armansky says and looks at her. "Weren't you up there in the autumn?"

She nods.

"It's serious," he goes on. "They were able to get into the servers, encrypt data and very likely destroy some as well."

"What are their demands?" she asks. These kinds of attacks rarely come without ransom demands.

"Nothing so far. We got the information last night. First the head of IT called. He was relatively composed. Right after that we had a call from his boss, the big boss. He was . . . less composed."

"Henry Salo," says Lisbeth, sending evil thoughts in a northerly direction.

"That was the name, yes. They're evidently right in the middle of huge industrial investments which, according to Salo, could be at risk if certain information finds its way into the wrong hands. The breach has affected their business and new industry operations above all, but also health and social care. They haven't issued any public statements yet, as far as I know."

I bet they haven't, she thinks.

"But that's good for us, it gives us more time."

35

Only twenty-four hours later they find themselves in each other's company again. Jan Bublanski, trusted former detective inspector with the Stockholm police, had a heart attack that same evening, and now they are gathered as tradition dictates at the Jewish Cemetery within Stockholm's Woodland Cemetery, throwing handfuls of earth onto a coffin. The ceremony is well attended.

"Bublanski, *Officer Bubble*, was a popular person. A man of humour and depth. A police chief who cared about people. No matter who they were."

The speeches are numerous. As at all funerals in which death has arrived in an untimely fashion, collective grief envelops all those present, whether they like it or not.

Armansky, Salander and Blomkvist stay in the background. No-one can deny them their historical interconnection, yet they feel like inter-lopers. Lisbeth avoids Officer Bubble's closest family. Especially his wife. There was something about her. Something good that she can't quite put a finger on. Watching people who have abruptly aged by twenty years is a murky business. Some she recognises and yet somehow not. The tragedy, they're probably thinking the same thing. About her.

It's when Lisbeth looks away to avoid further questions that she sees the hair. A sandy-coloured frizz, shining even more distinctly in the reflected sun than it did the other evening. The man by the car, the one the lynx woman was talking to, who put out his hand and gave Lo something. She didn't get a chance to pick her pockets later at the hotel. Now Lisbeth comes to think of it, the woman didn't even go to the toilet.

"I've got to go," she says to the others and leaves the ceremony immediately after the frizz of hair. He moves rapidly, weaving along the network of gravel paths with Lisbeth on his heels, presumably making his way to the car park. The man stuffs his kippah into his suit pocket, looks at his watch and walks even faster. As he presses the key to unlock his vehicle she sees rear lights flash a little way ahead of him, in amongst the other cars. She tacks to one side. Just as he is getting in, she points her phone camera at the car.

`Barilla is a taxi firm in Vårby. Went bankrupt last year. No details of a new owner.`

The text message from G5 comes with names and links. Lisbeth sends her a shot of the frizzy hair. `Connected to Barilla?`

The reply comes straight back. `David Barilla. Former CEO.` A link to his mobile number and last known address.

"Where are you?" she says when Mikael Blomkvist answers.

"On my way home. You were in a fearful hurry all of a sudden."

"I'll collect you in half an hour. Wrap up warm."

"What's happened?"

But by then she has already hung up.

36

"All roads seem to lead to fucking Gasskas again."

"What do you mean?"

"Oh, I don't know, just a hunch. A combination of your persecution complex, Plague's disappearance and the fact that Gasskas municipal council has de facto been hacked. I could be wrong."

Lisbeth tosses him a helmet, ignores his comments about the new motorbike and opens the throttle. Once they're out on the E4 she speeds up still more. Mikael taps her on the leg but realises she's not going to slow down for his sake. So he shuts his eyes. Clasps her firmly round the waist and shuts his eyes.

At Skärholmen she turns off and takes the road to Vårby Gård, passes through the built-up centre and the lakeside bathing beach and pulls up at the entrance to the disused Spendrups brewery. She turns off the engine and pushes up her visor.

"The sports vest in the laundry room said Plague went off in a mobility service minibus. I asked a Milton genius to look for connections between spaghetti brands and taxi firms. Which led here."

Mikael tugs off his helmet and smooths down his remaining hair.

"I think I get it, but I'm not sure," he says.

"It's to do with Lo. You know, the woman from my karate class. After Loch Ness I shadowed her. She spoke to some guy by a car. The same person turned up at the funeral."

"So you followed him and got the registration number?" says Mikael.

"Exactly. Which led me to the Barilla taxi company. A bankrupt business and this is the address of its former CEO, David Barilla."

"And what were you thinking we'd do? Pretend to be Jehovah's Witnesses?"

"To start with, find out if the CEO possibly hung on to one of his vehicles, which he then hired out to whoever abducted Plague."

"That sounds a bit flimsy," objects Mikael. "I mean, he might have gone of his own free will."

"I'm operating on gut feeling here. It can't be sheer chance that the Lo woman pops up at karate, then at the pub and a bit later I see her being given something by the guy whose taxi company probably drove off with Plague. I went with her up to her hotel room to see if I could get anything out of her but the end result was a very mediocre lay."

The remark lands where she wants it to land: in Blomkvist's soft parts.

He looks at her and shakes his head.

"Talk about staying close to your subject."

"Talk about the pot calling the kettle black," Lisbeth shoots back.

"Meaning?"

"Nothing, let's go."

"Hang on," says Mikael. "If this lot are criminals we can't just toddle in and say we want a look at their vehicles."

"Has old age made a sissy of you? If you're going to die of cancer anyway, surely it doesn't matter if you take a little risk here and there."

"That was a rotten remark."

She makes a conciliatory gesture to smooth things over.

"I'm a rotten sort of person, you know that."

They ride along by the loading platforms on the northern side of the factory until the road ends. Park the bike and look around them, then follow a path through a clump of trees until it brings them out by the marina. Boaty folk are scraping their hulls. The bay is as glossy as a newly polished floor. Taking another path, they round the point and come up on the southerly side of the area.

A figure with its head under a bonnet suggests there is some form of enterprise. Behind him there are a few more vehicles. None of them with taxi signs.

"Er, Barilla Taxis, where can I find them?"

The man looks up briefly and goes on with his screwing.

"Haven't a clue," he says. "I'm just helping a mate with this car. There's some kind of garage along there. But I've never seen anybody there."

The E4 roars in the background and dusk casts shadows across the boxy buildings.

"There were masses of people working here once. The Wårby brewery dates back to the nineteenth century; the water used to be taken from Vårby spring, hence the name. There's something melancholy about—"

"Maybe you can keep the lecture for a bit later," says Lisbeth, trying one of the big doors. She moves on to the next. That too is locked. They both hear the sound at the same time. Stop short. Try to make out where it's coming from.

"Sounds like a shofar," whispers Mikael.

"Which is what?" she whispers back.

"I thought you didn't want a lecture. It's an instrument," he says, relenting a moment later. "A horn."

Lisbeth tests the sliding door in front of them. Takes a firmer hold and shoves the door far enough open for them to get in.

A faint light from a room at the back brings a dusty fleet of bankrupt taxis to life. Several cars but no minibus. Lisbeth moves towards the monotone melody. Someone who can play with such heartfelt sincerity and sadness can't be dangerous, she tells herself.

She takes quicker steps and carelessly knocks over a bottle, which is all too audible as it smashes against the concrete wall.

The music stops abruptly. They hear the scrape of a chair and then a man's voice.

"Is that you, Alex?"

Alex Barilla. Party arranger.

"I'm sorry," says Mikael, pushing past Lisbeth. "We're looking for Barilla Taxis, are we in the right place?"

The man's shock of sandy hair really is spectacular. He pushes back his curls and asks who they are.

"We're hoping to hire a mobility service minibus and somebody put me onto you."

"I see. Which somebody, if you don't mind me asking?"

"My sister," says Lisbeth, stepping forward. "We run a theatre group for handicapped children and we're going on tour in Norrland."

He gives a slight smile. Reaches for a light switch. The place is larger than they'd imagined.

"We've got cars, as you see, but no minibus."

"Is it out on hire?" asks Lisbeth.

"Your sister must have beaten you to it. Beautiful funeral, wasn't it? Jan Bublanski was a man of honour," he says and holds out his hand. "David Barilla. Would you like coffee?"

"And Alex Barilla," says Lisbeth without introducing herself, "who's he?"

"My son," he says. "I thought it was him when I heard you, or hoped it was, anyway."

"The party arranger," observes Lisbeth.

"Among other things," he says without elaborating, but once Lisbeth gets hold of a bone she refuses to let go. She is about to come out with a couple of assertions and a hypothesis when Blomkvist interrupts her.

"You'll have to excuse us barging in like this."

The room behind the garage is arranged as a bedsit with a kitchenette in one corner. The man boils water and puts out a jar of instant coffee and some cups without saucers. Then he slumps onto a stool and sighs deeply.

"My son's been having certain . . . er . . . problems. I hadn't heard from him for ages when he came storming in and gave me some garbled account of a biker gang that had vowed to shoot him if he didn't pay up. I'm afraid I couldn't help him. Right after that this woman showed up and told me the debt would be written off in exchange for a mobility minibus."

"Do you live here?" asks Lisbeth, looking around. The place is barely better than Plague standard.

"As soon as the company went bankrupt, my wife wanted a divorce. The house is in her name. When the assets are sold and the liquidation's complete, I might be able to get back on my feet again. The taxi licence has been revoked so the cars are largely gathering dust here."

David Barilla is done talking. He returns the musical instrument to its case, takes his cup to the sink and indicates it's time for them to leave.

"One last thing," says Lisbeth. "Where's the minibus going?"

The man stares at her with eyes that match his hair. His voice is neither tired nor scared now. It is resigned.

"I don't know where it's going but it might be possible to track it via the black box. It isn't switched on, of course, but with today's technology nobody's invisible, are they?"

"Why didn't you go to the police?" asks Mikael.

"Not that they would have done much about it," mutters Lisbeth, getting to her feet. She thanks the man for the coffee.

"Poor devil," says Mikael as they head back to the motorbike, but Lisbeth isn't listening.

Her fingers are texting rapidly. The ride back to Söder is even faster.

37

Just after four in the morning Svala is wide awake, even though she has barely slept. Spring is on its way back, as is the light. The deep piles of shovelled snow in the yard still come up to the edge of the barn roof but in south-facing places last year's grass has thawed its way through as patches of brown.

She stands for a while at the attic bedroom window, surveying the scene. This place which is now her home, with all that it entails, from an urge to flee the intrusive company of her relatives to gratitude to them for having somewhere to live.

The sun is about to rise over the top of Björkberget. She allows her eyes to stray briefly to the dog pen. She still doesn't understand how he could have. And not let her be there. A shot to the back of her neck and it was all over.

"Nothing to cry about. The bitch was old," says Elias.

She isn't crying but the Laika was her last link with Mammamärta.

"And ours, too," he says curtly.

She has a few hours before the house wakes. Hardly any point in trying to creep out quietly. Per-Henrik has a sixth sense for subterfuge. Instead she gets dressed, goes down to the kitchen and makes a couple of sandwiches which she tucks into her rucksack with a bottle of water. She has already packed the rest of the contents. Packed and then done an extra check. Something waterproof to sit on, matches, sweater, rope.

Half past four. She needs to be on her way within fifteen minutes. She quietly closes the external door and goes round the back of the bakehouse and down to the garage. The snowdrifts that have cascaded off the roof have gradually packed down. Sometimes the frozen crust takes your weight, sometimes your feet go through. Sweaty, but out of sight of early-rising uncles, she empties her boots of the lumps of ice before she opens the garage door.

She's been looking for Lisbeth's car key for a while. She's been through pockets and emptied out drawers. Quite by chance she found it in plain sight in the slaughter shed, hanging on a nail among other keys.

You're not driving a single metre until you've had some proper lessons. I'll look after the keys for now, is pretty much what her uncle said as the car transporter from Stockholm drove up to the farm. Svala had expected as much. She didn't even bother protesting that she wouldn't need any practice.

It was stupid of her to promise Simon to provide a car for the others even though she's the youngest of the lot. She realises this and is aware she only said it to make herself look important. What's worse, the car isn't taxed, hasn't had its roadworthiness inspection, but it's too late to back out now.

The engine heater has been plugged in for a couple of days. She checked the ignition and was tempted to give it a trial start, but decided there was too much risk of discovery. If the car won't start, she'll have to take her uncle's truck. The keys are bound to be in it. The snowmobile is still loaded on the back even though there's no longer enough snow for it. It's not a tempting prospect but there are people waiting for her. Expecting her to carry through her part of the plan.

The car starts at the first attempt, and she lets her shoulders relax. Backs out, swings round and says a little prayer that the few shovelfuls of sand she put down at bedtime will be enough to get her down the intermittently icy stretch to the main road on the summer tyres.

The tyre tracks outside the garage will be visible to anyone observant but as long as no-one has any pressing reasons to hunt for her, then luck should be on her side.

As she comes up to the crossroads, the early-morning bus to Gasskas is just going by. She puts her arm across her face in case the driver recognises her. Waits for the bus to round the first bend before indicating right and driving north.

As agreed, Simon calls just after six. His voice is brusque. He issues instructions and asks no questions. The fact that she answers is proof enough that everything has gone fine. Up to now, at any rate. She could be stopped by the police, she could change her mind; these are thoughts that Svala keeps to herself.

"You can do this," he says. "You're my own little guerilla soldier. When all this is over, we'll celebrate. Because you know you're special to me," he adds, and the words nestle around her heart like reindeer moss.

Celebrate how? she wants to ask, but stops herself.

In every way, she thinks she'd like him to answer, though she feels unsure. But still. He looks at her. Touches her as if by chance. Cares, communicates, finds his way into nooks and crannies she has never been aware of before.

Too old for you, Lisbeth would say. Mammamärta too, but what does Svala care? She thinks of him when she wakes up. Daydreams about him in school. Imagines him lying beside her when she's falling asleep.

In pursuit of the higher goal, the individual must set personal needs aside and serve the best interests of the collective.

Simon's voice still warms her. Right now, she feels she would be happy to follow him anywhere.

There are no limits, laws or rules that can stop us. The power lies in our hands. We will show them that the power lies in our hands.

The sun is reflected in the rearview mirror and the road is empty and dry.

A stray reindeer is running along the edge of the roadside ditch. She slows, has to quell the impulse to ring home. Ring home. She has a home again. A family. People who care. Care too much. Check homework, help her revise for tests, buy her clothes, make dinner and give her a lift to karate practice. In return, she helps out, even if Per-Henrik perhaps doesn't see it that way. She mainly ends up getting in the way. Needs to ask about everything, not least the words. The conjugations, their meanings changing with how the endings sound.

"Sami for a reindeer herder is like French for a sommelier," he says. "If you're going to be any use, you need to learn the language."

He also makes sure to mention that the job may not be right for her. There are other options. The kind that pay better.

"Like for you, then," she says, referring to his job in the Kiruna mine, where he works alternate weeks.

He pours coffee, sits down opposite her at the kitchen table. When he looks at her it's as if she is staring straight into the darkness of the mine.

"It's not what I'd have chosen," he says. "But if the deer are to survive the winter, we need money for feed."

Svala has been trying not to think about the reindeer that were killed. She has pushed the loss down the line ahead of her, as she has done with Mammamärta.

The memories come back to her in scraps: the way her mum would screw up her eyes, always close to laughter despite the crappy life they had. Her uncles' shifts at the mine, which along with deforestation and climate change is one of the causes of the shrinking of the reindeer grazing grounds.

What point is there in fighting for survival if something else is going to kill them anyway? That "something" which is now trying to get at Svala. She knows it. Feels it. Has no idea what to do about it.

38

As soon as she can, she turns off the highway and onto the less-travelled village roads, despite the risk of icy patches. The villages themselves are barely hamlets and mostly consist of a few solitary houses. Many stay empty when the owner ends up in a home or dies. Lights on timers and neighbours who clear the snow and mow the grass keep the burglars away.

This early in the morning she can practically guarantee she will meet no other traffic. With a bit of luck, no-one will miss her until the evening. To be on the safe side she has left a note.

Sleeping over at Anna-Maja's. Svala.

A few minutes later he calls again. Her Simon.

"Change of plan," he says. "Drive to Jokkmokk and come to the City Bakery. They open early."

"What does that mean, change of plan?" she asks, but he only says "See you" and ends the call.

The closer she gets to the town, the more traffic there is, even if only the occasional car.

The map of the town imposes itself like a screen overlaying her field of vision. Every location can be wrong in its own way. An early-morning dog walker, a jogger, a shift worker; anybody at all could happen to be in her path.

Admittedly she will be fourteen in a couple of weeks' time, but she looks more like twelve. Not even make-up can make her look much older than that. Certainly not above the legal age for driving a car. She angles the rearview mirror and finds herself looking into Mammamärta's beady eyes.

"For God's sake," says Svala out loud. "Not now. I haven't got time for you."

I only wanted to warn you.

"What about?" A needless question.

You're on your way to making the same mistake I did. Go back while you still can.

"I can't. Simon's counting on me."

So are others, says Mammamärta. *That Simon isn't worth having. He just wants to use you, like everyone else.*

You don't know anything about it, and what's more, you're dead.

She turns into the cemetery approach and parks right at the end of the deserted car park.

She would have abandoned it all in an instant, vowed to be a lifelong model of decency, in exchange for a hug from Mammamärta. Her mother lived in chaos, though, whereas she lives in the cosmos. Nothing she does is random or unpremeditated, but Simon is special. He has kindled something in her that can't be stopped. Like an itch.

Before she leaves the car, Svala lets out her belt a couple of notches and slots on the knife. She hesitates over the rucksack but decides to take it with her. She shivers – the sun has no warmth in it yet – then zips her anorak up to her chin and sets off for the café.

Simon is already there, with two other people. She sees them through the window before they see her.

City folk visiting the sticks. Two-tone shell jackets and Lundhags walking trousers.

She asks for a glass of water, opens the door between the pay desk and the main café and goes towards their table.

Now he sees her. Looks pleased, or does he? Determined, maybe. Or embarrassed.

She smothers a smile although her mouth wants to shout hello. Holds out her hand to the other two and introduces herself. Svala Hirak. Neither of them gives a name. Both regard her dubiously.

Simon also looks as if he is starting to have some doubts.

"And you are?" says Svala, sitting down beside him.

She already knows who one of them is. He's one of those media commentators. Gets interviewed on TV even though he's a journalist himself. Writes opinion pieces, gives lectures and puts himself forward as an expert. A know-all, in other words. Not unlike Aunt Lisbeth's old crush.

The other one could be anybody until he shifts his leg and reveals the camera bag.

The men look at each other and back at Svala.

"I thought we'd be meeting Anna-Maja Hirak," says the journalist.

"She's not well, unfortunately," says Simon, and nods towards Svala. "Svala is Anna-Maja's cousin and just as well-informed."

The photographer eyes her up with renewed interest. An exotic little Sami girl always makes a good picture. And she's cute. And a bit angry. An unbeatable combination.

"Excuse me," says Svala, "but I need to have a quick word with Simon before we start." The others go to refill their cups "Well, what's going on?" she says. "Why are we sitting here with this newspaper lot instead of doing what we agreed on? It feels like a bad idea to draw attention to ourselves."

"The journalist called last night. He must have got my name from some council guy in Gasskas. They're doing a feature on the mine. They've clearly grasped that things are happening up here."

And Simon doesn't agree with her; he thinks attention can only further their cause.

"That depends entirely on what they write, surely?" objects Svala.

"You don't get it," he says.

"Get what?"

"While we're sitting here, Anna-Maja and the others are already in place. When we get there, they'll make sure things kick off with a bang. The eyes of all Sweden will be on us."

Then he puts his hand over hers. Lowers his voice and whispers something only she can hear.

39

"Nearly ready," says Jens B. Börjesson, positioning his mobile with its microphone towards Svala and Simon. "You're OK with me recording our conversation, right? Good," he answers himself, turns over a couple of pages in his notepad and looks up. "Let's start at the beginning," he says, turning to Simon. "Could you tell me what your organisation has against mines?"

"We're not an organisation," Svala leaps in, "but a loose grouping of people who want to safeguard the value of the natural world and human life. Establishing an entirely new mine that might have a lifespan of about fifteen years is out of all proportion to the harmful effects the mine would have on the natural environment and the people and animals who live here or are active in the area."

She speaks deliberately fast so he has no chance of interrupting her.

"The Sami village associations and the County Administrative Board have said a clear 'No', but the government has decided to disregard their views, although they are protected both in Swedish law and in international law on the rights of indigenous peoples."

"I very much doubt the County Administrative Board is protected by laws on indigenous peoples," chuckles Börjesson, and the photographer joins in with his mirth.

Idiot, thinks Svala, and smiles.

"Of course not," she says, "but the County Administrative Board takes its starting point in the people who live here and the nature that surrounds us, not in individuals or multinational companies who see Swedish natural resources as a moneymaking opportunity."

"I understand," says Börjesson, even though Svala can see that he neither understands nor cares. He wants juicier morsels. She has no intention of giving him any.

"But mines still mean more for wider society than a few people's interest in nature. Not least where job opportunities are concerned. Don't you think a lot of people will feel grateful to see new industrial projects established in their locality? I mean, there are hardly any jobs."

"4.6," says Svala. "6.2 in Stockholm and 7.4 in the country as a whole."

He gives her a bewildered look.

"Unemployment in percentages," she says. "This region has the lowest unemployment in the country. People commute, of course, but using unemployment as an argument for sanctioning a new mine is a distortion. Mining's about money and prestige, nothing else."

"But to look at it from a different perspective, then," he says, "like rare . . . er . . . earth metals, isn't it a good thing that Sweden can become self-sufficient?"

"Through the Gasskas mine?" says Svala.

"Exactly. Batteries, wind farms and a whole string of technological innovations need precisely those . . . er . . . metals for their production. I assume you haven't missed the fact that the green reset is about climate change? It seems very odd for some individual reindeer herders to be more important than the climate."

Svala is about to reply that new mines only accelerate climate change and themselves represent ten per cent of Sweden's carbon dioxide emissions, but here Simon breaks into the conversation. He has been squirming in his seat for a while. There are two of them on this, after all.

"Our view is that there are already sufficient rare earth metals up in Kiruna. The LKAB group have confirmed that themselves, not least through their investigations of slurry pools and slag heaps, which have turned out to contain high levels of lanthanum and cerium."

"Lutetium, holmium, erbium, samarium, dysprosium, europium, terbium, praseodymium," Svala continues the list of transition metals and would have been able to name several more if the photographer hadn't intervened.

"Look this way so I can take your picture," he says. "Smile a bit, too. You're probably really pretty when you smile."

Svala ignores his comment, turns to look at the journalist and goes on.

"In Stormyrberget, where they're prospecting for the new mine, that is, there's only iron ore and we already have an overabundance of that in Sweden."

The journalist's final question is one she is already braced for.

The Africa question.

"Isn't it better for us to have a Swedish mining industry with highly developed safety standards and higher wages as well, than exploiting poorer countries, and perhaps even children, to do our dirty work?"

She keeps her eyes pinned on Börjesson and does not drop her gaze until he himself looks away.

"If the Swedish state really wanted to do something for 'Africa' they ought to export their technology, but naturally they don't want to do that. And why is that, do you think?"

The question is left hanging in the air. She has no intention of answering it herself.

Simon's hand is running over her leg under the table, pinching the inside of her thigh. She's never told him she is incapable of feeling pain. Some secrets are best kept that way. But she gets it. He wants space. To be quoted. There's only one leader. A natural one. He wants to be listened to, maybe admired. It's the first time Svala sees him from another angle. She downs her glass of water, gets up and pats him on the shoulder.

"You take it from here," she says. "I need to pee."

Svala sits on the closed toilet lid. She doesn't like surprises. She gets out her phone and calls Anna-Maja, whose own surprise is obvious as she asks where the hell they are.

"Simon's entertaining the media. He says the plan's changed. Do you know anything about that?"

"You'd have known too if you hadn't missed the Teams meeting last night," she says. There is annoyance in her voice.

What Teams meeting?

"I couldn't make it," she says. "Did you decide anything in particular?"

"I'll tell you later, not over the phone."

She sits there for a while longer. Allows the disappointment to ebb away.

You'll always be on the outside. Even when you think you're inside.

When she comes back into the café the mood has changed. The three men are behaving like old mates, laughing so loudly that the old fellow a few tables away glares at them. She can't be bothered to get involved so she sits down and waits until they've wiped away their tears of delight.

"Simon just told us a funny story about you," says the photographer.

Svala looks at Simon. He opts not to meet her eye. A fresh gale of laughter.

"Are we done here?" she says, and makes to get up.

"Just a couple more questions," says Jens B. Börjesson, "then we can all go up to the mine"

"What mine?" she asks. "It doesn't exist yet."

"He means the Pit," says Simon. "Maybe you haven't had a chance to read it yet, but *Gaskassen* published an article last night about Salo's plans to reopen it. Not just transport the waste rock from the spoil heaps to Kiruna, that is, but resume mining operations. See for yourself," he says, holding out his phone.

I'll take them to the Pit. Check in at the Grand and I'll see you there later. Room 14.

"A toxic old opencast mine," says Börjesson. "Now there's something for you eco-muppets to get your teeth into. Could be even more fun than protesting at some road barrier in the middle of nowhere."

40

Svala Svala need not cry
Say who will sing her lullaby
Reindeer walk the high fells' feet
Their own roots tell them where to meet

Where has that rhyme popped up from? She doesn't know. It beats time like a conductor's baton as she walks towards the hotel.

"Room fourteen, here's your key," says the woman with a pleasant smile. "Your father's already checked in."

"He isn't . . ." She stops herself abruptly.

Pap Peder. The treetop hotel room at Britta's. The body sailing through the air to land with a reassuring crack as his neck breaks.

"Thanks. I'll go up and wait for him."

She shakes off Pap Peder. Not even a nice memory is worth preserving where her stepfather is concerned.

The room on the first floor is poky, and smells of dog and stale smoke. She opens the bathroom door, shuts it, looks down at the street below, opens the air vent and sits on the bed. Her phone has been on silent. A load of missed calls and messages, at least half of them from home, but those will have to wait. The damage is already done and what did she expect? That her uncles, who keep a daily lookout for the tracks of the reindeer's enemies, wouldn't notice she'd gone off in the car? There was a risk. She had taken it.

Now she must concentrate on the rest. Whatever that is.

She lies on the bed and tries to think of Simon the way she usually does. His hands that are always moving when he talks, his mouth she might want to kiss, his voice, things he says that are meant only for her. She can't do it. Time and again, Mammamärta's face pops up instead.

You're on your way to making the same mistake I did. Get out of there.

Then she must have dozed off. There's the sound of a key in the door.

Svala Svala need not cry.

Outlined against the light of the low afternoon sun, his body lacks all detail. For several seconds she doesn't know where she is, who he is.

"Can I trust you?" he says.

"What do you mean?"

"Somebody tipped off the cops by phone. They've confiscated anything that could be viewed as a weapon. Thermos flasks, penknives, even rope. Those who didn't disperse of their own accord were taken to the police station. Do you understand what this means?"

"Some good pictures for the article," she says, and he glares at her. One of his eyes is brown, the other green. Strange that it hasn't struck her before.

"Give me your phone," says Simon, holding out his hand.

She sits up. She doesn't like his tone and tells him so.

"What are we actually doing here?" she asks and gets a smile in return. The sort of smile grown-ups give children when they don't understand.

He sits down beside her. Puts his arm around her shoulders and pulls her to him. Strokes her hair and lets his hand run on down her arm, her thigh, up again and suddenly the hand is inside her shirt.

"Stop," she says, pulling his hand away, and what the hell had she been thinking, that he'd pay for a hotel room so she could take an afternoon nap? "You told me to wait here," she falters, but maybe he's right.

After all, how often has she thought about him exactly this way? About him touching her, liking her, thinking about her the same way she fantasises about him.

Svala feels guilty. His hand is back under her shirt, harder now, more urgent and not only inside her shirt; he yanks at her trouser button, gets the zip undone. Thoughts are pounding in her head, coming out as whispers although she wants to scream *No, NO, I don't want to!*

"You want this as much as I do, admit it," says Simon, and she admits it.

Admits it to win time and catch up with the guilt. This is her own fault. Hasn't she learned anything after all those years with Pap Peder? A little finger is a hand, a hand is an arm, an arm is a body and now he's lying on top of her, forcing himself between her legs and saying this'll be quick, it won't hurt and he likes her and he'll take care of her and in the end she can't stop him. He's big. She's little.

A man against a child. And although she wants to struggle, scream, hit out, defend herself, her body just lies still and waits for it to be over. That's all it can do.

Afterwards she counts the seconds. Minutes pass.

When his breathing turns to snores she extracts herself from his grasp. Puts her trousers on, buttons her shirt as she keeps a check on his sleeping face. Dribble is running down his chin. All of a sudden he looks very old.

His phone has ended up on the floor.

Now it's in her rucksack. The door closes with a slight hiss and then she runs. Down the stairs, out of the door, towards the cemetery.

She fumbles with the lock. Can't remember which pedal is the clutch and which is the brake. The car coughs and dies. She tries again.

Svala Svala need not cry.

She drives out of town. Passes the OKQ8 petrol station despite the fuel light shining red. She dare not stop. She supposes she'll have to park somewhere. Take a forest track. Gather her thoughts and call somebody.

She does all that, but somebody doesn't answer.

She leaves the car engine running. The fuel indicator shows she's running on reserve. Everything's gone to hell in a handcart anyway.

What crap you're talking, Svala. I warned you but you wouldn't listen. Don't feel sorry for yourself over something you could have avoided.

Mammamärta's eyes are as black as the waters of Gårtejávråsj.

"You're right," she says to the rearview mirror. "I only have myself to blame."

41

Svala does a U-turn, drives to the petrol station, pulls the hood of her anorak over her head and fills the tank before she drives back south. Down to Gasskas and the old pit.

Unlike the other members of the group, she'd known there was something going on. While the conditions still allowed it, she would take the snow scooter. Stop short of the mine and approach on skis or snowshoes to memorise everything she saw. Diggers, dumpers, a workforce in high-vis and helmets. She doesn't know why she didn't tell the rest of them. Maybe because she thinks keeping old mines in use is better than carving out new ones. If mines have to exist at all, that is.

On other occasions she saw familiar faces in the mining zone. Municipal boss Henry Salo for example, strutting around with a sneering, self-satisfied grin that sends Svala's thoughts in dark directions.

She has consciously let him be. Not for his sake, but for her own.

He has Mammamärta's blood on his hands. She has sensed it without precisely knowing why. He owes her an explanation. In good time she will force it out of him.

It is a few weeks earlier. Svala stamps the snow off her boots outside the municipal council offices and goes up to the reception desk.

"We've met before, haven't we?" says the woman behind the glass screen. "Are you doing another school project?"

"That's right," says Svala. "I need to talk to Henry Salo again. I got B plus last time, thanks to him. With luck and a bit more help I might even get an A for this one," she says, with one of those cutesy looks she can turn on at will. As fair and lovely as a summer's night.

"Go on up then," says the receptionist and opens the security barrier to the offices upstairs. "You know where to find him."

It is a new Salo sitting there with his feet up on the desk, munching on a cheeseburger with extra cheese. A stouter but more carefree version of the head of Gasskas municipality. Not even the hacker attack has done any lasting damage to his mood, although it did feel good to tear a strip off the security firm that had claimed to guarantee one hundred per cent protection against cyber attacks.

With his left hand he is googling foreign holidays to keep Pernilla happy. As usual she thinks he is working too much. A little bit of *viva España* around the dinner table wouldn't do any harm.

Their relationship is there. As stable as ice in spring but entirely possible. She came back. He took her back. That's roughly where they are now, between a thin crust of ice and a thaw.

It's only been a few hours since she rang to say the home test had come out positive. They have decided – she has decided – to try again after the miscarriage.

When there is a knock at the door he assumes it is Gabriel Johansson wanting to get something dull off his chest. He's a new face in the building. A southerner who's been dragged up north by his Gasskas-born wife. To crown it all, they're Pentecostalists. Why the hell can't he have his lunch in peace?

"Give me ten mins," he calls. "I'll come over to you."

"Hello," says Svala, closing the door behind her. "Perhaps you remember me."

Very carefully he gets to his feet, puts down his burger, brushes the crumbs off his sweater and wipes the drips of dressing from his chin.

Svala Hirak. That bird of ill omen. Memories he has successfully buried in the pile of rubble left by Branco draw themselves up to their full height and kick him until his legs crumple under him. He makes a grab for the desk and forces out "Oh yes, hi. It's been a while."

"It has," she says. "I'm writing an essay on the Gasskas mine and thought you might be able to help me."

"I'm not the right person. You need to talk to Hasse Eriksson. He was head of Business and Commerce here in the seventies and eighties. He's old but hale and hearty. I'll give you his number."

"I'm not talking about the old mine, I'm talking about what's happening there now."

"Now?" says Salo, looking as infuriatingly innocent as only he can if he chooses to. Dark and velvety as an evening in late summer. "The mine has closed down, you know that, surely?"

"Yes, but what are the diggers doing there?"

"I'm not aware of anything like that," he says, and realises it is a stupid answer. The girl is smart. Too smart for her own good. "Or do you mean the clean-up operation?" he adds. "There was a load of waste left behind when the mine closed. That's being cleared now, so no more streams get contaminated."

She takes a stroll around the room. Spends quite a while in front of the municipal map, saying nothing, moves on to the summer picture of Pernilla and Lukas that Pernilla put up with a drawing pin as an angry reminder of their existence.

"What luck that you got him back," she says. "Pity Mammamärta wasn't as lucky."

Fuck it. Back come the thoughts of the girl's mother that he has successfully chased away with the aid of high-proof alcohol. His guts writhe like taunted vipers. Images sweep by, forcing him to remember: a heap of human flesh, tied up in the back of the van.

At first he couldn't see who it was. She was in a cage. The features had been reduced to a bloody pulp. One arm was dangling strangely, as if on some loose-jointed shop-window dummy.

It was you who told us we could do what we liked with her and we've certainly done that.

Salo sits down.

"I loved your mother," he says, and she replies that he's said that before but it doesn't make any difference. Mammamärta is dead and now she wants to know what happened.

"I don't know," he says pitifully. "They took her to force the municipality to exchange her for wind farm shares."

"The municipality?" says Svala. "But the municipality is you, right?"

"No, not at all," he defends himself. "The municipality is politically binding decisions made by the municipal council. I'm only a civil servant."

She understands what has happened. With that knowledge comes a need for vengeance but vengeance is a lukewarm sensation and seldom worth the effort. She's older now, smarter. It's better to bide your time and let others do the heavy lifting. She has the language of an academic and the face of a fourteen-year-old. Somewhere between the two she can make the most of her skills.

"I see," she says. "It really was too bad things turned out the way they did. But as I say, my essay isn't about the past but about what's underway now. If you can't tell me more about what happened to my mum, maybe you can tell me what's *really* happening in the mine?"

The same exhilaration as over the wind farm has made Salo believe in the future again. The transition to green energy is part of the biggest move the politicians and investors have taken towards a cleaner world, and Gasskas municipality is on board. Local population numbers will rise, as will the tax income and other revenue. New jobs will be created, infrastructure improved. Personally, he can see nothing but advantages.

"The residual waste from mining operations most likely contains a lot of rare earth metals. If they can be extracted, that would mean vast amounts of revenue for the municipality and a big step forward for the transition to green industry."

Salo can see the sceptical look in her eyes as he utters the word "green", but he goes on:

"Over the winter we transported some material to Kiruna. If the testing stage produces results, the project proper could start as early as next year, but that's not all."

It turns out the mine was never exploited to full capacity. Times were hard, the price of iron ore was low. The ore-dressing plant can be brought back into use, and extraction can start up again. He keeps quiet about all the stuff like new roads, clear-felled forest, polluted streams and all the rest that gets eco-fanatics fired up.

"How much of that can actually be put into practice?" says the girl with a docile look. "Tell me a bit more about it. I don't know anything about mines or those special metals or whatever you called them."

"Electric cars and wind turbines are only a fraction of the industrial activity that needs metals like lithium, cobalt and manganese. The way it's looking right now, Europe is going to be entirely dependent on countries like China, the Congo and Madagascar. I assume you know that children of your own age are being exploited in the mines there. I think it would be better for everybody for the minerals to come from Swedish mines."

He's throwing her plenty of meat for her school project. His thoughts quickly divert to the Greek-Chinese businessman Kostas Long who, now that he has inherited his father's money, has decided to invest in the mining industry in Gasskas. With his substantial funds, he provides surety if the Swedish state were to pull out. They're meeting in Paris in a few weeks' time. A short break on the continent is exactly what he needs.

"Well, that sounds good," she says. "Does it involve building more infrastructure, too? I mean, we need better roads between Gasskas and Kiruna, don't we, if there's to be a new mine as well?"

Now they're on the same track. Salo looks at the girl with respect. She's clearly got her head around this, and here's his chance to have a positive influence on the next generation of Gasskas residents.

"In an ideal world, we'll build a road network that links up Gasskas with the old and the new mines and hopefully the Kallak mine north of Jokkmokk too, when it comes into being, plus Gällivare, Kiruna and maybe other parts of the mountains. Like you say, the inland needs infrastructure to create new job opportunities."

"And what happens to the reindeer herders' livelihoods, for example, if your plans come to fruition?"

Lapps and eco-Nazis. Lapps, eco-Nazis and now fourteen-year-olds too.

"Did you have anything in particular in mind?" says Salo with a flash of his best pike-fish smile.

"New roads, new mines, poisoned lakes, shrinking grazing grounds, swathes of clear-felling and so forth . . . but maybe they don't matter in the greater scheme of things?"

Is there anything worse than precocious brats?

"Special interests take a back seat when society is making progress, that's an important aspect to highlight in your essay," says Salo. "Individuals against the common gain. Social progress always has a price. The majority wins what the minority gives up. At a personal level that's unfortunate, of course, but for most people it's good."

"A bit like when Mammamärta had to give up her life for your wind farm, is that what you mean?"

They look at one another like equally matched combatants before their jaws clash.

"Unlike my world, which is based on sound political decisions and investors who stake their capital in the interests of society's progress, your mother lived in a criminal underworld built only on personal gain. It wasn't me that killed her; she asked for it. I chose the better alternative. Not for my sake, but for all of Gasskas."

"OK, fine," says Svala. "I only wanted to know whether she died on my lap for a good cause and now you've explained it to me."

She arouses that feeling of tenderness inside him. Right now he wants to pull her to him, snuffle at her baby head with its first curl. He lifts her onto his shoulders and walks towards the dog pen. They catch the scent of something fragile. Even the Laika bitch comes over and licks her feet. She laughs. Further off there is the sound of a car approaching. A few minutes later it is over. The screams fill his ears and the dogs are howling.

"You sat on my shoulders. You were like a daughter to me. I've told you what I know. There was nothing else I could do."

God knows he's doing the best he can. Salo clears his throat.

"So I hope you're not going to write anything inappropriate," he finishes.

She looks at him with her peculiar husky-dog eyes. For a fleeting moment, they are of the same kind.

"I never meant it to happen."

42

Svala is parked outside the perimeter fence of the mine, trying to understand the sensation that washes in and out of her. She has no vocabulary for the experience. She forces herself to put the thought of his body out of her mind, the hand pressed over her mouth, the uncut nails groping about between her legs, his – stop! She must blame herself. The self-reproach makes her angry and rage has energy. Feeling sorry for herself, being a victim, a little rape victim crying her eyes out to the police, would make her even more worthless.

Svala has always been on her own. This is no exception. She gets out of the car, skirts along the fence to its highest point and looks out over the industrial site. The water-filled opencast mine, the slag heaps alongside, the ore-dressing plant and the slurry pools extend as far as the eye can see, even though she is using binoculars.

There are signs of the demonstration here and there but no people, no roads blasted to pieces, only a scattering of possessions. A rucksack. A wooden cup crushed under the wheels of some vehicle. The STOP THE MINE banner that she helped to paint. She follows the fence down to the main entrance gate and picks up a scarf, almost sure it is Anna-Maja's. She hangs the chequered fabric on the branch of a birch and everything is unreal.

She sits in the car for a long time without starting it. Sits quietly, trying to summarise the last few months. Or to be more precise: where and when Simon came into the picture.

The mine protests aren't new. They started in Gállok and spread to Gasskas. They are basically about the same thing. Projects that are marketed as vital to the transition to green industry but are in actual fact no greener than the grey slag heaps.

At the start of January, Svala tags along with her cousin Anna-Maja to an information meeting where the municipality and the group of mining companies had agreed to answer questions from the public. Although Anna-Maja is around ten years older, they get on well. She is studying biology in Luleå but comes home for the weekends. They generally meet up then. Svala reads everything Anna-Maja tells her to read. Once she's done that, she carries on of her own accord, reading everything she can find in the Gasskas library on mining, geology, environmental pollution, history, the Sami languages, indigenous peoples around the world, and more. An assortment of reports. Dissertations and a book or two on numerical modelling also slip down nicely. She wants to understand the way calculations are done and how this can make a mine more environmentally friendly.

The school dining hall is full and the answers are few. At any rate when they get onto sensitive topics like reality. Svala puts up her hand.

"In the analysis carried out by an independent consultant to establish whether the consequences of a new mine are defensible in relation to the number of new openings for work, the consultant concluded that most of the work opportunities would be fly in/fly out jobs. That is, jobs that don't benefit the local population, or bring in tax revenue. So why are you still using the argument about an increase in job opportunities?"

The men on the stage exchange looks. They didn't see that coming when they let a child speak.

"Um, a consultant makes estimates that don't always tally with the real world. Certainly a number of jobs will be carried out by an external workforce, but there are also local gains such as the increased demand for places to eat and overnight accommodation," says the municipal council rep whose name she commits to memory. Johan Svedberg.

"Alright then," Svala goes on, "it's good that the City Hotel and the Kringle café can take on a couple more underpaid part-time staff, but you're contradicting yourselves. You just said the individual must stand aside for collective gain but that's not correct, is it? You lot are prepared to sacrifice our entire local environment for the financial profit of a foreign mining company."

"Well now, we seem to have a future politician with us today," exclaims Svedberg and he laughs. The audience laughs with him. And when other speakers who seem very keen on mines are chosen to speak for the rest of the session, Svala goes out. Her cheeks are blazing, she's finding it hard to breathe, but this is where it starts. The spark that ignites her.

She digs out Simon's phone from her rucksack. But as she starts to focus on the passcode, moving from the front seat of the car to the downy labyrinths of her brain, the phone dies. She only gets a glimpse of his home screen: a photo of a girl holding up the Sami flag.

She remembers the picture, where it was taken, exactly when and by whom: Anna-Maja. A change in the weather had made the roads icy. They took their kick-sleds up to Vaukaliden.

"Hold the flag up, Svala!"

She was even smiling. But Simon wasn't there, she's sure of it.

Afterwards they kick-sledded down to the Kringle café. Met up with the others. They were talking about the next mine protest when he showed up out of the blue. Sweaty, as if he'd been running, and he shook hands with them all, holding on to Svala's until she withdrew it.

He was soon at the centre of things. He had experience that the rest of them lacked. They listened to him like disciples. Everything he had to say, they swallowed it hook, line and sinker. Afterwards she couldn't stop thinking about the way his hands moved with his words, his eyes that fixed hers, his voice.

You're my own little guerilla soldier.

Simon is still such a natural part of everything that nobody wonders who he is, where he comes from or even whether he has a surname. She decides to start there. Switches her own phone back on and calls Anna-Maja.

"For God's sake, where have you been? Simon's looking for you. He says you're driving around in some illegal car and that you may have put his phone in your bag by mistake. I was worried something had happened to you."

Nothing happened.

"The group needed the car," says Svala, and realises she has fallen for a logical fallacy. *He* needed the car, and not the car itself, in fact – but her expectation, her belief that she had an important role to play.

His own little guerilla soldier.

Anna-Maja laughing makes her sense of shame even worse.

"That's the most stupid thing I've heard today. And I've just seen the newspaper's video clip from the demo. Thank goodness we'd shelved the idea of blowing anything up, but why didn't you come? Where are you? Shall I come and fetch you? Hello!"

Svala makes a U-turn and drives south with a vague notion that there might be someone who can help her, someone who would understand.

A while later, that vague thought takes a new direction. She pulls into a parking area for lorries and turns off the ignition.

The evening light is filtering through the fir trees. The lake below glitters with spots of reflected sunlight and it's so bloody beautiful someone ought to capture the moment in a painting.

The painting shows neither the truck drivers desperate for a pee nor the girl walking towards the water. She crouches at the shoreline. Feels the water, only recently freed from the ice. Holds her fingers under the surface until they go numb. Mammamärta's face is superimposed on her hands like a rippled mirror.

Are you here?

Of course. Always here.

Exactly . . .

Where are you, then?

Just somewhere. I need your help. That Simon, do you know who he is?

And Mammamärta laughs so hard that she makes waves.

But sweetie, she says, *you know I'm not real.*

But give it a go. Tall, same age as you, curly brown hair, ponytail.

Sounds like Simon Frisk. Hung out with Peder for a while. I thought he was dead.

He should be, says Svala.

Hung out with Peder for a while.

Pap Peder. Honestly, how naïve can she have been? But maybe she has a name now, and an opportunity to carry on looking. The only thing that matters.

43

Yesterday the first mosquitoes started biting. As Henry Salo drives home, it begins to snow. Completely normal but depressing all the same. By the time he turns into the driveway of the house, ten minutes from the council offices, the landscape is white.

He should be used to it. He was born here. Maybe they should move back to Uppsala. Or somewhere else where it's proper spring by now, as far away as possible from eco-Nazis and whining reindeer herders.

He turns off the engine and sits there.

The encounter a few weeks ago with the Hirak kid is sticking around like cat shit on the sole of his shoe. And soon it'll be time for the next one: Kostas Long is coming for dinner.

In the course of the day they have gone over everything from ground plans for the old mine area to environmental impact statements. Detailed estimates of what might really be lurking in the slag heaps and slurry pools are something he will keep to himself. The project is still embryonic.

Advance information from the LKAB mining company analyses looks promising, but the technical side isn't Salo's department. He needs Long as a financial guarantee against the Mining Inspectorate and the government, who will never give a reopening the green light unless the funding is already in place. What's more, it needs to be arranged before they even know the extent and types of minerals that are in fact there to be salvaged.

To crown it all, the cyber-attack on the municipality is making everything much trickier. The IT bods still don't know who the attack came from, or what they want. The latest he's heard is that Milton Security are sending somebody up from Stockholm, so in a few days the problem should be sorted.

Through the windows he can see Pernilla moving between the kitchen and the dining room. Presumably she's already laid the table. The cooking will no doubt be well underway too. She is leaving nothing to chance.

And now they're expecting again. A bunch of flowers is on the seat beside him. Red roses in a sea of frothy white. God Almighty, spare us any rows this evening.

He checks the time. A couple of hours to play with. Instead of going in he heads down to the sauna cabin. Lights the fire, sits on the cold bench for a while until it gets going.

Outside, the river is roaring with the verve of springtime, unlike Salo who is getting ever gloomier. He's tired. Fed up. He isn't clear what with. With most things. Not even the river provides much consolation to speak of. Or God, for that matter. He goes listlessly back up to the car, slaps his thighs with his hands like a slalom skier before his next run, grabs the flowers and steps into the house with a broad and gleamingly white smile.

"Thanks," says Pernilla, and tosses the flowers onto the draining board. "Perhaps you could see to them? I've got loads to sort out for this evening. I haven't even had time for a shower."

"You're lovely as you are," he ventures and gets one of her looks. The first time she's looked at him since he got home.

"What's he like, this Long? Chatty, quiet, fun, a drip?"

"A bit of everything, I'd say," says Salo, and she sighs.

"Tell Lukas he needs a shower, too."

Bugger. He'd promised to pick up the boy from the after-school club.

She stops what she's doing. Looks at him. Through him.

"You forgot."

Not waiting for an answer, she grabs the car keys and slams the door behind her. Silence descends. His shoulders fall a little lower. And lower still after a couple of whiskies.

The sauna is no longer hot but benign. He opens a beer and downs it. The alcohol raises his thoughts to a better level. A level where at least he doesn't feel like letting himself be swept away in the waters of the spring flood. A child. She could at least have asked what *he* wanted.

The door creaks. Lukas.

"Come in, it's just the right temperature now."

The boy sits on the bottom bench. Neither of them has anything they feel they need to get off their chest.

Afterwards they throw snowballs into the river. A female voice calls their names.

"We'd better go up," says Salo, putting an arm around the boy's shoulders. "Our guest's bringing his daughter with him, so maybe you two can watch a film."

"Girls are hard work," says Lukas.

Fucking tell me about it.

The guests arrive, the food is exquisite, the kids stay upstairs and the conversation flows, man to man.

If Salo hadn't carried on with the whisky and then had wine on top, he would have noticed Pernilla's rather odd behaviour. As it is, he laps up Long's praise of his attractive wife and lovely home.

Pernilla stands in the kitchen, gasping for air. It's him. Kostas Papadopoulos as he was then.

How is this possible?

There is nothing to indicate that he has recognised her. Her hair is a different colour now, she has filled out a little and her face is slowly but surely remodelling itself into that of an ill-tempered wife. The carefree blonde girl who went to Greece one summer for some island-hopping with a friend has been blotted out for ever. Not least in her soul.

And not least thanks to that arsehole sitting in the dining room eating panna cotta with cloudberries she picked herself and praising Henry for his excellent choice of wife.

She is clearing the table. Avoiding eye contact with Long. Suddenly Henry puts a hand around her waist and announces they are expecting a baby. This deserves a Champagne toast. She forces out a little smile.

That's great. Really great.

"Sit down and rest for a bit," says Henry. "I'll fetch the fizz."

All at once they are alone for a few minutes. His remarkable eyes. A luminous green, as if evil had a shade of its very own.

"Congratulations on the new baby," he whispers. "It'll be a comfort when I get my son back."

She pulls her cardigan around her. Tries not to keep looking. To find her voice, although the past is rumbling ominously: he caught up with you in the end. Now he'll never let go.

"You have no son," she finally manages to say, and hey presto, Salo is back with a bottle and glasses.

"Your wife isn't very talkative," says Long, "but my word, she's a brilliant cook."

The brilliant cook hides in the kitchen. Does the dishes. Waits. Takes a bowl of popcorn up to her son and the girl. She didn't quite pick up on the name. Mei, perhaps?

They are lying at opposite ends of the sofa, watching a film. Taking handful after handful of popcorn, tipping it into their mouths. The girl is a few years older. For Pernilla, an obscure part of Kostas Papado-poulos's life. An icy shiver of discomfort runs through her. If you are in the know, the similarities are striking. Neither of them looks particularly Asian. And yet there's something. The mouth. The hair. The gestures.

"Your dad has rung for a taxi. It'll be here in ten minutes."

"Thanks for having me and for the nice things to eat," Mei answers mechanically, picking up her phone to write something and then asking Lukas for his number.

"Lukas is too young for a mobile phone," Pernilla responds swiftly but the girl insists. "Then maybe I can get yours so he and I can stay in touch."

Stay in touch. Thanks for having me. How has she turned out this way?

Before Pernilla has time to say that they can be in touch via her dad, Lukas has reeled off the number.

The taxi moves off and Pernilla is ready. Henry Salo's face is flushed with fatigue, food and booze. He moves from the hall to the drinks cabinet.

"Long is an extremely important person. I think I'd made that clear to you, hadn't I? But you treated him as if he didn't exist. He even asked me if you were ill. Bloody embarrassing."

If she had been intending to say anything about "Long", this is clearly the wrong moment. She should have been scared but mainly she feels angry. Touch-my-child-and-I'll-kill-you angry.

"Next time you can take your guest for dinner at the hotel. At least they get paid for the food and the service there," she says, and starts on the customary tour of the ground floor, switching all the lights off.

He sits there in the dark. Pernilla goes upstairs and lies down beside her son. Before she falls asleep, she sends a text.

`Hi Dad. It's been a while. My fault. We miss you,`

especially Lukas. Couldn't you come up? P.S. They need a new editor-in-chief at Gaskassen. Love you.

The answer comes at once:

Applied for the job, moving up there next week. Meant to be a surprise but now you know. Love you too.

44

In the beginning was the ice.

When the ice receded and the land began to rise from the sea, the people followed.

Or to be more accurate, as the climate grew warmer, the animals followed their prey and the people came after them.

Elk, reindeer, bears, seals and birds were food and clothing.

The people who followed the animals were simply people. They had no epithets such as Swede, Finn, Sami or Kven. They found each other, broke into smaller groups with a single common aim: survival.

No archaeologist or anthropologist knows exactly when the first people arrived in Gasskas or where they came from. Probably from east and west, south and north. As people always have done up here.

The oldest settlement in Gasskas is around seven thousand years old. There are signs that hunters and fishermen have been here significantly longer, but they are not part of written history.

It is always the settled people whose stories are told.

Per-Henrik heads north without a clue where to look for a niece driving around in a car that is officially deregistered. For Christ's sake, she's still only thirteen and can barely see over the steering wheel.

He doesn't doubt that she can drive. She's as lithe as a weasel on the snowmobile and clearing the snow with the tractor has been her job all winter, but a car. He draws the line there and the line is where the law takes over. Kind of.

He sends dark thoughts to the person who presented her with the car and scrolls through to find her number. Calls it. Hears it ring but gets no answer. He calls again.

"Hello?"

"Is that Lisbeth Salander?" he says. "This is Per-Henrik Hirak."

"Is anything the matter?"

"Yes," he says, and suddenly everything sounds trivial. "Has she called you?"

"You mean Svala? Yes."

"So she called! And what did she say?"

"Don't know, I couldn't take the call," says Salander. Pauses, but when he says nothing, she asks her question again.

"Is anything the matter?"

"She's gone off in your car."

"Her car," says Lisbeth and yawns. She's evidently just woken up. Checks her missed calls when he asks her to. Nothing new from Svala.

"And what do you expect me to do about it, over a thousand kilometres from Gasskas?"

Per-Henrik's ear itches with irritation at her arrogant answer, but she's right. She can't do a thing. Responsibility for the girl lies with him and his brother now. Responsibility that means many eyes are on them. To be approved as a family home they had to attend a course. Answer hundreds of questions about everything from alcohol consumption and sexual habits to experience with children. Why they need to know about his non-existent sex life he has no idea. They should have asked about the reindeer instead. How it feels to work around the clock and still not know whether the animals will survive.

But Svala's arrival has given the work a new purpose. She has the skills and the interest, but the fact remains: neither he nor Elias has her under control. It's only a question of time, he's known that from the start. She's co-operative and does what she's supposed to. Goes to school, her sports practice, helps out at home. She's even picked up the language in the short time she's been with them. But she's like an iceberg. Only the tip is visible. She has that wild element to her. The same touchiness as her mother, a stubbornness that won't be shifted.

At the start it was charming that she wanted to go so deeply into her Sami roots. She asked about everything and they answered as best they could. And once she'd explored that as far as she could, she started to look outwards. He's not sure who those activists are, exactly. Maybe just young folk who want to make their voices heard. It's not that he isn't proud of her commitment, just the opposite, but there's something going on. He can feel it.

"Let me know if she calls you, OK?" says Per-Henrik.

"If she calls me it's presumably because she doesn't want to talk to you," says Lisbeth in her practical way.

"If she calls you, it could be because she's in need of your lawless superpowers," he retorts.

If you only knew what that girl's capable of on her own you'd be requesting military reinforcements, not calling me.

"Alright, I'll be in touch if she does," says Lisbeth and ends the call.

She gets into the shower, out of the shower, pulls on the clothes heaped on the floor by her bed.

Svala is a source of anxiety although she would never say it out loud. She misses her, and not only her. Having someone to be concerned about, to take care of, to focus on and forget everything else.

Sentimentality is washing around her cerebral cortex and it's all Mrs Ågren's fault. He puts his finger on tender points. Like a naprapath of the soul he applies pressure until the pain goes and if it doesn't he keeps on trying. The points have many names. Mum, twin sister, Kalleblomkvist and so on, but the weeks with Svala, that tiresome little brat, have left traces which can't just be swept over.

She is almost ready for the walk to the other side of Söder and her first therapy session of the week when who should call but the therapist in question.

"Oh, um, hello Lisbeth, I'm sorry to ring at such short notice, but I'm not well and I'll have to cancel this week's consultations. The same goes for the rest of the month, I'm . . . having an operation . . . and, well, the best thing for you would be to change therapists because I'm not sure when I'll be coming back. I'm afraid I haven't anyone to recommend, but I'm sure you can find . . ."

Then he hangs up. She gets it. Can't be much fun having her as a client. Someone who doesn't say a word for ninety per cent of the session and waits for the time to pass. That's how it looks from the outside, anyway. Inside she's processing every word or thought that slips through her internal censorship. And her body feels strangely light when she leaves.

But still. There's something odd about Mrs Ågren. His voice. His staccato delivery. The way he tailed off at the end of the call.

45

The fisheye perspective through the spyhole in the door shows an empty landing. Since Mikael Blomkvist got obsessed with the idea of being followed Salander has sharpened her senses, which is starting to get annoying. She's pretty sure he's just got the jitters. Being shot last autumn in Gasskas must have made him more hyper-vigilant than he cares to admit. She should suggest he consult Mrs Ågren. Or maybe not. Blomkvist would put his pensioner's head on one side and say, "How brave of you to go to a therapist, Lisbeth" or something equally pathetic, because that's the way he is. Always with Lisbeth tacked on the end as if she were some kid on the fringes of the school playground and he the worried teacher.

Back to Mrs Ågren. She can't get rid of the feeling that something's wrong. She calls him and it goes to voicemail. Tries again a couple of hours later, with the same result. And although she leaves a message he doesn't call back, which isn't like him. He normally goes over the top in his concern for her. Sends text messages with appointment reminders although she's never missed one and rounds them off with silly but touching phrases like "take care of yourself". She weighs the various possibilities and alights on the word "scared". Not ill. Scared.

If you're in a tearing hurry, the walk from Fiskargatan to Grindsgatan takes eight minutes. Trying to get her breath back, she taps in the door code and runs up the stairs.

There is no longer a name plate on the door.

The paper heart saying Welcome, which has annoyed her every time, is gone, leaving only a slight gluey mark.

She rings the doorbell and knows he isn't going to answer. His neighbour, on the other hand, is ready and waiting. In the opening above the security chain, all she can see is a nose.

"If you're looking for the therapist, he's moved," he hisses.

But when Lisbeth asks where to, he shuts the door.

Maybe nothing is wrong. It's only her who's fucked up. A freak, unwanted even by a therapist.

Getting home takes time. There's a demonstration in progress along Götgatan. On Folkungagatan she loads up a trolley with ready meals, uses her Swish app to give a hundred kronor to the Situation Stockholm vendor and walks home.

After her evening routine of press-ups, sit-ups and a shower, Lisbeth opens her laptop and logs on to the Milton platform. The geniuses have been putting their brains to good use. With some difficulty (of course, a pat on the head for that) they have been able to locate the minibus. Overnight it has been moving north. Since 1.20 a.m. it has been stationary, on an industrial estate in Sundsvall.

She checks the map. Three hundred and eighty kilometres. Three or four hours if she steps on it but the weather forecast gives a snow warning.

Wasn't climate change supposed to be making the world warmer?

The motorbike won't do, she needs a car.

Something thuds through her letterbox. The only post she generally gets is the free local paper, *Södermalmsnytt*. Barely readable. A load of twaddle about spry pensioners and shoe shops closing down, but the sudoku is fine with her morning Coke.

A padded envelope. Pristine, no addressee. Or sender.

Outside the door, the landing is as empty as before.

Few people know where Lisbeth lives, still fewer who she is. The name on the door isn't hers. She soothes herself with the thought that it's probably the Residents' Association making some kind of request. They usually pop a Christmas greeting through the door each year. It's a bit early for the invitation to the summer party she's never attended.

She squeezes and shakes it. Tears off the self-seal strip and puts the package on the kitchen table. Inside is a wrapped box, quite tiny. Like a gift for a very small child.

She tears off the paper. It's a matchbox. Solstickan brand, the longer ones, and then her phone rings. A relief, she admits it. Mikael Blomkvist doesn't even say hello.

"I've had a parcel."

"Me too."

"Have you opened it?"

"Only the outer envelope."

There's a rustling down the line.

"What do we do with the box?" he asks and she doesn't know.

"Open it, I assume."

Though she would far rather not.

"Shall I come over?" he says.

She sits on the floor. Leans against the fridge. The fatigue comes suddenly. A person crawling up a huge pile of sand and slipping back down just as fast.

"Hello . . . are you still there?"

"Yes, I guess so."

"Be with you in quarter of an hour."

Fifteen minutes later, she checks the landing outside. The stairs are quiet. Another fifteen minutes and the same again. The doorbell camera shows nobody at the front entrance. An hour passes.

Damn that Blomkvist. She calls and listens as it rings.

"You're through to *Millennium* and Mikael Blomkvist, say something or send a text."

You don't even work there anymore. Get a grip.

She even leaves a message.

Where the hell are you? Call me!

Blomkvist is probably one of the few people alive today who both leaves and answers voicemails in preference to texting. Right now she misses his wooden expression and there are only two possibilities. Blomkvist has other things in his sights besides her – this has happened before – or else something has happened to him. Which could be anything. Run over by a car as he crossed Götgatan. A heart attack . . . he's ancient after all.

She slides open the matchbox. A ring. But not only a ring. A ring finger.

The box bounces across the draining board and onto the floor.

Six hundred and fifty-two square metres feel menacingly huge all of a sudden. They can conceal a whole bunch of people who wish her ill, and there are quite a lot of those at this point. She locks the internal doors to the bedrooms, living room and all the other bloody rooms she doesn't use, has barely been in.

Plague. The ring. Plague. The ring.

And now she's got to get out of here. She's hazy about why but out is where she's going. She checks the peephole, rejects the lift, and runs until she is gasping for breath outside the entrance to Blomkvist's apartment block at Bellmansgatan 1.

1066, what else would you choose for your door code, takes the stairs up to the very top floor. Not at home. What the hell now? She's got a finger in a matchbox in her jacket pocket and no-one – fucking no-one – but Blomkvist can help her right now.

Lisbeth takes some deep breaths. Tries to think clearly. More rationally. They are not in the middle of anything. There's no reason to send severed fingers. She's about to go back down when she hears footsteps below.

Stay ice cool. Ready to fight. Weapon? Bare hands.

A few steps at a time, stopping, continuing, and now she hears other sounds too. Groans. Shuffling. Three or four steps, pause, shuffle, groan.

It doesn't sound like a murderer sneaking upstairs. She casts a quick glance down through the twists and turns of the stairwell. Mikael's longish hair plastered across his temples as he drags himself up with the help of the handrail.

She meets him on the stairs and puts an arm around his back. Together they limp into the apartment. She props him against the coat cupboard in the hall. Notes that he has sacrificed *fin-de-siècle* charm in favour of a security door.

46

"What happened?" she says, once she has manoeuvred Blomkvist onto the sofa. The wound is ugly. A big bump is starting to swell, extending from the ear and along the upper part of his forehead. He probably needs stitches.

"No, not the hospital. Surgical spirit. In the bathroom," he slurs.

It's a long time since she was at his place. Everything looks the same. The same fusty old den from floor to ceiling. A wall of vinyl, with a stereo and some outsize speakers. Piles of newspapers and magazines. Books everywhere, and not sorted according to the colour of their spines. A few paintings, coastal scenes, a framed Springsteen record, a sofa that could conceivably be called "vintage" if one were trying to be nice, which she rarely is in his company, plus a Philippe Starck armchair that was possibly cool around 1983. The kitchen is a corner of the living room. She doesn't inspect the bedroom but makes straight for the bathroom.

A bathroom cabinet can reveal many things. Blomkvist's cabinet is empty apart from everyday items such as razors, a spare toothbrush and a packet of condoms with an expiry date of February 2019.

Not much action in that department then, Micke my old pal? thinks Lisbeth with a certain degree of satisfaction.

"Can you turn round?" she says, dousing some cotton wool in surgical spirit.

She cleans his face, dealing with the blood and the scraped skin and embedded gravel.

"Did you fall over?"

He grunts something and asks for water.

"Water," he wheezes like a dying man, "water."

"For God's sake, Blomkvist, it can't be that bad."

Some water and a few mouthfuls of Coke later, his voice sounds better so she asks again.

"Well. What happened?"

"I was on my way to yours, but then . . ."

He looks at her with that look she still can't help being affected by, so as always she tries not to meet his eye.

"It was a pushbike, I think. The same one as last time."

"The superhero jersey and the cross-body bag," Lisbeth fills in.

"That's right," he says, and tries to smile.

This is slow. Too slow. Blomkvist may be sluggish, but she isn't much further ahead herself. She's got to find out where they belong in this mess, and why.

"As I see it," she says, "we're not involved in anything that would be a motive for murder. I'm not, at any rate."

She forces more Coke down him, the elixir of life. Between two gulps he comes out with: "Douglas Ferm, remember him?"

She shakes her head.

"Have you read any of the stuff I sent you?"

She has, but no Ferm was mentioned in it.

"Perhaps not," says Mikael, "but a couple of his companies were. When I was up in Gasskas I asked Plague to map his companies after I met Ferm at that gentlemen's club, the Tigertooth Order, but I didn't realise there was a link to Branco then."

"Have you opened your parcel?" she asks.

He hasn't. Fishes in his jacket pocket and brings out one like hers, only smaller.

"I thought I'd wait until I saw you. Opening presents on your own is sad."

"Yeah," she says, putting her own matchbox on the table and then withdrawing to the edge of the sofa.

"Have you opened yours?" he says.

"A finger with a ring on," she says, and empties out her box. "Plague's finger."

"Good God, Lisbeth."

His face is a picture of disgust.

"How do you know it's his?"

"Remember the trial?" she says, and he does, even though it was close to twenty years ago. "My whole body froze. My only chance was to get them to believe my story, but at the start I couldn't get a single word out."

It isn't hard for him to imagine the scene because he was there in person. Lisbeth in full war paint vs the court. Condescending people in suits and dresses against a rebellious spiky-haired punk.

"I looked for safety in people who believed in me. You maybe, your sister, Armansky, Bublanski – but it didn't help."

"I've always believed in you," he says, and she gives him a look.

"Suddenly I spotted Plague. He was the very last to come in. Bloated and greyish-green, on legs that could scarcely carry him. He'd risked so much in daring to come and I couldn't do any less. Through the whole trial I kept my eyes on him. Now and then he would give me a nod as if he was trying to say, 'If I can, so can you.' Afterwards I bought him a ring and asked a goldsmith to engrave a pi sign on the inside."

"And what does that signify for you two?"

"Just a fucking pi, what are you getting at?"

He reaches for his parcel. Strips off the paper with fumbling fingers. First the string. A matchbox. Solstickan matches, the smaller size. A slimy little object is sticking to the bottom of the box. The nerve fibres have attached themselves like suckers. A message has been slipped into the box, too.

Those who see too much can quickly go blind. The guilt lies where the finger points.

"Fucking hell!" says Mikael, recoiling and banging into the back of the sofa.

An eye. Very like a human eye and yet not quite. A bit narrower. A vertical line through the pupil.

"Who . . . the fuck?" stutters Mikael.

"A cat," says Lisbeth. "Or maybe a lynx."

"We had a cat when I was little."

"Presumably not that one."

"I mean, how the hell can anyone, an innocent cat . . ."

She doesn't know where to look, gets up and sits down again.

She hasn't a clue what to do. Pats him on the shoulder. Offers to put some Gorbys in the microwave and if he hasn't got any Gorbys, maybe she can order in some pizza. She opens another Coke and when none of this helps she puts her arm around him, like they do in films. He leans over and rests his head in her lap.

"It'll be alright, we'll fix this," she says when he moves his head up to her shoulder. "It's going to be fine."

Yes, fine, if only it weren't for that damn Blomkvist scent, his breath close to her mouth. His mouth finding its way to hers and hers which can't help . . .

"What the hell are you doing?" she says.

"Sorry," he says and sits up. "I didn't mean that to happen."

The power to decide, the will, the right, the choice. She kisses him back, moves her mouth down to his unshaven neck, drawing in all the memories of the smell of him, good and bad, and decides once doesn't count. Never again will she let herself be hurt, never hope or dream. She will just engage in *complete mindfulness*. Close, so bloody close that his stubble digs into the delicate skin of her groin.

Matchboxes go skittering across the table.

Condoms that expired in February 2019 are never put to use.

But when she comes, with an intensity like the ice melting on the River Gasskas, it isn't Mikael Blomkvist she sees but a red-headed cop in a leather jacket and boots, slamming a car door shut and walking away without looking back.

"Was that good?" he says.

"Tell me about Douglas Ferm," she says.

47

"OK," says Lisbeth. "So you linked up Douglas Ferm with Plague."

She is pacing around amongst piles of books and heaps of clothes, trying to get her thoughts in order.

"The person you and I owe our lives to, you've handed him to some goddamned venture capitalist. Why?"

Yes, why? Because he felt sorry for the man perhaps. And because of the information he got in exchange.

They run into each other in the NK department store, of all places. It's a pissing sort of day in the truest sense of the word. Mikael has had biopsies taken and endured an intrusive scan. Naturally it wasn't a man of his own age who stuck an ultrasound probe up his arse.

The shame hangs over him like a mouldy blanket. When somebody calls his name, he's tempted to pretend he hasn't heard.

"You look bloody awful," says Ferm. "What's up?"

It takes a few moments for Mikael to recall where they've met before: at the Tigertooth Order in Gasskas. But the directness of the statement and the genuinely interested expression make him tell things exactly the way they are. They go to the restaurant. Order a beer apiece, swiftly followed by several more.

Afterwards he feels better. They have a shared experience. Prostate cancer isn't a death sentence. He could emerge from this with a clean bill of health. They exchange phone numbers and resolve to meet again.

"And you did, I assume?" says Lisbeth.

"A few weeks later. It was me who called him, not the other way round. He happened to be in town again; I needed someone to talk to."

"You could have called me," she says.

"I did," he says, and she has nothing to add.

Ferm is interested in his job. That alone is . . . Here's someone who keeps up with current affairs. They discuss journalism and get onto Mikael's specialist skills, the ones that apparently aren't wanted anymore. Except by Ferm, it seems. He explains the situation: he has come across a scoop that might be of interest to Mikael. And they could work together, be useful to each other.

"And you bought it, just like that?" says Lisbeth, rolling her eyes.

"No, it was a significantly longer process than that. But I'm afraid of boring you."

He puts his hand to his temple, pulls a clump of clotted blood out of his hair and goes on:

"Ferm sent me some material, initially the sort I could have winkled out for myself, but it led to other things. I enlisted the help of an associate from Millennium, the *old* Millennium, Fredrik Stål, who we used to bring in occasionally when companies needed investigation. He pointed me to the right sort of questions to ask. The questions got Ferm a bit further but then he hit a wall. Branco has a finger in lots of unpleasant pies, but we know that already. In legal terms we were sitting on information that could have got a police officer somewhere, even the security services, but that wasn't the aim. Not at that point, anyway."

"Understandable," says Lisbeth.

"So I contacted Plague. But the contact was entirely via me, not between him and Ferm."

"And he found stuff about Branco that Ferm made use of?"

"I don't know. Plague went totally quiet."

"Until his finger came through my letterbox," says Lisbeth.

"And an eye came through mine."

They sit in silence. Engage in synchronised brooding over their own situations. She should go home. Needs to think in peace.

"Sorry," he says. Puts his hand over a hand that moves quickly aside. "I didn't mean to draw you into any more shit."

"So when do you start your new job?"

"The removal van comes on Tuesday."

A bit of distance never does any harm.

48

Lisbeth walks home. The light rain helps to clear her thoughts. In her mind, a strategy has begun to take shape. She needs a few hours' sleep first, that's all.

She opens the front door in Fiskargatan with certain misgivings. Creeps up the stairs. Stops. Listens. She's almost up to her floor when she catches a glimpse of blonde hair under a woolly hat. *Camilla* flashes through her mind before she sees who it is.

A swallow called Svala is hunched down on the landing, propped against the door. She's pulled her arms out of her anorak sleeves to tuck around herself. Her hair is a tousled mess. She is bleary-eyed. Flattened.

"At last," she says. "Where have you been?"

Lisbeth sits down beside her. The girl's knee is bony. The hand emerging from the anorak is cold and hard, as if it will never thaw and how the hell is she supposed to . . . The girl's other hand also finds hers. Her head falls against Lisbeth's shoulder. Lisbeth puts her arm around her, pulls her body close. The stairwell light switches itself off. Tears fall intermittently.

"Come on," Lisbeth says finally, "let's get you inside."

Among the thoughts whirling through an aunt's head, vengeance comes first, for some transgression as yet unspecified, and then food. Pizza, and not from the freezer.

"You must be hungry," she says, and orders for them both. "No, no fancy Italian tricks with charred crusts and mozzarella goo instead of tomato sauce. One capricciosa, one calzone, one . . . well OK, if you must . . . vegetariana and extra cheese on everything."

The girl is dropping off at the kitchen table. "Maybe we should . . ." Lisbeth begins, unsure what they are actually going to do. What the girl wants, needs, must do. She's materialised out of nowhere. Now she is someone's responsibility.

Of the twenty rooms, three are furnished: the kitchen, a living room, a bedroom.

She takes off one set of sheets and puts on the spare. The pizza is half-eaten and it's late evening, night really. She leads Svala to the bed. The baby swallow snuggles under the downy wing of the quilt. The forehead is a child's. Only a tuft of hair sticking up.

Something has happened and they are birds of a feather. She won't tell anyone. Not out of consideration for Lisbeth or anyone else, but out of concern for herself.

Lisbeth lies down on the other half of the bed. Scrolls to the photo of Lo she took surreptitiously.

If-and-then.

If we meet again. *And* it's between you and me. *Then* only one of us can win.

49

The next day, Svala's side of the bed is empty. Lisbeth listens for human sounds. In the window niche looking out over Skeppsholmen, a girl is chewing on leftovers from dinner and watching the world outside.

"Time to wake up," she says. "Why have you locked all the rooms? Or rather," she rephrases her question, "why do you have so many rooms?"

"I like space," says Lisbeth and braces herself for another aunt–niece conversation. "Did you drive down? Your uncle called. And if you did, where did you leave the car?"

"Outside the front door, of course," says Svala.

"In the disabled parking bay?" says Lisbeth and realises the question won't get her anywhere. "Doesn't matter," she goes on, and brings up the websites of the vehicle inspection and insurance companies. "We'll have to arrange the inspection on the way up."

Time is slipping by. She should have been in Sundsvall ages ago. She checks with Milton. The minibus still hasn't moved. Svala doesn't want to go back up to Gasskas. Nor does Lisbeth. But they must. For various reasons. They'll have time to talk on the way. If only she could think of something to say.

"Are things going OK at school?" she finally comes out with, some-where north of Uppsala.

"Ester's dead."

"Who's Ester?"

Doesn't she bother to read the papers, Svala asks, and is told in no uncertain terms that she can fucking well bet she doesn't.

"It's just a load of crap about idiotic people. I don't want to know what they've done or why."

"Ester Södergran wasn't an idiot. She was . . . great."

"What happened?" says Lisbeth in a less hectoring tone, and Svala tells her. Not everything. Leaves out the bits about the drone, the files she copied from Ester's computer and her own theories. It's too soon. She hasn't finished thinking it through and what's more, she knows her aunt. With the tenacity of a fighting dog she will hang on until she gets every last detail out of her. She's evidently already said too much.

"So you two worked together and belonged to the same group of activists?"

"I did work experience at the paper," says Svala, "and yes, she took part in the demos but that's no motivation for murder. I mean, we weren't exactly the Baader-Meinhof gang."

People will believe what they like about that, thinks Lisbeth and goes back to the earlier conversation with Svala's uncle. Whichever of them it was. Sad Per-Henrik or surly Elias.

She's mixed up in something bigger than shouting slogans and painting banners. We've lost reindeer. Svala's reindeer. An execution, you'd have to call it. We've reported the incident to the police.

And what did the police do?

They wrote it off for lack of evidence. If this goes on, we can't let Svala live here any longer. She isn't safe here. None of us are.

And where do you two imagine she'll go?

We'll just have to hope it doesn't come to that.

*

At Njurunda, Lisbeth turns down towards the Svartvik industrial park and follows the GPS on her phone. There's an older industrial area down by the water which, judging by the signs, serves as some kind of tourist attraction. Not a soul to be seen. But that hasn't helped the minibus, which has already collected two parking tickets. Parking attendants are an odd species; they never sleep.

"What are we doing here?" says Svala. "I thought we were getting petrol."

"You can stay in the car. There's just something I need to check on."

It's impossible to tell if the minibus had broken down or was simply parked. It's locked, anyway. Lisbeth wipes some fresh wet snow from the windows in the hope of finding something that can link the vehicle to Plague. A soiled item of clothing on the floor and a crushed 7-Up can on the front seat are all that is visible.

DNA analysis would no doubt reveal much more, but the question remains: is Sundsvall the destination or simply a vehicle change? The only thing she can hope for is a sign from Plague. Preferably in some form other than body parts. Sooner or later they will have to get the police involved. Hopefully later.

She knocks on the window of their car. Svala puts the window down.

"You're an ingenious little horror. Do you know how to pick the lock of a minibus?"

"Who's asking?"

"Someone looking for a lost friend."

"If you buy me a battery pack. I forgot mine."

She tosses the sweater and the empty drink can into the boot. There's nothing else to find. Just a strong smell of vomit.

They buy a battery pack, some snacks and cans of Coke. The phone in Svala's hand kicks into life along with the picture of the girl with the Sami flag, which flashes up for a moment.

"I'm going to get a bit of sleep," says Svala, turning her gaze inwards and setting off through the downy passages of her brain. At first she can't find her way. Keeps going down dead ends. Retraces her steps, takes another entrance, but all at once he's there, Simon, leaning against a corner and leering. He has something on his hands. It looks like paint. He says something. At first she can't hear. Or maybe doesn't want to.

I collect virgins.

How many have you taken?

I don't take them, I get given them.

And how many have you been given?

One thousand six hundred and forty-nine.

1649. The world gapes open. Simon's world. He's got here first. The phone has been wiped apart from the picture of herself and a couple of texts, sent in the hours before everything changed. When she still looked at him with admiring eyes, did his bidding, sacrificed herself for the cause, for him. It feels so long ago. She is a different person now.

She texts Petra from her own phone:

`Has Simon got a new mobile number?`

He has. She messages him. Asks if they can meet. When he has time. Hugs.

The answer comes instantly:

`At last! Missed you! Not sure exactly when we can meet. I'll be in touch! Hugs!!!!`

What a fucking rash of exclamation marks.

She sneaks a sideways look at her aunt. She'll tell her eventually, but not yet. There's a serious risk that Aunt Lisbeth will wreck the plan Svala's already drawn up.

"Can we go to the waterpark at Örnsköldsvik?" she asks. "Everyone's been there except me."

"Not me," says Lisbeth. "But no. We haven't got our swimming things or the time. Another day maybe."

Thank God for that. But it sounded right, at least. The kind of thing a child would want to do.

50

Paris in the Springtime. The rain comes down in buckets, putting Henry Salo in an even worse mood.

The mood has been brewing since first thing this morning. Pernilla's grumpy look because he's going away and leaving her with morning sickness and the school run stays with him as a guilty ache in the left ventricle of his heart, but it makes him angry at the same time. He is working for the best interests of a whole community, not just for his family.

"Let the boy take his bike to school, he's nearly ten!" he calls from the hall.

"Along a road with a ninety limit where people drive like imbeciles!" she calls from the kitchen.

Then the taxi arrives.

"See you in a couple of days, darling," he tries.

She doesn't answer him. Or his text from Kallax on the way to the airport.

Along with their legal adviser Katarina da Silva he is to draw up the continuing guidelines for the municipality's and the private investors' respective roles in getting the Gasskas mine up and running.

First up is Kostas Long.

Admittedly the world has enough Chinese mines, but Long has a different perspective. Greek mother, Chinese father whose fortune from property has been invested in mines. Not only in China but anywhere in the world with cheap labour and ineffectual human rights laws. Salo sends a silent thought of gratitude to da Silva, sitting across the aisle. Her glasses hang on a cord around her neck. Her earphones indicate that she doesn't want to be disturbed. She is a sly old fox. Retired for some years now, but indispensable. The sort you can call in when others get bogged down, or like now, when there are sums at stake that the municipality can only dream of.

At Charles de Gaulle, a driver is waiting with a name board. The traffic heading into Paris is sluggish.

Pernilla sends a picture of the bin he forgot to take out to the road.

But as soon as they shake hands, drinks are on their way into Long's office. A few swigs raise his endorphin level by a few degrees. Da Silva gives the almost empty glass a meaningful look. "Stay sober," it says.

But for Christ's sake, he thinks, they're not in Paris every day.

Long is fond of a drink, too. The conversation flows, da Silva takes notes. Puts in the occasional wise word as Salo's arguments become increasingly lacking in substance. So far, nothing's official. This is just the start of a slowly advancing process that will hopefully lead to lots of fresh new euros and an advantageous outcome for Gasskas municipality.

Most mines are owned by private companies, and in this respect Gasskas mine is an exception. In the early 1980s, when the price of iron ore hit an all-time low and the mine closed, the company in question did a bunk, leaving billions of kronor of debt and the mine area in dire need of decontamination. In return for a certain amount of state capital, the municipality took over ownership and responsibility for the clean-up, as well as for the individuals suddenly out of a job, who amounted to a considerable proportion of the male population of Gasskas.

Now that the mine has a future again, the municipality finds itself in possession of a potential fortune.

"That'll do for today. We have a few hours before the flight tomorrow if any more questions come up," says da Silva, getting to her feet.

Salo takes a shower, his second since leaving home that morning, and lies down on the bed. He has just dozed off when his phone rings.

"Henry! Kostas here. What are you up to?"

"Nothing much, working and watching the news."

"The jewel in the crown of all capital cities and you're watching TV? That won't do," says Long. "I'll pick you up in twenty minutes and we'll hit the city. We'll leave da Silva at home. OK?"

Salo's body screams: *No! – drink a bottle of water, call your wife and go to bed.*

"Sure," he says. "I'll come down."

First they drive along the Right Bank, then over to the Left and into a warren of roundabouts and arrondissements. He has completely lost his bearings by the time the taxi stops outside an entrance in rue Champollion.

Once they are past the door code and the lift has delivered them to the fourth floor, the world looks very different. No windows to let in light. Or let out secrets. Unobtrusive music and a low buzz of conversation open their arms to them.

Salo thinks it's a good job he's wearing one of his favourite suits and accepts a glass of Champagne.

Long, on the other hand, is less formally dressed than earlier in the day. He isn't even wearing a tie. With his open-necked shirt and boots that give him a few centimetres' extra height, he moves towards the bar with an easy familiarity.

"You're my guest here this evening," he says. "Everything's on me. Take a look around while I go to the gents."

Salo needs no second bidding The place puts him in mind of a costume drama set in the present day. Even the actors are there. Well-known faces, some older, some younger. An author he's just been reading, models, politicians and athletes. Mostly people he has never met and will never meet again. He stops beside a vast buffet with oysters and other delights, and caviar to be eaten by the spoonful.

"I saw you came in with Long," says a woman and tips an oyster into her mouth.

She must be the most beautiful woman he has ever seen.

"Do you two know each other?" he says, wondering how anyone can eat something as slimy as an oyster in a sexy way.

"You could say that."

For once, Salo is reduced to silence. He doesn't know what to say. Questions like "What line of work are you in?" feel wrong in such a setting. The whole place has an air of discretion. Some are barely wearing any clothes. He sweats inside his jacket, his tie feels constricting.

"Shall I show you around?" she says, taking his arm.

The place is larger than he first thought. Room after room, each opening into another. One for music, another for card games. The further they go, the darker it gets. In the end he feels as if they are in a maze.

The woman squeezes his arm, asks if he wants to take off his jacket. Stops and loosens the knot of his tie. The tie rather roughly straightened by Pernilla that morning.

Right now his wife feels as unreal as the place he finds himself in. He ought to leave. Make his excuses and go back to the hotel, but then another woman joins them.

"Are you Salaud?" she says and runs an appraising eye over his party outfit from shoes to tie.

"Naughty name."

"Salo," he answers with the stress on the "a". "Perhaps you have names too?"

They don't.

The intoxication of the Champagne is bubbling in his soul. He feels good. Better than for a long time and here comes Long with some of the harder stuff. He waves away the ladies and takes a seat on the sofa next to Salo.

"Nice place, eh?"

Henry Salo can only agree. It'll be something to tell them about in the coffee break on Monday.

"There are a few things I'd like to discuss with you while it's just the two of us."

"Shoot," says Salo, taking a small sip of the fine single malt.

"It's about your wife. Pernilla Salo. Or Pernilla Blomkvist as she was before you married her."

Now he is baffled. What could Pilla have to do with them?

"So she hasn't said anything? Well, that's understandable."

Salo still doesn't get it, but when he asks for clarification, it is some time coming. Long swirls his glass. Takes a sip and then another.

"First rate," he says, "just like your wife was, once upon a time. Now don't misunderstand me, time leaves its mark on us all, but picture Pernilla at twenty-two. Blonde, slim, innocent."

The uneasiness is gnawing at Salo's insides. A sensation that even spirits have no power to dull.

"Like every other young Swede she went to Greece to go island-hopping. We met in Athens. Very romantic. I even remember what we ate on our first date. Calamari and chips. With ice-cold retsina, obviously."

"What are you driving at?" says Salo. "What Pernilla got up to in her younger days isn't any of my business. But if you knew her from before, you could have said something. When you came to dinner, for example."

"If I hadn't known it was her, I wouldn't have recognised her. I've been trying to find her for years. Ever since she left me and vanished without trace a few weeks before we were due to get married."

"And she no doubt had very good reasons for leaving you," says Salo soberly. The stab of jealousy is making him queasy. His Pilla and Long, and not just some summer fling but a plan to marry. The thought of the dinner and both of them knowing when Salo didn't prompts a fury in him that wants to scream and lash out. Yet he manages to keep his cool, suspecting he might need it for reasons that overshadow the romance.

"Sure, but you have to see it from my point of view too. I'm an only son. Getting married was a real milestone in my life, even for my parents who thought I ought to have chosen a Chinese wife. Or conceivably a Greek one. They paid for everything. And all I had when she left was the sense of shame."

"So now you want your revenge," says Salo, "instead of accepting that life took a different turn to the one you'd planned."

"You're wrong there. When I came for dinner I already knew who she was, as I say. I didn't come for revenge, but out of curiosity. What I didn't know, however, was that she had a son. That *we* have a son."

The thought makes Salo's head spin. Lukas as Long's son. His and Pernilla's boy. Why the hell didn't she say something?"

"To return to the present," Long goes on, "we're close to reaching an agreement. If everything goes smoothly, the contract can be on its way to you within a few days. Along with the bank guarantee. I needn't tell you again that it is for an extremely large amount. Mines are expensive playthings. Nothing a municipality can run for itself, even if you were to use your whole annual budget."

Salo hears a "but" even before it's said.

"But. In return I want my son back. A son needs to be with his father. No offence, Salo, but with your alcohol problem it can't be much fun for either Pernilla or Lukas, even though you've no doubt got many good qualities. Blood *is* thicker than water."

Henry Salo really doesn't agree on that last point. How would his own life have panned out had he not ended up with that devoted couple, the Salos? Probably like Joar's, or worse. But this isn't about him.

He struggles to get his thoughts in order. Da Silva would undoubtedly have come up with a good answer.

"You realise, surely, that I can't haggle over Lukas? It's out of the question."

Long's look is green and cold. Salo senses this is not the final word on the matter, even if he were to back both the agreement and the bank guarantee.

"The boy is the easiest alternative. Admit it, you've often wished he didn't exist. He's sensitive. Needs his sister. Somebody like you wouldn't understand that."

Salo's life passes in front of his eyes. How often has he said that it would be simpler if . . .? How often has he sworn about the kid's whingeing and Pernilla's mollycoddling? Often. He cannot deny it.

But it isn't the whole truth. They have their shared interests, he and the boy. Fishing. The sauna. The railway. Somehow he's got to win some time. Make Long believe in a solution.

"How would that work, then? Pernilla must have recognised you. And she's on her guard."

"She did. And if you hadn't overdone the booze, you would have seen her fear. But anyway, we'll leave it there for tonight. You'll hear how the practicalities are going to work. I'll get back to you. It's good that we understand one another and that you've decided to put what's best for the community before personal interests. Only a true statesman acts that way."

51

When Salo is woken by a knock at his hotel room door, at first he doesn't know where he is. He tries to ease himself into a sitting position on the edge of the bed but slumps back against the pillow. There is an image of beheading before his eyes. His head is still attached, at least, even if hooligans with steel toecaps seem to be kicking his temples.

Another knock. Again he tries to sit up. Gets himself across to the door using the back of an armchair.

"Good morning, Mr Mayor. What happened to you?"

Da Silva. As bright-eyed and bushy-tailed as usual. Shower-fresh and with her hair blow-dried into a little grey puff.

"I'm sick, I think, running a temperature maybe, and . . ." He puts a hand to his head. "What time is it?"

"Ten fifteen," says da Silva and holds out a strip of ibuprofen. "You've missed breakfast. You'd have liked it. They even had oysters and Champagne."

He steels himself and makes it to the bathroom. He barely has his head over the toilet bowl before yesterday comes back up like some salt-sprayed toxic algae. At the smell of it, his memory returns. Of some scenes, anyway.

"You really are poorly," says da Silva. "I hope the worst is over by the time we have to leave for the airport. Long can't make the meeting, which is just as well."

Her words have an undertone. A stiffness. She certainly isn't stupid.

"You seem to have had a hard night of it in more than one respect."

She sits in an armchair and looks unashamedly at his almost naked body, which has collapsed back onto the bed.

"Tell me what happened."

"I'm not sure," he says with his nose in the pillow, feeling very small. "Long picked me up. The taxi took us to a private club."

He simply can't tell her. Tell anyone. It's not beheading he can see before his eyes now, but Lukas. A child with a price label attached.

Again his guts turn themselves inside out over a toilet bowl in rue de Rivoli. The sweat runs down his body. He splashes his face with cold water. Staggers out of the bathroom on shaky legs.

"You're in quite a state," she says. "It's almost as if you've been taking something."

"Like what?"

"Drugs of course."

"For Christ's sake, I'm not a drug addict," he says. "It's only a hangover. It'll pass."

Just after 10 p.m. the taxi turns into the drive. The house is in darkness. Henry Salo goes straight up to his study, pours a glass of whisky but skips the ice. Drains it and pours himself another.

Then she appears. In her nightdress and slippers. She pours herself a drop of brandy and sits in the armchair opposite him.

"Are you really going to drink?" he says, and she gives him a weary look.

"How was Paris?"

He'd decided not to say anything. Not tonight. But there's something about her voice. As ever, it's something about her voice and it's not only her. Women. Specialists in apportioning guilt. Basically, it's her own fault. She should have told him about Long. He says so and downs his second glass.

"You're right," says Pernilla and swaps the brandy glass for sparkling water. "But it isn't as simple as you think."

What is ever simple?

52

July 2011

As Pernilla Blomkvist gets off the plane in Athens and walks across the tarmac to the arrivals hall, the heat hits her face like a blast from a hairdryer. It isn't just the air that's different. The smells, the sounds, the people.

She has an address. It's the first day of a three-month adventure. She hasn't travelled much before. A school trip to Norway. A weekend in Berlin. Greece feels exotic.

In the room next door is Beate, an exchange student from Denmark.

"Let's go out," she says. "My father sent me some money for my birthday. The drinks are on me."

They end up in a karaoke place. At some of the tables sit lonely men with lonely bottles of spirits, drinking their sorrows away.

One by one they go up and sing. Mainly Greek songs in A minor containing different forms of the verb *s'agapo*. And even though Pernilla and Beate are the only women in the bar, nobody cares. The men are fully absorbed in themselves. All except one.

He's younger than the others. And he doesn't look particularly sorrowful either. He sings along to the songs. Drums out the beat on the table. They make eye contact.

Pernilla is drawn to his rather striking appearance. Greek and yet not. Apart from the eyes, which turn greener still as the rotating ceiling lights fall on his face.

When Beate goes to the bathroom, he gets up and comes over.

"Where are you from?"

"Sweden," she says.

"Ah," he says, "chocolate and cuckoo clocks!"

She hasn't the heart to correct him. From that day onwards they are inseparable.

"You're kidding me," says Beate. "I only went to the loo."

"We'll still see lots of each other," says Pernilla as she tells Beate only weeks later that she'll be moving out of her room.

They never see each other again.

What does she know about love? Not much more than that she is stricken. He is all she can think about. He is the air she breathes, the thoughts she thinks.

She is in a taxi with her possessions packed in a rucksack and a suitcase. The districts they pass through gradually change from houses with peeling facades and neglected high-rises to expensive properties. When the taxi pulls up to her new home, she is sure the driver must have gone to the wrong address.

She pays. Stands there in the street for a while and surveys the scene. The main entrance is inlaid with mosaic and she even finds her name on the entry phone at the door.

"At last," he says, and the door gives a click.

Overwhelmed by the luxury, his solicitude and this indolent life that makes barely a demand on her, she takes a while to wake up and be aware of other needs. Beate. Freedom. Impressions beyond those four walls. Girl talk.

She has been so wrapped up in him, but this carefree existence now starts to chafe against her ordinary old life.

"I think I'll go and see Beate today," she says to Kostas. He is shaving. She lies in the bath, watching him. Her eyes meet his in the mirror.

"The Danish girl, you mean? She's gone back home."

"Home, how do you know that?"

"Because I paid for her ticket."

The water has gone cold. Her brain has caught up. She is a different person when she steps out of the bath. It is a different look that meets his in the mirror.

"See you at five," he says from the doorway. "Wear something elegant. Dinner with business associates from Beijing."

She sorts through her dresses in the wardrobe. Feeling a spontaneous reluctance to please either him or the Chinese visitors, she rummages in her rucksack for a pair of faded jeans and a T-shirt.

This was me, she thinks. *Who am I now?*

He must have seen her arrive in the taxi. She is about to pay when he throws open the door.

"Go home," he says. "If I'd wanted to be with a slut, I'd have made do with the ones I fuck on the beach."

Still in a state of shock, she takes off her jeans and pours a glass of retsina.

The question is no longer only who she is, but who *he* is.

It's well into the small hours before he comes home. She pretends to be asleep. Hears him moving around the apartment. A glass smashes. Angry footsteps approach the bedroom.

Her pretence has no effect. He grabs her by the hair, yanks her out of bed. Hits her across the mouth. She is sent reeling and slams into the mirror. He pulls her up again, hits her again. This time with a fist. The fist can't get enough. It wants to keep on punching.

The next day there is a doctor sitting beside her bed.

"How are you feeling?" he asks. "You were attacked on the street.

Nothing's broken but you'll be in some pain. Three tablets a day. Drink plenty of water."

"Where's Kostas?" she slurs. Her lips seem to have glued themselves together.

"Your husband sends his best wishes. Look at those wonderful flowers!"

The bouquet has the same scent as Greece when she got off the plane. How long ago was it now? She falls asleep. Wakes. Dozes again.

In her dream she is fishing with her pappa. She is little and life is easy.

Now he is sitting on the bed, stroking her hair.

"Pappa," she says, "I'm so glad you're here." But there's something wrong with his hand. It doesn't smell of pappa. It smells of blood.

He begs her forgiveness. She wants to know why. Why, why, why?

In all his wretchedness he's afraid that she will leave him. Afraid of being deserted.

"Never," she says. "I love you, you know that."

Her face hurts with every word.

Play along. Get back home. Play along and get back home.

He rests his head on her breasts. Tears soak through her nightdress.

"You're everything to me," he says.

She pats him on the head as if he were a puppy. Good boy, good boy.

"I love you," he repeats. Certain phrases can't be said too often and bruises fade. Teeth straighten themselves out.

As long as she sticks to her plan, life is endurable.

She wins praise, is on her way to perfection. A cool, pleasant, considerate woman whose thoughts revolve entirely around how she will get away.

She sees things she didn't see at the beginning and learns what can push him over the edge. Usually.

There are mornings when she wakes up with a doctor at her bedside, but they are fewer.

The day after, it's incense and myrrh.

He needs to hit her to reset the relationship.

In the next breath, he proposes.

And so they go on. Pretending this is for real and for ever.

Pernilla could open the door and take a taxi to the airport any time. She isn't locked in, but she is under surveillance. One day her chance will come, but not yet. She still hasn't accustomed herself to the thought of dying.

Between times they live a normal life. Go to Paros on holiday. Make love in the pool and get engaged. He puts a ring pull from a drink can on her finger.

The next day he breaks her arm.

A couple of days in a private clinic after a cycling accident provides some respite.

Soon, she tells herself, the opportunity will come.

53

Pernilla pauses. Says they can go on talking tomorrow but Salo insists. He wants to hear the whole story tonight.

As is often the way with opportunities, this one presents itself when she is least expecting it.

It is evening. She has just undressed. Kostas receives a call.

"Put some clothes on. Wear your jeans," he says. "We're going out of town."

"Give me a minute," she says. "I just need to go to the bathroom."

She brings her passport, which she has hidden at the bottom of a make-up drawer, and a wad of banknotes. Stuffs them into her underwear and puts on her sweater.

They drive north, arriving in the early hours. They are not alone. There are two passengers in the back seat. To impose order. On her and possibly others.

His phone rings. Night is like a roller blind pulled down over the beach. The stars shine on the sea and it could have been very beautiful.

Kostas takes her aside.

"Now listen," he says. "There are people on their way here by boat. I want you to look after them. Make them feel welcome. Alright?"

"Who are they?"

"Refugees. We're going to help them to a better life."

She sees torchlight and boats putting in at the shore. Bewildered people with bundled-up babes in arms make their way towards them.

She hands out bread, fruit and water. Despite their exhaustion, they smile at her. Something is about to happen. As always she can sense it, but not in her stomach. Her index finger goes numb.

They stop in front of Kostas and his sidekicks. Produce documents and paper money. In front of her eyes, the unimaginable unfolds.

"Ten thousand dollars."

"We have only five."

"OK then, this is what we'll do," says Kostas. "Pick a child. We'll keep it until you can pay. There are plenty of jobs in Athens. You'll soon be together again. That's right, isn't it, Pernilla?" he calls to her.

Making herself forever complicit, she calls back: "Yes of course."

She retreats a few metres into the darkness and throws up. He is lurking right behind her.

"You're as implicated in this as I am," he says. "There are long jail sentences for human trafficking."

Now she can never leave him.

54

"But you did," says Salo. He hasn't even refilled his glass.

"That same night," she says, trying to find the words for what came next. "We were going on by minibus. I sat at the back with four children. The youngest was a newborn. The mother kept tugging at Kostas's clothing, imploring, weeping. He kicked her in the stomach. Hit another woman in the mouth. In the end, nobody dared do anything. They'd risked their lives in the Mediterranean for days and nights. Now they were left there on the beach, and about to lose their children for ever."

Salo moves over to the sofa. Puts an arm around her shoulders. She shakes it off.

"Several hours later we came to a house. There were people moving about in the yard. The children were screaming and I felt travel sick. I put the tiny baby on a girl's lap and moved slightly away from the group. I heard Kostas haggling over money. He wanted more for the youngest one. Nobody noticed when I went on walking. In amongst the trees, further and further from the house. I walked all night. Across fields, through olive groves, along little roads. At dawn I hid in a ditch and waited. Occasionally a car came by. When I saw a tourist coach coming, I went up onto the road and waved my arms. It stopped. It had come from Athens and was going to Thessaloniki. I said my car had broken down and they let me on board. In Thessaloniki I took a bus to the west coast and then a ferry to Corfu. From there I took a charter flight home."

He puts his hand over hers. It is warm against her cold one. He feels for her, forgives her, of course, but his feeling arouses others.

Long and Pernilla. He wants to throw himself on top of her. Pull up her nightdress and thrust into her. Do as Long did. Force her to love him. Now and for ever.

But he isn't Long. The distinction is in his capacity to control himself.

"And Lukas," he says, "is the child his?"

"When I first got home I didn't know I was pregnant. I thought the queasiness was to do with Kostas and the beach."

"So Kostas Long, as he calls himself nowadays, is Lukas's father. Just so I've got the full picture. You always told me his father was dead."

"Dead to me, anyway."

"He looks like him," says Salo.

"No, Lukas only looks like me."

He doesn't pursue the subject of green eyes and black hair.

"According to da Silva, Long is the son of one of China's wealthiest men," he says. "He's got a Masters in Economics and he's now CEO of the entire Long group. I find it hard to imagine him being involved in human trafficking."

"So you think I'm lying?" Pernilla says.

"No, no, not at all. I'm simply trying to take a sober view of the situation. Long has a lot to lose by going for you, and by extension me."

She decides not to comment on the sobriety.

"You don't know him," she says. "He's capable of anything."

The question is what Salo is capable of himself.

"There, there," he says to soothe the obligatory female tears. "Have you ever told anyone about this?"

"When I got home I went to the police. They said they'd look into the matter, but I didn't hear anything more from them."

Not exactly surprising, thinks Salo. Money and influence get you a long way. He feels sorry for Pernilla, but what about himself?

If Long doesn't get what he wants, it will all fall apart. He weighs truth against consequences. Tell her about Paris or stay silent.

"You may have to consider giving him shared custody. Even if he's a despicable bastard, he has certain rights."

"Are you joking?" she says. "Don't you understand the implications of what I've just told you? You've got to do something about it. Turn the tables, tell him he'll have to give up Lukas if he wants to be part of the mining project."

"I'll sort it all out," he says. "There's no need for you to worry. We'll take each day as it comes."

He goes to the kitchen, heats a plate of food in the microwave and wolfs it down, still standing at the counter.

Pernilla has fallen asleep on the sofa. He sits down beside her, lifts her legs onto his lap and switches off the TV.

Strands of hair fall over her cheek. Does he love her? How far do his feelings extend? Admire is a better word. She has everything he lacks but must be able to imitate. Thoughtfulness, assurance, honesty.

Indirectly, she makes him into a better person. Those are some of the qualities that hit home with voters and work colleagues. Not the traits that are growling in his innermost being. Anger ignited as easily as a match on tarred wood.

Salo strokes her stomach. His hand strays down to her thigh. She turns on her back. Fingers find their way inside her knickers. The erection swells inside his trousers, irresistibly driving away all thoughts of council minutes, negotiations, meetings, colleagues, mines and Paris.

But not Long. He is sitting there beside him.

She is wet. Possibly awake. He moves one of her legs into a better position.

Be my guest, says Long, *you first.*

55

How did it go?

Well, this is how it went:

"Where the hell have you been and what the hell were you thinking?"

Elias doesn't mention the car, there's no need. It's back in the garage, won't be going anywhere for years and Svala is on board with that, although she did have the foresight to ask Lisbeth to get the key copied. She squeezes out the requisite "Sorry" and says she'll never do it again. Lets him live with the road trip as the expression of a fourteen-year-old's rebellious yearning and Svala wishes it were true. That she was an immature teenager who drove illegally, got caught and must now mend her ways.

She feels for her uncles. They presumably never asked to look after her but agreed out of some vague sense of family responsibility. Felt guilty perhaps. Not on her account but on Mammamärta's.

She can't do things any differently. The process that was set in motion by Mammamärta's death, and even before that, can't be stopped. Not if she herself is to survive. Pap Peder is gone but there are others waiting on the fringes of his kingdom. She may not need to worry about the new upstarts, but the others, the *invisible ones*. Those who have been licking their wounds and recharging themselves. She knows a few things about them, but not enough.

They are after her. The dead reindeer sent a clear message. Sooner or later her family will abandon her. It is not strong enough to do anything else.

She stuffs a change of clothes, her laptop and some cash into Mammamärta's old Kånken rucksack, which she found in the attic. Elias looks up from the newspaper and down again. She can't see Per-Henrik anywhere. She heads off towards the school bus until she is out of sight of the house. Then turns into the forest and makes for Björkberget.

It is the sort of day that shows itself to best advantage in the forest. It is also six months to the day since Mammamärta's death in Branco's bunker.

In the forest, those who are living and those who no longer live share a common language. The words spread between budding leaves, along the wood ants' paths to the heap, through the moss, across the lichen, in whatever has found renewed strength after months of hibernation.

She sits on a rock at the top of the hill. The place where Mammamärta's ashes were united with other souls, others' last breaths. The eternal cycle that no-one can leave.

She gets out the binoculars. A great grey owl melts into the trunk of a blasted pine. A pair of ravens who have followed her from tree to tree alight in a birch. The fox is on the prowl and the hare is in flight. She moves the binoculars down the hillside, to the house where no-one lives anymore. Marianne Lekatt's red log cabin.

There are names on Svala's list. Of those who should have and those who shouldn't have. Died.

A flutter of the curtains. Or was it? She adjusts the focus. Too far away.

She carries on walking. Approaches the house. Now she is on the front porch.

The Cleaner has seen her through his gun sights. A child clambering down the straightest and steepest path from the hill.

He is ready.

He has allowed for the fact that people might show up. What they will find is an abandoned house. Possibly an abandoned house where a woman was found dead. That kind of thing can attract folk.

Svala has asked but no-one seems to know.

Probably an accident. Who's bothered about an old lady?

Svala tries the door handle. Locked.

Somebody's gone to the trouble of pulling the blinds down. She goes round the house. It's the same everywhere.

She sits on the porch steps, undoes her anorak. The sun warms this south-facing location. Things need to be done in the right order. She has a plan.

Use the spare key if you come in the afternoon. I generally take a nap then.

They didn't know each other very well. That trust gave her a warm feeling, as did the hug she would get at the end of the visit.

She has the key gripped firmly in her hand.

First Marianne was a victim, then Ester. If there's a connection, she is going to find it. Marianne refused to sell her land to the wind farm company. Ester played with fire.

Svala knows an awful lot about fire. Above all she knows how to put it out. That's why she is still alive.

She unlocks the door and steps inside. It smells unfamiliar. Different. Like a mix of sweat, mosquito repellent, and smoke from an open fire. Not flatbread and meat and vegetable broth like before. What's more, the house is warm. The sun is out, it's true, but the nights are still well below freezing. Shoes in the hall. A jacket on a hook.

"Hello," she calls, not too loud, "anybody here?"

She has time to register a movement. Breath that smells of coffee. He hustles her into the kitchen, sits her on a chair.

"What do you want?" he says.

Svala tries to collect her wits. Play the innocent. She *is* innocent.

"Nothing," she says. "I live on the other side of the hill. Felt like coming over here, that's all."

"And breaking in?" says the Cleaner.

She puts the key in his hand.

"No, I knew Marianne. And who are you?"

"So you're a Hirak?" he says.

"And you look like a Salo."

This was exactly what wasn't meant to happen. He has been careful. Come here now and then. Stayed for a while and then left again. The woodman's hut west of Spadnovaure is done for but he's found another. In a worse state of repair and even more remote from roads and people, if that's possible. Being identified by a nosy kid is the last thing he needs.

"OK," he says, "here's what we're going to do. You go back the same way you came and we've never met. I'm nobody. Do you understand what I mean when I say I'm nobody?"

She nods. Gets to her feet but can't help asking.

"What was the cause of Marianne's death?"

"According to the post-mortem, a stroke."

She asks whether he believes that, and he does. Maybe.

"She used to talk about you sometimes," says Svala. "She gave me your trousers."

She pulls up her anorak, pats the leather-patched knees.

A boy runs towards the forest. Trips and falls in the dirt, skinning his knees.

The situation is developing in the wrong direction.

Svala sees a Pap Peder type yet somehow not. There's no belly hanging out, no tattoos or tracksuit bottoms. Above all, he doesn't frighten her. He looks proper. *A professional.*

"Marianne didn't want to sell her forest. Ester didn't ask to die either."

"Who's Ester?"

"A friend," mumbles Svala.

Best to keep her mouth shut.

"You mean the girl who was found at the tip?" he asks, and instantly regrets the question.

Ester, it would be far preferable for her not to have a name. In the worse-case scenario, he could have been the one who . . .

"Maybe you know who murdered her," she says. "You look as though you could know."

And what should his answer be to that? Her assertion demands an answer. His potential answer would demand action.

"I was just going to boil some hot chocolate," says the Cleaner, clattering about among the saucepans.

She sits down at one end of the sofa and tucks up her legs, just like last time. Clasps her hands round her knees and watches his ineffectual search of the cupboards.

"The cocoa's on the left," she says. "And the sugar."

He opens the cupboard and the scents of childhood tickle his nostrils.

"Bless you," she says.

The question is what to do next. Shoot the kid and bury her behind the cowshed, the way his father did with useless dogs?

"You should never boil hot chocolate, even if that's the phrase. Only simmer it," says Svala. "It gets a disgusting skin otherwise."

She gives him the sort of look that makes him wash up the chocolate pan to avoid eye contact. He's seen it before. Must be quite a few years ago now. But still he remembers every detail of Branco's fascination with Märta Hirak and his evident longing to destroy her.

It's her who's the brains behind Peder Sandberg. A drugged-up whore who can't tell front from back. Maybe there is something after all in the saying that behind every successful man there's a dead woman.

So he asks a straight question and hopes the girl won't answer.

"Are you Märta Hirak's daughter?"

"You haven't introduced yourself," she says.

Her cockiness combined with that precocious I-know-better attitude is bewildering and irritating him.

"Henry Salo's brother, but you already knew that."

"But no name?" she persists.

"No name."

"Well, my name's—"

"Stop," he says, doesn't want to know, and now it is time for her to go.

She gets up and thanks him for the cocoa. Raises a hand in farewell and checks herself midway.

"I'm looking for someone and I think you know who they are. Mammamärta's murderer, Marcus Branco. Shall I go or stay?"

He is already weak. A shadow of his former self. He has rolled over for both Malin and Ferm. Nothing he can do to change it and now a child is standing there in front of him.

He more than anyone knows that childhood is a relative concept. She is a survivor.

In terms of the bigger picture, his own route to another life, it is possible that the girl has a value.

56

He drives them through the forest. Strangely enough, she still isn't scared, even though he has taped over her eyes and to be on the safe side perched her in front of him on the quad bike.

They round the hill and head north, Svala can tell that much. First along forestry access roads and tracks, sometimes entirely off road. It takes about an hour. They can't have gone further than twenty kilometres or so.

He switches off the engine and untapes her eyes. They are in a forest. Like any forest, only different. The trees are growing irregularly. Some are young, others dying.

Healthy trunks and sick ones plus the really ancient trees, a full metre in girth. The undergrowth is thick with moss, branches and spring shoots on their way up from winter's sleep.

It is an old-growth forest. She has been here before. In the late autumn before the snow was on the ground. They'd made a fire. Grilled Jokkmokk sausages on twigs. Rode their mountain bikes through the trees. Uncle Elias and Svala. Perhaps as a way of getting to know each other. Not that they said much. Words aren't generally needed.

They walk along an animal path, along the fringes of a bog. From a high point, a roof comes into view between the trees. Or the remains of one, passably patched up with sheet metal. Whoever's place it is and whatever its use, that was all a long time ago.

The sudden glint of a tarn, and they are there.

"So this is where you live," she says, scanning the hut. A couple of narrow bunks, a fireplace. A rickety table and some roughly made wooden benches. Drifts of dead flies, dust, soil and cobwebs. No electricity or water.

"Sit down," he says, pushing her towards a bench. "We have things to talk about. Does anyone know you went to the Holt?"

"I'm at school."

"What do you know about Branco?"

"Only that my aunt and I got into the bunker and found Mammamärta. She died as we were getting her out. Branco and his lot got out by helicopter."

She isn't going to give him everything, not yet. The more people that are involved, the greater the chance of a fuck-up. She works best alone.

"And if I were to tell Branco that you're here, what do you think he would say?" asks the Cleaner.

"I don't know."

Everything about the girl is pale. Skin, hair, eyes. Seen as a child she is innocent and fearless, the way children are because they don't know any better, lack the experience to imagine anything else.

But he knows there is another person hidden beneath the surface. Someone who has been exposed to a great deal. Has seen things. Been forced to defend herself and learned to read people's most private thoughts to stay one step ahead.

He realises he can't look on her as a child if he's going to get anywhere, but must treat her as an equal.

"OK," he says, "I'll start. Your mother was more than Peder Sandberg's girlfriend. She was the brains behind it all; that was how he was able to climb up the hierarchy. He didn't reach the heights, of course, but your mother did, Märta Hirak."

"What do you mean, 'the heights'?" says Svala.

She wants names. Wants to make him give too much away.

"The ones not involved in the extortion and drug dealing. The ones who've already earned so much that they don't need to mix with the dregs. Märta sort of wormed her way into Branco's favour. Partly with you as security."

"She'd never do that," says Svala.

"Would the words 'hard drive with cryptocurrency' jog your memory?"

She chooses not to answer.

"Märta claimed you had a sixth sense for figures and would be able to crack the code."

"That isn't even true," says Svala, getting up to pace around the hut. "We tried everything."

"Maybe so, though Branco thought it was worth a shot. But when it was time for the exchange of the hard drive and Märta's guaranteed route to success, it had vanished into thin air."

She comes back to the table. Sweeps some flies off it with her hand and tries to take in what he has just said, whether it's true or just a ploy to throw her off balance.

"How can you know all that?" she asks eventually.

"Because Märta Hirak fell into my hands before all this happened. On Branco's orders."

"And she told you her life story, you mean? She would never have said anything to someone like you."

The Cleaner leans forward, forcing her to meet his steely gaze.

"The hard drive saved her life. Only to take it later. When she realised you were in danger, she clammed up."

"And now?" she says in the voice of a beaten opponent.

"Now it's up to you if you want to leave."

"If it's the hard drive you want, then—"

"Stop," he says, holding up a hand. "We'll come to the hard drive later, but sure, it's part of the plan. No-one can get to Branco. But you . . . you're my bait."

She has gambled with her life before. Something in him is something in her, as well. The door opening a crack towards good which is then tripped up by evil. Pap Peder types, Branco people, bullies.

"OK," says Svala, "I'm in, but there are conditions."

He could grab the girl by the scruff of the neck and turn her into a voice that is never heard again. Let the birds of prey have a feast and then bury her bones deep under rocks.

"I've got a list. Of names, that is," she says. "Some are dead, others are alive. In their different ways, they're all guilty of Mammamärta's death. Branco was the one who put the last nail in the coffin. But others built it. There are some I haven't been able to get at. I think you'll be able to help me."

He doesn't know what to believe. Who is she, in actual fact?

"And I want to know why you want to get at Branco, your employer."

Now it's the Cleaner's turn to get up and pace the floor. He runs some water from a big container to fill a saucepan and sets it on the camping stove. Tosses in a handful of macaroni and slices a stub of sausage. Uncorks a bottle of whisky and puts out two glasses. Pours a drop into each and sits down again.

"Do you know how it feels to be free?"

She misses Mammamärta and would do anything to have her back. But as soon as she thinks of her, their life, other things come to mind. The months with her uncles are the closest to "free" she has known. But the past still haunts her. Mammamärta wasn't a bad person. She meant well and Svala can't forget. Can't put things behind her and start over again. Presumably it is the same for him. Branco is in the way, just as Pap Peder was.

"What do you suggest?" she says, rather than answering his question.

"Branco's a despot, an out-and-out psychopath who wants to get at your brain. He needs it. Needs both you and your cryptocurrency. Somebody has whispered in his ear."

"Who?" she says, and realises right away that the question is

245

irrelevant. Branco isn't the only one. To the last, Mammamärta insisted the hard drive was buried in the forest, which it no doubt was until it was transferred to a left-luggage locker at the station and the key went into Salo's safe, finally ending up for safekeeping in the backside of a cuddly toy monkey, now hanging on a hook in her room.

Someone could have put pressure on Salo, but it could just as well have been a drunken Mammamärta talking too much at the pizzeria.

The Cleaner does not intend to use a child as bait. In any case she is no ordinary child. She won't give up and has no limits. And is also extremely unusual, unless it is just idle talk, in that she can feel no pain.

He can only imagine Branco's delight.

"Alright," she says. "This is what we'll do. I'll hand over the hard drive and break the code in return for freedom. Mine, yours, everybody's."

And he can't help smiling at that.

Smile away. Do you think I care about your freedom? If the hard drive is the route to Mammamärta's murderer, I'm taking it.

"I get in and you get me out," she says. "Do we have a deal?"

"Yes," he says, though the odds are poor. "The risk is that you end up like Märta."

You little devil, what are you doing? Marcus Branco isn't to be trifled with.

Oh, it's you. Better late than never. I hear you've already met my friend here.

You can trust him. The Cleaner is a man with morals.

The Cleaner?

Joar Bark. The one you're about to say 'skål' to. Haven't I told you to stay away from alcohol! But never mind. Hard decisions are best sealed with the hard stuff.

Svala raises her glass. The Cleaner does the same.

With their eyes riveted on one another, they raise a toast for an inequitable plan.

She has nothing to lose. Nor does he.

57

"Nice to meet you all at the same time," says Mikael Blomkvist, surveying the *Gaskassen* editorial staff who have gathered in the changeover from day to evening shift to hear what their new editor-in-chief has to say.

He has scrutinised them one by one. Read, judged, analysed. He wouldn't say he has identified a style virtuoso amongst them, but there could be various explanations for that. Lack of time, boredom, inadequate leadership.

And soon there will be fewer of them. Over the next weeks it falls to him to present severance terms to the two who will have to leave: Roland Eriksson and Susanne Lahti. Two experienced journalists will go and be replaced by zero-hours staff when needed. How the owners have managed to sidestep rules like last in first out is incomprehensible, but the explanation is entirely predictable.

"We'll be phasing out the arts pages but extending the sports section. Gasskas is on the up in the SHL league and we're tapping into that."

For now he is keeping his own opinions to himself. He's going to find a way around the skinflints and build up some world-beating local journalism.

"There's no time like the present to put you in the picture about how we'll be working from now on."

He gives a presentation of himself. Sets out a structure and ideas for the future development of the paper. Nine reporters, three of them on

sport, plus editors, the photographer and the youngster on work experience yawn and fiddle with their phones, but when he gets to the
topics of the day they wake up: Ester Södergran's death and the explosion that damaged the bridge. Relentless reports of violence against
women, imminent cuts to schools' budgets and social care versus plans
to re-establish "the Pit".

"Excuse me, but is there any point digging deep into events that are
strictly speaking police business? I mean, we haven't got unlimited
resources and there's always talk of more cutbacks."

What was his name again? Ingemar, Roland . . .

Several others back him up. There's no time for this investigative
stuff. Anything that does get done in that department is thanks to individual journalists who sacrifice all their spare time and end up with a
breakdown.

"It's all a matter of planning and freeing up resources in the editorial
office," says Blomkvist. "We may need three on sport sometimes, but
not continuously."

Colleagues exchange glances. He can hear what they are thinking.

A bloody Stockholmer determined to stir things up and convinced
he knows best.

"We've won prizes for our sports coverage. Or maybe you're one of
those people who think sport isn't worth reading about? In that case
you should take a closer look at our reader surveys."

This isn't how he'd visualised his first day. He's coming across more
as an unfeeling asshole than a new spiritual leader.

"We should start a podcast," says Susanne. "All the major newspapers
have podcasts these days. Why not a sports podcast?"

The word "podcast" three times in basically one sentence is too much
for Mikael Blomkvist. He is aware of pressure in his bladder and fishes
the tube of painkillers out of his pocket. Excuses himself, lets a couple
of the tablets fizz and dissolve in his water glass and checks his phone.

Dinner at Pernilla's (and that infernal Henry Salo's). A delayed removal van and an empty rented apartment. Test results from the healthcare helpline number and two missed calls from the hospital in Stockholm. Exhaustion spreads its ragged blanket over him. Attacks of it that arrive without warning. He could fall asleep right there on the Bakelite toilet seat. In the gents' toilet at *Gaskassen*, looking in the mirror with its cracked plastic frame, he is depressed by the sight of himself. To think he used to like his face.

You are old, spent, runs the voice in his head. A has-been who may well soon be dead.

"Good idea, Susanne," he says on his way back into the editorial office, rolling up his shirtsleeves. "I'm giving you the responsibility for finding out everything you can about . . . uh . . . how to run podcasts."

The first concrete decision he's taken here that has actually made someone happy.

Blomkvist surveys the assembled employees for a moment before he goes on.

"I'm sorry if I sound like Mr Stuck-Up from the Big City."

Good, carry on like that.

"I'm used to working in a small editorial team with meagre resources and I'm not a dragon. *Millennium* has gone to the grave and *Gaskassen*'s shedding readers. It's up to us to keep it going. If it's going to work, I need you, and believe it or not you need me."

He's back on track. The headache recedes, along with the fatigue. The rest of the meeting goes better than expected. A beer to round it off wouldn't go amiss.

The taxi drops him outside the Salo residence at Gaupaudden. The sun is still up even though it's after eight in the evening.

He is suddenly in urgent need of a pee. To tell or not to tell?

58

While Mikael Blomkvist is warming up the editor-in-chief's seat at *Gaskassen*, Lisbeth Salander warms herself under the duvet in the bridal suite at the City Hotel in the town that gave the newspaper its name.

Nothing has changed since her last visit. The ostensible luxury still has its imperfections. Furniture with scraped and dented corners. Indelible stains. Most of it passes her by. This is the space she needs to be able to breathe. The sitting room with its sofas. The bedroom with its outsize bed. The corridor with a single door. Hers.

It is an evening for thoughts. Most of them are of Jessica Harnesk. Not out of desire, but for practical reasons. Or possibly both.

The bag on the table contains a puke-stained sweater and a crushed fizzy drink can. A DNA test would confirm that Plague had been in the vehicle and perhaps more besides.

The question is what she wants the information for. DNA traces won't lead her to Plague, but who knows, other things could come up to get the Branco gang up against the wall.

In this Norrland mishmash, Lisbeth is aware that Milton Security would be able to get the test done, but still she hesitates. She needs Harnesk. Wants to get near her, but until now she hasn't known how to approach it. A DNA test is a good excuse. Better than expecting her to respond to romantic invitations. After all, it was Harnesk who ended it. Turned her back on Lisbeth.

The evening – the occurrence – with Blomkvist is also still hanging doggedly around. Harnesk, Blomkvist. They blend together like some kind of compote of sour fruits. She is the milk curdling on top.

She has never been one for saying big words like "love". In her solitude she can permit herself the question: if either of them, then which?

Press-ups, sit-ups, eight *katas* and a shower later, the question is still in the air.

"You're through to Jessica Harnesk. I can't take your call at the moment but leave a message and I'll call straight back."

The hell she will. Right, that's enough.

When Mikael Blomkvist's name pops up on her display it isn't an omen. It's a direct confrontation.

"I can't stop thinking about what happened," he says.

"You mean the finger and the eye?" she says, winning time. A few seconds at least.

"No. What happened between us. I mean, we can't just pretend it was nothing."

"It's fine by me."

"But not by me. I can't stop thinking about you."

"And Birna, have you seen her yet?" she says, and when his answer doesn't come . . . "Exactly. You focus on your Icelandic friend, I've got other things to do."

But what they are is unclear to her. And even though she has put up defences, some things get through the cracks. *The eyes, the hair, the skin . . . the scent.*

"How about you, then?" he counters. "Jessica Harnesk can't be far away."

The battle evens itself out. One all.

"What happened between you and me was a mistake," says Lisbeth. "You were weak, so was I. Stick at it with the Icelander and it's bound to work out."

"You're talking crap," he says.

Now it's easy to hang up.

Almost right away there's a text from Jessica Harnesk.

`Working until 10 tonight, see you after that? J.`

As 10 p.m. approaches, there's another message.

`Running late. I'll be there as soon as I can.`

Come straight up to my room and let's take it from there, Lisbeth doesn't write.

The sensation of life repeating itself is bizarre. If everything were simple she would have capitulated long since. Appealed to Jessica's soft heart or at least got in touch.

Lisbeth takes the lift down to the bar. The same bartender. Probably the same bunch of roaring idiots as last time, there to celebrate making it to midweek. She moves away from the bar, sits on a sofa with a view of the room and all at once she's there. Tall, dramatic and looking very earnest. She doesn't order a drink but sits down opposite Lisbeth, checks all round her and leans forward.

"Svala's uncle just called. She's been missing since yesterday. She went for the school bus as usual, but according to the driver she didn't get on, and then she wasn't in school. Apparently she has a habit of disappearing, which is why Per-Henrik Hirak only called us now."

Lisbeth double-checks her phone.

One unanswered call from Per-Henrik but nothing from Svala.

Bloody kid and bloody Plague. All these people going missing, when will it end? If only they knew how tired she is of looking for them.

"And what are your lot doing to find her?" she says. "Having a drink while you wait for her to turn up?"

As always, anger is an effective barrier to fear. Anger keeps feelings at bay.

"I have to get back to work. I thought you'd want to know, that's all," says Jessica, getting up.

"Wait a minute. Do the police have any idea where she might be?"

"Not exactly," she says, sitting down again. "But you might have heard of Ester Södergran?" Lisbeth nods. "They were friends, it seems. There's probably nothing to worry about. As I say, Svala comes and goes as the fancy takes her. She can't really go on like that if she's going to stay at Björkavan. Social services are involved too, just so you know."

Jessica cannot say how the investigation into Ester Södergran's death is going. Or whether it's linked to other events – the bridge explosion, for example – that might point in the direction of the mine activists.

Anything is possible. At this point they haven't got any further than hypotheses. They've established the cause of death, but that's all, and she isn't at liberty to share it with Lisbeth Salander.

Lisbeth grabs Jessica's jacket sleeve, harder than she means to. The policewoman gives a small sigh and shakes her head.

"Pack it in, Lisbeth. Young people go missing sometimes but they generally come back. Faste wants us to wait at least twenty-four hours before appealing for information. I thought you might have some idea where she could be."

She hasn't. She dropped the girl and the car off at the Hiraks' place and took a taxi to the hotel.

"Didn't you go in to see them?"

"Nope. But if she didn't get on the school bus, where did she go?"

Jessica hesitates before answering. She reaches into her handbag and pulls out a transparent evidence bag containing something phone-shaped.

If you buy me a battery pack. I forgot mine.

Harnesk holds up the plastic bag.

"Is this Svala's?"

"Where did you find it?"

"Below Marianne Lekatt's house," she says. "She was the Hiraks'

253

closest neighbour, died last autumn from what's assumed to have been a stroke."

"Assumed?"

"She had a gash on her head, probably from a fall. There was no way to establish whether the stroke came first. In theory, she could have been—"

"Murdered," Lisbeth fills in. "Who owns the house now?"

"Lekatt had two sons. One of them, Henry Salo, went for adoption and lived elsewhere. We haven't tracked down the other one, he might have left the country. His name is Joar Bark."

"And you didn't find anything in the house itself, I assume?" says Lisbeth.

Jessica hesitates.

"We were up there a few hours ago in response to an emergency call. It was in flames, the fire had really taken hold. The fire brigade had no chance of getting in."

That can't be right. She would have sensed it if the girl were in danger – or would she?

Her thoughts shoot outwards, radiating like strings from a mid-point. Svala's disappearance, Plague, the ransomware attack on the municipal council (and Henry Salo). Ester Södergran, Marianne Lekatt and her missing son, what else?

"Per-Henrik Hirak also reported some reindeer killings. All this could be linked, but it isn't necessarily. There are plenty of Sami haters."

Lisbeth attaches another string to the origin point. Catches Jessica's eye. There's doubtless nothing wrong with her as a police officer but the police in general are not to be trusted.

That is Lisbeth's firm conviction, rooted in empirical experience. When she asks again what the police are planning to do about all this, the answer is already a given.

"Standard police work. We'll find Svala."

So it's basically a total screw-up and Lisbeth needs a strategy of her own. Unfortunately she also needs the help of the police.

"What would you say to a DNA test?" she asks. "I mean the phone, for example. Will you check for fingerprints and that kind of thing?"

"No. You said it was Svala's phone."

Lisbeth is trying to think as far ahead as possible and concludes that she can afford to tell her about Plague.

Everything is theoretical. There is no need for the police to be aware of the lynx woman's probable connection to Branco. Not right now, anyway. He's slippery. The least hint of discovery and Plague will be out of reach. Maybe Svala too.

Branco should have contented himself with Mammamärta, but what does Lisbeth know about his intentions? Nothing. And equally little about Svala's plans. She could be going after him. If she's happened on some clue and it's rebounded on her. She's a smart kid, but wilful.

The memory of a sleeping child with a tangle of fair hair on the pillow sends signals of anxiety to Lisbeth's brain. Again she considers initiating Jessica Harnesk into the events of the past month. If it weren't for the pitch of the woman's voice in reacting to her answers.

"So you've got a sweater and a drink can. Great, Lisbeth, but DNA tests are expensive, we can only do them when there are reasonable grounds. I realise you have your reasons. If you know a crime's been committed, I want to hear about it right now. I am a police officer after all, and it's your duty to tell me."

"Forget it," says Lisbeth, snatching up the plastic bag and heading for the lifts.

Behind her, a woman weighs up whether she should pursue or give up.

"You could at least have been in touch," she calls after her.

And yes, perhaps she could have.

59

It is late but the evening clearly isn't over yet. When Mikael Blomkvist calls, Lisbeth has retired back under the covers without getting undressed. Not to sleep, only to recover from her encounter with Jessica Harnesk.

Down the line, Mikael clears his throat.

"I'm still here. Salo was out, I'm glad to say. It was great to see them again, especially Lukas; he wasn't even shy, just pleased. He must have been missing his grandfather."

"And Pernilla?"

"A bit distracted. Tired. If she was glad to see me again it wasn't obvious."

Mikael's attempts to talk to his daughter were far from fruitful. There was something about her, he could sense it. She avoided the subject of her husband, but also more basic topics like the boy's approaching summer holidays and her own obvious fatigue.

"We can talk once Lukas is asleep," she said.

But they didn't, because she fell asleep at the same time as her son.

It isn't only Pernilla he's struggling to talk to. Lisbeth seems just as evasive. He tries picking up the threads from their previous call but gets nowhere.

"Did anything special happen?" says Lisbeth. "You got yourself into a fucking mess as usual and I patched you up a bit. That's all I'm aware of. By the way, Svala's been missing since yesterday and, well, I know it's the kind of thing youngsters do, but Svala isn't just any kid."

"Missing? That's odd. She contacted me earlier today. Wanted to meet up, about some pieces she'd written and had on a USB stick. You might not know, but she did some work experience at *Gaskassen* recently. In fact, the weekend supplement published rather a charming piece she'd written about food and space travel."

Lisbeth sits up.

"What the fuck . . . did you see her?"

"She didn't turn up and I couldn't stay and wait."

"And you're telling me this now? Marianne Lekatt's house burned down yesterday. Did you miss that too, while you were tied up with your snuggly family evening?"

A couple of hours with his phone switched off and the world is on fire.

"The police found Svala's phone on the ground near Lekatt's house. Does the celebrated journalist have any theories about that?" she goes on.

Maybe he has. If he could only think in peace.

He hears someone come in at the front door. Footsteps on the stairs. The door of the study closing. Like a thief, Mikael sneaks out of the house, makes his way to the main road and rings for a taxi.

Ten minutes before closing time he arrives at the City Hotel and summons the lift. She'll be in the same room as last time, he presumes. On some levels, Salander is entirely predictable.

He is prepared, has thought out what he wants to say and how, but still it comes out wrong. She is prickly. Worried, is his guess. Svala has left her mark in corners he has never had access to, he notes with slight sadness, pulling his notebook out of his pocket.

"It was something Douglas Ferm said about someone known as the Cleaner. When we met up in Stockholm. He mentioned him in passing and immediately regretted it, but I made a note."

He flicks back and forth through his notes as Lisbeth paces up and down looking annoyed.

"Worked for Branco. Ferm met him in Copenhagen. They have some kind of agreement. He didn't specify what, but he said the Cleaner has a brother in Gasskas. Hypothetically it could be Salo. If that's correct, the Cleaner is Joar Bark."

"Marianne's younger son, who according to Jessica Harnesk has left Sweden," Lisbeth says.

"Have you met up with her?" says Mikael in a voice that could be jealous but is most likely merely his standard journalist's tone.

"We had a passionate clinch just before you arrived," she says automatically, but her mind is on Svala. The phone, the fire, the Cleaner, and she messages the police officer.

Try again tomorrow?

"Someone called a 'Cleaner' is a systematic killer," says Mikael. "Shall we assume it was him living in that hut where they found all the bones in the autumn?"

Early the next morning Mikael Blomkvist and Lisbeth Salander drive north-east in a hired car. The roads grow narrower and change from tarmac to dirt tracks. Harnesk sent the coordinates by text the night before.

They take a forestry road that ends at a turning place, then walk along an animal track until the young forest turns to something older and more densely tangled with other growth.

"They found the remains of four people," says Mikael. "One of them was never identified, probably a foreigner."

It is a beautiful place. Lisbeth can understand why the Cleaner chose it.

"Look, an eagle," she says, shading her eyes from the sun and following the bird's circling flight as it seeks potential prey.

"When they searched the area, they found a feeding tray. The person living here, the Cleaner or whoever it was, fed the birds human flesh. Sea eagles can't overwinter inland without supplementary feeding."

"You seem to know a shitload on the subject," she says.

"Part of the job."

They wander around but there's nothing to indicate a human presence.

"If the Cleaner's got Svala . . ." she says, and leaves the sentence hanging. The eagle dives. Clouds move across the sky. The wind seizes hold of the treetops. Soon afterwards, it starts to rain.

They make their way back to the car. On an impulse, she logs on to the Hacker Republic platform. He's asked her not to use it, but what are her options? She tosses out a question.

Anyone know an Ante? Based in Luleå.

There's an Anteremit, but no Ante.

Plague, can you contact me?

She waits a few minutes. No answer. But when she is about to log off, the answer symbol pops up.

Hi, can we meet?

Where are you?

I took a holiday.

In Norrland?

That's right. Can we meet? he asks again.

Considering that they have only met IRL three times in the twenty-five years they've known each other, the question is strange.

Why? she asks.

Got info.

Meeting place?

I'll get back to you.

Then he is gone.

"If Branco's got Plague and Plague wants to meet up with you, it's you they want," says Mikael, and she gets that of course. "So you have to say no thanks," he goes on.

"Exactly," she says, barely listening.

"Svala's our number one priority," says Mikael. "Drive us to the police station, it's time for them to do some work for all that taxpayer money. Or actually, drive us to where Svala lives first. We ought to talk to her uncles."

60

Per-Henrik is plainly pleased to see Mikael again, but he answers questions about Svala evasively. How it's working out with her living here, whether she's behaving herself at school, and so on.

"Tell it like it is: you've both had enough of her," says Lisbeth.

"If I'm being honest, things aren't working out at all well. There's nothing wrong with the girl, but she attracts trouble, just like her mother."

"Harnesk said something about reindeer being shot and hate crimes. What's going on there?"

"There are people who hate the Sami right enough, but we've never had anything like this before. For most people, reindeer herding is a natural part of the community. Wild animals are more of a problem for us than racists. This is something else."

"Linked to Svala?" says Lisbeth.

"We think it could be," says Per-Henrik as he assembles cups and saucers and pours coffee from the pot on the stove. "And we can't be doing with it. It's hard enough to afford the animal feed. My brother called social services. They're coming on Monday."

"Right now there's no Svala to find a new placement for," says Lisbeth. "So for you it looks as if the situation's going to resolve itself."

Per-Henrik looks at her, meets her reproachful eyes.

"You think we had anything to do with her disappearance? That we'd deliberately harm our family?"

"You have to admit it doesn't seem entirely far-fetched, but no, I don't really think that. Svala says she's happy here."

"Then let's concentrate on finding her," says her uncle. "Social services aren't coming here for our sakes but for hers. If anyone's trying to harm her or what belongs to her, it's best she doesn't stay here."

Lisbeth concedes that there's something in that, but says she's far better suited to protecting the girl than social services. Images of severed fingers and cats' eyes flash through her mind. She has to find a way of understanding all this in its totality. Where the kid fits into the picture, herself, Plague, Mikael, the Cleaner and all the other names that crop up on the fringes.

"Is it OK if I take a look in her room?" she asks, getting to her feet.

"Upstairs, the one with the dormer window."

The bed is made with army-barracks precision. In the wardrobe, the clothes are standing to attention. The sun is shining on some newly awakened geraniums. An uncle crosses the yard.

Lisbeth sits on the bed. Runs her eyes around the room and stops at the threadbare monkey moping on a hook.

In addition to a considerable sum of money, a hard drive, a passport, assorted trinkets, presumably from Mammamärta, a notebook and a diary, there are various bits of paper. Folded into tiny squares.

She picks one at random. All the folds make for slow reading. It is a letter dated 7 May 2022. It reeks of painful romantic absorption in a certain individual.

S.

Deep in the bowels of the monkey, the unmistakeable shape of a gun.

The stairs creak. She just has time to scrabble up the items, hang the monkey back on its hook and sit on the bed again before Elias puts his head around the door.

"Ah, there you are," says Elias. "Have you found anything interesting?"

His eyes scan the room, taking in the fact that the plant needs watering.

"She's a tidy girl, Svala. A real rock in most respects. Mikael said to tell you he's waiting in the car."

61

The lift lumbers up to the fourth floor. As the doors open, they come face to face with Hans Faste.

"Well I never, look what the cat dragged in. I thought you two had had enough of Norrland. If it's Harnesk you're looking for, she's on the third floor these days. Things were getting too cramped up here."

"I can understand that," says Lisbeth. "And it doesn't smell very good either," she adds, just before the lift doors close again.

"We think the Cleaner's taken Svala," says Lisbeth, one floor down.

Jessica Harnesk looks baffled.

The *Cleaner*?

"Alias Joar Bark."

"Left the country in 2001." Jessica's fingers rattle over the keyboard. "There are clear indications that he died in combat. Mali 2017," she says over the top of her computer screen. "So he's dipped his last mop, that's for sure."

"Resurrected, and sitting on his brother Henry's right hand to pass judgement on the living and the dead."

Jessica shakes her head.

"No shortage of imagination, anyway."

"I'm serious. If the Cleaner's the same man who was doing his dirty work in the hut outside Spadnovaure, where all those human bones were dug up last year, maybe he's found a new place to live.

Because it was never clarified who killed them, was it?" Lisbeth goes on.

"Not directly," Jessica admits. "No DNA was found apart from that of the dead. All except one were already known to the police, so the working assumption was that this was the underworld cleaning up its own shit."

"Fucking cynical way of looking at people," says Lisbeth, "but whatever. You've got to agree it sounds plausible. Lekatt's house burns down. The owner is Joar Bark, alias the Cleaner. Svala's phone is found right outside. Then she vanishes without trace. You lot need to get moving and find her," insists Lisbeth.

"Of course," says Jessica, "but how come you two had access to information about an individual called the Cleaner, who may be Salo's brother Joar Bark?"

"I was researching something," Mikael says swiftly. "Looking into a couple of companies in the mining sector. Nothing particularly noteworthy. Purely journalistic stuff."

Using the National Land Survey they search for buildings on maps dating from 1875. The sea-eagle cabin is marked, along with a lot of hangovers from the heyday of lumberjack huts and new settlers' land.

"Wait a minute," says Jessica. She leaves the room and comes back with an older colleague.

"Nils-Erik knows the forests better than anyone."

After a good half-hour and without saying a single word, Nils-Erik prints out the maps, puts crosses over some of the buildings and rings around others. Then he leaves.

"Chatty type," says Mikael.

Nice and quiet, thinks Lisbeth.

"One of our best," says Jessica. "About to retire, unfortunately."

They pore over the maps and despite Nils-Erik having crossed out anything that has collapsed or been pulled down, they are still left with a profusion of rings.

Jessica checks her e-mail. "OK, so we've unlocked the phone. It's been almost completely wiped. But we have established one thing – it isn't Svala's."

"Whose is it, then?" says Lisbeth. "I'm sure she had it with her in the car on the way up."

"A Simon Frisk."

S as in Simon.

"Who's he?" asks Lisbeth.

"Seems to hang out with the mine activists. He's twenty-nine. Registered as a student at the Luleå University. Two convictions, 2017 and 2019. Assault and battery, and document forgery. Suspected of manslaughter in 2020. Case dropped on the grounds of lack of evidence."

62

"Hi, I'm Irene Nesser and I've just moved up to Gasskas to start the developing countries programme at the folk high school. Next term," Lisbeth adds. She is glad to have packed the blond wig.

She shakes hands with people sitting on sofas and chairs. Commits names to memory. They could come in handy.

Simon Frisk's handshake is as limp as the sole of a sweaty foot after a run. She squeezes extra hard to get his attention. His eyes glitter. He's well trained in this.

What does the kid see in him?

After two minutes of introduction from Petra, he takes over. Clears his throat and surveys the gathering.

"Anna-Maja and Svala aren't here. Has anyone heard from them?"

Anna-Maja Hirak? Shit, that's Irene Nesser's cover blown.

"You said we ought to keep Svala out of it because of her age," says Petra. "She called yesterday but I didn't answer. I didn't know what I could say."

"Who's Svala?" says Lisbeth. "Unusual name."

"Probably the cleverest of the lot of us, but she's only thirteen. It could reflect badly on the group if we have children as hangers-on," Simon explains, and moves on to the action planned for the weekend.

Lisbeth realises there's something big coming up. More than tree hugging and slogans.

"Is it alright if I join you?" she says. "I really loathe the mining companies."

They exchange looks. Surely there can never be too many of them?

"Of course. I can brief you afterwards," says Simon quickly.

When the meeting is over, they walk together towards the car park. He commends her hair. She commends his self-assurance. Several times, his hand happens to graze hers. She has to control herself in order not to pull it away.

"See you on Saturday then," he says. "Unless you fancy a drink tonight at the City?"

"I'm meeting a friend, I'm afraid, but let's speak tomorrow. Give me your number and I'll be in touch."

"Only fair for me to get yours too, then."

"I'll call you," says Lisbeth.

He walks away and she follows him as he moves towards his car.

The simplest thing would be to get Milton Security to check both vehicle owner and phone number, but she gets the engaged tone from the switchboard and Jessica Harnesk answers straight away.

"Could you check a mobile number for me, and a vehicle registration? Preferably today," says Lisbeth, sounding brusque.

Nice leaves room for manoeuvre. Brusque has gravitas. Usually.

"You'll have to ask me nicely," says Jessica. "Much more nicely."

"Please."

"The mobile is pay-as-you-go. The car, however, is registered in the name of Mimer Mining. If you felt like it, we could . . ."

Lisbeth drives out of the car park. Her eyes scan her surroundings: an area of low apartment buildings with plaster facades, a few blocks from the town centre. She is on the lookout for a silver Volvo and suddenly almost every car is silver, including the one a short distance behind her on the road.

Instead of turning right at Köpmangatan she takes a left. The car sticks with her through roundabouts and along one-way streets. If she speeds up, it speeds up. If she brakes, it slows down and stays sufficiently far back to keep her from making out the driver.

She brings up Milton's number again. Puts in her earpieces, curses the switchboard's litany of opening times and sees that the fuel gauge is down to reserve. With one eye on the road and another on her phone she finally gets through to Dragan Armansky. She interrupts his friendly greetings and asks him to put her through to one of the company geniuses.

She stops at a red light. The infernal sun in the goddamn sky sends its blinding evening rays over the contours of the Volvo. It could be anybody at the wheel. And now she's on the main road out of town.

"Mimer Mining. The make of car and the registration number. Find out everything you can. Address, car dealer, whatever the fuck you can."

"I'm sorry," replies a genius. "There's only a box number. The company's registered in Great Britain. And so on."

For a second or two Lisbeth's eyes are on her phone, selecting Blomkvist's number. When she looks up, her pursuer has gone.

Her pulse calms down. With any luck she's simply paranoid. She turns her car in a driveway and heads back to town. Just before the town centre turn-off she catches sight of the other car again.

It is facing onto the road as if in wait for her.

63

The Cleaner packs his rucksack with the appropriate gear, undoes his wristwatch and asks the girl to keep a close eye on the time. After three hours she is to follow the map he has put on the table. Neither earlier nor later.

"Have you got that?"

She's got it.

He has heard helicopter blades whirring above the trees. Left a fire as a glowing signal. They ought to spot the smoke. And find a girl who is counting minutes. In other words, he has changed his mind. Has decided to exclude the girl from the plan.

The girl can be just a girl when she wants to. Sit meekly on a home-carved wooden bench and wait.

She waits fifteen minutes, then starts walking. The map gives her the direction. First she follows a narrow animal path. When that peters out at a bog, she has to turn back on herself, climb a hilly outcrop, slither her way down over a succession of flat rocks and go on through the irregular geography of the ancient forest, negotiating trees uprooted by the wind and unexpected dips in the ground.

Branches whip her in the face. The scent of the forest is deep and agreeable. A nesting capercaillie flies up in alarm. There's the sound of a car in the distance. She sticks out a thumb. And yes, it's unwise to hitch-hike, but she missed the bus.

The driver lets her out at the turning down to Björkavan. In her room there is a monkey dangling from a hook, waiting for her. Arse-heavy with an assortment of hidden treasures. The time has come for her to need them all.

According to her calendar, one brother is in Kiruna and the other in the reindeer forest. An unfamiliar car is parked in the yard. She keeps out of sight behind the slaughter shed on her approach to the house. A quick glance at the dog pen and on down to the garage.

The area around the house is quiet, strangely quiet. The dogs are generally jumping up and barking.

She resists the urge to go over there. Pulls up a plastic chair with a cracked seat, climbs onto it and looks in through the kitchen window.

Per-Henrik is sitting on the sofa. The kitchen chair is overflowing with his visitor's thighs. She has met him before. Social services' caseworker Eric Niskala. Protector of all the children in Gasskas who are going through the wringer. He has kind eyes but at the same time he always comes with an unpleasant agenda.

Like now, clearly. The signs have all been there for her to see. Not just the obvious ones, like dead reindeer. The looks her uncles exchange, their attempts to make her listen to reason. Even to force her to keep to times and routines.

They can't cope with looking after her. They live in the belief that Svala is a headstrong teen with needs they can't meet, and who can blame them? She skips school. Goes missing. Keeps her mouth shut.

The kitchen smell is tainted with uncertainty. She nods to them, hangs her coat on the back of a chair, asks if there's anything to eat.

"Come and sit down," says Per-Henrik, patting the sofa. What he would really like to do is hoist her in the air and shout with joy because she's come back home. She ignores his words. Makes herself a sandwich, pours a glass of milk. Lets her eyes stray to the dog pen. Still so remarkably quiet.

"Are the dogs with Elias?"

She perches on the sofa next to her uncle.

"Yes," he says, "they are that."

He puts his arm around her. His sweater smells of forest and sweat and mosquito repellent and resin and snuff, safety, care, love. His gaze is like Mammamärta's, she tries to catch his eye, he looks away.

"I'm so sorry, Svala, we want you to stay with us but it isn't safe for you to be here. Or for us."

Niskala takes a gulp of his cooling coffee and clears his throat.

"Your tutor says you're neglecting your schoolwork and you're going to miss your targets for Year 7. You've scarcely attended school these past few weeks. When you were placed with your uncles it was on condition that it would be beneficial to you developmentally. Per-Henrik tells me he can barely get through to you anymore. Is there anything in particular bothering you?"

Is there anything in particular bothering you?

"No, only that my tutor doesn't know who Kierkegaard is, or that black holes are places where time stops existing, for that matter. That my classmates treat me like I've got some contagious disease and that I've frankly had enough of nicknames and idiotic comments I've decided to ignore and that . . . never mind the rest."

The rest, meaning Simon.

She is trying hard to be smart but her feelings are taking over.

"I'd rather go into keeping reindeer than go to school. It has nothing to teach me."

Niskala gives her an indulgent look; he can see a foundation for change. But however accommodating he is, school is a clear boundary line. No education, no chance. Some of the teachers claim the girl is intelligent, but if she makes nothing of it, it can only count on the minus side.

"Your uncles and I have agreed that you living here isn't working. Until we find a more permanent home, you'll be placed in a residential centre not too far from Gasskas. I'll take you there this evening."

He is braced for protests and a lot of fuss. Instead she just nods, says she's going up to pack her things.

Per-Henrik holds her closer to him. Comfort and consolation are badly needed. Eventually she pulls away, puts her hand on his shoulder and says maybe it's just as well. They've done their best but she has made it harder for them.

This will get sorted, I promise. I'll soon be back.

She conveys the message in their own language.

Niskala looks up from his guilty conscience.

"Does the girl speak Sami?" he says.

"She picked it up in a couple of months. They must have mighty good home-language tuition at the school."

64

A room is to be emptied of life. She packs a karate bag. The last thing she stuffs into it is the carrier bag full of brightly coloured Mammamärta clothes. Not that she will wear them. But she might not be coming back.

Per-Henrik calls from the hall.

"Five minutes," she answers. "I'm just packing the last few things."

Pap Peder's Glock is wrapped up in an old T-shirt. She unfolds it, presses the fabric to her nose, counts cartridges, finds room in her bag for a new notepad and other items of survival gear.

The stairs don't creak.

She can hear them talking heatedly in the kitchen, something about dogs.

No-one notices as Svala flies down the yard and stops at the dog pen.

Whoever did it. However they did it and why. A human being's right to life is always up for discussion. Never that of an animal.

She opens the gate. Puts her face to Aiko's chest. The body is still warm. The coat gritty with sand and earth. She wants to lie down beside him. Wants him not to be alone. She moves on to the young male. His tongue is hanging out of his mouth. The sand around the body is stained with his blood. She closes his eyes.

A minute later she is backing the car out of the garage. The tyres leave gashes in the newly thawed ground. She doesn't even stop at the crossing.

Drives straight out, off and away. She doesn't slow down until her pulse has shifted from her throat to her abdomen.

She pulls into a lay-by. Opens the door and throws up.

All these deaths are Svala's fault. The reindeer's, the dogs' and Mammamärta's. She could have opened the hard drive, allowed her thoughts to roam through the downy passageways of her cerebral cortex and find the code, but she didn't want to. Imagined that as long as the money was in the bank vault of her brain, that would be Mammamärta's life insurance. In the end she couldn't. Maybe she got too tired. No-one was watching when Svala the swallow broke her wing. How much it hurt. Hurt in the only way she can feel pain.

There you are again, feeling sorry for yourself. Haven't I told you it doesn't help?

I'm not feeling sorry for myself. It's hard work having to do everything on my own, that's all.

Call Lisbeth Salander, she can help you.

And at that moment, Levi Grundström rings. There's that thing he wants to show her. He's ringing to remind her to come to the Pit. She's late.

"Did you forget?" he asks.

"No, I'm on my way. I couldn't come any earlier."

In the course of the spring the activists' meetings have grown less frequent for no obvious reason. But it's different with Levi. They generally meet at the library. Talk books and writing. She lets him read chapters of her "memoirs", as he calls them. And he tells her about his life. What little is left of it. Last time he didn't show up. Now she can hear from his voice that it's a real struggle for him to keep going.

She turns onto a forestry track a few kilometres south of the mine. Just as Levi told her, there's a barrier, but he's left it open. She parks at the turning area behind his old Saab and continues on foot. It isn't far but it's steep. Levi must have got himself up there by a sheer effort of will.

At the highest point she finds him sitting propped against a pine with a rucksack beside him, breathing oxygen through a tube. She sits down next to him. The waters of Davidsjaure stretch out beneath them. To the north they can make out the slag heaps, looking like black mountains.

"I grew up by the lake. The house has been demolished but the cowshed is still standing. When I was little, it seemed so big, but I think it only had room for three or four cows and maybe a pig. To start with there was no road leading up here, only some fairly decent paths, but my dad didn't have far to go to work, at least."

"In the mine?"

"Yes, just like me. I started there when I was seventeen. After it shut down I had jobs at other mines. Boliden. Adak, Kristineberg, Renström . . ."

He pulls the rucksack towards him. Fishes out a Thermos flask and two wooden cups. Cuts off flakes of dried reindeer meat to eat with the coffee.

"Our drinking water came from a spring, a bit of a walk away. The animals got theirs direct from the lake. When the first cow died, nobody thought of the water. A few years later, Pappa died of leukemia and we moved into Gasskas."

Svala and Levi watch the sun go down over a dead lake. The leaching of minerals over decades – like arsenic, zinc and copper – has wiped out the fish. There are warning signs at intervals to prohibit swimming. Because although the mine area has been largely decontaminated, new discharges reach the lake and stream as the opencast mine expands outwards.

"The mine giveth and the mine taketh away," he says, and tries to stand up. He staggers and falls headlong, face down in the moss.

Svala fights to get him to his feet, but he is too heavy and he can't control his legs.

"Those bastards took my life and now they want to take other people's, but I won't damn well let them."

He hauls himself up against the tree trunk. His breathing is laboured, as viscous as resin in his chest. He looks at her as if seeing her for the first time.

"Who are you?" he says. "Are you a wood sprite, or a little siren of the forest popping into sight among the trees?"

"I'm Svala, you know that," she says. "You fell over. Maybe you bumped your head. Should I call somebody?"

"You know what," he answers with an effort, "I'm in a bad way, that's for sure, but if you really want to help me it's not emergency services you should be calling."

He points to the rucksack, asks her to open it.

In days of old, rock blaster Levi Grundström would have talked about his job. Gone into detail but never mentioned his mates. Since he retired, they've hardly been in touch. They know he's sick. Maybe they're frightened of their own death sentences.

"But not you Svala, you're not scared of death."

With shaking hands he takes out a mobile phone.

"This is where you set the time. The charge itself is in the boot of the car. The key's on the front tyre. Park where this road forks. That's where it'll have the greatest effect."

"So it was you who blew up the bridge? Everybody thought it was Simon," she says, and feels ashamed of herself and the others.

How impressed they all were even though he only dropped hints. Most of all she's ashamed of her own childishness, the diary, the scraps of paper.

"Take a dying old man's advice. That Simon is no catch. Stick to the silent types who only speak when they've something sensible to say."

A prolonged coughing fit robs his voice of breath. Another follows straight afterwards. Then a third and his body slumps to one side. His throat rattles a few times and then stops.

"Hello," cries Svala and she gives him a shake. First carefully, then with more force.

But like Mammamärta, who has taken her last breath, Levi Grundström has now departed this earthly life.

She knows it. She puts a hand on his stubbly cheek. Tries to find something to say.

"Rest in peace, Levi. This bomb will do some good. I promise."

By the time the ambulance takes the body away, the sun has almost set.

People have called. Worried. Demanding. Insistent. But not one of them remembers that today is her fourteenth birthday.

Svala angles the rearview mirror downwards. Pulls her hair back into a knot. Nothing has changed. She still looks just as childlike.

She fires off a few lines to the number the Cleaner gave her.

`I know you changed the plan. Sweet of you, but it won't work. I'm your only chance.`

When the time comes she will walk into the jaws of the lion with a monkey on her back. The way she sees it, she has no choice. First the reindeer, now the dogs. She has got the message.

Yet she still can't help hoping the Cleaner is with her. Which means she won't have to encounter Marcus Branco. She's been hearing about people like him all her life. Those who stay invisible. Those who do as they please. Those who never get caught.

Fear is an unfamiliar feeling that rarely comes to the surface. So when Lisbeth Salander calls again she chooses to answer. Like some little brat, she can't keep the tears from catching in her throat. But she can't help smiling when Lisbeth launches into "Happy birthday to you."

"You're a fucking useless singer."

"Dearie me. The fourteen-year-old has learned to swear. I've got a present for you. Come to the hotel and you'll see."

65

Simon Frisk is seated in an armchair in the hotel suite. Lisbeth hasn't stinted on the duct tape. She called, he came. Like a lovesick suitor he stood in the doorway and turned on the charm. His fringe fell perfectly over his forehead. His eyes glittered and Lisbeth struck first.

There is a gun on the coffee table.

"It's his, in case you were wondering," she says to Svala. "I'm a pacifist. Happy birthday. Surely you didn't think I'd forgotten?"

Lisbeth holds out a parcel. For now it's just Svala and Lisbeth. They have disconnected from Simon Frisk's grunts and groans.

The parcel is soft. She fiddles around and gets off the string and sticky tape. A monkey's arse is the first thing she sees.

"I thought the other one looked a bit shabby. This one's got more compartments. There's something inside, but you can check that out later. What do you think we ought to do with your big present?"

Until now she has avoided looking at him, at Simon. To be honest she doesn't see any point in him being there, still less know what to do with him. He looks so tragic that thoughts of vengeance feel over the top.

Lisbeth rips the tape off his mouth. He gulps air as if he had no nose. Svala doesn't remember it being so big. Everything about him feels big and unattractive now. His big toes are poking through his socks. His ears are sticking out through his hair. His flies are open. His belly is bulging over the top of his trousers like any other Pap Peder's would. How could she have missed seeing that he's one of them?

"Help me Svala," he says in a pitiful voice. "You know me, you know I've always looked after you."

Lisbeth's hand delivers a smart slap. She tells him to shut up. Threatens him with the tape.

"I'm sorry Svala, this is going to hurt, though not so much you as . . ."

Lisbeth can't bring herself to say his name. She unfolds one of Svala's little notes and reads it aloud.

I went to the hotel. When S came he was different. Started groping me all over. I didn't want to, but he said he did and I only had myself to blame. He's right. I blame myself.

"Stop," says Svala, grabbing the note.

"He raped you."

"Like hell I did," yells Simon. "She wanted it!"

Now his nose is bleeding. Blood is running down his chin, dripping off him.

"Do you have any conception of how fucking scared she must have been?" says Lisbeth, picking up the gun. "I bet you don't."

She forces open his mouth and thrusts in the weapon. His throat gives a gurgle. His eyes widen.

Svala gets up. Places her hand over Lisbeth's. Slowly she pulls the gun out of his mouth and sets it on the table.

"It's not worth it," she says. "He's a little scumbag who's going to die young. Others will make sure of that, but not you, Aunt Lisbeth. Simon Frisk works for Branco," she goes on. "They got him in with the mine activists to keep a check on us. To make us do things we wouldn't otherwise so we'd look like fanatics. All to keep the focus on the old mine and speed up the process for the new one."

"How do you know all this?" says Lisbeth, trying to stop the train of thought thundering along at two hundred and ninety kilometres an hour with defective brakes.

"Through Ante. He made contact with a hacker who works for Branco. Though Ante thinks there's something shady about the whole thing. We were meant to meet up yesterday but some other stuff got in the way."

"And where is this Ante?" says Lisbeth.

Plague, Ante, Ante, Plague.

"I don't know. He's stopped answering. But thank you for my present."

Svala is still for a few seconds, contemplating the tearful heap opposite her. He looks away. The Cleaner was right.

Some kinds of justice you can only administer for yourself.

And that is why she has to ask the question that has been nagging at her ever since it happened.

"Have you got others apart from me on your CV?"

"No, no, of course not. I was so carried away by you, that's all," he says.

There's a new energy in his voice. Maybe he detects a way out.

"You're like an adult, I didn't think of you as a child."

"'1649'," she says. "'I don't take them. I get given them. They come voluntarily.'"

Now he doesn't understand. He recognises the words. He said them himself. But definitely not to her.

And 1649 is the passcode on his mobile.

Her crazy aunt is sitting next to her with his own gun in her hand.

But it's the girl who frightens him most. Who she is. What she's capable of.

To start with the stories were fragmentary, more like a myth. Things were stirring in the underworld. When Peder Sandberg was found with a broken neck under a treetop hotel, the map was redrawn. A leader was gone. He was no genius, but his operations had grown organically; he collected loyal people around him. Without him, they tended to writhe around like decapitated snakes.

Märta Hirak would have been his natural successor, but Branco went too far. According to Räv, who incidentally is the only one of Branco's Knights who talks to Simon, he wanted to subdue the woman, make her acknowledge his supremacy, which she never did. Any more than she told him where she had hidden the hard drive with its fantasy money.

Somewhere along the way the girl was tossed up like some magic coin from the Hirak Sami tunic. She found a way into the bunker. Got her dead mother out and the rest is history.

This is where Simon himself comes into the picture. Recruited directly by people whose real names are unknown to him except as characters in a story. He has a specific task: to map Svala Hirak.

But not for the reasons she thinks. Branco doesn't give a flying fuck about mine activists and keen reporters who think they've landed a scoop. The death of the kid's friend, the girl at the tip, is a mishap. It's Svala they want to get at. He doesn't know why. They issue instructions. Never explain.

This leaves Simon in a rather uncomfortable position. It's far from the first time, he admits, but he has no choice. He's the kind the world wants to hang up by the cock and whip until he's dead. And yet he can't stop. Svala was a tasty morsel he couldn't subjugate. Verging on overripe but irresistible.

"That was a joke," he says. "A silly boast."

"Very impressive," says Svala. "One thousand six hundred and forty-nine child rapes would be considered a record-breaking feat in some circles, I'm sure."

If only she knew.

"Sorry," he manages to get out. "I didn't mean any harm."

And what does one answer to that? Svala looks away, trying to choke down her distaste before she asks her next question:

"Were you there at the tip?"

He doesn't answer.

"You were there at the tip and found time to amuse yourself with

Ester before you pushed her in. Admit it," she says, her hand hovering over the gun.

He is small now. As small as she felt with his puffing and panting bulk on top of her, the hand pressing her down into the pillow, the air running out along with the will to defend herself.

"No. Others were there, not me. They say she stumbled and fell over the edge."

Kierkegaard considered that every individual has the potential to become great. He can't have meant for "great" to imply the right to dominate others. Yet Svala suspects that he, the philosopher, did not attach any moral weight to the word "great". A man who rapes children and pushes women off cliff edges, is he "great" because he has power? No, it's unfair to invoke Kierkegaard in the same breath as Simon. A human being is always responsible for their actions. The question is where the world around them comes in. What her duty is right now, if an individual's highest duty is to help their fellow human beings towards a better life.

"Do you believe in life after death?" says Svala. "I do," she goes on without waiting for his answer, "and I'm going to help you be reborn. See it as a service. In the next life, you'll get a chance to do better."

Before Lisbeth has time to react, the gun is in the girl's hand. The barrel against his temple. His body squirms like bait on a hook.

When Svala takes off the safety catch, Simon Frisk faints. The fun is over.

She searches his pockets, takes his phone and stashes it away. Lisbeth comes out into the corridor with her. Puts her arms around the reluctant frame and holds her until she softens.

"We'll take them down, every last one. But you've got a whole life ahead of you. Don't waste it on morons. Go home to your uncles."

"There's a USB stick in your jacket pocket," whispers Svala. "Make sure it gets to Mikael Blomkvist. I've copied over Ester's files and Ante's are on there as well. Try to contact Ante, find out who he is."

In the inside pocket of Svala's jacket Lisbeth has left something too. An appalling little invention for parents to keep watch on their children, jealous husbands their wives and aunts their nieces.

Lisbeth Salander goes back into her room. Cuts off the rest of the duct tape and throws Simon a towel.

"You squeaked through today, but if I hear of you going anywhere near Svala or her family, or for that matter if you rape anyone ever again, you're dead."

Fifteen minutes later he staggers out of the front entrance of the City Hotel with his collar up, wearing a cap and a pair of sunglasses.

Svala ducks as he passes the car.

A few moments later she observes a police car turning into the hotel forecourt.

Lisbeth has barely had time to tidy up after the birthday party.

Some knocks at the door and everything around her evaporates. The uncertainty, the mortification at Jessica Harnesk's attitude, Lisbeth's own doubts.

Jessica smells as if she has just stepped out of the shower.

Lisbeth takes off the other woman's trousers. Entangles herself in those arms and legs. In the witchy hair that binds them together. In the flesh that is almost electric with desire. In the longing she realises she has had in her since she left Gasskas last autumn and went home to Fiskargatan with her tail between her legs.

But when she comes, when her hips are braced against Jessica Harnesk's thighs, it is Mikael Blomkvist she's thinking of. His head of curls with a receding hairline, resting in her lap.

66

The delay has left various parts of the Swedish state administration playing catch-up. The police are looking for a missing child. A helicopter has observed smoke from a cabin. The police officers on board confirm that it is empty. A sea eagle swoops on its prey. It is a beautiful place. The tarn glitters in the afternoon sun.

But no Svala and nothing that could be interpreted as a trace of her. To Birna's ears, "the Cleaner" sounds more like a local legend, but someone has clearly been here. Could just as easily be fishermen. If she had made more effort she would have found a hair tie with some light-blonde hairs caught in it.

Jessica Harnesk has cashed in her overtime and is taking a day off in lieu. She has switched off her phone and is lying on the sofa with a cup of tea. Her thoughts wander between Faste and Lisbeth Salander. Both of them problematic. The latter significantly sexier. She feels the tingle inside her as she thinks about their encounter. About their bodies, words, mouths and . . . Stop. It was only one night. No promises made. No next episode to get hung up about.

Mikael Blomkvist makes two colleagues redundant and shuts himself in his office. Tonight he's babysitting. Pernilla has gone to the summer cottage to do the spring cleaning.

When Blomkvist finally plucked up his courage and rang Söder hospital, the doctor was very upbeat. Wondered why he hadn't called sooner. Would he like some good news? The good news was that the cancer had not spread and that radiation treatment would be a gentler alternative to chemo.

A hesitant smile twitches at the corner of Blomkvist's mouth. Maybe he isn't as close to death as he thought.

Salo has arranged to meet Long and gets through two strong beers before he shows up at City's à la carte restaurant. Long's shirt is neatly ironed. His trousers have sharp creases. The whole man is as clean-cut as a Mormon at summer camp in Salt Lake City. They shake hands. Menus and a bottle of Chardonnay are brought. The girly drink tastes acidic on his tongue. Long speaks first.

"Good to see you again. Did you notice the down payment that's gone into the municipality bank account?"

They talk like the good business associates they are. Sweat trickles from Salo's armpits.

The first course arrives. Long pushes the vendace roe to the side of his plate. The main course. A bottle of red. Long takes a few mouthfuls of the reindeer fillet. He recognises the dessert.

"As delectable as last time," he says. "And talking of last time, I assume you've ensured that Pernilla will voluntarily relinquish custody of the boy? She's had her years with him. She has deliberately kept the child from me. A violation of the law. Swedish law included," he concludes.

"But you know I can't. She would never give up the boy voluntarily. And bearing in mind your past record, I'm not so sure a court would judge you to be an appropriate parent."

"My past record?" says Long, looking disinclined to understand.

Alright then. Salo will have to play this game a bit longer. They have their given roles. The good venture capitalist vs the loyal municipal servant. The yearning father vs the stepfather. There is no perfect outcome, but he owes it to the municipality to close this deal.

"Pernilla's gone to the cottage, but I'll talk to her as soon as she's back. Everything will work out. You have my word on that."

"So you and she have a cottage too? Not bad. Public service clearly pays well in Sweden."

The waiter pours the final drops from the bottle of red wine.

"What were these berries called again? Really delicious."

"Cloudberries," says the waiter. "Picked locally, lightly sweetened and delicately cooked to preserve the aroma and the vitamin C. With them we have a lovely vanilla ice cream made of skimmed milk from mountain herds with a sprinkle of liquorice powder from Kemijärvi."

Salo would like to murder somebody. Why not the waiter?

"For Christ's sake, we can see what we're eating," he snaps. "Bring us the coffee and brandy instead of rabbiting on."

"You seem annoyed," says Long. "The cloudberries are exquisite. Here, do you want to try?"

As if there were something to toast, they raise their brandy glasses to each other. One day the residents of the municipality will thank him personally. Neither God nor Pernilla is ever likely to forgive him.

67

The cottage is cold. Spring comes late in the mountains. There is still snow on the ground but the terrace has been warmed by the sun. Pernilla is sitting on a reindeer skin, her face turned to the light. The silence around her is thunderous. A distant neighbour beats a rug. Solitude is an absolute must if she is to take any decisions. At home, everything is a mess. Henry is drinking more than usual and Lukas doesn't want to go to school.

The girl has called a few times. Lukas's so-called sister. Talking to her makes him happy. Through the voice on loudspeaker, Pernilla can detect the girl's father. Small messages. Innocently formulated in the mouth of a teenager.

"We'll be coming to Sweden again soon," it says. "Hope we can meet up. Your mum is very pretty; Dad thinks so too."

Since she and Henry had it out with each other . . . nothing. He is as closed as the buds on the birch trees. She thought he would open up, talk to her, hold her. But the opposite has happened. He comes home. Heats the sauna. Bolts down his dinner, if he eats anything at all. Goes up to his study and stays there until she is asleep. Always with Lukas, now. The boy turns away from her, wanting to sleep in peace. He's too big to share a bed with his mother and she knows all this.

She puts a hand on her belly. She isn't showing yet but her breasts are swelling and she is on her way into that protective bubble of pregnancy where the world around her is less important.

Kostas Papadopoulos, or Kostas Long as he calls himself, has come into their lives to stay. She understands that much. He will never give up Lukas now he has caught the scent. The question is how he will act and what he intends to do with her. Presumably he would never touch the boy. She herself has no value. On the contrary, she is an obstacle.

The sun disappears behind the clouds. She goes back into the cottage and puts more wood on the fire. She feels her lower abdomen contracting in a cramp. Only natural, says the midwife, nothing to worry about. She couldn't bear to lose another child. Still, she didn't listen to the doctor's advice to wait at least a year before trying again. She wants another child and not just that; something to bind her and Henry together again.

As evening draws in, she calls Mikael. He and Lukas have built some Lego models and they've just had dinner. They're watching a film and soon it will be time for a bedtime story. He wants praise. Is asking her to pat him on the head, but she can't.

"Good to hear you're sticking to your task," she says and hangs up. Perhaps Lukas can benefit from what she herself never had.

The sheets are cold. She heats some water, fills a PET bottle and cuddles it to her like a warm body. The log walls creak and click. The night-time temperature has dropped to below zero. She feels tired and would really like to fall asleep but those sounds, is it the wind or . . . no, something else . . . a snow scooter slowing down as it approaches the cottage.

For a second she thinks "Henry" and her spirits lift, but she knows his scooter is locked away in the shed. This could be their neighbour. He's bound to have noticed there's somebody here. She keeps a firm hold of the water bottle and gets up. Christ, those cramps. She has to sit down again. She waits for the pain to subside and listens for the sound of the snowmobile, which has stopped.

Now there's someone on the porch. She puts on her sheepskin slippers and creeps into the living room without lighting the gas lamp. Feels around for the axe by the stove. Settles for a lump of wood. Shielded by the bedroom door, she waits. A window smashes. Someone curses. Maybe it's only a burglar but her thoughts tug her in other directions and her panic rises. Where the hell did she leave her phone?

She sneaks back into the bedroom. Calls Henry's number. It goes to voicemail and she leaves a message. Calls emergency services and finds herself in a queue. Just as she gets through, she is cut off. Damn. The gale is making the connection even less stable than usual.

Whoever it is, they have given up on the window and are moving to the door.

Another shooting pain. Pernilla puts a hand over her mouth so as not to scream. Keeps out of sight by the bedroom and watches the front door slowly yield to a crowbar, the snowmobile boots, the ski suit, the gloves. Once inside, he stands still. Listens for sounds. Gets his bearings. He has two rooms to choose from. He goes for the one on the right.

She came to the cottage for some decision making. In an instant she decides. The moment the intruder catches sight of her, Pernilla raises the block of wood and brings it down on his head.

A direct hit.

The moonlight illuminates his balaclava. She pulls it off him. Ready to strike again if need be, but his body is still, his face young and without distinguishing features.

When he fell, he dropped something. A kick sends the object skidding under the sofa.

He starts to move, tries to sit up. Another decision.

The blow lands awkwardly. His body thuds back onto the mat. The chunk of wood bounces across the floor.

She grabs her coat, runs in her slippers down to the car.

Nobody locks their car up here. If anything were to happen, rescue would be far away. Looking for keys is the last thing people need. And yet she has locked it. The key is on a hook in the hall. That leaves the visitor's snowmobile.

She isn't dressed for it. Barely knows how to handle one. She tries to recall Henry's cocky instructions.

Push the start button and use the throttle, that's all you need to know.

Nothing happens. Damn. She looks over at the cottage. Is there movement at the door or not? A figure makes its way unsteadily down the track.

Don't forget to push in the kill-switch that's connected to the safety tether. You'll get nowhere otherwise.

The man is close now, the crust of the snow bearing his weight. But all at once the scooter starts. She presses the throttle. The front rears up and slams back down as she releases her thumb hold.

"Hope you freeze to death, you fucking slag," he yells after her as the machine finally does what she wants.

Freezing to death seems the likeliest outcome. Her coat flaps in the wind. Her face rapidly goes numb, her fingers too. Her nightdress has ridden up over her thighs.

She could drive to the neighbour's place. But if he is away and the bastard finds her car key, he'll soon catch up with her.

She drives out onto the trail. Stops before the track that leads across the lake and lets the engine tick over. Zips up her coat with stiff fingers. The treacherous ice of spring extends below. Around the jetties twenty metres away there is open water. On the far side she can make out the holiday cabins lined up along the shore. In the opposite direction, towards the road, a car is approaching parallel to the shore.

Drown or be shot?

Pernilla drives on. As the scooter reaches the edge of the ice she gives it full throttle and ploughs through the churned-up slush.

Behind her, the ice cracks like brittle glass.

68

The evening's babysitting at Gaupaudden is coming to an end. The boy has no trouble falling asleep. He makes it half-heartedly through his reading homework, turns on his side and puts his arm across Mikael's stomach.

There is no distance between them. At least not when Pernilla gives her consent. Between her and Mikael there is more of a distance. At times, a yawning gulf. Right now he is grateful for whatever he can get.

He pulls the quilt over Lukas's shoulders. Creeps out of the room, sits at the kitchen table and opens his laptop.

After a few days at *Gaskassen*, his inbox is once again satisfyingly full. Even the e-mails from management asking how he's getting on with the redundancy notices feel relevant. Anything's better than that sense of being left outside, as he has since *Millennium* discontinued its print publication.

Initially he expected offers to rain down on him from the Stockholm press. But in fact no-one is interested in a reactionary of sixty plus. Except *Gaskassen*, that is. Mikael feels slightly ashamed at the thought of the workshop he gave them the year before. His failure to register that the reluctance they displayed had nothing to do with incompetence, but was rather a reaction to his own inflated view of himself as a benchmark for outstanding journalism.

Six months later, his self-confidence isn't exactly top-notch, but on a clearly rising curve. In the pipeline there are deeper investigations into recent events that have hitherto been treated as individual news stories. The bridge explosion, for example. And Ester Södergran's death, which according to Birna Guðmundurdóttir looked like an accident, or possibly suicide.

Quite why he's got this idea about them all being linked he doesn't know, but hunches can be worth taking seriously.

Engrossed in thoughts of great future exploits, he jumps as the front door slams and Henry Salo's voice echoes from the hall.

"Are there any hacks in the house? Come on out and I'll give you something sweet to get your teeth into."

He throws his jacket over a chair and goes straight to the drinks cabinet. Finds two glasses, pours a finger into each, and sits down opposite Mikael. Who then closes his laptop and remarks that Salo seems to have had a successful evening at the Tigertooth Order.

"To put it mildly. Construction of the new ice rink's going to get approval. The cotton field will have to wait a few years for its arts centre, though."

"The cotton field?"

"White-haired old biddies who flock to subsidised cultural events. Is the boy asleep?"

"Yes. We called Pernilla. Lukas wanted to say goodnight but she didn't answer."

"She goes to bed early these days. She's expecting . . . we're expecting another nipper! She hasn't known for long and she's probably worried it'll end the same way as last time."

Still, Mikael feels a stab of resentment that she didn't tell him. What does her husband think about that, or does she never actually talk about her father? But Salo is now glued to his phone.

His complexion is changing from club-night pink to red, with sweat beading his brow and trickling down his face. He leaps to his feet so suddenly that his chair falls backwards, and heads for the bottle but stops at the sink. Puts his mouth under the tap and splashes his face with water. He keeps running his fingers through his hair and gulping for air.

Something's wrong, Mikael can see, but Salo doesn't say a word.

"What is it?" he prompts, receiving only some choice swearwords in reply.

Surging inside Henry Salo there is a volcanic outburst he cannot contain. The lava must find its outlet, laying waste to everything in its path until it solidifies.

"I assume Pernilla never told you who Lukas's biological father is?"

This is correct. At first he asked questions, but they were never answered. That's her business, thought Mikael. They haven't touched on the subject since.

"To cut a long story short," says Salo, and gives him an account of recent events, including his own dubious involvement: Kostas Long realising that a custody battle will never give him the boy. Not with his background.

"So, if I understand this right, you promised him he'll get his son back if he goes ahead with financing the old mine?"

Mikael forces himself to sound neutral.

"Initially, yes, but I'm not entirely heartless, if that's what you're thinking. I checked up on Pernilla's human trafficking story. It turns out that an international alert has gone out for Kostas Papadopoulos. That person died the same instant Long came into existence. His narrative as the son of a rich Chinese father with an unlimited fortune built on property and mining is most likely invented. Long's money is a lot dirtier than that."

"And now he knows that you know?"

"Pernilla," says Salo, looking wretched. "I told Long she'd gone to the cottage."

He presses voicemail, puts the phone on speaker. The voice whispers: *He's getting closer, I can't start the snowmobile.*

The same sensation as when Lukas was abducted by armed men is rising in Mikael. His grandson was under threat, and now his daughter is, too. His voice has a dull resonance as he notes that the message was received four hours earlier.

"How the hell can you bear to live with yourself?" he demands.

"I can't," says Salo, and gets to his feet. He scoops up his car keys and with an unopened bottle of Lagavulin Single Malt in his other hand he disappears out of the door.

With Lukas asleep upstairs there isn't much Blomkvist can do. Beyond calling the police.

The door of the cottage speaks volumes. He calls her name although he knows she won't answer.

A snowmobile has arrived and left.

Henry trudges through the melting snow and out onto the trail. He breaks into a run. Although he can hardly catch his breath he continues until the fresh track turns off towards the lake. He falls, gets up, shuffles as best he can down to the shore, where the telltale outlines of ice floes are like a mosaic against the black open water.

He has no voice left to shout with. He kneels as if he were praying and maybe he is. Praying that somehow, miraculously, she got across although he knows it to be impossible.

At the edge, the ice is still hard. The bottle is bulging under his jacket. Henry untwists the cork and lets the smoky whisky run like milk down his throat. He moves slowly towards the point where the density changes to a fluid form.

As the ice finally gives way and his body is sucked down between the ice floes, the stars come out. The water puts its tender arms around him, carries him through an ever-narrowing tunnel that soon reduces to a minimal opening. He squeezes through the hole. Head, shoulders, trunk, legs.

A mother looks at her child. In her eyes there is nothing but love.

69

Lukas wakes. Goes downstairs. Sits on the sofa in the dark. Something has happened. His tummy senses it, aching and hurting. And now it wants to be sick.

"Never mind," says Mikael. "Did you have a bad dream? Hang on, I'll get you some dry clothes."

He has locked the front door. Switched off the light in the kitchen. Looked out to scan the area around the house. Listened for any noises and called the police on Birna Guðmundurdóttir's private number. She took in what he was telling her and asked a few questions, told him she was at the far end of the district but would come as fast as she could or send some colleagues.

The boy's body is stiff and chilled through. Mikael puts him in the bath. Then gets him dressed. Chats about the summer and fishing trips, the rowing boat that needs a coat of tar and the bilberries they'll pick and the sun that will always be shining except when there's a light summer shower, and the dew on the grass.

"Where's Mum?" Lukas says and Mikael wants to lie. Has to lie. Not only for the boy's sake, but because there's someone knocking on the door.

Some sort of relief at last. And they were quick, too.

"Get your rucksack and pack a few clothes and any other bits you want. We're going to sleep at my place tonight. Coming!" he calls towards the door, and switches on the hall light.

A foot in the door, a shove and a voice that needs no introduction. Kostas Long.

"Didn't your mother teach you never to open the door to strangers?" he says, holding out his hand. "You must be Mikael, Pernilla's father. Nice to meet you."

"I've called the police," says Mikael. "They're on their way."

"In that case, please call them again and tell it like it is: there's nothing wrong. The police can get on with more important things."

When Birna calls, Jessica Harnesk has come off shift and has just picked up Lisbeth Salander outside the City Hotel. They have barely had time to say hello, let alone talk, but Birna insists. It's Mikael Blomkvist. Can she drive out to Gaupaudden? Birna herself is forty-five minutes away. There was something strange in his voice and, sure, maybe she's exaggerating, but just to be on the safe side.

"What's up?" says Lisbeth.

"Probably nothing. Her old boyfriend's scared of the dark. He must be babysitting Salo's kid."

Lukas pads silently down the stone stairs. If he can reach the hall and get outside without attracting their attention, they'll never find him. Gaupaudden is his fort. Hideaways are his secret places.

"Lukas is my son," Long says. "I'm going to take him to a richer place on earth than Gasskas."

He spits out the "s" sounds in Gasskas.

"A dreadful place, ought to be burned to the ground. My son deserves a better life, don't you think?"

Lukas doesn't understand. He hears the words but cannot grasp them.

Lukas is my son.

And somehow, it's as if he has known all along. Dreamed about the girl who phones now and then. Seen photos of her and thought how alike their mouths are.

"Mum, who is my dad?" he tries, but she just laughs and always gives the same answer: "You were born on a flower. You came sailing to me on a lily pad."

Then they read "Thumbelina". She says the story is about him and no, you daft thing, you're not going to marry a badger or be taken prisoner by a beetle. But she has no name for his father. So perhaps this is him, the man leaning against the sink with his arms folded.

Lukas cranes forward to see better. His foot knocks against the cast-iron boot remover, which . . .

Both men jump and look in his direction. Long drags him into the light and places his hands on his shoulders, says something to him about look-alikes.

Long's phone vibrates. He has been expecting company. Words rattled off, sounding like an order. Time for them to go.

"Lukas isn't going anywhere," says Mikael. "He's staying with me."

"Are you sure about that?" says Long. "Isn't it enough that he's motherless?"

70

They drive to Gaupaudden in total silence. Jessica waits for Lisbeth to make the first move; after all, she was the one who made contact.

Lisbeth loses the thread and doesn't know where to start. Letting the police into her private affairs goes against the grain. Particularly when Svala is involved.

Just after the turning to "Salo's Ranch" she asks Jessica to pull over. No more engine noise.

"What did Mikael actually say?"

"Not sure, because this is second-hand information from Birna. Something about Pernilla and Salo. Mikael was agitated, but perhaps he is generally?" says Jessica, and gets a sceptical look from Lisbeth in return.

To be honest, Jessica hadn't really listened very carefully. Since Mikael Blomkvist turned up again she has grown thoroughly tired of Birna going on about the journo's many assets, even the more intimate aspects. The stopper is out of the bottle for the introverted Icelander. She's in love. Jessica wishes her every happiness, but even romance has its limits. Other people's, at any rate.

"What?" says Lisbeth. "Are Blomkvist and the cop a couple now?"

"Evidently."

Is Lisbeth surprised? No. Disappointed?

If so, she's not going to let it show.

Lisbeth opens and closes the car door as quietly as she can. Under the cover of the trees she creeps towards the house until she is about twenty metres from the front door.

A Mercedes with a foreign numberplate is waiting just below the front porch. The tinted windows mean she can't see how many people are in the car. She rapidly notes the reg number and sends it to G5.

Registered in France. A company car. Long S.A. Can't find any more.

A deleted memory of a mediocre night last autumn in Rovaniemi flashes through her mind. Kostas Long, wasn't that his name?

There must be thousands of Longs.

Thousands of Longs, and Kostas is one of them. To spare the child, he hadn't intended to make this so dramatic. But when the old man attacked him physically he had no choice. Things turned a bit bloody, but it could have been worse. It only took a light blow. He has no desire to see headlines about serious businessmen with lives on their conscience.

Long hooks the rucksack over the boy's shoulders and takes his hand.

"The car's waiting outside. We've got a long journey home. I'm sure you're going to like your new room."

Dragging feet, small hands trying to hang on to the door handle. Screams that hopefully cannot rouse dead mothers – Long's patience is not unlimited. Gripping the boy by the scruff of the neck and clapping a hand over his mouth, he steers him to the Mercedes. He is about to open the rear door when he hears the familiar click of a hammer being cocked right behind him.

"Let go of him," says Lisbeth.

He slowly loosens his grip.

Lisbeth meets Lukas's eyes.

"Run down to the car that's parked by the road and tell the woman inside to take you to the police station. Don't be scared."

And Lukas runs. But when he reaches the car, it is empty. He slips into the back seat and onto the floor. His heart is pounding. His inhaler is still on the worktop in the kitchen.

71

Jessica materialises behind Lisbeth. Unarmed, as befits a fine upstanding police officer who has come off shift and locked away her service firearm.

"Why the hell have you come up?" hisses Lisbeth. "I told you to wait down there."

"What the fuck are you two doing here?" says Long, his eyes darting between them.

Then he smiles. Broadly. He is on the verge of laughter.

In the confusion that follows, while Lisbeth attempts to orientate herself in the shared basis of their acquaintance, he throws a punch, lands it on her shoulder and wrenches open the car door. He hurls himself into the seat and the Mercedes roars off down the slope and onto the road.

Lukas has changed hiding place. Under the floor of the old boathouse he bites his arm to stop himself crying, breathing or coughing.

He was born in a flower. Came sailing in a walnut shell. Set up camp in a waterlily and was brought home by his mum. He will never need a dad. But a grandpa is a different matter.

Grandpa was on the floor.

There was blood streaming from his head.

His body couldn't raise itself even though Lukas kept shouting.

When they were Christians and lived in Uppsala, miracles happened all the time. The sick were cured. The paralysed stood up and walked. He never saw it for himself. But it was definitely true. His mum isn't in the habit of lying.

For the first time since they moved to Gaupaudden, he puts his hands together and prays.

Rise, take up your bed and walk.

Under a rotting plank of wood, on ground that has barely thawed out, a miracle happens. At first the voice is so distant he can scarcely hear it.

"Lukas," it calls. "Lukas, where are you?"

He squeezes out of his hiding place and runs towards the voice. Buries himself in the embrace of a man who, like the boy, still does not know the extent of his loss. Pernilla's phone is switched off. Salo's as well. Long is lurking among the reeds and everything will be like before. He promises.

Lisbeth and Jessica are waiting in the car. There have been developments on other levels too. They travel in silence to the City Hotel.

"You two are sleeping in my room," says Lisbeth. "This lady will make sure they send a proper police officer to Salo's cottage. One with a gun."

"That's bloody unfair of you. You must see that I can't just make free with my—"

"No, but fucking Greek-Chinese psychopaths is fine, apparently."

"Well thanks. The same to you."

Their voices are rising. Mikael Blomkvist plugs in his earbuds. The boy has fallen asleep against his shoulder. Birna reports that a car is on its way up to the cottage and no, they don't want Mikael Blomkvist to join them, and yes, they'll keep in touch.

Amidst all the misery, Birna's voice provides welcome warmth. She's good. Better than most. The silent type. Not entirely unlike Salander.

Or Pernilla for that matter, and his thoughts have circled back to her, his daughter.

The prospect of never seeing her again. Stroking her hair. Chuckling with her over some bad joke. Seeing that serious face suddenly break into a smile.

No, that can't be right. She's a survivor. She's endured Salo, Long, him, her mother. Miscarriage and a son who survived a kidnapping. For Lukas's sake, his own and even Salo's, it can't be right.

There's comfort in the thought. Feeble comfort, but still.

The boy goes back to sleep on Lisbeth's sofa bed. They sit on opposite sides of the bed. She passes him a beer. Opens a Coke.

"Good job Long whacked you on your left-hand side. It makes you more symmetrical."

"Thanks for the sympathy," says Mikael, grimacing. "I saw your message. Did you want anything in particular?"

She digs in her pocket and puts the USB stick into his hand.

"From Svala. The kid's ahead of you. Maybe she should be editor-in-chief at *Gaskassen*." And yes, Lisbeth has copied over the files and had G5 go through the material.

"Who's G5?"

"Milton Security's genius number 5. I number them, it's easier that way. Five is good. I'll get the material back tomorrow. There's something going on at the sanatorium. Svala twigged it several weeks ago."

"I didn't even know there was one."

"Exactly," says Lisbeth. "Ester Södergran did an innocent feature on haunted houses. Two days later she was dead. I assume Svala got wind of it when she saw the photos. Taken with a drone. The kid's Christmas present."

"From you?"

She nods.

"Who else? Svala and Ester were in touch with a hacker from Luleå.

Calls himself Ante. I think he happened to get on Branco's track and drew Ester into the whole thing."

"Sounds like the sort of journalist I'd have liked to work with."

"Yeah, you could do with someone to fire up the old brain cells," says Lisbeth.

"Meaning?"

"Since we met at the Åsö café you've lined up a whole series of scoops. Branco, Ferm, Salo, Malin, Lo, the Cleaner and so on. But you're not doing anything about it. If I were you I'd start with Svala. She knows things, and don't say she's just a child because she isn't. She was the one who did Ester's research, wrote the articles about the mining industry and even committed to joining the activists to find out how people think. It's all on the flash drive, including the kid's investigations of Ferm's and Branco's involvement in some fucking disreputable stuff that words can hardly describe."

Old pickup trucks rumble past on the street below. The bars are closing and people are weaving unsteadily home.

Mikael Blomkvist opens his laptop and slots in the USB stick, all but oblivious to Salander, who is doing her statutory fifty press-ups and the same number of sit-ups before she gets into bed. There she puts on her headphones and shuts out the world around her.

72

Strictly speaking Per-Henrik should have left the day before for his week working away. But when a friend rings and asks for help, he isn't one to refuse. Not so very far up the lower slopes of the mountains there is still snow on the ground. Emaciated from the lean winter months, some of the stray reindeer have ventured further north than usual in their search for food.

They've been on their snow scooters all day, taking out fodder. The melting snow makes the going unpredictable and bodies have to work extra hard.

Partway through the afternoon, they make a fire. Cut some slices of bacon and cook pancakes. Boil up the coffee and chat about this and that. Each of them stretched out on a reindeer hide until their muscles recover and the sweat has cooled.

Per-Henrik offers to do the next round on his own. Unlike his friend, he has no young children to consider. The landscape rewards him with its magnificent expanses. On the spur of the moment, he decides to let the job take its time. He drives slowly and enjoys the freedom of his stolen day.

The sun goes down before he gets back to where his truck is parked. It is dusky rather than dark. He switches off the ignition, removes his helmet and listens to the keening urge of the ice breaking free from the jaws of winter.

On the other side of the lake there is smoke coming from a chimney. A scooter passes at high speed. An unusual amount of activity for the season, he thinks, and tilts the flatbed. With his own vehicle loaded, he casts a last glance down at the lake. Unsure of what he is actually seeing, he gets out his binoculars and focuses them.

A woman on a scooter. She must have come down the track with a view to cutting across the lake. She is standing on the slope a few metres from the shore, looking hesitant.

"Don't chance it!" he yells, as if she could possibly hear. "The ice won't hold!"

Then he hears the engine revving and sees the machine's skis fighting their way through the slush, almost hovering like a hydrocopter. Behind her, the ice cracks into thin floes. By the time she reaches the other side, it is open water. Seconds later the engine sound cuts out abruptly and nature reverts to its usual self, as does Per-Henrik.

He jumps into his truck and drives a few kilometres but his thoughts won't leave him alone. There was something about the woman. Something abnormal.

At first he can't place it. No helmet, but then he doesn't always wear one himself.

'Shit," he says out loud. She was bare-legged.

He stops abruptly. Turns the truck and drives into one of the cabin parking areas. Backs the scooter down from the flatbed and weaves among the houses towards the place where she would have come ashore.

He catches sight of the machine a little way ahead. The engine is still ticking over. One ski has run into a young birch and got jammed there. The woman is wedged underneath it, between its plastic belly and the snow. She looks as if she is asleep.

Using his own weight, Per-Henrik tips the scooter back upright.

She mumbles something. She's still alive.

"I'm going to pull you up and it might hurt," he says, trying to find a decent hold as his boots slither on the snow.

The woman weighs no more than a reindeer in autumn. He puts her in front of him. Knots the lasso around them so she won't slip off if things get bumpy on the way up.

With a reindeer hide across the three front seats of the truck and another over her knees plus his own padded jacket, hat and gloves – everything he can find – and her head in his lap, they head for Gasskas.

The heat is turned up full blast.

Under the reindeer hide, the woman thaws out. She raises her head, asks where she is, who he is. Per-Henrik stops in a lay-by. Hoists her up onto his arm, pushes the hair off her face. She isn't in any pain. She can wiggle her toes. She doesn't want to go to hospital. Doesn't want to go home.

So he drives straight to Björkavan. She sleeps the whole way. Sits up when he switches off the engine and asks where she is.

"At our place. Me and my brother Elias. And Svala, but we never know where she's got to."

Perhaps he should phone the police. Or get the woman to A & E. She's sleeping now, in the double bed. She still hasn't said who she is. As if she's taking a break from her life.

"Svala?" he says as Elias comes through the door.

"Still missing. The car too."

At a turning place down by the old logging docks, a newly minted fourteen-year-old has reclined the front seat and zipped her jacket right up to her chin.

In the last light of the sunset she takes out her notebook. Turns back through time and reads the diary of her life, even though some of the entries make her feel very queasy. And Simon isn't even the worst thing, or Ester's death or the reindeer and dogs. Not her uncles wanting her to move out, either, or Aunt Lisbeth who doesn't know how to relate to people. No, it's the tone that's the most upsetting thing of all. A kind of indifference guiding her pen.

While Mammamärta was alive there was something to look forward to. A life without Pap Peder, her mum's promises to stay sober; her assurances that with the help of the bitcoin money they'll be able to start afresh in some other part of the world. Some place where nobody knew them.

"Tell me where you want to go and we'll go there," she would say, and Svala would spin the globe. "Finland."

"Finland? Couldn't you opt for somewhere more exotic while you've got the chance?"

"According to the UN's World Happiness report, the Finns are the happiest people in the world," Svala said, and Mammamärta laughed so hard there were tears in her eyes. Then they went to Buongiorno and had pizza.

Hello pet, what's going on?

Nothing much.

Are you fed up?

A bit.

Tell me what the matter is.

I don't want you to be dead.

I get that, but you know, don't you?

Know what?

We'll always be together. I'm here whenever you need me. Never forget that.

Svala stows away her notebook and presses the button to lock the doors. Mammamärta is there. But then why does she feel so lonely?

73

Ante has e-mailed. He hasn't been well. Was tied up with an exam. Says sorry.

`I made contact with somebody called Plague. Best thing might be for us to meet. You say where. I can be in Gasskas in a couple of hours.`

The relief makes Svala feel happy. Ante is the link back to Ester. He brings her to life again. Her voice, her laugh.

`The Pit is a good place. They shut it all down there after the bridge was blown up` writes Svala, and gives her phone number. `Call me if you can't find it.`

Until their meeting, she whiles away the time in the cemetery.

She puts some daffodils in a vase on Mammamärta's grave. There's nothing else in bloom in the beds of the town park.

Thirty-nine years old. Probably older than she will ever get to be.

Not far off, Ester is lying under a sea of wilting funeral flowers.

Twenty-three. That too is probably older than she will ever be.

Svala went to the funeral. Arrived last, sat at the very back and sneaked out first. Now she slots a scrap of paper with a handwritten message between two roses.

I shall finish what you started. Svala.

*

Lisbeth Salander has been tracking Svala's erratic course around town for a couple of days now. As long as the dot is not moving towards the sanatorium, she lets her be. Walks past the car when it is parked by the docks for the night, hangs a plastic bag of food on the wing mirror. Makes herself known in various ways and thinks the girl will be in touch when she needs her.

She has eased the uncles' anxiety by assuring them that Svala is alive and well. They'll have to deal with social services themselves.

In the end she swallows her pride and calls Harnesk. They meet over a beer. She comes up to Lisbeth's room. And despite the thought of Long's hands all over the policewoman's body, Lisbeth can't help . . . well, what . . . falling, perhaps. Falling headlong into the woman's arms and legs and the silky folds of her skin until reality catches up.

Harnesk promises to take reindeer and dogs seriously. Lisbeth passes on the leads she has. Simon Frisk's blood on a ball of cottonwool, for example. Search paths on the darknet that lead to his sickening activities with minors. It's going to take time before they can apprehend him. Time enough for Lisbeth to investigate his links to Branco for herself. He is her way into the sanatorium and the question is, what's worse: disappearing with the help of Branco's cleaning staff or falling foul of Svala's revenge, for herself and for Ester.

Mikael Blomkvist has been through all the material on the flash drive. Lisbeth is waiting for G5's report on Ante the hacker while making her own enquiries on the side. Her theory is that Ante and Plague are the same person. She hopes it isn't just wishful thinking.

Since Plague's suggestion of a meeting, she has heard no more.

The call was not traceable and the platform's lying there as deserted as a Norrbotten County railbus station in the middle of the night.

If they are right that Branco and his menagerie are hanging out at the sanatorium, it isn't simply a matter of barging in. She needs a plan. Old ground plans of the place, for example. She draws a blank with the

National Land Survey. It would be so easy to get into the municipal council's data systems but in view of other recent incursions they have suffered she decides against it. Instead she asks in person at reception if they wouldn't mind making some old-school copies for her. The receptionist's reaction is revealing. She rolls her eyes and wonders out loud why everybody suddenly wants the plans of a building that has been out of use these past twenty years, but a faint gleam comes into those eyes as she describes the individual who requested them before Lisbeth.

"At first I thought it was Salo, but I'm sure he's on sick leave."

Joar Bark, alias the Cleaner.

In the council's IT department, chaos still reigns. Lisbeth has to admit that the problem is more far-reaching than she'd thought, but one thing remains clear. Addresses, including her own at Fiskargatan, have fallen into the wrong hands.

So much for social services' confidentiality policy.

Men with restraining orders can buy the secret addresses of their terrified wives and children. As for her, she can be sent severed fingers through the post.

When Milton Security sends up a couple of geniuses she feels no indignation, only relief.

She goes back to the hotel and draws up a list of questions.

Plague: Are you alive?

Lo: How dangerous are you?

Branco: Will you be pleased to see me again?

The Cleaner: Who are you working for?

Svala: Where are you heading now?

The dot is on the move again. Turning north and not slowing until the exit to the old mine.

G5: What have you found on Ante?

G5 replies instantly:

"It was seriously hard let me tell you, but we've been able to localise that hacker. He's quite well concealed behind hidden IP addresses and a false identity. Looks like your niece, the one with the bird name, has a date with him tonight. Smart girl. Could be a future Milton, what do you reckon?"

"Where are they meeting?"

Lisbeth receives the location, briefly heaps praise on G5 and is about to end the call when she exclaims:

"Hang on Lisbeth, there's one other thing. That Ante made a mistake when he was messaging someone else. We've apparently got his real identity here. Stay on the line!"

The dot is moving more slowly now. She's probably on foot.

"Hello Lisbeth, are you still there? The guy's name is Simon Frisk. Have you got that? Simon Frisk."

74

Svala gets there first. She wanders down to the Pit. The only sign of activity is a fox that has got through the wire fence and is running around following a track on the ground, until it slinks off behind the miners' huts where Levi Grundström changed his clothes, heated up his lunch and had his coffee for the first fifteen years of his forty-seven-year working life.

They didn't have time to talk properly. They'd only just got to know each other. In his company she was never too young, too weird or too quiet. She was simply Svala. As for him, he never took a sick day in his life.

She picks up a stone. Rubs its smooth surface against her cheek, thinking about the last thing he said. Perhaps the nicest thing anyone has ever said to her.

Your best time isn't now, but it's coming.

On her way back to the meeting place she dismisses a call from Lisbeth and then another. When she calls for a third time just as Svala hears the car coming, she switches off her phone. Lets down her hair and runs her fingers through it.

The delay between expectation and surprise means it is a few seconds before she registers that it is Simon Frisk getting out of the car, not "Ante". He is in no hurry. With only a few metres between them, he stops and looks about him. Pushes his sunglasses onto his head, fixes his gaze on her.

A few weeks ago this gaze was warm, a comfortable place to be held. Now she has to force herself not to look away.

Her mistake. She should have suspected. Deep inside, maybe she didn't want to. She saved herself the effort, wanting to salvage a bit of her pride.

She was the one who let herself be swept up in a pathetic teenage crush. The one feeling something like that for the first time. The one who wrote little notes whose gist was that he ought to see her as a woman, not a child.

"Good place you've picked," he says. "Quiet. Nobody else here. But what do you say, shall we take a stroll? Mine activists can never get enough of slag heaps and slurry pools, can they?"

Is this the way it's going to end? Just because she didn't make the most of the chance when she had it, listened to Lisbeth who then let him go?

She stuffs her hands in her pockets. Feels the shape of her own switched-off mobile and a pay-as-you-go phone that can call, text and . . .

"Give me your phone," says Simon. "Do you think I'm stupid?"

She does as he says. Drops her iPhone at his feet. As anticipated, this sets off the emergency call. It's happened before. Embarrassed, she has had to explain to the call centre that she dropped her phone by mistake. Here they are now, calling her back. No-one will answer, but who knows? Maybe they'll get it. Sense her telepathic desperation and call Lisbeth.

He mashes the phone under his shoe until it stops ringing.

Inside, Svala is fighting against her awareness of how little she is. She has allowed it to surface sometimes, but little is weak. Weak is a child and in the voice of a child she appeals for his sympathy. Says she's sorry about before, and now they're quits.

"I genuinely liked you," he says. "It's a shame it has to end like this but I have no choice. You of all people should know that."

"If I disappear, you're the first one Branco will come down on, and not only you. Your little sister and your mum, too. Your dad's already dead so not him, Pap Peder's so-called master. In my notebook I call him C. He was a bastard, just like you. Genetics truly has its ugly sides. Or do you prefer me to call it social conditioning?"

He is rattled and her confidence grows correspondingly.

"If you plan to dump me in the slurry pools, I suggest we take your car. It's quite a long walk and the first night-time security guard will be here in half an hour. But maybe you didn't know that? I brought us a snack, by the way. We ought to have a little chat before you shoot me. It would feel right."

"Shoot and dump," he laughs, shaking his head. "There's nothing wrong with your imagination."

But sure, they can have her snack, now she's gone to the trouble.

"My rucksack's in the boot of the car," she says. "Coffee and dried reindeer meat."

She loosens the cord of Levi Grundström's rucksack. Lets him see the Thermos flask, wooden cups and plastic bag of flatbread before they get into his car.

"May I?" she says, making to withdraw the knife from its sheath.

"Go ahead."

She spears a piece of meat and passes it over. Unscrews the top of the flask, apologises for the coffee having gone cold and pours them each a cup.

Win time. Get him to change his mind.

"Apart from being useless at coffee-making, you're a reliable sort, Svala. We would have made a great couple," he says, opening the door. He tosses out the cup and puts his hand on her thigh.

"Get your clothes off," he orders. "You owe me something to feast my eyes on. This could be the last time we see each other."

Win time. Get him to change his mind.

Svala tugs off her jacket. Undoes her top. His hand moves up to the button of her jeans, but when it won't immediately yield he takes her hand and presses it into his groin.

"Admit you liked it and want to do it again."

She swallows her feelings of disgust as Simon unzips his flies, undoes his trouser button. He puts her hand around his hard-on and she could make it easy for herself: stick the knife into his pumping carotid artery and let him bleed to death.

Then his phone rings. Reluctantly, he is obliged to answer. His cock goes limp in her hand.

"Totally," he says, "we're on our way. Twenty minutes."

He backs into Svala's car. Curses, engages first gear and screeches off at speed.

"If we're in a hurry, the quickest road is through the forest," says Svala. "You know, the one we were going to block with our bodies. The other way takes at least half an hour. I know the route," she says, seeing in her mind's eye the map she has memorised. "Pap Peder used to do rally driving around here and I was his navigator. Straight for about four hundred metres, then it bends round to the right," she says.

The wheels slip and spin on the loose ground.

"Three hundred, two, one, fifty, twenty-five metres to go . . ."

Simon takes the bend with both hands on the wheel, changes down on the next straight stretch and the trees swim by like a solid mass of green until they reach the last bend before the fork.

"Fifty metres, tight bend, after the bend there's a barrier but I know the code," she says, holding Levi Grundström's mobile in front of her like a GPS. It's an old model. A cover to slide up. Digits to enter. The car bumps and lurches. He brakes and stops at the barrier.

Before Simon Frisk has time to react, she hurls herself out of the car, rolls down the sandy slope towards the pools and counts to five.

For the second time in the spring of 2022, those sleeping Gasskas residents are woken by the detonation of an explosive charge big enough to demolish a tower block. And big enough to blast the municipality's mine plans back to the future.

Levi Grundström had been generous with the gunpowder.

Svala lies there with her arms covering her head for protection. The shock wave sends car parts and other parts raining down over a flattened forest. A foot in a Nike Jordan bounces off her hip, rolls on and stops by a root.

When the place has reclaimed its silence and the pressure in her ears has eased, she slithers the rest of the way down to the pool.

For soap she uses fistfuls of sand. She scrubs the smell of him off her hands, rinses them off and scrubs again and again, but she needs to hurry now. Get around the crater and run back to her car even though she is burning up and would like more than anything to throw herself into the coral-green water and cool off in the glitter of rare earth metals.

Just before Gasskas she meets the flashing blue lights.

Nobody takes any notice of the child who can barely see over the steering wheel.

Nobody except Lisbeth, who's been following a GPS dot that is no longer moving.

75

What is a warrior, a *busho*? Someone who defies their fear and meets death in combat, or someone who picks their battles to survive at the expense of others, as she does?

The only safe place she can think of is the Cleaner's hut. She turns into yet another of the municipality's innumerable forestry roads, built solely for tree-felling, hoping to grab a few hours' sleep. Her ears are bleeding from the detonation. Her whole body feels as if it is going to burst. When daylight returns, she empties the car of all belongings and sets off on foot towards the hut.

Birds stir from their sleep. The images recede. Car parts and other parts.

She walks along the margins of the bog, over the hill, over the state-funded drainage ditch, through the forest.

Birds fall silent. Images flicker. Simon's eyes. The way he looked at her. The surprise. The fear everyone shares.

She dumps her possessions on the floor. Takes the whisky from the shelf over the stove. Puts the bottle to her mouth and drinks. Drinks the way Mammamärta, Pap Peder and all the other soaks have taught her, when sometimes. Often. There's no other solution but to opt out.

The liquor is doing its best to come back up, but she really wants to keep it down. She lies on the bunk. Her head is spinning but she can't care. Can't care about the vomit that splatters onto her hand on its way to the floor.

About the fire that isn't burning properly.

About Mammamärta's hair that was caked with blood, which normally fell in a shiny black mane down her back and the back that she always held straight and her hands that would plait Svala's hair and tell her she was the most beautiful creature God ever made.

I shan't leave you all, I shall come to you.

Help me then because I can't do this anymore and . . . and . . .

She is panting for air like a rabid dog for water. A draught blows into the hut. Hands lift her. Arms hold her close and she squints, tries to see, but her eyes insist on closing and she is so little now. A seed falling out of a husk.

She ought to cry because she is so new in the world but her tears are dry. Instead, she vomits. Drinks some water and vomits again. A hand on her forehead. The last spasms ebb away.

"That Simon," she says, and however hard she tries to conjure up his insistent hands, his words, the coercion, male parts, smell, the pictures she sees are different ones. "That Simon, he didn't deserve to die. He was only a little shit who wanted to move up in the world and I pressed the button."

"Aren't we all little shits who want to move up?" says the Cleaner. "And when it's a contest between them, someone has to press the button."

He asks her to hold out her arms. Pulls off her top. With hot soapy water washes off the smell of sick, carries her over to the other bunk, covers her shoulders with a blanket.

"Don't think so much. Tomorrow's another day. Stay in the hut while I deal with Branco. There's enough food to see you through."

"What are you even doing here?" she mumbles.

"A swallow flew me a message."

"Can it fly a message to Lisbeth Salander, too?"

"Who's she?" asks the Cleaner.

"My aunt. She may think I . . . don't exist any longer."

When sleep comes, it is quiet and colourless. A gap has widened and closed again and he is right. Tomorrow is another day.

76

On that new day she is alone in the hut. She tries to remember and when she does it is only the foot she sees. Simon's foot. But no Cleaner.

Be that as it may, a warrior has a mission. There is no allowance for the luxury of being little. Her top is still damp. She ties a piece of rope around her waist to keep the Cleaner's T-shirt hitched up. The one he removed at some point during the night and put on her instead. It smells agreeably of sweat and washing powder.

The car is still parked outside where she left it. There are two ways to the sanatorium. A shorter route through Gasskas and a longer one through a series of small villages. If they are looking for her, the first is risky.

As long as she doesn't run out of fuel.

If it comes to it, she can walk part of the way, and for a while everything feels normal and fine. Pop music pours out of the radio and then a news bulletin comes on.

An explosion detonated late last night on the southern approach to the Gasskas mine has caused serious damage to roads and nearby buildings, according to a statement from the council press department. An individual who has not yet been identified was reportedly found dead at the scene of the incident. The National Bomb Protection Squad is carrying out a post-blast investigation.

The police can currently offer no comment on potential perpetrators or speculate as to why the mine has again been the subject of a bomb attack. "We are of course investigating whether there is any link between the two attacks," says Hans Faste of the Serious Crime Unit at Gasskas police.

Svala's thoughts circle the clues she has left behind. The police will make a thorough search of the area. As the crow flies it is only a couple of kilometres between the meeting place where she offered Simon coffee and the site of the detonation. On the other hand there won't be much left of her jacket. She saw the smoke, felt the heat of fire. Her eardrums still have difficulty making out certain sounds.

She has to ring Lisbeth's number several times from Levi's phone before she answers. And yes, of course she realises Lisbeth has been worried, and no, she can't say where she is but she needs help.

"Check the map. There's an overgrown road leading down to a farm at Davidsjaure. Only the cowshed is still there but a path leads uphill from the farm. Follow it directly north and you'll come to a turning place. He mashed up my phone."

"Which he?"

"That Simon. You've got to find it. The police are going to think it was me who—"

"Whose number are you calling from?"

"Levi's. He's dead too. Cancer. Anyway, I need to hang up now."

"Wait," says Lisbeth. "I've already . . ." but Svala has gone.

On the table in front of her lie the remains of her niece's mobile.

Lisbeth got there too late. Most likely only by minutes. Initially she took the wrong track off the road. Up at the turning place stood the old Honda. Locked and abandoned. She went down to the Pit and shouted Svala's name. In the fading light she happened to step on the phone.

Seconds later the bomb went off. The earth shook beneath her feet. She ran back to the hire car, made for the point of impact but realised it would be impossible to get up close. The fire, the heat, the smoke, the trees, the hunks of broken road.

On the way back to Gasskas she met the oncoming blue lights. She tried to call Jessica Harnesk but only got through to voicemail. She left a message and hung up.

Two hours later, a knock at the door of her hotel room.

Lisbeth knew immediately.

"We found the remnants of a jacket," said Jessica, and threw her long arms around Lisbeth. "I'm so sorry, but I think it's Svala's."

Now she's applying thick black stripes of eyeliner. Painting her lips black and fastening her leather jacket. Doing one last check through the contents of her rucksack and everything's there. The ground plans. The gun, cartridges, a rope, a torch, knife, Coke, duct tape and pepper spray.

If the roads lead to the sanatorium. *If* Svala is already there. *Then* there is no time to lose.

77

Svala's plan ultimately consists of not having a plan, because there is no way she can get an overview of the situation. Her unique value is the hard drive. Assuming everything is as simple as Mammamärta claimed: break the code and let Branco cash in the money.

Svala is not so sure. She has tried. Gone astray in the labyrinths of numerical memory and emerged just as poor as before.

Just as well, maybe. Branco is never going to give in. The money is hers. In theory she could take it and make herself scarce, but that would leave Per-Henrik and Elias, along with the reindeer, and the misery of the Hiraks would be repeated all over again. Mammamärta's debt to Branco is Svala's. She owes her uncles a better life.

Alternative outcomes are something she tries not to think about.

As is the woman who contacted her, said she knew the uncles and arranged to see her by the fountain in the town park. They sat on a bench. The skin of her hands was like cracked leather. Her voice low and friendly.

"You have something that belongs to my employer. He wants to meet you."

"And if I refuse?"

"I wouldn't recommend it."

She drives up a side turning towards a field lying fallow. It is almost June, chilly and mosquito-free. She rummages in her bag for Mammamärta's *kolt* and pulls the belt tight. The fabric makes her feel itchy and warm. She shoulders her new monkey and walks in the direction of the sanatorium.

Like other places where life has hung by a fragile thread, the building exudes something powerful, reverential and far from pleasant. People with consumption came here to get better or to die. On the wide terrace overlooking the lake the patients lay under thick blankets to drink in fresh air. Or they turned to ash in the oven of the crematorium. The chimney sticks up between the birches in the avenue.

Long before she reaches the door, they know that she is there.

The woman from the park puts an arm around Svala's shoulders. Praises her for her sensible decision. Tells her that she needn't be scared, that she'll soon be leaving there as a free person.

The pair of weatherbeaten French doors conceal another door behind them.

Svala realises the building is nothing but a front. Once inside, sheet metal and bars. The possibility of escape is minimal.

"Excuse the mess. We're based on the upper floors. The previous tenants didn't bother to clean up when they moved out. You have to see it as a sort of museum. Great outfit, by the way. The colours suit you," she says, and asks her to take off her rucksack.

Apart from the hard drive, there is nothing in the rucksack of interest to anyone but Svala. Pap Peder's Glock is still in the car along with Levi's phone, and Simon's for that matter. The plan had been to throw it in with the bomb but she didn't have time. Things got in the way.

It would have been reassuring to feel Pap Peder's Glock in her back pocket. But just as she anticipated, she is made to stand against a wall with her legs apart while hands are run over her body.

"Haven't you got a name?" says Svala. "Everybody has a name."

"Lo," she says. "As in Lotta, Louise, Lolita, Loreen. And you, why are you called Svala?"

"Mammamärta wanted to call me Hirundo but nobody could pronounce it right, so she settled for Svala."

The woman isn't the same as she was before. She moves more quickly. Talks fast. Avoids eye contact, but Svala has to ask.

"How is he?"

Lo is uncertain. Branco's mood of recent days is beginning to be a problem. Surprisingly enough, the hacker is the only one able to keep him within some sort of check. Presumably because the creature has nothing to lose.

The hacker has been bedridden on the top floor for a few days now, in one of the rooms that has survived intact since the sanatorium was built. The dying were sent to the top floor, to receive the palliative care of the time.

Branco visits him daily. From outside the door she can hear them laughing, but the boss's good mood only lasts as long as it takes him to get back down to everyday life.

Everyday life in the Branco Group companies is a constant struggle to strike a balance. It would be odd if it were otherwise, in an operation that treads the thin line between sun and shadow. But even so. Marcus Branco as founder, majority shareholder and all-powerful decision maker is heading downhill. The information was there, she knew what she was letting herself in for, but she hadn't reckoned on the full range of his demons.

Like the other Knights in Branco's innermost circle, Lo has special skills. Hers are in legal matters, but until now they have barely been called upon. He says he trusts her, and only those he trusts are given operational assignments. Operational in the sense of Svala, for instance. Getting her to voluntarily hand over the hard drive in exchange for the protection of her family.

Lo is doubtful as to whether he is going to be satisfied with the money alone. He is fixated on the girl, fascinated in an unhealthy kind of way. His lewd talk of her attractive looks and amazing brain is growing problematic. He wants to have her, to own her soul with all that it entails.

In Lo the girl stirs memories of a child nobody wanted. Herself. Svala's thin teenage body with its innocent face is a shell. Inside the shell other powers lie in wait, she can sense it.

"Branco's no problem as long as you stick to your side of the agreement."

She stops the lift door from closing and presses 3.

If the entrance hall is a waiting room in a clinic, the third floor is the Grand Hotel.

"Marcus Branco will see you shortly. Please have a seat."

Marcus Branco will see you.

For all the world as if they had scheduled a meeting.

78

"So we meet again, at last," Branco says, and invites her to sit down at a table laid with elegant teacups and a matching teapot. "I've been longing for the opportunity to make you a pot of Da Hong Pao, or Big Red Robe as they call it, after a legend that the tea cured the Emperor's mother of a serious illness and he protected the plants with his robe out of gratitude. One of the world's most exclusive teas with a deep earthy base note and hints of chocolate and smoke."

He describes the rituals around the picking and fermentation of the tea leaves and then pours a few drops for himself before serving Svala.

"In 1972, Mao Tse-tung gave Richard Nixon four hundred grams of Da Hong Pao when he came to China on a state visit. But being a simple American he didn't realise that four hundred grams from the mother plant amounted to half the annual production and was worth around a million dollars. Talking of dates, your mother was born in 1972, was she not?"

She can see what he is driving at. She sips the steaming tea and lets the liquid fill her mouth with earth and chocolate before she swallows.

"I prefer hot chocolate or a bar of Marabou, and you're wrong, Mammamärta was born in 1982. If you hadn't killed her she'd have been forty in two weeks' time."

Svala forces herself to look him straight in the eye. He is a man who makes noises. There are little grunting sounds as he breathes in through his nose.

If it weren't for his eyes, he would look likeable enough. She has seen that gaze before, in other individuals who are sick in the head. *Keep-away-people* as Mammamärta called them.

Then Branco smiles at her infantile comment and engages his adult voice.

"Märta Hirak would still be alive if she hadn't been so infernally stubborn. She could have gone a long way. Courage is an exceptional quality, but it was courage that was her downfall. Right up to her death she refused to tell me where the hard drive was. It was a secret she would have taken to the grave if somebody hadn't whispered in my ear, and now here you are. Present and correct with both the hard drive and your brain."

"Don't expect too much," says Svala. "I don't have the passcode; if I did, I'd have had the money a long time ago."

He sets down his cup. Reverses his wheelchair and brings it round to her side. He takes hold of her by the chin and she concentrates on his eyelashes. They are long and black. He runs his fingers over her face, down her neck and up through her hair.

"I knew your father," he says, "but evidently it's not him you're like, or your mother for that matter. Your father was an interesting person who had a very unusual condition. Or should I say ability? Tell me Svala, have you inherited it?"

He yanks a little clump of hair from her head. She lets out an "ow" and Branco shakes his head. He watches the hairs falling gently to the ground. He moves his hand to her arm and wrenches it backwards. Holds it in a dislocated position until he tires, returns to his side of the table and presses a button on some kind of two-way radio.

"We're done. Tell Varg to come up."

Looking at Varg, Svala is sure they have never met before but his wolf name fits him to a tee. Only the tail is missing.

"Hmm, something nasty seems to have happened here," he says, raising her arm with a hairy paw. "Poor you, that must have hurt a lot, but I'll put the bone back in its socket. I'll just give you something for the pain first," he says, holding the syringe upright and letting a single drop out of the needle before he dabs her upper arm with a ball of cotton wool.

79

Apart from a thin shaft of light forcing its way in through a knothole in the wooden board covering the window, the room is in darkness. The bed creaks as Svala tries to get up. She loses her balance and falls back into a sitting position. Between her meeting with Branco and the room where she is now it is all a blank.

She focuses on the meagre ray of light to regain some sense of balance. She shifts onto her knees and shuffles towards the window. Pulling herself up, she puts one eye to the knothole. The birch trees are coming into leaf. A few more days and the bird cherry will be fragrant. The grass needs cutting and a squirrel scurries up a tree trunk, a moment before a human figure crosses the yard. He is carrying something heavy. A sack. He rests it down, takes a fresh hold and goes on, out of her line of vision.

Her need to pee is getting more urgent. She concentrates on the peaceful world outside until she can't focus anymore. Crawls away until she can see the shape of the opposite wall, the bed. A key in the door. Preferably Lo the Lynx, please not Branco.

"Good morning honeybunch. Did you sleep well?"

Varg. She remembers him now. Her shoulder. The injection.

"What are you doing on the floor?"

"I need the toilet."

"I thought you might," he says, putting down a bucket. "Sorry, it's a bit basic, but I've brought you some food too. Branco said you like hot chocolate. Eat up and I'll come for you a bit later. We're getting ready for a meeting so it might be a while. Use the time to rest, it's going to be a late night."

"Could you leave the door open? I can't see a thing."

"I'm sure you'll get used to it. Don't burn your mouth on the chocolate."

And he is right, Svala's eyes grow accustomed to the gloom and details emerge. A bedside table, a wardrobe.

She lies in the bed thinking about Levi Grundström. She wants to think about something positive. Levi is that. Was that. He wanted to know stuff, like her. Sat in the library and looked things up in books. She's thinking about something he said and can hear his voice.

"In 1945–6, when the sanatorium was built, around three hundred people died of tuberculosis in the Norrbotten region. A significant number of those deaths occurred in Gasskas, because of the flow of refugees from central Europe. People already drained by war and famine had the worst chances of survival. The statistics showed that the death rate in Norrbotten was over forty per cent higher than in Stockholm. Even though overcrowded living conditions were a contributory factor in the spread of disease.

"My eldest brother was sixteen years older than me, born in 1940. When he was eight he got TB, even though that was a time when children were being given the Calmette vaccine. My mother got infected, too. My dad, who was an anti-vaxxer of his day, managed to keep the family away from the authorities' eyes. We lived in a remote place and he had his faith. Anyhow, my brother was in the sanatorium for a couple of years but he pulled through. When I was born he'd already moved out but every time he came home to visit I would ask him to tell me about those days. I didn't really care about the disease but I wanted to hear about death. Well, maybe not death in itself, but the tunnels under the sanatorium. The route they used for transporting the dead bodies out to the crematorium, where they cut them open and removed their diseased lungs before they sewed them up again and took them back to their next of kin."

80

Hours pass. Through the knothole she sees the sun move westward. When the key rasps in the lock again she is sitting ready on her bed.

This time it is Lo. She asks how she feels. Says they're going for a little walk. Wants to know if she is hungry. No, not hungry but fed up. Svala has given them the hard drive. If they want the passcode she will try to work it out for them. But this is not part of the agreement.

"Is there such a thing?" says Lo.

They take the lift and descend one floor. Lo walks ahead, apparently confident that Svala does not intend to put up a fight or try to escape.

"Put the rest on, too," says Lo, setting down the carrier bag of clothes that Svala had in the car. The trousers, turned-up shoes, cap.

"We're off to a party. You're the guest of honour."

In the hall the buzz of party conversation stops as Svala makes her entry. Even the sick need amusement. In 1948 they were suffering from TB. A music session with local big names like Jokkmokks-Jokke would no doubt have livened them up. In 2022 the sickness profile is rather more diffuse. Below her, twenty or so besuited men have just finished dinner. Now they want some entertainment.

Marcus Branco emerges from the crowd and brings his wheelchair up a ramp onto the stage. He stops beside Svala and takes her by the hand.

"Allow me to present Svala Hirak. A real-life Sami girl who we will take a closer look at in a moment. In 1922, a state-financed race-science institute was set up in Uppsala by the legendary doctor and eugenicist Herman Lundborg. In view of the continuing migration that has afflicted the whole of Europe, there is good reason to mark this centenary. Brothers and sisters in the civilised world have seen with horror how Muslim values and their barbaric culture are infiltrating our society at the cost of our freedom and democracy. In the background lurks a left-leaning elite, the Jews, whose aim is to create chaos in order to seize control of our beautiful homeland, our Europe. But we have not allowed the Jews to take over and we will continue to fight against the dilution of our race. But do not misunderstand me; we do not hate immigrants. On the contrary, we believe that they have a right to live in peace in their own countries, in their own culture, just not here."

"*Ausländer raus*," yells someone. Others join in.

Svala's eyes scan the group of men below her. They come to rest on a suit and red bowtie that distinguish one of them from the crowd. There is something familiar about his face, but the recognition is so fleeting that she returns to concentrating on Branco's deranged speech.

"What we have achieved today is a historic milestone. With shared resources and capital, we have an opportunity to transform the playing field. Invest in core activities and achieve such a measure of success that our voice is heard above all the others. No-one will be able to ignore us, or dare to keep us out of decisions. Our collective capital will make us guarantors of a white Nordic pact, and you all know as well as I do that we have many kindred spirits out there. They have been waiting for us. Have begged us to come. And now here we are. Here we are!"

"HERE WE ARE!"

"HERE WE ARE!"

Branco raises his arms in a gesture of humble acknowledgement. Hushes the assembly and turns to Svala.

"A colourful girl, isn't she? A hundred years ago, Herman Lundborg had Sami heads and bodies measured to see if they deviated from the Swedish norm. Their nomadic culture, reindeer herding and language sat strangely with the rights they had appropriated. What was more, they were at the very bottom of the socio-economic ladder. Unfortunately, Lundborg found himself hoist by his own petard. He fell in love with a Sami woman, married her and had children. But . . . if his children were as lovely as Svala, I suppose we have to forgive him."

A few people laugh, brandy glasses are raised and eyes are glued to her body as everyone waits for something to happen.

An uncomfortable feeling settles in the region of her stomach. It's not just the hard drive he wants; now it's something else too.

If Marcus Branco could have heard Svala's thoughts, his answer would have been:

I'm going to force you out of your clothes, item by item. Once you're standing naked in front of these drooling, boozed-up right-wing extremists I shall pick one of them to come up here and measure you.

He holds up a slide caliper for the audience to see.

"The long Germanic skull is considered superior to the short Sami skull. The question is, where will Svala end up on the scale? Her father was German. A splendid specimen. Big, strong, decisive. Svala's Sami mother, on the other hand, climbed the criminal career ladder like a rat, but she had one stroke of brilliance. She bought six thousand bitcoins when Svala was a baby. As of today, they're worth the incredible sum of 4,553,406,000 kronor. And Svala is going to donate every last öre of it to the Nordic Assembly. Deserves a round of applause, wouldn't you say?"

81

The Cleaner has seen the cars arriving, individuals travelling light. Before them the catering deliveries and cleaning service vehicles.

Twelve hours earlier, the kid had strolled blithely across the forecourt. She was admitted and has yet to come out. The fact that the building is crawling with people complicates matters.

Since he took up his position in the forest north of the sanatorium, he has devoted his days to reconnaissance. Apart from Branco, who he has sighted once or twice, there appear to be four other people there from his inner circle, possibly five.

He knows Varg of old, Björn too. Neither of them is easy to deal with. Björn is perhaps the most reasonable. Varg has no boundaries. Both are psychopaths.

The woman is new, the one the Delivery Man says is called Lo. The fourth is unknown to him, as is the fifth, who does not fit into the group. Fat doesn't begin to describe him. Like a TB patient he occasionally sits out on the top-floor terrace with a blanket over his legs.

The Cleaner has also spent time studying the plans of the complex. The main building comprises four storeys above ground, with a floor area of about two hundred and fifty square metres on each level. The ground floor has doctors' consulting rooms, a library and a reception area. On the first floor there is a kitchen, dining room and an assembly hall. The second and third floors consist of rooms for patients. The fourth is reserved for those who are most sick, the dying. The basement is a maze of cold-storage areas, storerooms, showers and, in the middle of it all, a chapel.

From the chapel there is a connecting passage to the crematorium. Two other passages seem to connect to nowhere.

When night comes, the Cleaner moves off through the forest. A setting sun would have made life easier. The dusky light makes visibility poor, but the risk of discovery remains high. In his years away from here it was the midnight sun he missed most. Now he wishes himself back to black nights.

Twenty-five metres from the crematorium he sees something be-tween the trees. Not an animal, a human being. The figure is moving towards him.

His binoculars track the body's progress. The closer it comes, the harder he finds it to define the individual. Like a child, a child in warpaint.

He waits for the sounds. When they are right beside him he grabs the body by the neck, drags it to the ground, presses his knee to its chest and puts his hand over its mouth in case it decides to make a noise. At that moment, he realises who it is.

The aunt. Lisbeth Salander. He lets go of her.

She sees it as a chance to hit him on the jaw. He pins her down again, restrains her by the arms.

"Take it easy, we're on the same side."

"And whose side is that?" hisses the black-painted mouth that extends down towards her neck. She looks diabolical but her body is strong despite its size, and size is of marginal significance. He knows that much after his years in Africa.

"Svala's side."

He can see in her eyes that she understands. Over the past year his identity status has gone from unknown to that of any other fully registered citizen. The notion is a relief but also horrifying. Being ordinary means being held responsible.

"According to the plans, there's a passage between the crematorium and the sanatorium," Lisbeth says when he releases her again. She sits up and brushes herself off.

"I know, but it would be odd if they weren't using it themselves."

They ponder in silence. Lisbeth has questions. Most of them will have to wait.

"As far as I can see, there's no alternative."

"Maybe not, but there's this legend," says the Cleaner. "One passage for the dead and one for the souls."

"Sounds exactly like a legend. If the soul exists, it doesn't need underground passages to get out."

"But that's the point. This was the post-war period. Rationing was still strict. What if there was a secret tunnel that was used for smuggling stuff in? Oranges, tomatoes, alcohol, tobacco, coffee. Things for the soul."

Although he has said the questions will have to wait, she can't help asking.

"Henry Salo was found drowned yesterday. You're his brother, right?"

82

At around 4 a.m. the baying stops and the Nordic Assembly retires after a night's hard drinking. The elation, the belief in the future, have set their stamp on the evening. The last of the bunch is an ICA supermarket owner from west Sweden, who throws up under the table.

Marcus Branco takes the lift to the third floor.

The evening has not been all sing-songs and back-patting. When the mood is at its most exuberant, Varg taps him discreetly on the shoulder, asks for a few minutes of his time.

"These pictures have just come in. Picked up behind the crematorium. A bit fuzzy, but you can still make them out."

The creature presses its ugly face to the camera lens and gives a broad, toothy smile. It backs away, waves and is gone.

Now the face pops up whenever he closes his eyes. The subsequent search proved fruitless. It was not unexpected for Salander to locate them. They had factored it in. But at this stage she should have been on her knees, pleading for her niece's life.

A lack of sleep turns his thoughts black. He wants to throw things around, maim, torture, destroy, kill, but mutiny is brewing in various quarters. He can sense it. The easy familiarity there has always been between him and his Knights is reduced to politeness. They tiptoe around him, keep him out of day-to-day problems for fear he might explode.

Varg has warned him. Asked him to dial it down, *be a bit more professional*, but he can't. All he can do is wait. Wait for *the cruel one* to lick his paws and withdraw, but *the cruel one* wants food. He can feel the hunger.

Sleep would therefore be a blessing. These last weeks, rest has been hard to come by.

Branco goes to bed and is just falling asleep when his body starts to jerk. The legs are the worst. He dreams of long, muscular limbs, already brown although the sun has barely shown itself.

"You rang," says Varg, stepping into the room. "Can't you sleep?"

"Bring the girl here. We've already wasted so much time."

Varg stifles a yawn. Can't it wait?

He takes the stairs up to the fourth floor. As expected, Svala is asleep.

With a little help she has dozed off, and rather than waste time rousing her he carries her down to the room and lays her on the sofa. Her head rests comfortably on a cushion. The rest of her body is at grabbing distance for a wheelchair user who taps her on the shoulder, and when the shoulder doesn't answer he slaps her face with the back of his hand.

"I thought you were only pretending to be asleep. Up with you, it's time to get to work."

She sees the sofa beneath her. A wheelchair, a face close to hers. Branco hits her again.

There is a log-in for the platform, a passcode selected the day a person creates a user account and buys bitcoins. When Märta Hirak takes it into her head to buy six thousand units at a krona apiece she is in a state somewhere between dead drunk and unconscious. In the gap between the two she can see Svala. The top of her head covered with a light down. The nose that barely sticks out. At that moment she thinks six thousand bitcoins might conceivably double in value. That is, if she can repress the code so that neither she nor anyone else can get to it at any point when money is in short supply, which it often is.

"You've got an hour," says Branco as Svala's brain clears little by little.

"And if I can't?"

"If you can't, you'll feel the consequences," he says with a smile. "Now get going!"

This time it is Svala who must smile.

She remembers. Coming in at the end of the day with broken arms and legs. Climbing onto roofs that give way. Getting into fights. Coming home with bleeding gashes, twisted limbs and concussion, not having noticed them in terms of any pain, but only as physical limitations.

The hospital is her safe space. The refuge where she discovers she is a child. Sometimes somebody enquires where her parents are, why they never come to visit.

Dead, she says. Partially true.

Her return home is a transit stretch until the next visit to A & E, but there comes a day when everyone stops being a child.

Twelve is a good age. Peder's fixed up a summer job for you. You have to leave a bag, pick up another one. No weeding for the bloody council for you, be grateful for that. There might even be some pocket money.

"The room", which they refer to in the definite form, is more than just a room, she realises that. What they do in there is harder to fathom. It reminds her of a chemistry lab. Computers, machines, gauges. Burettes, pipettes, glass vessels. Spoons, spatulas, tongs. They all look too new to be left over from the TB era.

"What happens in here?" she says.

"Biomedical research," says Branco, and summons someone.

That someone appears right away. He pulls out an instrument on wheels and asks Svala to move over to a narrow bed. That too is on wheels. "Take off your top," says the person who is neither Varg nor Lo.

His appearance is more like that of a fox. When she refuses, he pulls off her *kolt* with hard hands.

"Nobody cares about a child's body," he says, taping electrode pads to her chest and upwards, around her head.

Nobody, except possibly Marcus Branco.

"In a few years' time you're going to be a very beautiful woman," says Branco. "Have you thought about what you're going to do with your life?"

"Reindeer herder," she says curtly.

"Hope you'll have some reindeer left to herd, then."

83

At Björkavan the uncles are sitting in the kitchen. The police have just been there. The jacket found in the car that was blown up is Svala's and there are human remains, but the technical investigation is not yet complete.

The blast was enormous. It was heard all over Gasskas. They are sorry. The brothers must prepare themselves for the worst.

"Well, we knew this was how it could end," says Per-Henrik.

"I suppose we did."

Outside, the rain patters against the windowpane. They should be cooking a meal. But they can't bring themselves to do anything except just sit there. Sitting and staring is all they can do now.

"It was a mistake to get the authorities involved in all this," says Elias. "We should have sorted it out ourselves."

"Right enough, but how?"

"We could have sent her west. There's plenty who deserve a bit of extra help during calving, not just us."

When the phone rings, Per-Henrik answers, even though the call comes from a withheld number. He hangs up without saying a word. Nods to his brother.

"It was her. Marika Vikström. Calls herself Lo these days. Weren't you and she a couple, back in the day?"

"Yes," says Elias, "at upper secondary. A shrewd sort of lass. And good-looking. I think about her sometimes. What might have been. How about you?" He glances into the bedroom. They have barely talked about her. The woman Per-Henrik saved from certain death, who stayed on long after she had recovered.

"You mean Pernilla?"

"Yep, the Salo woman from the other side of the mountain."

A look comes into Per-Henrik's eyes. He sits there, saying nothing. Gets up and refills their coffee cups. Because although they are brothers and have lived together for almost forty years, work side by side and eat most of their meals together, they rarely talk about anything other than everyday activities like feeding the herd, clearing snow, hunting and dogs. Women – or feelings, for that matter – are not part of their vocabulary.

"There was something," says Per-Henrik, "but since she went home I haven't heard from her."

"So what do we do now?" says Elias, bringing them back to the more familiar reality. "The kid needs bringing home, somehow."

"Same as we've always done to protect ourselves against wolves, bears, wolverines and lynx. We defend those closest to us."

84

Svala shuts her eyes and turns inwards. Shutting out reality started as a survival strategy. For as long as she can remember she has had the capacity to transport herself between the chaos of her surroundings and inner peace. Inside the boundary, nothing can get to her. They can shout in her ear, yank her arms, hit her. She isn't there.

She can no longer see or hear them, Branco and the others. She is walking in the forest. It is one of the hottest days of summer. The mosquitoes have died from lack of water. Little flies buzz around her face. She is on her way to the bog. The cloudberries should be ripe soon. On its margins the marsh rosemary tickles her bare legs. She pulls off a few leaves, rubs them between her fingers and breathes in the smell.

Mammamärta is standing in the middle of the bog, her back bent to her task. Always first in the cloudberry patch.

Svala calls out, she waves back with a *come this way, they're ripe here* and Svala starts making her way over.

The surface is dry beneath her feet, like one of the mowable bogs. But the longer she walks, the further away Mammamärta seems. Then she is running, calling, running. Barely registers the peat getting wetter, her shoes sinking into the ground, deeper with every step. She has to make it, has to get there. She slows down, is about to say something important when her feet land in a hole. She grabs hold of a birch sapling and tries to pull herself out. The ground answers by sucking her back with a squelch, down and down until only her head and her hands, still hanging on to the sapling, are sticking out.

"Did you want anything in particular?" says Mammamärta, clearly unconcerned by Svala's predicament.

"The passcode for the bitcoin account."

"Oh that . . . well you've come to the wrong place. The passcode is with the akkas, the goddesses. It's Jahbme akka you need to ask. She who rules over the underworld and the realm of the dead. Because that's where you're heading, isn't it? I can see you're sinking."

"Can't you go instead? You're already there. I'll wait here for you to come back."

"That's not how it works, but don't be afraid. Death isn't bad."

"You mean I've got to die to get the passcode to a bitcoin account?"

"One will die, another will live."

"Wait," calls Svala as Mammamärta's back recedes towards the edge of the forest. She can't hold herself up any longer. She lets go of the birch. With a plop, the ground closes over her head.

When she wakes she is alone in the room. With the *kolt* wrapped around her. No wires or instruments. She can hear voices outside. Keys jangle. The door opens. The whirr of a wheelchair and following it some slow, shuffling footsteps.

Plague. It must be him.

Some light on the horizon. At least she isn't alone with Branco.

He fixes his gimlet eyes on her, asks how it went and she nods. Fine, it went fine.

One will die, another will live.

"Good. I'll leave you two for a moment." Branco looks at his watch, keeps looking at his watch as if he wants to say: "Look, superb isn't it, and incidentally the world's most expensive Patek Philippe."

"Looks as good on you as on Patrick Bateman," mutters Plague.

85

Once the guests have departed, the catering firm's van comes up the avenue. The cleaners are just behind it. They park outside the trades-men's entrance, unload buckets, mops and an assortment of other equip-ment, and are admitted by a woman with skin like a sunburnt viper.

For a few seconds she allows her eyes to meet those that in the distant past looked at her with warmth and sympathy. Now they are neutral, puzzled. How did you end up here, they ask, what pushed you over the boundary? "Life itself," she wants to answer. A poor excuse. "Greed and a lust for power," would have been more accurate. She could tell them something about death, too. That the part of herself which could feel, engage with others and take sound decisions died in a house fire. That she was only the exception that proved the rule: without feelings, the individual is free.

"The main hall and kitchen are your priorities," she says, "and then the bedrooms upstairs. Don't forget the toilets."

One hundred and sixty-three metres away, another cleaner is tracking this activity through thermal-imaging lenses. In the darkness they are an excellent tool for locating a living creature. By day, a standard pair of binoculars with optics that produce an image as sharp as the eyesight of a snake.

Everything is going to plan. At 18.00 on the dot he begins to skirt the area covered by the CCTV. According to Salander, all the outdoor cameras have been disarmed, thanks to some genius she says she knows, but better safe than sorry. She is fearless, he'll give her that, but restless too. She is all for dashing in, shooting everything that moves and rescuing the girl. A fantasy he hopes he has dissuaded her from.

"You want to die?" he asks.

"I guess not," she says.

They both agree that their only way in is underground. The moment the scant darkness touched this part of the world, the Cleaner went back to the base of the building, located a discrepancy with the help of his thermal imaging device and dug until he uncovered a trapdoor which he then concealed with spruce branches.

At 18.05, Lisbeth puts a hand on his shoulder. Her make-up is even more striking than before. At least she isn't in a skirt and high heels.

What the hell is he doing? He has asked himself this so many times that the question barely exists any longer. Or the answer, for that matter. He must trust her, and she him.

Shielded by a hedge of firs, they crawl through stinging nettles and brushwood. Remarkably, the trapdoor opens without too much resistance. He pulls it up a few centimetres and scans the hole. No sign of human presence. Only a strange, rank smell.

"Eleven metres," he whispers.

Salander climbs in first. The Cleaner closes the trapdoor above them and switches on his torch.

According to the plans of the complex, there is a distance of a hundred and twenty metres between the way in and the way out. Whether the latter still exists is unclear. As is whether the stated distance reflects real conditions or means as the crow flies. On the other hand, there are several possible routes. He straps his thermal binoculars to his head and takes the lead. The tunnel has many eyes. Luckily they only belong to rats, which scatter into hidden cavities.

At the first choice of tunnel they take the left, and then left again.

"What's that stink?" whispers Lisbeth.

He doesn't know. Sewage, maybe, or the corpses of rats that have died recently. She keeps close to his back. Stops when he stops. Falls still when he hushes her.

With twenty-three metres to go, they reach an arched gate. On the other side of the gate the tunnel is wider, with a concrete floor and graffiti on the walls.

"How can we be sure it's old graffiti?" whispers Lisbeth.

"No-one writes 'prick' these days."

He notes, however, that the padlock is new, and cuts it off with his bolt cutters.

"Stay here," he says, and passes her the torch. "I'll do a recce first and come back for you if it's green for go. If I'm not back in five minutes, you take the same way out. Understood?"

She sets her watch.

"Understood."

Five minutes can race by. Five minutes in an underground tunnel with rats running around your feet really drags.

She spends the first minute thinking about Mikael Blomkvist. What he's going to do with Svala's reflections on Simon Frisk and similar scum.

The girl has an eye for things, the sort of intuition that strips those wolves to the bare skin. Fourteen years of experience have refined this ability to perfection.

Four minutes pass. Still no Cleaner. Another UFO, she thinks. No doubt a hundred per cent ruthless when the need arises, but not devoid of empathy. She had seen it for herself, the forced self-control when she flung out the news of Salo's death. He began to say something but clammed up. Turned away to tie his bootlace. She put a hand on his shoulder. He let it lie there.

But what he personally hopes to gain from rescuing Svala is far from clear. Lisbeth has asked. He hasn't answered. She assumes the truth lies somewhere beyond Svala, in the snakepit of Branco's people and anyway, it's immaterial. They have a common goal, she must trust him on that.

When her watch tells her time is up, she starts walking. Not back as she was ordered, but who the hell is the Cleaner, with his warlike choice of language, to decide things for her?

Understood?

No, unfortunately. The kid is coming out of this ramshackle mansion. The kid and hopefully Plague too, if he's still alive.

86

Paradoxically it is one of the animals that Plague has to thank for still being alive. A mouthful of pills every morning has bucked him up. The nature of his complaint is unknown, beyond the fact that he is horribly obese. Something to do with blood pressure maybe? Or diabetes?

His recollections of the past few weeks are blurred, probably because he is actively trying to forget. Yet the guilt still thumps away inside him. Even though he never had a choice. Did he? Well, yes, sure he did, but cowardice took over. The question is whether he can put any of it right, turn back the clock and help the only person in the world who genuinely means anything to him: Lisbeth Salander. And if not her, then maybe the person slumped in the chair beside him with her head in her hands, staring dejectedly at the screen.

He plugs Svala's hard drive into his own laptop and clicks into bitcoin.com.

Take control of your money. Buy your first bitcoin today.

"Why are you here?" she says, instead of talking passcodes.

"You need me. For as long as you go on needing me, I get to live."

"Yes, but what for?" she insists. "According to Lisbeth you're a good person, the best, not like Branco and his brutes."

The only part of his bloated face that shows any sign of life is his eyes. They regard her sorrowfully.

"Thank you," he says. "It's kind of you to say so. Lisbeth is . . ." He can't get it out. Simply can't. So he switches to giving her some sort of explanation of the job he's been given to do. Nothing grand. Some disruptive ransomware attacks on the municipal council, that's all, but now its boss is dead so maybe that doesn't apply anymore.

She sits bolt upright, asks if he means Salo and yes, that's right, that's his name. She seizes the laptop and finds the online edition of *Gaskassen*.

The man who was found dead on Tuesday at Randi power station in the Lilla Lule River has been confirmed to be Henry Salo, CEO and head of trade and industry at Gasskas municipal council. The police do not view the death as suspicious, but believe he is likely to have fallen in by accident and drowned.

In his five years as municipal CEO, Henry Salo made a name for himself as a proactive leader who put Gasskas on the world map. The first stage of what is to become Europe's largest wind farm recently had its inauguration and it was announced shortly before his death that the old Gasskas mine is to reopen.

"Our thoughts naturally go out to Henry Salo's family. On Friday the municipal executive board will mark his passing with a moment's silence in the town square. Many of us will miss Henry's enthusiasm and energy," said board chairman Oskar Boström.

"I don't understand," says Svala. "I was up in his office a few weeks ago. We talked about the new mine."

The combination of Henry's relationship with Mammamärta, with her herself when she was little and the present situation is too much.

"He wasn't a bad person, not deep down."

Plague gives her some moments with her memories but the clock is ticking; the wheelchair is waiting in the wings. In Plague's world, the people out there have no names. They are mere words, like "eat", "shit" and "die".

Not really sure what he is doing, he brings up private correspondence between Henry Salo and Marcus Branco. He angles the screen towards the girl and lets her read in peace.

```
Regarding the hard drive, I believe it to be in
the possession of Svala Hirak, Märta Hirak's
daughter. The person in question currently lives
with her relations at Björkavan 1.
I take it for granted that this information will
stay between us and that the demands previously
stipulated by you for compensation for wind-power
shares that were not forthcoming will now be
dropped.
Yours sincerely
Henry Salo
```

Yours sincerely Henry Salo . . .

She brushes aside her emotions. Grief turns to anger, anger generates energy. Again she takes over the laptop, her fingers pattering over the keyboard as she dashes off messages to Lisbeth Salander, to her uncle Elias who has e-mail unlike his brother, to Mikael Blomkvist and to the police tip-off website.

"They can see everything you're doing," says Plague. "My instructions are to stop you doing precisely what you're doing right now."

Svala stops and meets his eye.

"But I'm not going to, of course," he adds.

"Good, because something needs to happen. I haven't got the passcode. I found myself in the kingdom of the dead and then I woke up again. According to Mammamärta, or was it Jahbme akka, one of us must die first. It's Branco or . . . no, not me."

The sound of a gunshot makes them both jump. Loud voices are coming closer. Sporadic words that sound like orders. The last of them issued right outside the door. "Only the hacker," says the voice. "The kid's not to be harmed."

Plague sees a child, its eyes open wide. Without thinking he throws her to the floor, covering the girl with his lardy bulk.

Seconds later, Varg kicks open the door.

The very first shot is fatal.

Plague's arms spread outwards onto the floor, his hacker fingers stiffen. Beneath him, a swallow fights for breath, not knowing if it is her blood or his.

This is how odd she is. Her classmates throw stones, the well-aimed ones hit her head. There's nothing wrong with her blood. It flows like other people's.

Don't let yourself be bullied. Walk away with a smile. Never snitch. Pay them back whenever you can.

She breaks wrists, wrecks kneecaps with a kick. They claim she's violent. As for her, she barely reacts when they break her femur and knock out her teeth. It wasn't that bad really. In spite of everything.

Don't let yourself be bullied. Walk away with a smile. Never snitch. Pay them back whenever you can.

"Svala Hirak or Marcus Branco. Who shall we pick?" The akka goddesses rustle and whisper amongst themselves. The volume rises. The voices grow clearer.

"You all know what happens if Marcus Branco gets his hands on the code. Those billions of kronor go straight into the hands of evil. Svala can do better than this. All she has to do is stand up. People need her to be strong now. Her uncles, Lisbeth, the Cleaner."

She wrenches her arm free. Tries to push Plague aside, but it's as if a house has fallen on her. She is trapped and gasping for air. Far away, Svala hears voices. She could swear that was Elias. "No," she tries to yell. "Get out of here! I can cope on my own." But the oxygen is running out down there. Her voice has no sound. Her arms will not obey. Or her legs. Might just as well give up.

"Jahbme akka will look after us," she whispers to Plague. "Death isn't that bad, don't be afraid."

87

Lisbeth Salander comes to the stairs which should lead to a trapdoor in the kitchen, according to the blueprints. Cautiously, she sticks up her head. Listens and looks all around, notes the CCTV and flashes her best smile: *I'm here now. Happy to see me?*

She slowly follows the floor plan she has memorised. Moving through the scullery, serving area, hall and up the first flight on the main staircase.

Marcus Branco is ready for one last session with Svala and is about to go to her room when Räv attracts his attention. The first thing he sees on the screen is a man with a rope over one shoulder and a scrubbing bucket in his other hand. Someone from the cleaning company, presumably. But he is moving stealthily, not walking naturally. And the rope, what the hell is that? Like some fucking cowboy with a lasso.

Räv zooms in on the picture.

"The cleaners all have clearance but I'll tell Lo, to be on the safe side," Räv is saying when another picture pops up on the screen that makes Branco's eyes narrow and his lips whistle as his breathing gets heavier.

At first he can only see the hair. Short, swept back. It's when the creature turns its ugly mug to the camera and laughs like a crazed hyena that he completely blows his top. He grabs the plate with Räv's half-eaten lunch and hurls it across the room. Spaghetti bolognese runs down the walls. On the bank of screens, linked both to cameras and to motion

357

sensors, more figures appear out of nowhere. But Branco is focused on one person only: Lisbeth Salander.

There is a crackle as Lo answers.

"Remove that ugly snout from the face of the earth unless you want to find yourself in the fire again," he says and turns to the others.

The sound of a shot, and then another, is reassuring.

Initial security plan activated. The hard drive remains in his safe-keeping, with its rightful owner. Time to get going. A shame about Svala, he thinks, but no doubt they will have other opportunities to meet.

Lo has understood the command. She just needs to get a hold of herself. It was Elias or her, she persuades herself, and he shot first. The first-floor corridor has white walls and stone floors. She squats beside the lifeless body. Puts her hand in his. The man who once stroked her burn-scarred skin with calloused fingers and promised he would always . . . no. This won't do. Thinking back is like giving away your strength.

She goes down to the ground floor. Asks for positions. No-one answers. In the reflection off a window she detects movement. Salander.

"Put down your gun and turn around," says Lo.

If, and, then.

"How does it feel to have a child's life on your conscience?" says Lisbeth, turning slowly towards Lo. "After whingeing on about your own lousy childhood, I mean."

"Shut it if you want to live," she says as she bundles Lisbeth back to the kitchen. "Now you listen very carefully. I tried to get Svala out before Branco attacked her physically and I'm not talking about cuffs around the ear or broken arms. He's a monster. I've seen him with girls Svala's age. Films he shows to a chosen circle. This wasn't what I expected when he recruited me and I can understand if you think I'm a creep, but I wrote to you. You didn't answer. I'm sure the police are on their way, and I'm getting out myself now."

"Where are Svala and Plague?"

"Room 12, fourth floor."

"Are they alive?"

"I don't know. She never managed to crack the code."

Lisbeth freezes at the sound of a shot echoing from one of the other floors.

"Who's shooting? If Svala and Plague are harmed you'll be held responsible too, you know that."

"OK, it was my idea to bring him up to Gasskas, but it's thanks to me he's alive. I got him the meds he needed. The girl is Branco's own project. He's never going to give her up."

'Touching," says Lisbeth. "Kidnapping Plague and then trying to save him."

"He was useful. He found me your address, for example. With a friend like him you don't need many enemies," she says. She shoulders a rucksack and opens the trapdoor in the kitchen floor. As she goes down, the same way Lisbeth recently clambered up, she keeps her gun trained on Lisbeth.

"I'm sorry it's had to end like this. In another time, another life . . . I liked you Lisbeth Salander, but I can't risk you—"

There is a click as she cocks the hammer. The sound as a bullet goes through Lo's head and ricochets off the trapdoor cover sends shockwaves through Lisbeth's body. Her eardrums feel as if they will burst out of her ears; her stomach turns inside out. Instinctively she shields her head with her hands, curls up like a little grub and waits for the next shot.

There isn't one.

A hand is placed over hers, pulls her up from the floor and into arms that let her stay there until the grub has uncurled, regained its poise. The embrace smells of sweat and mosquito repellent.

The Cleaner.

"Five minutes," says Lisbeth, once she can trust her voice. "Where the hell did you get to?"

"I prefer to work alone."

She feels like remonstrating. The Cleaner's gaze is already on the future.

"No more fucking five minutes," she says. "Bring me up to speed. Do you know what happened?"

"No more than you. Shots fired on the upper floors."

She doesn't ask about Svala, doesn't want to know. The kid is alive. The kid is alive because the kid must survive because if she doesn't then Lisbeth has no idea if she herself . . .

Don't think, just walk. One step at a time, up the stairwell. The wallpaper, with marks where paintings once hung, following the curve of the banisters, is a greenish colour. The smell of something ingrained, something dead. She presses her arm to her mouth, stifles a cough. Gets a sharp look from the Cleaner, but the building remains silent. The Cleaner goes first. Every so often he stops to listen, then proceeds.

Second floor, clear.

Third floor, clear. Fourth. The lift.

They point their guns at the protective box as it creaks its way down.

There is only one person who would need the lift when fire is licking at his arse: Marcus Branco. The Cleaner takes her arm. Keeps a tight grip on the leather with its metallic clink of rivets and chains.

"Right, this is what we'll do," he whispers. "You go on up to Svala, I'll take Branco."

As long as Branco is alive, Svala will be in danger.

If Svala isn't alive, his focus will shift to someone else.

The Cleaner's motives are somewhat different. He can't risk escalating the situation by dragging along a half-crazed woman who wants vengeance for her niece.

In his mind he has rehearsed the plan so many times that it feels feasible; Branco is the primary target. Preferably Varg and Björn as well, the two closest to Branco. The lynx woman was not on the list. No great loss.

Step two is harder. If Douglas Ferm is right that he, Joar Bark, has been made to front Branco's darkest business secrets, he'll need the help of a hacker. And without his own intervention, the hacker would have been dead by now. At least she is doing as he says, continuing up the stairs.

Lisbeth runs to find room 12.

Below her, war breaks out again.

The sound of sirens is getting closer.

She rounds the corner of a corridor and almost trips over a body in a sitting position, slumped against the wall. When her brain catches up with her she realises who she has just passed, stops, retraces her own bloody footprints, squats and turns the face towards her.

The late Elias Hirak, reindeer herder. Beside him lies his hunting rifle. His lasso is like a bag strap around his shoulder.

Svala must be here somewhere.

All the rooms have numbers, but there is no number 12.

She frantically tries doors. Most are locked. Other rooms are empty. The one at the far end has no number, yet still she hesitates, sensing that this is it.

Svala's turned-up shoes are in a neat pair just inside the door. Plague's bullet-peppered body lies beached on the floor.

Lisbeth has come too late. Again there is nothing she can do. At least, not for Plague.

She puts her arm over him. Her face to his. His stubble is prickly. His lips are still soft. The years flash by. Without Plague, she would not have survived.

"You were my best friend," she whispers. "I'm so sorry."

Then she feels his body shake. A hand appears. The slim fingers of a girl under Plague's vast wing.

"Svala?"

She takes hold of his sweater, tries to turn him over, to make space. She braces her feet on the slippery floor, tries to lift the body to free the girl, slips, loses her grip, starts all over again.

She puts a hand under his ribcage. Feels the contours of a face, hair – the kid.

"Are you hurt?"

Svala can't tell. She doesn't know what's what. She did try to get up. One leg isn't really working. Or could it be her back? Her arm?

"Help me Aunt Lisbeth, I can't breathe," she whispers.

What does a man like Plague weigh? Two hundred kilos? More?

Lisbeth battles with the weight of him. It's no use. She isn't strong enough. All she can do is yell. Shout for help. Keep shouting and someone will come.

Someone with a lasso like a bag strap around his shoulder. Per-Henrik gets the rope over Plague's head. Manages to work it over one of his shoulders too.

"Are you ready?" he says to Lisbeth, and pulls as hard as he can. Imagines he's catching an irascible bull reindeer that's fighting against its loss of freedom. Imagines Elias is at his side, although he witnessed his brother take his last breath. Now they are winding in. Pulling. Winding in, until Lisbeth has pulled Svala's bloodied body from under Plague's protective mortal bulk.

They sit on the floor. Svala with her head on Lisbeth's lap. Around them, the building will soon be crawling with police. A Cleaner with a gunshot wound comes to his senses and slinks into the underground tunnels, like the decimated group of animals that has already taken the same route.

The girl is weak, barely moving. With a trembling hand she reaches up and runs her finger down Lisbeth's cheek.

"Aunt Lisbeth. Your make-up."

88

The Gasskas River flows gently past Björkavan. It pauses on the bend around the bay, gathers itself and hurls the rising spring flood onwards to the sea.

In the Hirak kitchen, Anna-Maja and Svala are sharing the final preparations for the coffee party after the funeral. There are sandwiches to be made, sponge cake to be decorated with cream and last year's berries. Coffee to be brewed on the stove and poured into big Thermos flasks. Between them there are words that need to be said but they will have to wait. Between them stand Simon Frisk, Levi Grundström, the group of activists and Ester Södergran.

"Let's leave that for afterwards," says Anna-Maja. She is burying an uncle on her father's side. Svala an uncle on her mother's. Outside, Per-Henrik has brought the car to the door and early summer is a picture painted in green. In a frame as black as a raven.

When Svala asked who killed Elias, he replied that he does not know. Because if he does know, it is best to stay silent. The girl won't give in. That list of hers grows longer and longer. Sometime it will all have to end.

He watches her unwieldy leg in plaster, bobbing down the stairs. Her crutches stand unused in the hall. For ease of movement she has trimmed off the plaster around her toes. As stubborn as her mother. Still partially dressed in Märta's clothes, which she refuses to take off. Her uniform, as she calls them. She has been allowed to get a new *kolt* for the funeral.

She will be staying on at Björkavan, at any rate. He feels guilty at the thought of what lies ahead. She'll be needed to help with the reindeer. She'll have to start doing her share, filling Elias's shoes. Otherwise they might as well give up now.

On the way to the church they pass Gaupaudden. A boy is standing with a bike at the roadside. He raises a hand and waves. Despite the wretchedness of everything, a smile passes across Per-Henrik's rugged face. He waves back. Thinks about the boy's mother, with her reddish-blonde hair and uneven front teeth. Slowly thawing until some life came back into her eyes. Which then came to rest on him.

Svala sees Lukas, too. At Henry Salo's funeral, he wept at his mother's side. Pernilla, by contrast, maintained the same severe expression throughout the service.

She did not join in with the hymns. Did not lay a rose on the coffin. Left before the burial.

No-one can blame her. Least of all Mikael Blomkvist. All the inessentials that have perpetually monopolised his time have been consigned to a past of no significance. Even *Millennium*.

He knows that she is suffering. That she loved Salo in her way.

And yet, happiness rejoices within him. His daughter is alive. Everything will be alright. She will, he will, everything will.

Pernilla took the boy by the hand, walked to the church door without looking to either side. Not until the back row where Svala and Per-Henrik were sitting. A swift nod. A look meeting his look.

And now Svala knows why he is smiling at his brother's funeral.

The procession of cars makes its stately way to Björkavan. They park in the yard around the house. Guests take a seat wherever they can find space, in the kitchen, in the dining room. Some have had long journeys. Most are united by their clothes, language and memories.

If the service was sad and muted, the mood is all the lighter now. Svala does her best to keep up with the language, politely tells people all they want to know. Excuses herself, takes a scoop of drinking water from the bucket, goes out to sit on the front steps. The mosquitoes are back in earnest now. Elias's shadow takes a turn down to the dog pen.

Lisbeth sits down beside Svala, and shortly afterwards Mikael Blomkvist joins them.

"That wasn't a bad story you submitted, and as I said, it'd be great to have you on work experience at *Gaskassen* again this summer," he says. "Perhaps we can put our wise heads together on a few matters. One thing I still don't understand, for instance, is why Simon Frisk blew himself up, but perhaps he had his reasons."

"He must have," Svala says.

"And Marcus Branco is another mystery. An early-morning swimmer came across the wheelchair in the river, but they've found no body as yet. And incidentally, I met Douglas Ferm the other day. He brought some evidence confirming Branco's involvement in the disappearance of Ingvar Bengtsson's daughter Malin. Although the body's never been found, she's been declared dead."

"Are you planning to write about it?" Svala says.

"Yes, of course, but we'll have to work our way through all the material from Ferm first. There are other things in there that the public will want to read about."

"Such as?"

"The fact that Ferm was the leading financier of the scheme to reopen the old mine, for example. Where there's money, blown-up bridges and roads are not a problem. Paradoxically enough, he's even slated to be the new head of Gasskas municipality. However that's supposed to work. Financier and CEO in one and the same title."

Ausländer raus!

Out with the vermin!

Memories of that evening have been skulking in the darkness. Svala has tried to pin them down, snatched at words as they danced away into the nooks and crannies of oblivion. But now she can see the raised stage where she herself is standing. Marcus Branco raising her hand. The men below, merged into a chanting mass. Dark suits, white shirts. All except one who is wearing a red bowtie.

Douglas Ferm.

"He was at the sanatorium," says Svala. "They were going to measure my skull."

The picture is shaky, distorted at the edges, but she is sure.

"They've formed a new party. The Nordic Assembly."

Now the earth is spinning too fast for Mikael Blomkvist. Way too fast. If the girl is right, this brings everything crashing down. His first major scoop at *Gaskassen* and his already somewhat tarnished honour will be at stake, but still . . . hopefully it is not too late. There were signs that everything was not as it should be. Perhaps the cancer got in the way. His loneliness. His willingness to confide in someone like-minded.

He asks if she is sure. She is. An eternity ago, when Ester was still alive, she showed Svala a blurry photo from a club meeting.

"Check out this picture," she said. "Someone mailed it in anonymously. The cream of Gasskas, all gathered in the same place. Politicians, trade and industry, bankers, insurance companies, media. Men only."

She knew the names of several. Ferm was one of them.

"And the Nordic Assembly, who are they?" says Mikael.

"People with money. New money. Not the upper crust, I don't think. The aim is to infiltrate society by investing in companies. They elected Branco as their chairman. Then they sang a song. Thou ancient, thou free, thou mountainous north, now we assemble for the final battle. For the day has come for our proud white race. *Ausländer raus*, now the Nordic countries will be ours. That sort of thing . . ."

"Holy shit," says Mikael several times. "Holy shit. Thanks, Svala!"

He bends to give the girl a hug, nods to Salander, takes the steps two at a time as he rings for a taxi and almost breaks into a run on his way out to the road.

"How are you feeling?" asks Lisbeth.

Svala shuffles up beside her. Rests her head on her aunt's shoulder. A mass of words is pouring through her body but nothing comes out. *She was standing on the stage. Garment after garment was peeled off her body. The eyes of the exultant crowd below her were shining with drink and arousal. A chosen individual was asked to come up. To place the metal gauge around her head and other parts of her body.*

"OK," Svala says. "A bit tired, that's all."

A police car comes slowly up to the house. The Icelander is at the wheel. The other one unfolds her legs to climb out of her seat. She has something in her arms.

Svala shades her eyes. Jessica Harnesk's armful is moving; it is alive.

"We had an idea," Jessica says, and passes the puppy to Svala. "A pathetic little scrap, but she'll bounce back soon enough. If you want her, that is. You don't have to say yes. We call her Tiddler but I'm sure you can think of a better name."

"Laika," says Svala. "I'll call her Laika."

Dusk draws its rapid brush across the hills and forest, across the lakes, river, town and the people, awake and asleep.

Svala takes out her exercise book. Sharpens a pencil.

EPILOGUE

On election day, 11 September 2022, Erik Larsson goes through passport control at Arlanda airport. He takes the lift up to the lounge; he still has a couple of hours before departure. Several whiskies later, he looks up and around him. Businessmen are engrossed in their laptops and newspapers. Holidaymakers are dressed in colourful clothes. Police officers and security staff drink mineral water and scan the room at regular intervals. Then there are those like himself. Indefinable.

He drains his glass and meets a pair of eyes. A woman. A brown-haired thing with battered trainers and a Ramones T-shirt under her leather jacket.

There is a dull ache in his groin. She's beautiful in an ugly way. Presumably Swedish, which surprises him. He isn't normally attracted to Scandinavians. Above all, she isn't smiling. Not even when he asks if he can get her anything. A beer, perhaps?

"Sure," she says, "if it's no bother. Lager, in that case. I hate IPA."

"Maybe you'd like a gin and tonic. Or a Bailey's?"

"Hardly," she says, and carries on scrolling on her phone.

"My gate will be opening soon," he says, handing her the beer. "Where are you off to?"

"Quebec."

"Me too," he says, and gets a "mmm" in reply. "On holiday?" he ventures.

"No."

"Uh-huh. So why Quebec, if you don't mind my asking?"

"I'm getting tired of your questions," she says. She pushes her glasses up onto her head and gives him an expressionless look.

Her face is pale, almost white. She wears no mascara, her chapped lips look as if they want to speak, possibly say something like: "Why can't you shut your face, you little creep? I don't want to talk to anyone."

So he returns to his own business. Has another whisky. He is aware of her behind him when it is time to go to the gate, but refrains from checking.

At the door of the plane they go separate ways and he is helped to his seat in first class. Only to be reunited fourteen hours later at the baggage carousel. He gives her a nod.

She looks away. Collects her case and walks off to the exit.

The air is cold and clear.

Five minutes later, Malin Bengtsson leaves the airport in a taxi.

Erik Larsson, alias Marcus Branco, guides his wheelchair into Fairmont Le Château Frontenac and takes the lift up to the Charles de Gaulle suite. He notes that his special requirements have been met. A pot of Huang Da Cha from Huoshan province, Champagne of who bloody cares what kind and an under-age female sitting on the edge of the bed, looking becomingly terrified.

The cruel one has awoken.

KARIN SMIRNOFF worked as a journalist before quitting her job to buy a wood factory in her home county in northern Sweden. Her debut novel, *My Brother*, was nominated for the prestigious August Prize and has been optioned for TV by the producers behind *The Bridge*. Two more novels followed, and the entire trilogy has now sold more than 700,000 copies in Sweden. *The Girl in the Eagle's Talons*, the seventh in the *Millennium* series, was translated into more than thirty languages and was an international bestseller.

SARAH DEATH studied Swedish at Cambridge University and University College London (PhD 1985). She is a three-time winner of the George Bernard Shaw Prize for translation from Swedish, most recently in 2021 for *Letters from Tove*, the correspondence of Tove Jansson. She has also been awarded the Swedish Academy Translation Prize 2008 and the Royal Order of the Polar Star 2014.